A Union in Thunder

Hannah Eaton

ISBN: 979-8-9931692-1-7 (Paperback)

ISBN: 979-8-9931692-0-0 (Ebook)

Cover Design: Samantha Sanderson-Marshall

Proofread: Golden Editorial

To my mom, forever my first reader.

HALORAN

WESTERN
SEA

Cape of Tempests

ELVOR

TYTHMORE

THE WASTES

PROVENTIUM

PETRA CLIFFS

SOUTHERN
SEA

MESGARA

SILVER ROCK

CONTENTS

This story explores themes of gender and power imbalance. There is a scene of coercive SA. The act is not graphically depicted nor is it committed by the love interest. Please read with care.

CHAPTER 1
LAVINIA

Magic to freeze a dog's age should have been impossible, too, I reminded myself. If my magic could do that, then surely, I could do this.

The magic I held now was far greater than that burst of untrained power that preserved Remus forever as a puppy, but I would never complete such a feat again. Some abilities were for the Graces only, lest they be abused. I hoped the Graces forgave me, that they understood. Maybe they had pets of their own, living happily alongside them forever.

Well, for Remus, forever was yet to be seen.

I hoped that it had tied his life to mine somehow. I hated the idea of him living on forever after I was gone. *Who would understand his fear of rushing water? Who would sneak him leftover bread?*

Looking away from Remus's sleeping form, I returned focus to my task. I could fix this. I could.

Standing for over a century, the elm tree my parents married under had been ravaged in last night's storm. A singular strike of lightning scorched the tree, black bark loosening its grip on the life within. The energy that had felt like a rising tide pushing against me was now a faint trickle, a stream where there had once been an ocean.

Healing magic was one of the more common powers, low levels

were spread throughout the kingdom. Common, unremarkable, weak, despite the strength of my own power, it would always be just that. Average. The best I could be was useful.

The kings of Proventium had long valued offensive powers. Centuries of infighting had left the strongest fighters and families in power. No matter the use of a powerful healer, nobles wanted marriages that would beget sons with a power of use to the king.

A power that would bolster their house's standing. A power that would win wars.

Healers saved men, but they did not save crowns.

Of the healers I had met, the power in most had been dulled, leaving skill only for minor ailments and injuries. The palace healer, Padgett, was the strongest in Proventium. His wife, Mariana, was second. My father believed with time I would come to rival their skill. He had thought the same of my mother, though the Graces had not been so generous as to let her discover the true depth of her power.

Bringing the dead back to life was a fool's gamble, impossible for even the strongest healer. But the elm wasn't dead yet. The core of the tree still echoed with the life that pulsed under the soil. I felt that beat in my palms getting stronger as I worked.

A drop of sweat trailed down my temple. My long black hair was stuck to the nape of my neck. Clinging to my damp back, my slate blue day-dress fared no better. Pausing, I squinted up at the sun descending from its perch.

Steeling myself for a last push, I took a deep breath. I pictured silver threads of power wrapping around the life still within the tree. What was in the elm rushed back to me, greedily accepting more. All sound and light seemed to drain away as I poured my strength into the tree one final time.

Light began to come back, but no outward sound could compete with the rush of my blood in my ears. Instead of standing over the tree, I found myself kneeling, bracketed by the fallen trunk and branches that seemed to embrace me in gratitude. With shaking hands, I pushed myself up to touch what remained of the standing trunk and was met with the glorious buzz of life.

I had done it. I collapsed back on my haunches and closed my eyes, a smile on my lips.

At Remus's sharp bark my attention snapped away to watch his small grey body bound toward two approaching figures.

"Lavinia," my brother scolded as Remus darted around his legs. He was still too far away for me to see the exact expression on his face, but close enough to see the shake of his head. "Do you have any idea what time it is?"

I didn't deign to raise my voice to match his. Waiting until he stood at the fallen trunk, I said, "I may have lost track of time." I grinned wide and insincere—the way I knew got under his skin.

"What have you been doing all Grace-deserted day?"

"Healing this." I stood on trembling knees. Expending that much power had left me light-headed. "I've done it. This part was beyond repair." I waved a hand to the destruction between us, "but this will live on."

"Amazing," breathed the man accompanying my brother.

The man I had avoided looking at.

Though with my cheeks already flushed with exertion, maybe now was the time to look at him.

Oran's mouth hung slightly agape, his grass-green eyes alight. Meeting his gaze transformed his mouth into a grin. The kind that brought a blush to my face despite my efforts. I bit my lip to quell a matching smile to the one currently carving dimples into his cheeks and softening the sharp edges of his jaw. The right side of his smile lifted higher than the left. My favorite crooked smile, one I could paint from memory with my eyes closed. Warm, tan skin lit by the afternoon sun and the freckles across a strong nose were a distraction that I had to gather my remaining strength to fight.

At Leith's voice, I tore my eyes away. "What a miserable waste of power. Honestly, Lav." He accompanied his scolding with another shake of his head. "If it matters so much to you, we could have sent for someone." With his hands on his hips, he looked so like our father: broad shoulders and a lean, wiry frame, tense with disappointment when speaking to me. Leith's honey-blonde hair was in sharp contrast to my raven locks, but our eyes were the same. Our mother's eyes. Icy, crystal blue, the center iris so pale it verged on being colorless, ringed in deep navy.

"Vin is not at war. No one is sick. What else is she supposed to do with her magic?" Oran asked.

Leith snorted, "I suppose you're right. I could beat you in a match each day if she needs something to heal. Not a damned tree."

"You've never beat me," Oran dismissed.

Some of the frustration left my brother. "Are you bored, Lav? Was that it? All the books finished? We can find you a better hobby than botany."

"Do healers spar? She and I could have a match."

I rolled my eyes at Oran's offer. As children, Oran was the one who declared me a lady not fit for roughhousing long before Leith recognized me as a girl and not simply a sister. Oran would sooner incinerate himself than spar with me.

"Please," Leith huffed a laugh. "Lav has never been built for that. I'd like her to not be turned into a pile of ash. Father would have my head." His grin contained a touch of malice that made me grit my teeth. Leith, as adept at being funny as he was at being cruel, was a dichotomy of good and bad humor.

"If you're quite finished," I interrupted, waiting with raised brows until Leith focused on me. "If Oran is allowed to waste power," I sniped, "this part is dead." As soon as the words left my mouth, the fallen trunk burst into flames under Oran's open palm. The ruthless heat made me retreat a step. At the close of Oran's fist, the flames were extinguished as quickly as they ignited. Untouched grass beneath a pile of ash was left at our feet.

"Something like that is not taxing for Oran." I wondered how Ruby was able to stand Leith's mercurial moods. "How long have you been out here?"

"Have we not already established that I don't know what time it is? The day got away from me." I shrugged.

"We've been worried," Oran grumbled. "None of the staff knew where you were." He studied me with concern, not annoyance.

"Come." Leith waved a hand to me before turning to begin the walk home.

"Pardon?" I took a swaying step forward to be caught by Oran's gentle hold above my elbow.

"Leith, have the carriage pick us up here. It's a long walk after Lavinia's day."

"We're already late." Leith's stride didn't slow.

With a sigh, Oran guided me along. Remus cheerfully set off, lumbering grey scruff nipping at my brother's heels.

"Leith," I bit out. "Slow down and explain."

"We're leaving tonight. The maids have packed your trunks."

"No, we're to leave tomorrow morning."

"King Alaric has invited Father, Oran, Lord Lennox, and myself to the hunt tomorrow. Unless you'd like us to deny the king on your behalf, then yes, we will leave tonight."

"Enough." Oran's voice was stern before softening. "Vin didn't know. None of us knew until earlier today."

Oran had spent years mediating between my brother and I. Twenty-six to my twenty-two, when we were children, the four years between Leith and me had seemed an insurmountable chasm, one that was only bridged by Oran's efforts. To Oran, the three years between us were as inconsequential as the single year between him and Leith.

"As the king demands," I muttered under my breath.

"That is how being king works. You demand, and others do. This is important to Father," Leith warned.

I raised my face to the fading afternoon sun. The field of high grass released the day's heat like an old friend, safe in the knowledge that they would reunite tomorrow. Our dark brick manor, still only the size of my palm in the distance, was an imposing sight against the endless expanse of worn blue sky.

I didn't want to spend our walk arguing with my brother, and yet… Leith, confident, outgoing Leith, was transforming into a courtier, manipulative and single-mindedly focused on ingratiating himself to the king. Power and influence had become Leith's principal concern, just like Father and Lord Lennox.

In my younger years, my behavior had been the source of Father's disappointment, but now, with each season that I ended unmarried, his stress lay with my powers. Marriage to a healer was a liability. I felt more and more of a burden with each passing day.

Of the four domains of magic, Spirit was considered the common power, under which lay healers and those with a power over the body. Nature wielders had power over plants or weather. Element magic gave power over ice, water, fire, and metal. Seers, truth wielders, and illusion wielders comprised Mind magic.

Despite the utility of Spirit wielders graced with speed or strength, the lower classes were largely comprised of those with lesser Spirit powers or no magic at all. Despite the strength of my healing, I would always be seen as common.

Leith made no effort to hide that he thought me a weakness in the Bruis line. I'd mended his injuries more times than I could count, but he valued magic for its brutality. He saw unforgiving, offensive strength as the way for House Bruis to hold unchallenged standing.

Most noble houses were large, extended family all proudly bearing the name, but each house fell under the rule of one head passed from father to son. The members of each house ranged in their ability, the strong seeking the strong for marriage, hoarding power for themselves. The weaker members were left to each other, to fade into obscurity lest they draw attention to their vulnerability.

My father had married my mother, a skilled healer, for love. The story, love at first sight, was as romantic to me now as it was when I was a child. To Leith, it was a politically inconvenient marriage, but also a triumph of Father's power that House Bruis was not weakened by his choice.

"The hunt is important to my uncle as well, but that won't stop me from besting the king." Oran didn't boast. He spoke it as fact. "Leith, do try and not make it so obvious that you're missing so as to not offend King Alaric's ego tomorrow, will you? I personally think he appreciates the competition."

Despite myself, I found it irresistible to take a jab at my brother. "Leith cowing to the king? Shocking," I drew the word out, letting it drip with sarcasm. "Should you go out on the hunt or simply wait at the castle to shine his boots?"

"So very funny," he drawled back. "When he has you strung up for treason, I'll not weep for you." Leith pointed a finger at Oran. "Well, maybe a tear or two." The pair laughed in a harmonious rumble.

"I'd like to be burned after my death, if you will. Seems fitting."

"I'll see it is so. Or you could simply let King Alaric have a singular shot over you tomorrow?"

Oran groaned. "If Alaric wants to show how superior he is, he should just go with the old guard who have no hope of keeping up. My uncle barely remembers how to string a bow. If Alaric wants competition that he can easily best, only Hugo need be there."

"Being around the heirs helps him feel like he is still the young king."

"When did you become so astute?" I asked with a retch of disgust. "I miss when you were fun." I looked to Oran. "Remember when Leith was fun?"

"I've always found his presence to be dreadfully dull." Oran kept his voice and face smooth, masking the laughter that danced in his eyes.

"Fun? You should be thanking me that I don't have time for fun," Leith, quickly turning to anger, sniped. "Securing your future is not an amusement for me. I don't have time for the luxuries you do."

I froze. He spoke as if a marriage were imminent. "There is no haste for me to marry." I softened my tone to placate him. "If this is weighing on you, it need not. You'll marry this season. I can wait till the next or the one after. There's no rush, truly."

Leith was engaged to another Lennox cousin in hopes that the strength of her wind magic would ensure House Bruis a powerful heir.

I was not so easily matched.

Father, I hoped, would be kinder than Leith would in marrying me off. Surely there were houses that could see the benefit of a skilled healer, or, more likely, the benefit of aligning with the Bruis. Someone whose offensive magic was strong enough without the need for a wife to match. A husband who could knock Leith down when he was rude was unlikely, though the daydreams made a fun diversion.

"If anyone will have you," he spat. "Oran and I have protected you, in case you have forgotten. The only reason your prospects have not been completely ruined is because we have made it so."

"The dramatics are not of interest to me." I lifted my chin. Leith had done far worse than I, with far more paramours.

"You know nothing of what court is really like. Father shelters you from much. We can only hope whoever he picks to take you off our hands does the same." Leith looked down on me with a stern glare. "The world is not as kind as the one you've experienced."

Oran's hand flexed on my arm. "Leith, mind how you speak to her."

"Oh?" The word exploded out of me in a huff. "Cause my life has been so perfect? You don't actually know everything, Leith." I ripped my arm out of Oran's grip to push past Leith.

My brother, my first friend, saw me as something to be rid of. I ignored the hurt blooming in my chest, focusing instead on anger. I ground my teeth together as his words replayed in my ears. To speak as if my life were full of luxury and frivolity when he was the one with the privilege of deciding his future. Leith would have a life of his own even after marrying. He would still be Leith, soon to be Lord Bruis. Once I was married off, I would be reduced to 'wife'. A wife, a mother, a hostess, my life would be confined to the walls of my husband's home.

My father and brother expected me to be grateful that anyone would have me, that any man would risk his child being a pathetic healer like me.

"Watch your tongue!"

I ignored the burning in my lungs and legs as I hurried toward the manor. Leith should have caught up to me. I didn't slow but chanced a glance over my shoulder to see Leith, seething at my retreat, held in place by Oran.

I sucked in a trembling breath as I entered Bruis Manor. Hands braced on my hips, black spots danced in my vision.

"There you are!" The words were spoken with impatience. Father remained trim in his age. His honey-blonde hair, still thick, was streaked with white along the temples. The lines around his eyes and mouth were a permanent fixture despite his lack of smiles. Dark brown eyes peered down a straight nose to survey the state of my appearance. "Where've you been?"

I gripped my skirt in sweaty hands. He shouldn't be waiting. I should have had time. Time to get home before he could see any evidence of how I spent the day. "The elm was struck. I was fixing it." Righting my posture, I gave him a closed-lip smile. The one Aunt Clodia had said was that of a well-reared lady.

"Yourself?" He stared at me in shock. "We could have gotten a Lynx to come and look at it."

"A Lynx?" Lord Lennox snorted a laugh. "A Lynx doing a favor for any of our houses would be a sight to see."

Our lands bordering each other, my father and Lord Lennox grew up together just as Leith and Oran have. Fire and ice long held power in Bruis and Lennox. The two houses should have been rivals, opposite powers for opposite goals, yet they were the closest allies within the Six. Befriending the power most opposed to one's own preemptively neutralized the biggest threat House Bruis or Lennox could face. What began as strategic allyship almost two centuries ago had transformed into real kinship.

"Yes." Father's mouth twitched, his closest proximity to laughter. "Or a Rudyard. They have a few talented members. The woman who grows the oranges, perhaps."

"Certainly not Clodia," Lord Lennox mocked. "She can barely keep more than a few flowers alive."

"It would be too late for it by the time you could get a nature wielder," I corrected quietly.

"Forgive me," Lord Lennox began, "but I was not aware healers could work on, well, anything other than humans."

"Life is life. I've found the principles are the same, humans, animals, plants."

Father turned to scrutinize me with a pinch in his brows. Despite the flush of embarrassment that I felt at my appearance, I pushed my hair behind my ears. He expected me to be more composed. A lady, not a child. His thumb and forefinger came to hold my chin. The smile he gave me was sad as he searched my eyes. Mother's eyes.

Everyone who knew my mother always remarked on the striking resemblance. He typically avoided looking at me unless he was feeling particularly melancholy. Whenever he was already thinking of her, his gaze would pin me, a crushing weight of dissatisfaction. *She should be here, not you.* The words were never spoken aloud but had stood in the cavern between us for years.

"You'll ride with the boys. We must be off." He released my face to place his hand on my upper back, turning us to the door.

Leith and Oran were walking to the line of carriages as we stepped outside.

"Leith, help your sister into the carriage. You'll see her straight to our chambers, and then you'll stay there. Both of you."

"I'm to ride with Lavinia?" Leith repeated the command as a question.

"Malcolm and I have much to discuss," Lord Lennox said. He dismissed them without a glance. My father's eyebrows raised until he received a reluctant but dutiful nod from Leith.

"Come," Oran held a hand out to me. Warm hands on my waist guided me into the second carriage. He then bent down to Remus, mumbling, "Up you go, little monster."

At court, Oran was stern. His usual confidence became aloof and intimidating. Whenever we were at the palace, I observed him like a stranger who had traded his grins for glares. I delighted in the sight of my favorite sideways smile adorning his face as he passed Remus to my lap. Once we entered the palace grounds, it'd be a rare sight.

I had only a moment to contemplate which would be worse, if he sat next to me or across from me before Leith made the decision by taking the seat across from me. At the brush of Oran's arm against mine, I decided next to me was worse. His scent, amber and warm whiskey vanilla, was a familiar vice. The heat he radiated made me long to lean into him, so I instead pressed myself against the window and crossed my ankles over each other to avoid the brush of his thigh against mine.

"Have you eaten? Where is the dinner the cook packed?"

I closed my eyes, listening to the sound of our trunks moving as he rummaged through them. I only opened them once I heard his triumphant "ah." Oran unwrapped each sandwich before handing me one.

"Thank you." I smiled. Cucumber slices on top, my favorite.

Leith grunted as Oran passed him his own. The continued brooding was excessive for being left out of a two-hour carriage ride. If he was going to stew in rage, I'd let him—at least while I ate. I never benefited in any way from rising to match his anger. As I inhaled dinner, I wondered if he was so upset that I could have his as well.

"Are you going to pout the whole ride?" I dusted the bread crumbs off my hands and wiped the corner of my mouth with the napkin Oran had placed on the seat between us.

"You missed a bit of drool," he snapped.

I kicked out at his shin. "Honestly, Leith"—I rolled my eyes—"A hunt cannot be that important. King Alaric doesn't expect you to solely ensure there are deer to shoot."

"It's not just a hunt, Lav," he sighed.

I waited in silence. I had asked enough times. He could tell me, or he could be miserable on his own.

Finally, he sighed again. "The king is displeased, and that makes him volatile. Unless we want to be on the receiving end of his ire, it is crucial we all do our part to remain in his favor."

"Why is he so unhappy? The court season has just begun," I scoffed.

Leith eyed me with exasperation. How he expected me to hear the rumors the men of court do was beyond me. "There are rumors about the queen. They are getting worse with each day, and the king is doing nothing to dispel them."

"What are the rumors saying?"

"She has not just fallen out of favor with the king. There are whispers of her failure to aid the Wasting."

My head shook frantically in dismissal. "If a nature wielder was all that was needed to cure the Wasting, it would have been done years ago." It was absurd to expect Bryony to make a difference. The Wasting had been ravaging the land for my entire life and would continue until the Graces were satisfied.

"Yes," Oran agreed, "but he is desperate. He is nearing forty. She has delivered neither a son nor a cure for the Wasting." Oran's square jaw was clenched, making him look older than his twenty-five years.

"They've been wed for two years. It's preposterous to demand a son immediately. She'll become pregnant with time."

Oran ran a hand through his chestnut brown hair, pushing the soft waves back from his face. "Or she won't. Sevasti was his wife for four years and never gave birth. Queen Margaux only had a living daughter to show for their decade of marriage."

Leith's voice was cold as he said, "A daughter, a dead son, and a string of failed pregnancies. The king has lost his patience."

Fear shot through me at his tone. The way he was speaking was as if it were already decided. Not Bryony. She was kind, she didn't deserve—*no*, I couldn't let myself think it.

Concern for the king's temper had always seemed exaggerated to me. Father believed him to be a just ruler. It was one's own nervousness that made them fearful of King Alaric.

The carriage hit a bump, sending me jostling into Oran's side. My arms tightened around Remus, holding his napping form to my lap. My entire right side pressed against Oran's left. He made no rush to move me. His hand ran down the back of my head, ending at the base of my neck with a gentle squeeze.

It was to Oran that I said, "Not a second wife." Bryony betraying Proventium as Sevasti had was unthinkable.

He said nothing, but the tick of his jaw told me he believed the king could.

CHAPTER 2
LAVINIA

"Come on, give me a challenge!"

The taunt made me raise my attention from the book in my lap. No blood. Yet.

Rhode Thallium circled Caius Vaux in the large competition ring on the grounds of the palace. He had promised me with a wink that he would do no bodily harm, but I trusted his intent more than his execution. Luckily, the two were practicing without magic.

"Your left is open," Caius reminded as he smacked Rhode's flank with the flat of his sword.

"I kept it open because your right is so weak."

"See, when I step here, you want to put your right foot there. And then, yes, exactly that."

Another pair sparred on the far-right side of the ring. Two Vaux, Antonius and...what was the other cousin's name? I'd mended a broken wrist for him last year during the Solstice games. He had looked more in pain from having to accept the help of a Bruis than the broken bone. Jupiter? Junis? Justinius? If he needed help from me again, he'd have to ask nicely.

The competition ring was slightly removed from the intricate gardens that took up the majority of the western grounds behind the palace. The breeze from the sea beyond was a constant presence. A few ladies and their maids whispered as they eyed noble sons from their seats in the sparsely populated stands surrounding the ring.

I was often on hand for the nobles sparring at the palace. Should there be blood or broken bones, the palace healers needn't concern themselves with lesser sons. Rhode was more often than not involved in taking sparring one step too far. His powers were easy to unleash but harder to rein in.

It was important for heirs to prove their skill in the ring. Houses, especially the Six, remained poised to fight for position with the crown, or for the crown, should the royal house weaken.

Power in the kingdom was condensed into seven houses: six noble and one royal. The nineteen other noble houses lacked influence in magic, land, money, and standing. They followed the hegemony of their allied house in the Six: Bruis, Lennox, Delphi, Thallium, Lynx, or Vaux.

At twenty-nine, Julius Vaux was the youngest head of house. Graced with the power of speed, like his brother Caius, his magic made him formidable in battle. The House Vaux army, comprised of Spirit magic, speed and strength, had won favor with the king during the Conquering. In close combat, they were said to have defeated rebel factions triple their size.

House Lynx held a long line of Nature magic. The current head, Alder, was strong enough to level an orchard in one blast or create one anew in minutes. Queen Bryony was one of Alder's many distant nieces.

The Graces bestowed House Thallium the ability to manipulate metal. Cadmium was my father's age and rumored to be the most powerful his house had ever seen.

House Delphi, despite having no offensive magic, held the crown until a century ago. Holding the power of sight and fortune, the Delphi Kings of past could see outcomes and futures. They used this to preserve peace and forge alliances. It was said that each decision of House Delphi was guided by the Graces to hold the throne.

The last Delphi king foresaw nothing that would prevent his usurper.

The previous queen, Sevasti, was of House Delphi. I had always wondered if her fate had been as unavoidable as the house's overthrow all those years ago.

House Delphi conceded defeat to the storms of House Harald. The

Graces installed the Harald line on the throne for expansion. House Harald assured the people of Proventium prosperity, hand-picked by the Graces to safeguard and lead.

"Lavinia!"

Ruby Southton Lennox breezed toward me. Her signature red gown complemented her tawny brown skin. Ruby's mother, Sapphire, was the sister of Amethyst, Lady Lennox. The sisters had wed brothers. Her father, Hercule, was Lord Lennox's younger brother.

"Ruby." I smiled. "Did you just arrive?" I closed my book and handed it behind me to where my maid, focused more on embroidering than chaperoning, sat. Simonette, Ruby's maid, joined her with a soft greeting.

Ruby fluffed her caramel-colored curls. "Yes. Do I look a fright?" Sitting next to me, she arranged her skirts, smoothing the folds to fall in a perfect line. Ruby was a radiant beauty. I had never seen her look anything less than immaculate. "I wanted to ride with you and Leith, and Oran," she tacked her cousin on as an afterthought, "yesterday but Papa insisted I ride with him. He was quite miffed at not being invited to the king's excursion. Between you and me, of course." She paused until I nodded. "Mama told him it was small, Lennox, Bruis, and Vaux, heads only, but still he was furious."

I felt a pang of sympathy for Caius. Despite being unwed and childless, his brother failed to treat him as the true heir to the Vaux line.

"You mustn't tell Oran. His patience for my father is very thin. I suppose that soon enough he'll start angling as a Bruis instead of a Lennox with the marriage," she mused.

While men trained their magic to protect their house and Proventium, women were to train their magic for marriage only. We were to test its depths and control, but no further. A woman's dowry was to be her power.

"Did I tell you?" Ruby clutched my arm. "Our fathers are going to ask the king to approve the wedding date! Next month, we'll be wed!"

Ruby's enthusiasm was infectious. No matter the arguments with my brother, I was happy for her. "We'll officially be sisters!" I squeezed her hand with a grin. "Leith is very lucky to have you. You're far too good for him."

She demurred. "We're lucky to have each other." Looking out at the ring, she grew contemplative. "I had spent so long terrified of being wed to someone old or cruel. When I pictured the kind of man that we'd need an alliance with, it was always someone dreadful. I'm so relieved that it's Leith. He's handsome, charming. He makes me laugh." She looked back at me for approval. I hoped the smile I gave her was enough. "I do think we'll be happy together."

"You will," I murmured. Ruby nor Leith had ever dreamed of marrying for love the way I had. Marrying for politics, for power, was expected. Getting attraction and friendship was a gift beyond their expectations.

"Has your father said any more about a betrothal for you?"

Two years ago, I had thought I was on the brink of a betrothal. Though it was not one my father knew of. My eyes returned to the sparring ring against my better judgment. I allowed myself one inhale and exhale before I tore them away. "I know he is plotting something. Egos pose a problem. Most of the higher sons don't want a healer, but my father struggles with the idea of a Bruis, no matter the power, with a lower son or cousin. Or Graces forbid a son not of the Six." My father and brother would see it as a personal shame to have me lowered so.

"Graces forbid!"

A mass of sunflower yellow caught my attention. Meadow Haase waved to us as she walked along the side of the ring. "Lady Lavinia, Lady Ruby! So lovely to see you both."

"It's been too long," Ruby gushed. "We must have tea soon, so I can hear all about what you've been up to." Ruby fluttered her fingers in a parting wave before turning to me. "Insufferable," she muttered. "You'd think her family would have learned to employ some subtlety. Everyone knows that they want Caius, but he's still never spoken a word to her. She should feel humiliated."

Rhode's shout of pain pulled our attention back to the ring. He clutched his arm to his chest while his magic ripped the sword from Caius's hand. The clatter of the sword drew all eyes to them.

"I'm sorry! Are you alright? I said we should take a break! You were getting sloppy. It's not my fault, I did try and warn you." The words rushed out of Caius, frantic and worried. "I'm sorry!"

The weapons rack on the side of the ring began to shake with a rattling clang. Rhode was unaware, still doubled over in pain. "Rhode," I shouted. "Come here and stop acting like a child. It's just a bit of blood for Graces' sake."

"Do you need an escort, my lady?" Caius offered his elbow to Rhode, the jest another apology.

"Piss off," Rhode laughed.

"I really am sorry."

"Nonsense," Rhode dismissed with a smile.

Caius's frame relaxed as he returned one of his own.

The two were above average height, equal in size and build, but opposites in coloring. Rhode was fair with white blonde hair and eyes so dark they were almost black, while Caius was dark-skinned with piercing, pale grey eyes. They had both cut their hair since I had last seen them over the winter, leaving only a close crop of hair.

Rhode used to have enough hair to weave my fingers through, to tug and guide.

"You've been very kind to train with him. He's a wretched student," I told Caius when he stopped in front of Ruby.

He nodded in gratitude. "He needs all the help he can get."

"I take it back. Say sorry for that," Rhode ordered with a huff. He shot his injured arm out to hit his friend, before drawing it back with a hiss.

"The dramatics could not be more unattractive," I told him. "You're lucky there isn't a bigger audience."

"Please, there's nothing unattractive about me," he purred. An opportunity to flirt was the fastest way for him to forget an injury.

"No blood on my dress, please." Ruby blew a gust of wind into his face as she scooted away.

"It'd match." He slumped down next to me and dropped his arm in my lap.

"Ew." Ruby grimaced, averting her gaze.

"It's not too bad," I assured. Damp with blood, the sleeve of his maroon shirt stuck to his arm. The color did its best to disguise the wound. "Could you please get water and a rag?" I asked Caius.

As Caius left, Rhode leaned his head closer to mine. "I kept my promise, didn't I? I didn't draw any blood."

"A kept promise from Rhode Thallium? A first." My tone was light, though both he and I knew the depth behind my words.

Undeterred and ever shameless, he grinned. "I'm happy to make and keep a few more promises if you save me a dance or two tonight." His light brown eyebrows danced on his face.

"I promise you that would end with Leith making you into an ice sculpture in the courtyard."

"Ah, well…then you could warm me up." He winked. The smile he gave me brought my mind back to the summer we were twenty. The whispered promises, the brush of his hand against mine, the soft searching kisses pressed against the garden hedges.

A wink, a touch, a kiss, all given to many eligible ladies at court.

I shook my head as Caius returned. Even if the current of attraction still hummed between us, I was not the same girl, so eager to be loved that she deserted her judgment. I refused to be. Rhode would do as his father instructed, no matter the misery it brought him.

"No rag," he said, handing me a water flask.

"Fine," Rhode answered. He made a show of rolling his eyes before removing his hand from my lap to strip his tunic. "Not a true rag like Caius's, but not one of my nicer ones." He handed it to me before placing his arm back. "All yours, my lady."

Ruby gasped. "You're going to cause a scene!" She didn't avert her gaze from the newly-revealed expanse of ivory skin.

I tracked the drop of sweat that ran down his stomach, following the line of dark blonde hair into the waist of his trousers. Sweat I had tasted from the side of his neck. I shook my head again, ignoring the smirk I knew adorned his face. His vanity needed no further encouragement. Dumping water on the hem of his tunic, I was relieved to find that the blood had made the injury appear worse than it was.

I placed my hand over his cut, feeling the pulse of his blood as flesh and skin slowly knit back together under the silver threads of magic. I filled my lungs again, as a final push smoothed his skin.

"Thank you," Rhode said softly.

"You're welcome," I replied in the shared breath between us. Too close for being in public, I leaned back to create distance. Rhode remained where he was.

"Not a single mark," Ruby praised.

"Lavinia is too talented to leave a scar," Rhode scoffed.

"That was," I stuttered, "that was actually quite nice." I had never before received a compliment from Rhode on anything other than my physical appearance.

"I am nice. I can be very, very nice. If compliments are what you'd like to touch me some more, I have more than enough to last us the whole evening. Maybe even through to the morning."

"Oh, stop." I flushed. I removed my hand from his arm, but he was content to leave it resting in my lap.

"Your footwork really is appalling." Caius's voice held a hint of worry.

"I can't be good at everything. Wouldn't be fair to the rest of you."

"Footwork is your failing?" I raised my brows.

"Footwork," he nodded with resignation. His voice dropped to a murmur low enough only for me to hear. "I'm not great with gold either."

"Haircuts are another failing," Ruby chimed. "You both had lovely hair. What happened?" Her eyes widened in exaggerated horror.

"Did you two cut your hair together, or do you match on accident?" I asked.

"I'm shocked you're able to tell us apart," Rhode joked.

Caius pointed at Rhode. "He copied me. He's so desperate to be like me, it's worrying."

"Cai, you begged us to match. Your letter, I remember it well, read: 'My dear most handsome friend, I won't cut my hair until I have your agreement that you will as well.'"

"That's not right, the letter said—"

A shout of "Thallium" ran out from the edge of the ring.

I squeezed my eyes shut with a groan.

"Oh, Graces," Ruby breathed at the tone. Raising her voice, she cheered, "Darling!"

Leith's stride did not break. "Get up!"

Rhode made a slow show of standing. Unbothered by my brother's fury or his own nakedness, he remained relaxed and a little smug.

Caius took a step back, eyes bouncing nervously between me and Rhode.

"You should go," I told him lowly. Caius wasn't built for conflict.

"I'm fine, Cai. I'll see you later." Rhode gave a shrug for good measure.

Caius shifted his weight, hesitating for a moment before retreating with an apologetic grimace.

Ruby grabbed Leith's arm to stop him passing. Pressing against his side, her voice was saturated with adoration designed to distract. "How was the hunt?"

"Calm down." I too stood. "I was healing his arm."

"I don't care if his arm was falling off. He can find Padgett, or better yet, he can drop dead."

"Bruis, come now," Rhode chided. "Lavinia and I are old confidants. You know this."

"You don't want to get into what I know."

"Nothing untoward would happen in front of an audience, Bruis. If that's your preference, I pity Lady Ruby."

Leith took a menacing step forward.

"Darling, don't cause a scene," Ruby begged. Her eyes darted around the grounds as she faked a thin smile.

Before Rhode could respond, he let out a curse. His hand flew to the side of his neck as a spark burst.

"Thallium," Oran's voice boomed behind us.

Embarrassment pooled in my stomach as I turned to watch his approach. Leith seeing me with Rhode had anxiety tapping at me like a sudden rain, annoying and inconvenient. Oran seeing me with Rhode sent humiliation crashing through me like waves in a storm, overwhelming and inescapable.

"You lost the right to speak to Lavinia," Oran growled.

"Why don't you and Bruis run off?" Rhode sighed. "We were having a lovely time until you arrived."

Leith crossed his arms. "We so missed you at the hunt this morning. Such a shame," he lamented with a grin as icy as his voice. "Your dear old father will just have to keep using *you* as his target until he gets an invite."

Sympathy was an ache twisting in my chest. Lord Thallium's harsh hand was widely known but never discussed.

Oran stopped next to me, bicep brushing my shoulder. Rhode was tall for the men of court, but Oran still had the advantage in height and breadth.

"Rhode," I cautioned. Oran still had his dagger strapped to his waist. It would be too easy for Rhode to use it himself. "Don't." Before I could touch Rhode, Oran reached a hand out to shove him back. His other hand, hot through the fabric of my dress, came lightly to my waist, guiding me a step back.

"We've been forgiving," Leith said, "but all forgiveness has its limits. It's almost as if you don't care about my friendship. Really, Rhodium, I thought we were closer than that." Leith's hand came to his chest in mock dismay.

"So forgiving." Rhode straightened, a smirk proudly adorning his face. "I would never want to jeopardize a friend like you, Bruis."

I felt Ruby's confusion. She hadn't known. Now, Leith would have to tell her. And I would have to pray that she was the friend that I thought she was.

"Leith is forgiving." Oran rolled his shoulders back. "I'm not."

"I think that is quite enough." I raised my brows at my brother. The grounds had emptied further, but we still risked an audience. "We should all return to our rooms."

"Yes," Ruby agreed. "Lovely idea! We must get ready for tonight, darling." She sent me a kind smile as she guided Leith away, Simonette dutifully trailing after them. "Oh, I need to tell you about that wretched Meadow Haase."

The relief loosened the worry knotted in my gut. "Off you go," I tossed at Rhode over my shoulder.

"Gorgeous, it's always a pleasure." The grin on his face was filthy in suggestion. "Lennox"—He looked Oran up and down—"it's always an obligation." The swathe of bare skin as he left garnered a gasp from two ladies leaving the rose gardens.

"What did you see in him?" Oran whispered the admonishment as he came to stand in front of me. I noted the clench of his jaw, that familiar tick told me when his mood was more than just his usual brooding.

"He doesn't speak to me the way he does to you," I excused. Oran was the last person on the continent that I wanted to speak of Rhode.

"We must work on your taste in men before you marry," he grumbled.

I took his extended arm with a smile. "Are you offering?"

"Ah, Vin, if only you were ready for what I had to offer."

I felt heat from his flirtation rise to my cheeks. Rhode flirted constantly and baldly. His tone lascivious and brash. Oran's flirtation contained none of what made the game familiar to me. Straightforward, almost earnest, but at my blush, he always let it drop.

I didn't push for fear of rejection. A childhood crush hanging over us was mortifying enough. I would never again be able to look him in the eye with acknowledged, unrequited love staining his gaze.

And Oran didn't push because, despite the way he flirted, he didn't want anything more with me. My mind knew that Oran saw me as nothing more than a friend at best and a responsibility at worst, but my heart, racing at the sight of him, had yet to accept that.

I fought not to think of *that* moment. The moment that I thought was the start of the rest of my life. Despite my efforts, a masochistic part of me often revisited the hope and the devastation. The regret I had seen on his face had long been my favorite bruise to press.

"So," I began as we walked back to the palace, Leith and Ruby visible in the distance. "How was the hunt?" As we made our way toward the north wing of the palace, shade from the imposing towers blocked the sun that beat down on the ring. The eagles carved into the grey stone spires peered down at us.

"Fine. You may thank me for the venison that will be served tomorrow."

"Wonderful! I'm glad all was well. I knew Leith was worrying for nothing." I breathed a laugh that was quickly interrupted by the tick in Oran's jaw. "What aren't you telling me?"

He paused, the muscle in his jaw fluttering. "He did not speak directly of the queen. He wished Leith happiness in his upcoming marriage. 'May it be more fruitful than mine.'"

"Poor Bryony." She needed to get pregnant quickly. Or at the very least, say whatever lies he wanted to hear to earn enough time to endear herself to him again. "And I assume the men all laughed."

"I found nothing to be remotely funny. For any man to speak of his wife that way is dishonorable. King or not."

"Yes." Oran never laughed out of pity, cruelty, or social convention, only true amusement.

"Lavinia, listen to me." He stopped. His right hand ran down the back of my head to squeeze the back of my neck. His hand was gentle, but his face was pained. "Until we are back home, it is best for us all to avoid drawing the king's notice. Don't be a part of any talk that could garner his attention."

"Of course. I don't...I've not spoken to him since I was a girl."

Before I was old enough to formally be at court, King Alaric was larger than life in my mind. Bright copper hair, a booming laugh, and richly colored attire. At my formal introduction to court at sixteen, he may as well have had command over the sun, for I could barely look at him. His presence was so overwhelming, my hands shook as I curtsied before him. His smile had been kind. I remembered that, the relief I had felt at the kindness of his welcome.

"Talk of you and Rhode is included." His voice was stern. "Your father is on edge as well. You don't want to push him into making a hasty decision on any upcoming betrothal."

"Of course!" I wanted to stamp my foot in anger. There was no me and Rhode. "The only ones that could make a problem are you and Leith. You act like brutes. That is what makes people talk. Rhode and I certainly aren't going to say anything. That leaves you two. If I'm speaking with him, you need to trust that it is innocent. And I need to trust that you'll not cause a scene."

"Agreed." He nodded slowly, in time with the tick of his jaw. "It will not be a problem for much longer. Your father and brother are looking to have you wed soon. I expect in six months' time, you'll be safely married."

A breeze, far too cold and violent for summer, lashed through the gardens, whipping my hair and sending a chill up my spine. As bumps rose on the exposed skin of my chest, I felt a prickle of apprehension lay root in my gut.

CHAPTER 3
LAVINIA

Ugly. Outdated. Hideous color. Itchy fabric. What in the world was I thinking?

Each season, the dresses I left behind in my room at the palace were seldom missed. I could hear Thomasina in my head already: *I'm not sure the girls in the village have need of velvet or silk.* They likely didn't, but I knew she'd take them anyway. I studied the floral embroidery on the gown in my hand. The hem was too short on me now, but it would make one of the village girls a charming wedding gown.

"I'm looking for my niece. Do you know her?" The familiar song-like cadence of the words washed over me like the comfort of a warm bath.

"Aunt Clodia!" I gasped as my aunt glided into my bedroom. Throwing myself in her arms, we stumbled back a step at the impact. Her laughter rang through my solitary chamber like windchimes on a spring day.

Aunt Clodia's hair, once as dark as mine, was pulled into a bun at the nape of her neck. Soft streaks of silver marbled the strands around her face. Keeping her arms around me, she pulled back, the lines around her eyes deepened with joy. "Sweet girl." Our eyes matched in color, but unlike mine, which dominated my face, round and overlarge, hers were narrow with a feline tilt at the outer corner.

"I didn't know you were coming this season." My aunt lived

between Proventium and Elvor.

"Your father invited me." Her expression was heavy with sympathy and regret. "He'll be here in a moment to discuss."

"Aunt Clodia, I don't... I'm not ready." I knew I sounded childish. Many women were married much younger than I, yet that did nothing to quell my panic.

"You will be," she said the words lightly, not a command but an assurance. She looked behind her to the door. Her emerald earrings bounced against her jaw with the motion. "Listen to me." She raised her eyebrows expectantly. "No matter what he says, you are not powerless in this. Beauty is power. Use it yourself, or it will be used for you. Or against you."

I nodded loosely. A numbness settled in my limbs. I'd been a fool to pretend this wasn't imminent. My forced ignorance had done me no favors.

"I know that you are like your mother. Marrying for love." Her nose wrinkled in disdain.

She had told me my whole childhood the merits of marrying for your own purposes, the freedom that comes with being a widow. When I wouldn't be swayed, she had instead begun giving advice on who to fall in love with, as if even then I had any choice.

"You can fall in love after the marriage," she offered. "My first husband suited my purposes. I grew fond of him." Her tone suggested otherwise.

"I don't want to marry an old man," I breathed.

"Yes, Octavia couldn't be convinced either. I keep hoping," she lamented. "My second husband, it wasn't love at the start, more so passion. Oh, I was mad for him. Boredom only set in a few years before he died, so it was a great success all things considered," she trailed off with a purse of her lips. Clodia shook her head, dismissing an errant thought. "Pick someone good. You can fall in love with anyone." She smiled as if the solution to my problem had presented itself.

Before I could reply, Father entered the room without looking at either of us. Dressed in pale Bruis blue, he sat in the armchair of a matching shade. The soft blue surrounding him made his eyes darker in his pale face.

"Sit, my girl," the order was given as he adjusted his cuffs.

I took the chair opposite him in front of the hearth while Clodia perched on the edge of my bed with a smile. Sitting off to the side, I would only be able to spare her the occasional glance as I faced my father, denying me the confidence that emanated from her.

Father studied the hearth. The pinch in his expression told me he wasn't finding what he wanted in the flames. Even still, the crumple of his brow was less pronounced than when he looked at me.

His eagerness to marry me off, I knew, included that he'd be free of my presence.

"I'm not in the mood to look at you."

He'd said it one evening when he'd been drinking. I was no more than ten years old, but the pain it inflicted was still fresh: wet blood dripping down my chest after all these years.

I had left the library with tears blurring my vision. In the entryway, Oran caught me by the arm. I was never allowed out after dinner, but as long as the sun was up, the boys could do as they pleased. If the sun were setting, then I could go to bed. I wanted to cry alone and bring an end to the day without having to answer questions. Thomasina would look at me with pity; I needed to get into bed before she saw me. Oran pulled me into his arms without a word. My head barely reached the middle of his chest, he was growing quickly into a young man, leaving me a child alone.

"Please stop crying. Please don't be sad. Please."

"Tell me something happy."

"I snuck Elvor chocolates out of Uncle's trunk for us."

I could feel sympathy for Father's grief now, but as a child, I had needed more from him than the blame and burden of his mourning. He tried his best to love us, but Mother's death took too much of him. The man Clodia remembered from his courtship with Mother didn't survive. He, too, was buried in Bruis Mausoleum.

The man who remained poured himself into politics. With that came responsibility. One Leith and I worked toward every day. Father was a smith, his expectations a forge.

Leith's good humor honed into a cunning blade by Father's disappointment. The man Father wanted Leith to be was powerful and unapologetic. Charming, not for the joy of it, but for what it could get him.

Where Leith was sharpened, my edges had been whittled away; rounded and softened, designed to please and appease.

Leith could become a courtier Father wanted, that he'd be proud of. Father's disappointment in me would not be solved on my own. It would continue to carve away at me until there was nothing left. Unless I found a husband whom he could be proud of.

"Your aunt is here to help me in finding you a match. It's been put off long enough, and it will be done this season."

"But Leith is getting married this season." I fought to keep the pleading out of my voice. Begging would not sway my father.

"Ruby is two years younger than you." Even commanding, Father's cadence was measured.

"Yes, Father."

"Lavinia, my patience is not infinite." He finally looked at me then. His regard a harsh, unyielding bronze. "I forgave you your folly. I understood it was the Thallium boy's fault."

Clodia's nod brought the prick of tears to my eyes. I had begged Leith not to tell Father, but I had not been shocked when he had. The sting of betrayal had been soothed by its inevitability. But Father telling Clodia? The humiliation amplified betrayal's bite, leaving me raw and aching.

"Yes," I whispered. I stared at fire crackling lowly in the hearth.

"You didn't want Lord Merrifield, and I agreed." He crossed one booted foot over his knee. "The Merrifields have just lost a large portion of their lands, so that decision was fortuitous."

I nodded loosely and forced my lips upward. I hoped the smile didn't look as pained as it felt.

"Your mother wouldn't have wanted that for you," Clodia said as a chastisement of Father. "Graces rest her soul. Her beautiful Lavinia with that toad? He's older than you, Malcolm."

"Your first husband was how old?"

She gave a light laugh. "Far older than my father," she purred, "that was the point. The wealth and power of his title without the dull confines of a husband. Lavinia wants to be a wife. I wanted to be a widow."

Father sighed but didn't respond to her. To me, he said, "I know your aunt has told you stories about your mother and I. Love like I felt for your mother is rare." He cleared his throat, the motion doing nothing for the raspy quality of his voice. I often wondered if his voice had always been so, or if it was a mark left from the howling grief of Mother's loss. "Even rarer were the circumstances. My father was dead. It was my choice alone. I took a risk because I was confident in my standing. Thankfully, that risk was worth it. I got to love your mother. Leith inherited my powers by the fortune of the Graces."

The relief in his voice made me grit my teeth.

"Others aren't willing to take such risks, Lavinia. Sons need to be strong. The Delphi were overthrown because they weren't strong enough. The Thallium line was not a member of the Six until they overthrew the Irons. Lord Vaux survived his challenge because his father chose a wife who would give him strong sons. No family is secure by chance. It is strategy that keeps power within the right bloodlines."

"I understand the burden on you and Leith." I had known that fact since I was a girl. Not only was I a wraith haunting Father with his late wife's image, but I was also a liability to the Bruis name. "But I could find someone who doesn't think of it that way. Who thinks of me the way you thought of Mother." I looked to Clodia. She could be swayed by pleading.

"The Thallium boy was lying to you." A slap would have been kinder than Father's tone. "Cadmium will not risk weakness, not when unrest over the Wasting is worsening. The traitors grow bold. The Merrifields would have no land left if not for the Ravens sending aid." He shook his head with frustration. "Thallium land is some of the richest in the kingdom. They will not risk a healer heir losing it all."

"Not Rhode, but someone else," I mumbled. It was easy for Father to shield me from the effects of the Wasting. Our land in the east was safely removed from the destruction in the west.

"There are a few who are not heirs but could be suitable for you. A Vaux or Delphi boy."

"Come now, Malcolm," Aunt Clodia chided. "You know men. There are more than a few who can be swayed by a beautiful girl with a sweet smile. Men lost their heads around my sister as they will around Lavinia."

"Be careful with what you are suggesting."

"I'm not implying anything untoward. Men have done far more extravagant gestures than marriage when infatuated. Lavinia simply needs to pick a man she wants to charm."

"Clodia," he reprimanded. "A beautiful face that comes with a gamble is not as simple as you'd lead her to believe."

"Not simple but possible. I did it twice. My sister did it."

Father rubbed a hand along his brow. "If only Hugo or Hercule had had a few sons. One of them would have to take you."

Heart stuttering, I chanced. "He has Oran."

"That boy is a liability. Obstinate and careless. The stain of his parents is something he'll never escape. Other fathers may tolerate a Lennox at a price, but not me."

"But you just said…if my prospects are so low, then the price of Oran's father would be worth it."

Coyly, Aunt Clodia reminded, "Not caring about the opinions of others sounds quite like how you were as a boy, Malcolm."

"I could do so because my standing was secure. The traitor's son is an arrogant fool if he thinks he is in the same position. A healer is better than a traitor. I don't trust the boy, and neither does the king."

"I think the Lennox boy is very handsome. Something about a fire wielder that I've always liked."

"Clodia," Father snapped.

"I wasn't speaking about how fire wielders are as lovers, though my experience was pleasant."

His throat rumbled with disgust.

"Come now," she reprimanded, "the private life of a widow cannot be so shocking to you, Malcolm. I birthed a son, but you want me to pretend to be a virgin? Lavinia should—" she continued until Father cut her off.

"Lavinia will not act like you."

"Honestly, Malcolm, I'm trying to help."

I looked down at my hands. Foolish every time. I never learned to stop hope flickering in my chest. A flame as warm and enticing as if conjured by Oran himself.

"You're right. Of course." I felt guilty as I said the words, but the way I felt for Oran was a secret I jealously guarded.

"You will be amenable to whomever I choose."

"But," Aunt Clodia interrupted, her tongue clicking in punctuation.

Father held her gaze for a long moment before continuing. "If you find a worthy suitor on your own, I will support you," he conceded. "Worthy," he emphasized. The finger he pointed brought my eye to the silver wedding band that still adorned his left hand.

My own choice. I had so few in life. This, I knew, was an illusion. A mirage in the desert urging me to continue walking toward an oasis that would never be. To behave, to be good, to do as my father said. But without this illusion, there was nothing to keep me from falling into despair. At least with this, this possibility to choose my own husband, I had action and purpose. I had a goal. Find a husband who was handsome enough, kind enough, good enough. A marriage of love was out of reach, but maybe I could find someone whom I could come to love.

If the love that currently consumed my heart with a crooked grin could fade.

"The Vaux boy." He shrugged. "I'd be delighted. With you, Julius could ensure his brother's children never usurp his own."

"Caius Vaux?" Aunt Clodia looked thrilled. "Lady Lavinia Vaux has a lovely ring to it. I knew Lady Philomena before she married Lord Vaux. When she was Philomena Telis, she was great fun. I can speak to her. Arrange tea for the four of us?"

I shook my head. "He's my friend. He's Rhode's best friend."

"That makes it even easier." Her face lit with victory. "I've never had a male friend who wasn't half in love with me."

I'm sure that was true for Clodia, but it wasn't true for me. "I'll find someone else. I will."

My feet would carry me onward. Even if I never reached the oasis, I'd keep walking.

CHAPTER 4
ORAN

It was so miserably loud.

I could depend on several occurrences during a season at court, one was too-loud balls and banquets.

Also stationary atop the list: my uncle maneuvering at the right hand of King Alaric, young noblemen making asses of themselves at the feet of the Crown and the eligible ladies of court, and Lavinia healing those same men after they lose to me in the sparring ring.

The latter two I enjoyed greatly—an amusement and one of the few precious joys to be found within the confines of the palace.

The first, I benefited from. I acknowledged that even if I was still loath to participate. Uncle Hugo's name and standing shielded me from the repercussions of my father's death and my mother's subsequent banishment. Though only a fool would believe it out of the kindness of his heart.

Magic was not bound by the laws and whims of man. Children received one parent's power by the choosing of the Graces. As a response to hubris or just the fickle nature of magic, unions could occasionally produce children of incongruous strength. Opal, my uncle's only child, had no more than a drop of power, limited to lighting a candle.

I filled a role Uncle Hugo desperately needed. Whatever guilt my uncle had felt over the fate of his sister tempered the rage I knew he still felt toward my father. That guilt used to be my only protection when his resentment toward my father turned on me. Now, it was fear that stayed his hand.

Fear of me finishing what my father started.

For many, my uncle's standing was more than enough to forget that I was a traitor's son. Those who painted me with the brush of my father feared Lennox influence too much to do more than whisper.

My father had been a powerful illusion wielder capable of projecting entire battlefields, new terrain, or legions of men that did not exist into the mind of the enemy. He had been a formidable leader on the battlefield, and yet he had failed. But my uncle had long known that I would surpass both my parents and him in power. If I wanted to, where my father failed, I would succeed.

My mother had sent me to live with her brother when I was five years old. I was named his heir at ten. Claiming me as his own was a way of keeping that power on a leash, a pampered hunting dog to do his bidding. So well-kept, there would be no need to bite the hand of his master. Though he held a few threats over my head to ensure compliance. A dog who understood starvation or the sting of a whip would be grateful even under a harsh master.

Uncle was drawn to anyone with immense power and wealth. It was why, even as a boy, he had taken Malcolm Bruis to be his friend and ally. It was why I was the obvious and only choice for his heir.

I was confident that my power was enough to keep House Lennox firmly in place without the extra machinations. Uncle Hugo was aware that I would never jockey for any political standing. He made no secret of his frustration with that fact, but he also knew that it was my magic House Lennox rested on.

The truce we were in was sustainable. Uncle would not act upon his threats, and I would not publicly undermine his efforts. He would leave my mother in peace, and I would marry someone for standing. He would not send me to the border, and I would maintain our current alliances.

As for the rest, I was free to do as I pleased. Without causing scandal.

What I really wanted was not something Uncle was denying me, nor was it something he could give me.

Lavinia sat across from me. The top half of her hair was twisted at the back of her head in an intricate braid, affording me a clear view of her sculpted profile. The rest of her hair was left to pour like midnight silk down her back, brushing the top of her waist. Three pearls dripped from each ear, drawing my attention to the heart-shaped point of her chin and the pout of her rosy lips. Her gown tonight was rich azure with accents at the waist of a blue so pale it almost matched the crystal of her eyes. Enraptured, I watched as she smiled at something Ruby said.

Bruis had ushered Leith from his right to place Lavinia at his side. He kept a proprietary hand on the back of her chair as he scanned the hall. Her aunt was on his other side, her whispers to Lavinia behind Bruis's back going ignored but not unnoticed if his frequent eye rolls were any indication. My uncle was across from Lord Bruis, granting me an unimpeded view of the way the wine brought a flush of rose to Lavinia's creamy complexion.

She was so inconveniently beautiful.

No, Lavinia was not something that could be given to me. Nor something I could take for myself.

I would not allow further weakness for exploitation. Uncle lay like an executioner's blade over my mother's fate, a familiar brand of torture. Painful but endurable, expected, and without finesse. The thought of him exercising the same threats over Lavinia was a refined and insidious torture I would not survive. A brutal, slow poison, corroding through me inch by inch.

I was selfish, but even I was not selfish enough to put her in the position of traitor's wife.

The seating change, placing Leith to my left across from his betrothed, had sent him into a mood.

"Stop scowling," I told him.

His lips quirked. "Far be it from me to encroach on your signature appearance."

"Hugo," Uncle Hercule huffed from the other side of Hugo and Aunt Amethyst, "get him in line."

"Pardon?" I took another sip of wine. The boredom on my face was one I perfected in my first year at court. "How will *you* get me in line?" I knew dogs smarter than Uncle Hercule. They learned from a kick to the ribs. Hercule did not.

"Enough," Hugo dismissed us both. Grey and thin, only a glimpse of our chestnut hair remained. Weight and time had padded his jawline and stomach. His heavyset frame was still imposing, but the fit man of my youth had slowed. "Leave him be," he instructed his brother in a low voice. He kept a pleasant smile on his face as he said it. He'd never air Lennox laundry for any at court to see.

Hercule quieted not at his brother's reprimand, but at the hand Aunt Sapph ran down his arm.

King Alaric stood from the table to our right, pushing back with a force that made the table shake—a poor imitation of his magic, the thunder that the whole of Proventium trembled under. A hush of reverence and trepidation fell over the banquet hall.

"Thank you, thank you!" His voice was deep and perennially smug. "Forgive the interruption, I know we are all excited for another season to commence. Tonight, we have the most joyous of news. News to begin our summer celebrations with an eye toward unity, toward prosperity." One long arm extended to gesture at our table. "Please join me in toasting to the betrothal of Leith Bruis and Ruby Southton Lennox!"

Leith, brooding forgotten, smiled and raised his glass to the king, before extending his hand across the table to Ruby. Kissing the back of her hand, he brought an even greater smile to my cousin's face.

Leith stood smoothly. "Thank you, Your Majesty." He winked at Ruby. "And thank you to my beautiful betrothed for saying yes." Chuckles rumbled through the hall. "We are both thrilled to wed in one month's time. I speak for all of House Bruis and Lennox when I say we couldn't be more delighted to formally join our two houses. I feel so very fortunate not just to have House Lennox as family soon, but to have found such a wonderful woman to spend my life with. To Ruby," he toasted.

My glass froze at my mouth as I watched Lavinia lean over to kiss Ruby's cheek. She deserved to be that happy for her own betrothal. The few times it was raised in my presence, Bruis's attention had felt too knowing. He already thought I was a negative influence on his son. His daughter? I'd never be qualified to be her husband. He wouldn't relinquish her. And I wouldn't betray Leith or Lavinia.

As the banquet finished and dancing commenced, the hall felt even more crowded. The evening air, soft and cool through the veranda, caressed Lavinia's hair, amplifying her intoxicating floral scent.

"It's disgraceful," Ruby whispered to Lavinia. "And on my night no less!"

They eyed Lady Aspen's low-cut gown. "I just don't know how she is still standing," Lavinia agreed. "I can barely breathe as is. How did they get her corset so tight?" She pressed her hands to either side of her own ribs in contemplation.

"Lack of shame," Ruby huffed. "Do you remember when she gave Leith her favor at the winter solstice three years past?"

Lavinia's answering hum seemed to indicate the incident was not one she remembered. It was a week after Lady Aspen had been in my bed. Enthusiastic but needy, she had gone to Leith in the misplaced hope of spurring jealousy.

Ruby continued, "Now look at her. Desperate for a match. The latest rumor is that she has bedded the king. Her own cousin's husband! If I were Queen Bryony, I'd have her banished. Or beheaded."

"Ruby," I cautioned.

She ignored me and continued, "Well, I've yet to see the queen, so maybe…"

"No, don't say it." Lavinia shook her head.

Leith leaned forward with a grin. "It's true. Queen Bryony has been ordered to remain at Borras Palace."

Lavinia's face crumpled with concern while Ruby's eyes widened in shock.

"Surely, it will only be temporary," Lavinia mumbled.

"Unless," Ruby began.

"Enough," I groaned.

Ruby squinted her eyes at me in annoyance before tossing her hair in dismissal. Looking to Lavinia, she gleefully reported, "Lady Temperance looks like she wants to throw her drink. She hasn't had competition for the king's bed in months."

"It couldn't happen to a nicer person," Lavinia joked. She seemed distracted, her moonstone eyes scanning the room. Occasionally, an enticing smile would come to her face only to disappear as quickly as it arrived by the bite of her teeth into the plush of her lower lip.

"What was it Temperance called you? Plain? It was something very mean and very untrue," Ruby assured.

"Plain and ghostly," she said the words with no emotion or inflection. "Or maybe it was ghastly? Either way, I've not worn a black gown since. I didn't think I looked so unnerving." Lavinia finished with a self-deprecating laugh.

I remembered the black gown. Matching her midnight hair, the gown had enhanced her striking beauty. The ivory of her skin against the dark gown wasn't ghostly, it was sirenic.

Though I was always a man drowning in her presence.

I had fallen in love with Lavinia like falling into a lake; submerged in an instant, swimming and drowning all at once. No matter how far I swam, I had yet to reach the bottom. The depth was so endless that I no longer remembered how to breathe above water.

Lady Temperance, pale in comparison, was pitiable. A viper of her father's design, whored out to the royal bed just so Lord Sanctas could have the satisfaction of the king knowing his name.

Ladies of lower houses were increasingly primed to follow suit. The families who encouraged this were worse than beggars or common courtesans. Desperation for power, for the king's notice at any cost, was a pervasion corrupting the lower houses.

After the execution of his second wife, the idiots believed their daughters had a chance of being elevated not just to mistress but to queen.

Desperation bred delusion.

I heard his laughter before I saw him. King Alaric swaggered as if every room were a stage. He made his way to stand behind Leith's chair with no shortage of fanfare. I kept my eyes forward. I'd not wrench my neck in an act of deference.

"Leith, congratulations!"

"Thank you, Your Majesty." Leith stood eagerly to clasp his hand.

"What a beautiful bride Lady Lennox will be. Lucky bastard," Alaric laughed, clapping Leith on the shoulder. Ruby gave a bashful bow of her head.

"The luckiest."

Uncle and Bruis had trailed behind Alaric. "Well done, Bruis, Lennox."

Uncle's posture was too stiff to match Leith's relaxed stance. Though he was quickly approaching his fourth decade, King Alaric wanted a performance of friendship from the young lords. From the older lords, he wanted respect.

"Thank you, Your Majesty." Bruis and Hugo bowed.

"Will Oran be next?" The grip that came down on my shoulder was too firm to be pleased.

I inhaled slowly before standing. Ruby and Lavinia remained seated with perfect posture. "Next? I don't know how one is supposed to pick."

As expected, that drew a laugh. "Smart man. The picking is easy"— The king dropped his voice—"for a night." Uncle and Bruis dutifully chuckled. "When you want to pick anew is when things get tricky."

"I would hate to make my life harder. Picking without any promises to weigh me down is much preferred." The words were as hollow as my voice. I felt Lavinia's gaze on me, but I didn't want to see disappointment or even worse, indifference.

Bruis cleared his throat. "Your Majesty, you remember my daughter, Lavinia."

My eyes snapped to her then. She rose gracefully, though I could detect a hint of nervousness. She smiled prettily at the king before dropping into a curtsey.

"How could I forget?" Alaric bowed over her hand, pressing a kiss to the back of it. "My lady, please forgive my crass humor, shameful in the face of such lovely ladies." His sight remained fixed on Lavinia as he addressed Bruis. "A spitting image of your late wife, is she not? A remarkable beauty like her mother. I remember I fancied myself smitten with Lady Octavia as a boy."

If Bruis felt any pain from the mention of his late wife, he did not show it. "Yes, strikingly like her mother."

"Is she an ice wielder as well?"

Lavinia stood with her hands clasped in front of her, the picture of serenity while they discussed her like a new mare.

"A healer. Like her mother in that regard as well."

"Ah, yes, forgive me. That is right. Padgett's excuse for growing lazy. I hope he doesn't work you too hard, lady?" I recognized the wolfish grin he gave her. It was more often directed to Lady Temperance. My teeth snapped together with an audible clip.

Lavinia's laugh was a shaky exhale. "I'm honored to help when he is otherwise occupied. The lords' sparring is excellent practice."

King Alaric revealed large white teeth through his copper beard. Looking to me, he joked, "I can't think of a more distracting sight for them." His leer returned to rake down Lavinia's body. "I'm glad to hear it. If he ever gives you too much work, just let me know. I may happen to know the man in charge of Padgett," he finished with a wink.

I felt warmth rising in my hands but smothered it. We all had no choice but to endure him.

"You're very kind, Your Majesty." The flutter of Lavinia's lashes reminded me that she was raised a good noblewoman. 'No' was not in her vocabulary. Despite our childhood days as heathens running through the fields, her father and aunt had raised her to one day be the ideal wife for a lord. For a king...I couldn't bear to think it. Feeling a spark dance over my knuckles, I clenched my fists at my side.

"I'm looking forward to seeing more of you this season, Lady Lavinia." With another too-low bow at the waist and kiss to her hand, he left.

Bruis stared after him with assessment, Uncle with the hint of a smirk playing at the edges of his mouth, Lavinia with a flush to her cheeks and bewilderment in her eyes.

"Shall we have a dance?" I interrupted. I held my hand out to Lavinia, jerking my head toward Ruby in silent command to Leith. I didn't let her hesitate before I swept her among the throng of dancers.

"Let me guess. I'm in trouble? I can in no way be held responsible for that. I was doing as you asked, that was extenuating and unexpected circumstances," she informed me with a determined tilt of her chin. "You're all so dramatic about him, honestly. I think it's completely out of proportion. He's a man, not a rabid animal on the loose."

"What a guilty conscience you must have to immediately launch into excuses and justifications." Despite myself, Vin always brought me back to the young boy who would tug her braid when she looked away. Anything to have her full attention.

I had no smiles to give of my own; I was too busy searching for hers.

She snorted a laugh. As we spun, her hair brushed the hand I anchored on her waist. "You're so annoying."

"Yes, you've only been telling me that for two decades."

Her smile widened, making my own taunt the corner of my lips.

"Impressive that you have managed to be such a pest for so long."

"My stamina is impressive in other ways." It was my most treasured hobby—drawing first a blush to Lavinia's cheeks and then earning a laugh. The sound reminded me of the sparkling, dancing bubbles in wine. The effect just as intoxicating. "You look gorgeous," I told her. The answering blush made her complexion raspberries and cream. "I cannot blame the king for noticing. As long as it stays as simply admiration. Looking at a beautiful woman won't enrage him. No matter how precarious his temper."

"Just looking," she told me primly. "I don't know what you've come to think of me, but I'm not going to be a mistress."

"I would never think that of you." I had to consciously keep my feet moving to avoid a standstill among the other dancers. "I didn't mean that. I'm sorry, Vin. I'd never think that of you."

"Thank you," she murmured.

Our years together had not dulled the knife of her displeasure. It cut through me, a freshly sharpened blade, each time I earned it. I searched for what to say to make amends. With each turn and step in silence, her shoulders loosened until, eventually, her eyes met mine again. Dancing. I didn't need to say any further apology as long as we were dancing. She'd loved it since her first childhood lesson.

Those crystal eyes pierced through me. "Stop it. You're thinking far too much."

"On the contrary, when I'm with you, my mind goes quite blank." I flexed my hand, squeezing her waist.

"Ah, that's why you're so terribly..." she drew the word out as if in lament, "unproductive."

"Tragically so."

"You could take up a hobby. The flute," she mused, "or perhaps painting?"

"If you'd like me to write songs for you or paint you, you only need ask."

She giggled again. "You'd write something lewd or give me a hideous mole."

"Never." I smirked. Her skin was so smooth, it took all my strength not to stroke her cheek. "A mole wouldn't make you hideous. Some pox marks..." I trailed off.

She threw her head back in delight. The movement made more black silk caress my hand. Combined with her laughter, my heart felt like it may burst through my chest. "So that's your plan!"

"Damn, I always say too much around you, Vin."

"Maybe this new pox mark painting career could be good for you. Ladies could hire you to sabotage unwanted betrothals. Since you have all this time on your hands to spend worrying." She dramatically tossed her head with a grin.

"Exactly. I'll be so busy that I won't have a single care in the world."

If only there were a cure for what Lavinia did to me. It was more than just my waking moments. My dreams, too, were consumed by her. Every worry, every hope, every heartbeat was set to the rhythm of *Lavinia*.

"What do you know about the little Vaux?" Leith crossed his arms over his chest. He was content to let his fiancée dance with one of her Southton cousins. He was less content to allow his sister to dance with anyone associated with Rhode Thallium.

As was I.

"Seems to be Thallium's closest friend. Speed, like his brother. Has good strategy in theory, but in actual matches, he loses his head."

The Vaux boys had been spoiled by their parents. Seven years ago, when Darius Vaux passed unexpectedly, Julius was challenged by Andre Alexandrite. The houses of the Six could only be challenged when an heir inherited their seat. The Alexandrites thought the coddled boy now leading House Vaux their best chance to ascend to the Six. Julius shocked court when he not only won the challenge but spared Alexandrite's life. Alexandrite would not have done the same. The harsh welcome to the Six had hardened Julius, and he was determined to do the same to his brother. Lord Vaux needed an heir, not a little brother. Better for the little Vaux to learn the reality of this world at the hands of his brother than at the hand of another. His brother would stop before it killed him. But Julius's efforts had the opposite effect.

The little Vaux, once a pampered second son, was now a meek younger brother. He only seemed remotely happy around his mother, Thallium, and Lavinia. I knew she was fond of him. Friendship, I thought, maybe tinged with pity, though she'd protest me saying so. Lavinia took in birds with broken wings and blind kittens, of course, she'd befriend the hunched, hand-wringing boy.

He used a burst of speed as he spun Lavinia, sending her into a fit of giggles. The sound beckoned a smile to my face, muscle memory that I bit back.

"Is he the sort who would pursue a friend's former dalliance?" Leith's scowl lifted slightly. "Well, with a friend like Rhode that'd leave no one left for the little Vaux."

"You're not wrong," I conceded in a grumble. Thallium was blind and ungrateful.

"I know how he feels. You're lucky your cousin is so pretty, as you left me no options save for your relatives. You've pillaged every other house of their ladies." Leith was gleeful in his quip.

Anything that kept him from looking closer at who I wished to pursue helped me. Dalliances were not because I was resistant to marriage, but because I knew the only lady I would ever want to marry was not in my reach. "I'd prefer not to be grouped with Thallium, thank you."

"Well?"

"I think the little Vaux sees Lavinia as a friend." I needed that to be the extent of it.

"He looks like that could easily change. We could ensure Thallium wouldn't kill him in a courtship."

"Pardon?" I stuttered. "You want him to pursue Lavinia?"

"Is he not in a convenient position? Only an heir until his brother marries and produces one. He is well-ranked but not so highly that a healer son would ruin him."

"The little Vaux?" My voice rose beyond what was appropriate. Swallowing harshly, I lowered my voice. "He looks like he'd cry if he tried to bed a woman."

"I said courtship. I don't want to speak of him bedding my sister." Leith hacked in disgust.

"You think they'd just play cards were they to marry?" My heart pounded dangerously fast.

Lavinia had had her fair share of suitors ever since she turned seventeen. None were as serious as what she felt for Thallium. Her family allowed her these past two years with no promising, public courtship. Her father had accepted her denial of Lord Merrifield's abrupt proposal last year. Now it seemed he and Leith had decided this would be the year she wed.

"I think that someone her age whom she considers a friend, is better than the present alternatives."

"Matchmaking should not be a burden on your shoulders. You're marrying soon. Lavinia's prospects can wait until after that is complete."

"And leave it to my father?" He challenged.

"Is he so determined that it is to be this season?" The thought of my fate being sealed so soon brought a cold sweat to the back of my neck. It was one thing to accept that I could never have her. It was a dull ache, one that I only let consume me when I wanted to indulge in misery. For her to truly belong to someone else would be a pain capable of driving me mad.

"Why do you think my aunt is here? He floated the idea of Hemlock Lynx the other day."

"He's twice her age." The Lynx was the lord's younger brother.

"But he has a son from his first marriage. He need not worry about the magic of his heir. It keeps her in the Six. It would be a gesture of friendship, of alliance with a house that has always had a strained relationship with us both. The Ward boy, Porter, was the other option. But only his mother is a Delphi."

"She is not in danger of becoming a spinster before the year is done."

"That's easy for you to say. Opal ran off with Dean and got herself pregnant before you or Hugo had any say in the matter. I'd throttle Lav if she tried that."

"Be grateful Vin hasn't tried that. She is a woman who knows her own mind. She should be allowed to pick for herself."

"She tried to pick Rhode Thallium!" The ice in Leith's eyes hardened further in anger.

My jaw clenched with a snap. I needed no reminder of that. Comparisons between myself and Rhode did nothing but dig into a festering wound. The night Leith and I discovered them together, I went to bed with a bottle. When unconsciousness had finally claimed me, it had felt like a mercy. Happy, charming, Rhode Thallium made sense for Lavinia.

She radiated kindness and beauty in a way that was addictive. The shine of Lavinia wasn't blinding. It was hypnotic. Not just stars, she held entire constellations, twinkling in a pattern I wanted to learn like a secret language. My eyes had adjusted to staring at everything bright, and good, and *Lavinia*, leaving all else dull and out of focus. I wanted nothing more than to look at the light for the rest of my life.

I was well aware that I was one on a list of admirers, of moths crowding the light. She deserved someone similar, whose light she could share in.

Not someone who would only take. Greedily soaking up every smile. Hoarding her laughter. Coveting every shining piece of her for himself.

I shook my head. Leith was not someone who deserved my ire.

"Are you nervous about the wedding night? Is that it? Trying to distract yourself?" Goading Leith was all too easy. "Ruby won't know any different, so however horrible in bed you are, it'll be fine. She'll probably be thankful at how quickly it's over."

"Piss off!" He pushed me with a laugh. "Your standard for the women you bed is lower than mine. She's gonna be begging for more." He winked.

"Two virgins together, it really is sweet." I smirked.

Leith sent a blast of ice to me. I grinned back as I evaporated it into a puff of steam.

CHAPTER 5
LAVINIA

"Ow," I muttered. My failing efforts to evade the thorns resulted in a single pearl of blood on my fingertip. I never liked healing myself; the pulse of my magic combined with the heat of mending skin wasn't painful but odd.

Roses were a poor idea. Petunias would be better.

The morning was bright and clear as I walked out of the gardens toward the stables. The wind off the Petra Cliffs ruffled my braided hair. Thick with the garden's heavy floral scent, the air was cloyingly sweet. Dewy grass kissed the hem of my sky-blue day-dress in farewell.

Positioned in the southeast of Proventium, the expanse of the Cirrus Palace grounds was enclosed by the sharp drops of the Petra Cliffs and Southern Sea beyond the gardens.

Court was slow to rise. The sun allotted several hours each morning with only the servants for company, affording me the opportunity to walk the palace grounds alone. By noon, my lack of chaperone would be fodder for the other ladies of court, but now with the forgiving dawn as my only companion, I was free.

I bent to begin picking the petunias that grew along the path to the stables. Hay diluted the floral air, tickling my nose. Under the pleasant din of stable boy chatter and horse whinnies, a high-pitched bark rang out.

"Early, is it not?" Oran's voice brought a smile to my face.

"We can't all be gentlemen of leisure." I remained crouched, looking up at his approaching figure. He trailed after Remus, who fared far better in the mornings than Oran.

Remus bounded toward me on gangly legs that made his eager run more of a clumsy lumber. His large paws hinted at the hound he would have grown into had he not, twelve weeks after his birth, been purchased by my father. We'd not had Remus more than a week before my power claimed his future years for myself.

Stopping before me, Oran placed his hands on his hips. "Leisure? If you could tell my master that"—he pointed to Remus—"I'd appreciate it."

"Hello, my darling!" I greeted Remus with a kiss as he placed his front paws on my knees. "I wondered where you were." I scratched along his ribs, earning a pleased wiggle.

"I got him this morning from the sitting room. Thought we'd have a nice walk while you slept in. Clearly, we should have all just gone together."

"That was so kind of you," I told him.

Through my soft smile, an ache unfurled in my chest. It was hard enough to try to maintain a distance between us. When he reminded me of how thoughtful he was, it was a pull I had no hope of fighting. I rarely had to ask Oran for anything. He was observant, anticipating how he could help before ever being asked.

"My mind painted a lovely image of you in bed." His eyes sparkled.

"In *your* bed?" My lips curved in the familiar game of flirtation.

His gaze heated as it trailed down me, kneeling in the grass. "This may be the only sight that could rival that."

"Oh? On my back, on my knees." I grinned wider as I watched his throat bob with a swallow. "Such narrow fantasies. We'll have to give you some more inspiration lest you get bored."

"With you, I'd never be bored." His dimples deepened in my favorite crooked smile. "You wouldn't either, I can promise you that."

"Such promises," I purred. "I prefer a man of action, not talk."

His mouth opened to retort but closed just as quickly. I watched the moment he decided things had gone past jesting settle into his brows. He studied my face with a concern and regret that made me think I wasn't as good at hiding the true depth of my feelings as I hoped. I averted my gaze, hiding embarrassment under the pile of flowers in my lap.

"Did they not have flowers in your rooms? I have white ones in mine that I can give you."

"These are for Ruby." I stood after a final stroke to Remus. "I'm going to do a portrait of her as a betrothal gift. I thought the red would be a nice touch. More Ruby than the green of the Lennox rooms." It was easier for me to paint a clear vision, a scene in front of me, a memory. I struggled with creating an image entirely anew in my mind. "Then she can also have the flowers to keep. I can ask Aunt Clodia to preserve them." Unlike my mother, Clodia was a nature wielder like their father had been. Flowers were her specialty. "If she likes them," I finished in a mumble. I'd never put together a flower arrangement before.

"I am sure my cousin will love it." He nodded with a certainty that made fondness tighten its grip on my heart.

Even though I didn't have all of him, the piece of Oran I did have was a gift beyond measure. Oran had always believed in me. He was the person I felt safest with. Being truly seen by him was like a warm hearth. No matter where I went or what happened during the day, I knew I had that comfort waiting for me.

"I hope so." I smiled. "Are you and Remus returning?"

"Actually"—he gestured me toward the stables—"I have some business in the stables. If you don't mind waiting a moment, we could go for a ride?"

"Yes!"

With a hand on the middle of my back, he led us in. Each pen was divided in dark wood and black iron. Oran tied Remus with a length of rope to an empty pen by the entrance. Unperturbed, he began happily rolling in the hay.

"Hello!" I greeted the first stable hand we saw, a boy who couldn't have been out of his teen years. "May I leave these here for a short while?" I placed the petunias on a small beam near the entrance.

The boy's eyes were wide in his thin, acne-spotted face. "Of course, my lady," he sputtered anxiously.

"Thank you ever so much!"

That brought more redness to his already ruddy cheeks.

"Come," Oran told me. "Watch him until we are back," he ordered with a glance at Remus. At the strike of my elbow to his gut, he added, "Thank you."

"Don't be a bastard!" A stern voice commanded.

"Is he talking to you?" I joked in a whisper.

Oran's lips twitched as we approached the pen holding a massive blood bay stallion. A stout man, face shrouded by unruly dark brows and a matching beard, stood in front of the beast.

"Fintan," Oran greeted.

"Oran!" When smiling, he looked to be not much older than Oran or Leith.

"Did my new mare arrive safely?"

My head whipped toward Oran. His stallion, Declyn, had already fathered several foals on mares owned by Father and Lord Lennox.

"Yes, sir. She's in the last stall while she decompresses. I tell you, I don't think she's much broken."

"No, not at all to my knowledge."

I inched closer as the stallion threw his head with a stamp of his hoof. He was far taller than the dapple-grey mare I had at home or even Leith's black stallion. His eyes met mine with a snort of hot air.

Oran's hand pulled me a step back by my bicep.

"Give me a moment," Fintan drawled, turning his back on the stallion as if it were a house cat.

Once Fintan was in reach, Oran clapped him on the shoulder in greeting. "I'm actually here to discuss a job I have for you. I'll compensate you well, if you can spare the time."

"I'd be happy to help with any task you have, my lord." He bowed his head.

"I need the new mare to be trained and can think of no one better. She has a good temperament. I merely need your help ensuring it stays that way. I'd like her to be a horse you'd feel comfortable entrusting with your wife."

"It'd be my honor." An eager determination filled his brown eyes.

The mare was beautiful, silky cream with a matching mane. She eyed the men nervously, retreating until her haunches touched the back of her pen.

"Vin," Oran cautioned.

I scooped an apple from the feed barrel against the wall, extending it to her on my open palm. Oran's chest pressed against my back, enveloping me in his scent of vanilla whiskey. Strong hands, poised to pull me back, gripped my waist. She took a cautious step forward, then another. Stretching her neck to take the offering, the barest scrap of teeth and tickle of tongue touched my palm. A smile bloomed on my face even as she quickly retreated once more.

"See, she'll warm up just fine," Fintan said.

Oran nodded. "I'll come back tomorrow when it's quieter to discuss. I'll need regular updates."

Fintan's face grew solemn. Something very different from his earlier enthusiasm settled in the hard line of his mouth.

Oran gave a single swift nod in return before asking, "But for today, what can we have for a quick ride?"

I slowed the paint mare, Camelia, to a trot alongside Oran's dark bay gelding. The sea air whipped my skirts and hair. This view was my favorite part of court. The jagged cliff and sprawling ocean made everything else seem insignificant. Breathing in the smell of salt and brine, I relaxed. The pressure to find someone before Father's deadline had taken all the air out of the palace.

"This was so nice," I told him. "Thank you."

"It's good to get out of the palace." He looked around the cliffs with a wrinkled brow.

"We've only been here a week," I laughed.

"Even still," he sighed. "Do you miss being home?"

"Ask me in another week and I'll be begging for the quiet of home." I looked behind him to survey the endless green we'd ridden. The rolling hills stretched to caress the clouds dotting the mid-morning sky. "If you only look that way"—I gestured behind us—"it almost feels like we are home. It doesn't look so different from our usual rides."

"It doesn't," he conceded. His eyes left the horizon to meet mine. The color of them put the sprawling hills to shame.

In the soft silence between us, I wondered if I should confide in him about Father's deadline, but dismissed the thought as quickly as it came. In this moment with Oran, I wanted to pretend that fate wasn't waiting for me, a fate married to a man I didn't love. I didn't want to spoil the happiness I felt as the sole object of his attention.

Around Oran, I felt like a woman that I could only dream of being. The best version of myself emerged only under his gaze. As if his self-assurance seeped into me. Oran was unapologetically himself. He was kind and fair, never cruel or rash. He was honest and bold, never false or acquiescent. Clodia had long told me to pick a good man. *A woman can fall in love with anyone, so you must ensure he is good first.* But I feared that falling in love with Oran, a man who was so good to his core, had spoiled love for me. How could anyone else compare?

"So why the new mare?" I asked as a distraction. I wouldn't waste the precious time I had with him ruminating on far-fetched dreams.

He cleared his throat before rushing out the words, "She's from my mother."

"I'm sorry?"

"My mother wrote me that she had a lovely mare that she didn't have room for. I sent her money to have one of the village boys deliver her here. Fintan's a good man. I like giving the money to him, and he'll do a good job."

"How do you know him?"

"A fellow Tyth." He shrugged. "I like giving him the work."

Understanding was heavy and solemn. He wanted to help a Tyth. He couldn't give charity, but he could pay well for a task.

At the start of King Vidar's reign, Proventium had absorbed Tythmore. The Conquering was celebrated each autumn on the anniversary. Proventium's grip on Tythmore had seemed absolute until his death. King Alaric, nicknamed the Teenaged Tyrant when he took the throne at sixteen, was nineteen when the largest rebellion since the Conquering was attempted and crushed under his storm. That nickname was then replaced with a host of others—the Conquering King, the Tempest, the Ruling Thunder.

Though he had proven himself equipped with a magic mightier than any of his formidable forefathers, Tythmore continued to revolt. Each time, the rebels were crushed under an unforgiving torrent of thunder and lightning. Those who came to Proventium to escape the scarcity and turmoil of their home were convicted as traitors for the crime of being born in Tythmore.

Oran was protected by his standing. He could help them in small ways without jeopardizing his reputation. He held his shoulders back, chin proud, but the clench of his jaw told me he didn't want to discuss it further.

"Will you visit her again this summer?" At the end of each summer since Oran was sent to live with his aunt and uncle, he traveled west to visit his mother.

"Yes, I'll make the time." He nodded. "She'll be happy for an update on the mare."

"And on you. I know the circumstances are…" I paused, searching for the word.

"Marrying a Tyth was the foolishness of youth. Marrying and having a child with a Tyth who was going to lead forces against Proventium was idiocy bordering on suicidal." His voice held a bite that I so rarely heard from him. His smooth, deep voice was gravely with barely contained anger.

For love. She had done it for love, but put her child in the position of being a traitor's son. I had heard disdain and scorn for Tythmore from Father as long as I could remember.

Rotten people, the lot of them. The Wasting bred from their depravity.

Looking at Oran, however, I couldn't believe them to be bad people. Born from love, Oran could not have been created by evil people. Misguided, perhaps, but not bad. Nothing related to Oran could ever be bad.

"Do you miss her?" His mother was never a subject Oran wanted to speak of. When he'd return from his short visits, he'd recount the journey, the horses, the house, but nothing about her.

"I hardly know her." He tried to dismiss the subject. "She is kind. Always very kind but nervous. I think she doesn't know what to say to me. I certainly don't know what to say to her."

I remained silent, studying his face. The furrow of his brow deepened, the tick in his jaw fluttered, the clench of his hands tightened on the reins. I leaned forward to brush the tips of my fingers down his forearm. When his eyes met mine, he heaved a sigh. "But I think I do miss her. Which sounds foolish."

"It's not foolish." I shook my head. "I miss my mother, and I never knew her at all."

My mother had held me in her arms for only a moment before the bleeding became overwhelming. Drained from labor, she died in my father's arms within the hour.

I thought of her often. If she'd be proud of me. If she'd *like* me. It took years of using my power, our power, before I was able to heal anyone without thinking of her. Of the cruelty of the Graces that she could not heal herself, like my birth stole the power and left her with nothing.

As if reading my thoughts, Oran said, "She'd have been so proud of you."

"You know your mother is proud of you, too." I couldn't stop the note of pleading that permeated my voice.

He quirked a brow. "That I'm like her estranged brother?"

"You're far better than him," I reprimanded, "and she couldn't have hated Hugo. Not if she trusted him with you. She might not know how to connect with you now, to be what you need now, but what you needed then was to be protected. She loved your father and she loves you. She sent you away because of how much she loves you."

The death of Larkin Cahill did nothing to lift the stain on Helene. Everyone knew, despite the Lennox name, that she had married a Tyth rebel. Her distance made it easier for court, for the king, to forget that Oran was Hugo's nephew, not his son. Oran Lennox, not Oran Cahill, was safe from the wrath the king exacted on any Tyth rebel.

It was selfish of me, but I was thankful for Helene's empty life. Oran could have been with her, exiled in the valley between the mountains and the Wasting. And then my life would have been empty.

Yes, it was selfish. Pity and sympathy for her loneliness tapped an insistent rhythm in my head, but the gratitude for Oran that drummed with each beat of my heart would always be louder.

"The older I get, the easier it is for me to understand her. Her choices."

"She had to make an impossible choice. I know she wouldn't have been able to do it if it weren't for how much she loves you."

"Yes," he mumbled. "Love is…agonizing when it isn't enough."

"Love can be enough. Enough for a happy life."

Love.

Everything in my life revolved around it, chasing it, wanting it, keeping it. Even unrequited, it was something I zealously protected. The thought of loving and being loved in return not being enough, was far more depressing than the loveless marriage that awaited me.

"But not always. Pursuing love doesn't always mean happiness. Sometimes you have to choose between love and happiness." His eyes held a pleading that was out of place in their steady depths. Oran, sure, constant, Oran, shouldn't look so desperate.

"That's a sad thought."

"I don't want to make you sad."

"Tell me something happy then," I breathed.

It was a game we'd played for as long as I could remember.

Don't be sad.

Tell me something happy.

"You can name our new horse," he offered. Everything in him seemed to soften at my laugh of surprise.

"Our horse?"

"Ours."

"I'll come up with something good for her."

At that moment, I didn't care if my expression revealed just how lovesick I was. Not when it brought my favorite crooked grin to Oran's face. Not when it crinkled the skin around his eyes. Not when he looked at me like I was his favorite sight.

My cheeks were still warm and aching when I sat in the Lennox rooms to paint Ruby.

CHAPTER 6
LAVINIA

"Dreadful!"

The ballroom was a sea of jewel tones: ruby red roses, emerald and sapphire gowns, onyx and topaz doublets, and the citrine glow of the chandeliers. Typically, Zaid's music was light and melodic, but tonight it was ominous and heavy.

"Very," Ruby agreed with Leith. She clasped her hands at his elbow to rest her head against his shoulder.

"It's interesting," I defended. We were close enough for Zaid to see us, so I kept a pleasant smile on my face.

Leith snorted. "That is certainly a word that could be applied. I don't know why King Alaric is bothering. The decision isn't going to depend on our entertainment. If he sold Gaëlle faster, we could have had a proper party."

The decision was the betrothal of the king's only child, Princess Gaëlle, to the heir of Elvor's throne. Mesgara to the south was more adversary than ally, making Proventium's tie to Elvor in the east vital. The nine-year-old princess had been brought to court for the week from Borras Palace. Sat in a too-large chair next to her father, the copper-haired girl was a statue. Her posture was perfect, eyes unwavering from the stage. Weighed down by a ruby and diamond necklace and matching tiara, her already small frame was dwarfed by the trimmings of her title.

Her father lounged in the throne next to her, jesting with the Elvor ambassador, a slight figure with narrow shoulders. The ambassador's bald head glowed distractingly bright under the candlelight. It was a baldness that he seemed to compensate with a swooping mustache.

"Poor girl," I murmured.

"Lucky girl, more like." Ruby gave a light laugh. "Her future as a queen secured before the age of ten? Nothing poor about it. She'll have seven years to prepare for her future in Elvor."

"So, I should have asked your father for your hand when we were children?" Leith asked with a grin.

"Exactly," she giggled. The light twinkle twirled above the heavy drone of Zaid's performance.

"It's so intimidating. She's a child, but she can't enjoy that because she already has years of expectation laid out before her," I argued.

"Better than the fate of others," Leith scoffed. "Ask a starving wretch on the border if they'd like to keep their childhood or be sent off to be a queen."

Leith would never understand what it was to be a girl. Forced to wait for men to decide your fate, feeling the weight of expectation crushing like a boulder that will never truly be lifted.

"Drinks?" Ruby was already tugging Leith's arm to lead him away from the stage.

I followed slowly while they traded soft words between each other, affection curving their lips.

Assessing the crowd, Father's words from earlier in the week taunted me. An insidious whisper that was as insistent as the pressure of his impending decision digging into my spine. Sitting back and allowing Father to pick made me just as anxious as the thought of selecting for myself. I couldn't bear to move forward, but sitting still was just as painful. I told myself I needed a plan first, but each day that passed without a potential suitor allowed dread to sink another claw into me. Spine contorted in pain, I was unable to brace for the next blow.

Chemistry and attraction were natural, but courtship was to be built on artifice. With each glare or reprimand from my father, I had learned what was expected and improved in the act of a lady. Like shoes that pinched, I could walk, but it was unpleasant. It threw into stark contrast the relief of being barefoot. I could count on my fingers those around whom I could truly be myself. The men I was supposed to attract? It would be a performance—playing the part of Clodia to make them desire me and the part of Ruby to make them view me as a suitable wife.

What do you have to offer? Only the Bruis name.

Musical windchimes danced through the room. I sought out the sound of my aunt's laughter.

The ambassador held one of her hands, leaning over the table as if he couldn't get close enough. My aunt bent forward for a moment, only to sway back, drawing him in further. The edge of the table digging into his stomach didn't interrupt the look of rapture on his face. I studied her in earnest, her movements and smiles effortlessly sensual. She fluttered her lashes, tilting her stance to give the ambassador a subtle view of her cleavage.

Clodia was skilled. A spider gracefully crafting a delicate web. In the light, the beauty of it was entrancing. Men were eager to get a better look, so much so that they didn't even notice they were caught. Some would even plead with the spider to keep them longer, to keep only them. Clodia was as adept at weaving the web as she was abandoning it for a new one. Men still hung in webs long discarded.

Clodia chose men who would suit her purpose. *She had a happy life.* That reminder gained no strength in repetition.

My eyes skipped over married and older men, bouncing between eligible lords. With a deep breath and a toss of my hair, I glanced back one more time at my aunt. I breathed as deeply as my corset allowed. Her words in my head drummed like a battle march.

This is the power women have in this world. There is no shame in using it. Your father wants you to believe that you can do nothing but wait for your fate. Your mother saw what she wanted, and she took it. You can do the same.

My romantic heart, bruised and fragile, had long held the foolish hope that things would fall into place.

My life and future lay in Father's hand. Not outstretched, but clenched at his side. I had accepted having no control over my life, telling myself again and again that I'd miraculously fall into the life I dreamed of.

No longer. I would take control. I would act. If I failed, I could enter a loveless marriage knowing that I tried—that I hadn't given up on my happiness.

Dracaena Lynx, handsome, intelligent, a bit short, but a nice smile.

Chord Growley, charming, good dancer, drinks too much, but always in good cheer.

Arrow Burgundy, tall, easy to laugh, secluded much of the year in the north, but quick-witted.

Not tall enough. Eyes the wrong color. No dimples.

My plan to take control and pick a husband for myself had one fatal flaw. The husband I picked in every daydream since childhood, distracting me from realistic prospects. Longing and desire haunted each conversation as I searched for that familiar, enchanting warmth. Comfort, attraction, friendship, and something indescribable— calloused hands, whiskey vanilla, and a rumbling laugh.

Oran.

The truth, sinking in my stomach like lead, was that Oran was not beholden to either the opinions of his uncle or court. He charmed ladies at his uncle's suggestion but more often picked paramours for the sole reason of his own pleasure. If there was any part of Oran that wanted me, he would have done something about it.

He was playing dutiful heir with his uncle and several Alexandrite. My eyes found him in every paused conversation, but never was he looking back at me.

Rhode was the only man who gave me hope of finding a different love. Lesser, but still love, which was the best I could hope to find in another. Rhode had dangled the possibility in front of me, taunting a cat with a string before taking it out of reach. This time, I would grab it before it could be taken.

After several rounds of conversation, my cheeks ached from false frivolity. I let the mask of simpering maiden fall as I finally found a friendly face. Caius knew the sort of husband each man would truly make.

"Lady Lavinia," he greeted me with a bow of his head.

"Cai." I smiled.

The Sanctas sisters, Temperance, Honor, and Patience, outfitted in gold and white, had been inching toward the Vaux brothers but froze at my approach.

Temperance's husband traveled as one of the king's secretaries, delivering letters across the kingdom while his wife warmed the royal bed. Her younger sisters were eager to upstage her, angling for a husband in the Six. I had never before felt any kinship with them. Until now. I understood the pressure they must feel. A defeated part of me also envied them, their confidence in the game they must play. If I were to be successful, theirs was a determination I must emulate.

"Brother." Caius cleared his throat. "You know Lady Lavinia Bruis. Lavinia, may I present my brother, Julius?"

"Lord Vaux." I curtsied.

From a distance, only their stature and the length of their hair set them apart. Julius was taller than his brother. Standing with the relaxed confidence of a man who was certain of his place in the world, Julius's shoulders held none of the nervous tension of Caius's drawn frame. The elder allowed two inches of tight curls on top of his head, the rest closely shaved. Up close, Julius's pale eyes were wider set, his lips fuller, and his chin more pronounced. One of the favored topics among the ladies of court was why Julius Vaux had yet to take a wife. Looking at the handsome harmony of his features, he had everything to have his pick of ladies even without the prominence of his title.

"Lady Lavinia." Julius's gaze held a rigidity not found in that of his younger brother. "I hear several members of my house have you to thank for their good health."

"I'm thankful for the practice." I smiled.

Lord Vaux pinned his brother with a stare. "I'd prefer their practice was better done so that it didn't require yours." The words were kind, but spoken like a criticism.

"I've spoken to them. I already, that is, I told them, but I'm happy to do so again." Caius ducked his head.

"Yes. You'd do well to remind them of how I feel and remember it yourself."

"Of course, brother." Caius met his brother's eye for a heartbeat before looking back to his feet with a nod.

"Enjoy your evening." Julius bid us farewell.

Honor Sanctas slinked forward only to have her greeting dismissed with a quick bow of his head. Julius continued through the ballroom to where Cadmium Thallium stood with the Ward house's second son, Poet.

"What was that about?" I asked.

"My brother"—He wrung his hands together—"just, he doesn't want us to be seen as foot soldiers. Getting bloody in the ring with each other makes us look like brutes."

"You certainly aren't. Lucius, though," I mumbled.

Caius snorted a laugh that was quickly smothered by his hand.

"Don't," he warned with mirth in his eyes.

Of his distant cousins, Lucius, a flaxen-haired, ruddy-faced bully, was Caius's least-favorite.

"Has he been blessed with the power of speech or grunts only? It's like a boar." I made a low sound in my throat. As expected, it drew another chortle from Caius.

"Lav," he laughed. "Stop, he's here somewhere."

"I don't see him." I made a show of looking around the room.

"Maybe he is out in the sty after all." He smirked at his joke. "I've never met his mother, but every Appian woman I've met has broader shoulders than mine. I cannot say with certainty that she isn't a sow."

"Caius, did you just make a joke? About your cousin, no less? For shame! Where is your house loyalty?"

He pulled my arm as I made to walk away, the two of us dissolving into giggles.

"Find some decorum." Leith and Ruby's approach made me jump.

"We are being the height of decorous," I told him. "You're old and unfun. We"—I waved a hand between Caius and me—"are unburdened by such shortcomings."

Caius shrank back in on himself. "Bruis."

"Vaux."

"Caius," Ruby sang, "I heard a rumor that your brother is looking to marry this season."

"Oh, no. I wouldn't say that." He looked to where his brother now stood on the other side of Poet Ward.

"No? You then maybe." She cut her gaze to mine. The idea of marrying Caius was laughable. "As long as any betrothals wait until after my nuptials."

"My brother and mother will pick a bride for me when the time suits them." His attention shifted to where his mother stood. "Not that that will be anytime soon," he hurriedly added. "Your nuptials are safe from any news of mine."

Lady Philomena Vaux's bright white hair was easy to pick out in a crowd, as was her violet gown. Both enhanced the glow of her golden-brown skin. Standing with the Thallium twins, her poise was in contrast to the surly boredom etched on the faces of the identical blondes. At sixteen, Rhode's younger sisters were in their first season. I couldn't blame them for being unhappy about it. They were too young to be serious marriage prospects, so their time would be spent observing until they could return to Thallium Manor.

"He certainly has his pick of ladies," Ruby said. "You both do."

"Lady Honor has been eyeing him all evening," I whispered to her.

"Of course, she has! Their father is a fool to think any of his daughters will marry into the Six. Look at Temperance. It's a disgrace."

"Her son is rumored to have red hair." Leith leaned closer to us. "Her husband said it's a strawberry blonde," he spoke the color as if it were a humorous joke, "but Martin saw it and said it was copper."

I gasped. "No!"

"The king's bastard," Ruby confirmed.

"But that's…" I couldn't find words. Lady Temperance was poised at King Alaric's shoulder. She tossed her head with a laugh at a joke from the Ambassador.

Temperance was lush curves contrasted with a harsh, angular face. The line of her cheekbones and nose was as sharp as her hips were round. Her thin lips were only ever pursed in distaste or curved in a taunt.

"See, Lav, when a man and a woman," Leith started.

Ruby smacked his arm with a wrinkle of her nose.

"That's why his mistresses are married," Caius told me in a whisper. "Any children are passed off as the babes of the husbands. Even if they look nothing like them, it's, well, it'll be nothing more than rumor."

"Shameless," Ruby seethed. "Is there no propriety anymore? Any pride? I'd never be able to look my family in the eye."

I felt a sharp flash of anger. Toward the king, toward Temperance. Bryony's kindness was being repaid with humiliation. The whispers about the boy wouldn't harm King Alaric. They wouldn't harm Temperance either, each whisper another adornment, rumor and notice shimmering under the light.

But Bryony would be harmed. She needed no more pressure to birth a son, but here it was in the scrutiny of Temperance's red-haired boy.

The wine was a pleasant buzz in my veins. My body felt light, my head heavy on my neck. After one too many and too loud laughs, Leith insisted we retire for the night. As we made our way to where our fathers stood, a command halted our progress.

"Lady Lavinia!" My feet stopped, but my heart galloped in my chest.

"Your Majesty." I curtsied.

Leith's eyes cut to me, but he did not pause, tightening his leading grip on Ruby's arm.

"Come," King Alaric beckoned me to the table with a hand outfitted in heavy gold rings. "Are you enjoying the evening?"

"Yes, very much so."

The king's dismissive glance at Temperance lasted only a second, but she understood, rising from her perch on the arm of his chair to curtsey. "Your Majesty," she simpered.

"The Ambassador was just remarking on how fortunate we are to have such beautiful ladies. Proventium is graced with beauty such as yourself." King Alaric did not need pretty words for his compliments. He had been denied nothing from birth. He knew that any single moment of attention from him was worth more than a dozen sonnets from another.

"You flatter me, Your Majesty."

"Lady Lavinia Bruis, Ambassador Gregor Vante of Elvor."

I curtsied again before offering my hand.

"I recognize your aunt in you. We've been honored to have her in our court in Elvor. Have you been to Elvor, lady?" the ambassador asked over the hand he still held. His hand was coated in a light layer of sweat that mirrored the perspiration on his brow.

"No, sir. I hear it is lovely. My aunt has nothing but praise for Elvor and its people. My father traveled there with the late king. He, too, said it was a beautiful kingdom. He spoke of the most magnificent waterfall." I extracted my hand and clasped my palms in front of me.

"Ah." He smiled. "We are indeed graced with a landscape of unrivaled beauty. Unlike here, where the land tries to kill you." His laughter resembled the honking of a goose.

I inhaled sharply at his callousness.

"Funny." The king's tone was devoid of amusement.

"Well"—the ambassador cleared his throat—"should your king here finally decide to visit, I hope you'll be able to join."

"She certainly will be," King Alaric declared. His voice was light once more, but the weight of his words took the breath from my lungs. "We'll visit soon for the official betrothal." He drummed his fingers on the arm of his chair.

Gaëlle simply straightened her posture further.

I felt a deep sympathy for the young girl. Her mother and her younger brother had died in childbirth. The loneliness she felt was familiar—the face of a desolate young girl I sometimes still glimpsed in the mirror.

The daughter of one of Tythmore's most revered houses, the marriage to Queen Margaux had been a gesture of unity between Proventium and Tythmore. Now, Gaëlle would walk that same path by solidifying Proventium's relationship with Elvor. I wondered if she would find any comfort in that. If she could feel her mother's presence the way I sometimes felt mine when healing.

"It must be so difficult to imagine your only child living in a foreign land." The Ambassador's words had the effect of a dagger. *Only child.*

The laments grew louder with each year that passed without an heir. The king made no effort to conceal his growing desperation. Where court whispered, he thundered.

"It is what is done with daughters, with princesses. I know my precious girl will be treated well. Maybe my dear friend King Nasir will have a daughter for Proventium one day. I hope he should be so blessed."

"One day," the Ambassador demurred. "Three sons keep him busy."

I stepped to be in front of Princess Gaëlle. "Are you enjoying the evening, Princess?" I asked softly.

"Very much, my lady." She looked at me and gave a single nod before straightening again.

"I hope you've had time this evening to try the caramel cake," I lowered my voice conspiratorially.

She assessed me from the corner of her eye. "Oh?"

"It's delicious, I had to stop myself from eating the whole thing."

"Lia," King Alaric beckoned the princess's maid from where she stood off to the side of her chair. "It is time for Princess Gaëlle to retire. Please see she gets some cake on the way." He shot me a wink.

The princess smiled for the first time that evening, revealing a gap where her front teeth had been. Gaëlle dutifully allowed her father to press a kiss to her forehead before she snatched Lia's hand and descended the dais with a skip. The king's obvious fondness for his daughter softened his intimidating posture.

I smiled watching the little girl look like just that: a little girl, free from the expectations of a crown she didn't ask for.

"Where is your queen tonight?" The ambassador's voice was smooth as spilled oil.

"Ah, I fear you don't wish to hear the inner drama of Proventium." The words were spoken with a friendly dismissal.

"I was looking forward to meeting your third wife. Your second paled in comparison to your first." He smirked. "May the Graces rest her soul."

"Queen Margaux is dearly missed."

"Maybe the fourth, eh?"

King Alaric sat forward. The twist of his lips was a spiteful jest of a smile. "Maybe."

I looked away lest the pain in my chest show on my face. Poor Bryony. To speak of casting her aside… maybe Leith was right to be worried about his discontent. I glanced back to where my brother stood. Oran had joined them. The intensity of his stare made my chest stutter. Leith was focused on Father, who, in turn, was observing me with an expression I couldn't decipher. I was familiar with his disappointment, but this scrutiny was foreign.

"I think my father needs me. If you'll both excuse me? It was lovely to meet you. Your Majesty." I curtsied again.

His large hand, warm and smooth, grasped my wrist as I turned to leave. "Call me Alaric, Lady Lavinia. Please." The request was whispered like a secret.

"Alaric," I murmured back.

The smile he gave me was boyish, lacking any of its usual arrogance. I was so disarmed by it that I felt the unease that scalded me at the mention of a fourth wife extinguish like a candle in a breath.

Several ladies boldly turned their heads to follow my walk from the king to my family. I plastered on an overly cheerful expression as Father took my arm. The memory of court was short. One conversation, that was all. It'd be forgotten by the next gathering.

CHAPTER 7
ORAN

"Oran, come look. Isn't it lovely?" Aunt Amethyst looked away from the doublet to eagerly watch my reaction.

"Yes." I rubbed the thick black fabric between my fingers. On the chest, a patch with the Lennox crest was embroidered: a pine green shield with a dark L burnt in the center. The letter curved and twisted at the ends like flames, capable of protection and destruction.

"I know you prefer to wear black, even though you look lovely in green, but it'd please your uncle if you wore it occasionally." She took the doublet and held it up in front of my chest. "So handsome."

"Thank you." I pressed a kiss to her temple.

I had clung to Aunt Amethyst's kindness in those early days. In screaming, kicking tantrums, I had still gripped her skirts to keep her near. Ripped away from my mother, Aunt Am had been stitches on a gaping wound; jagged and imperfect, able to slow the bleeding if not stop it.

I remembered the silent carriage ride. Leaving Tythmore, my mother's hollow eyes remained fixed on the window even as she held me in her arms. Once we descended into the Wasting, the pain had started.

The Wasting had begun as a small patch at the border of Tythmore and Proventium. Beyond being barren of life, the land was also barren of magic. Rotted and black, the land pulled and drained any magic wielder who stepped foot on it. I had been warned, but was too young to prepare.

The Wasting didn't just take, it carved. It was an enraged monster with talons and fangs, digging and slicing to remove the well of magic, potential still lying dormant, in my chest. I was suffocated by the pain and by the black dust kicked up by the carriage. My mother had tried to soothe me, but shuddering gasps stole her comfort.

Punishment, penance, purge, no one knew why or how the Wasting came to be. Or how to cure it.

My aunt and uncle had been waiting just outside the bounds of the Wasting. My mother had still been shaking when she placed me in Aunt Am's arms.

My mother. I remembered the way the sun picked up the auburn gleam in her hair. I remembered the way she smiled through the tears in her eyes. I remembered the lavender smell of her skin.

And I remembered the way Uncle had assessed me like a new foal for the stables. *It affected him already? That's good, he'll be powerful when he comes into his magic. You should be happy that he'll be useful, Helene.*

His assessment then held none of the wariness it did now. "Don't baby him, dear." Hugo strolled to the center of the Lennox receiving room to place a hand on his wife's waist.

"Oh," Aunt Am tutted. She lightly batted his chest in reprimand.

His face softened with a smile that was only ever for her. Uncle Hugo's devotion to Aunt Am was never matched nor diminished. Glancing at me, his face sobered. "You and Ruby, both so opposed to Lennox green."

Hugo was never seen outside our house colors.

"The green doesn't flatter Ruby's complexion," Aunt Am shook her head. Instead of the dark green of House Lennox, Amethyst tended to a lighter, pastel green, or the cherry red of House Southton.

He grumbled in acknowledgment before bending to press a chaste kiss to her cheek. "I'll see you this evening." Straightening, he snapped his head toward the door in command. "Oran."

We walked side-by-side through the halls of the palace, Uncle's steps hurried to match my longer stride.

"What have you to report so far?"

"Lord Raven still knows his place," I assured. "Cobalt is skilled when fire is already present, but not powerful enough to sustain a blaze on his own for long. Onyx is aiming to marry his son to one of the Iron nieces, but Cobalt is singularly focused on getting into Patience Sanctas's bed."

Hugo smirked. "And?"

The other prominent fire wielders outside of House Lennox were the Ravens and Placinos. "Ember Placino can barely find his bed at the end of the night. If you'd like me to challenge a drunk, I can, though it'd be boring." The alcohol on his breath would take a mere spark to incinerate.

Uncle bestowed a pleasant greeting to the two Sands conversing in the hall. Lowering his voice, he asked me, "and who would you challenge instead?"

"I haven't decided," I lied, "but I prefer someone who can hold their own." The exertion of sparring was the only modicum of relief that I could give my magic at court.

"Not someone who can beat you," he warned. He looked over his shoulder to ensure the Sands remained where they were, now out of earshot.

"That's not something I'm worried about." For over fifteen years, the constant wildfire in me raged and scorched the walls of its prison. Containing it was exhausting. Sometimes I imagined the reprieve it'd be to burn until there was nothing left.

"Don't be arrogant. I'll not have your ego shame this family. Lennox don't rest on talent. They prepare. They plan."

I nodded but said no further. There was an odd sense of satisfaction in my uncle accusing me of being an over-confident boy. The man had scrutinized me for twenty years, yet still saw nothing.

My silence angered him as it often did. As I often did. "You will continue to be useful. You will continue to remind the king why House Lennox is so valuable. If you cannot do so here, I know where to send you to make the most of your power. Don't think that I won't, Oran."

The threat to send me to the border burned under my skin. My mother loved the people of Tythmore. The death of my father did nothing to turn her against his people or his cause. Hugo would ensure she'd hear if I killed any of my father's countrymen. The threat to force me to hurt my mother, was that of a coward. But Hugo was adept at using his cowardice to get results.

The tenderness I felt toward my mother was an illness Hugo had hoped to cure. When it became clear the ailment was irremediable, he learned to employ it to his advantage.

I was once a biddable horse led forward by a carrot, now a headstrong horse whipped onward. He cared not for the motivation as long as the motion stayed the same.

I stopped walking. Hugo halted a few steps ahead of me. Anger contorted his features. Cowardice had worked for his purposes. Now it only worked when I allowed it to. He took the few steps to meet me where I stood, as I knew he would. I kept my face stoic even as satisfaction sang a cruel song in my chest. Stopping in front of me, his neck craned back to meet my gaze.

"Don't think I won't," I repeated his words back.

His green eyes, murkier than mine, squinted, no doubt searching for the little boy who used anger to hide his fear. The little boy whom Hugo could grab by the ear and cow into submission. The boy who screamed in terror at the sight of fire. The little boy who was long dead.

He dropped his gaze to the floor. A single moment of deference was all his pride could allow. It was enough for now.

"And what of the ice wielders?" he asked as we continued.

"The Growley and Quinn alliance is of no concern." The other ice wielding houses had joined in marriage over the winter. Bartholomew, the Quinn's second son, had married Harmony Growley. The latest rumor Ruby had passed along was that Bartholomew would have preferred his bride's younger sister, Melody. "A child, I think, will be some time coming. The two are said to spend little time together. As for the Growley sons, Reed and Chord are either weak or nervous. Either disposition is easily dealt with."

"Good. You two need to remember that houses like the Growleys, the Quinns, and the Ravens have multiple sons to rest on. You and Leith need to be better than them."

I kept my eyes forward through the weight of his scrutiny.

"Yes, sir," he prompted me.

"Yes, sir," I mocked back. I didn't keep the smirk from my face even as his nostrils flared with anger. Hugo knew I *was* better. Than the Ravens. Than *him*.

The doors to the private royal study opened before us. Two men, wearing the uniform of the king's personal guard, a grey so dark it was almost black, stood on either side of the door. The eagle of the Harald crest was stitched over their hearts. The only insignia indicating that they were relatives of the royal house was found in the crimson diamond sewn on their right sleeve.

Leith, Bruis, and the Vaux brothers sat at the long table waiting for King Alaric.

"Nice of you to join us," Leith snarked. Leaning back in his chair with an arm draped casually over the seat next to him, he was at home in the royal suite.

Bruis shot a blast of ice to sting at the back of Leith's neck. From sparring with Leith, I was all too familiar with the burn of frostbite.

"Fuck," he whispered lowly. Rubbing the back of his neck, he straightened his posture to match his father's.

Lord Vaux watched with disinterest. His pale eyes were observant but edged in caution. Despite his standing, his gaze held the caution of a cat who never knew when the dog would again start chasing. He kept an open seat between himself and the chair designated for Hugo. The little Vaux sat next to him instead of in line with Leith.

Uncle feigned an apology. "Apologies, Lord Vaux. You know how young men can be." He adjusted his cuffs as he sat next to Bruis. "Though your brother seems to possess admirable decorum."

Vaux's eyes bounced between Leith and me. What he was searching for, I couldn't tell. If he were waiting for a bark or bite, we were not the hounds he need watch.

The little Vaux's absence was noticeable on the hunt, but I understood why Vaux found the imbalance preferable to the meek misery next to him.

"Young Caius, so good to see you. We missed you at the hunt." Uncle's smile was as friendly as it was false. "It's vital for boys to learn early how best to fulfill the demands of their position. Leith and Oran here started at fifteen and fourteen."

"Caius." Vaux's voice snapped the cowering boy's spine upright.

"Thank you, Lord Lennox. That is, well, I'm, I am happy to be here. Honored to be here?" He looked to his brother for guidance or reprimand.

"We needn't concern ourselves with the personal affairs of House Vaux." Bruis laced his hands together on the table. "They've continued to do an admirable job at the border. Should that falter, then there would be need for concern."

"I assure you it won't," Vaux's voice gained a lethal edge.

"We have the utmost faith that the Vaux army will continue to serve our beloved kingdom well," Uncle assured.

Vaux was saved from replying by the entrance of the king.

"Forgive me, but I fear this no longer fits me as it once had." He smoothed a hand down his doublet with a grin aimed at disarming his audience.

We rose in unison, standing until he took his place at the head of the table.

"Your Majesty." Bruis bowed his head from his position at the king's right.

"We have much to discuss. I had hoped, foolishly perhaps, that the season could be focused on bringing levity back to our kingdom. Dancing, dining, games, enjoyment. Instead, we are being battered on all sides." With a heaving sigh, he sank back into his chair.

"Are we waiting for Lord Delphi, Your Majesty?" Uncle failed to cloak his glee at Delphi's exclusion.

Delphi, Bruis, and Lennox had been King Alaric's closest confidants at the beginning of his reign. After Lord Vaux inherited his father's seat, he slowly joined Alaric's right hand. If Delphi was being pushed out, Uncle and Bruis would be elevated as his most experienced advisors.

Alaric's eyes narrowed, an eagle watching the scurrying creatures below. "I maintain the utmost respect for House Delphi, but Ambrose seems interested in a battle of wills. Please, believe me, I would avoid such unpleasantries if I could."

"Oh?" Uncle's brow wrinkled in faux concern.

"Ambrose wants something." He drummed his fingers on the table. Looking to Bruis, he asked, "Have you heard anything from your dear neighbor?

"No, Ambrose only speaks when it suits him." Bruis's hands laced in front of him.

"That can be influenced." Alaric looked between Uncle and Bruis, debating how much to say before he continued. "He's withholding, and what he does say recently, I am hesitant to trust. The Graces," he grumbled, "make it complicated with him, so I need to give him whatever it is. Lest he become another problem to deal with."

"Yes. My wife and Lady Delphi were quite friendly, and Ambrose and I have had a cordial relationship since I inherited the Bruis seat. Though lately there have been rumblings on our border. I would hate things to become further strained over any unrest his—"

"Believers," Uncle interjected.

"Incite," Bruis finished.

The Delphi Believers held the house as the ordained rulers of Proventium. The sect remained quiet and therefore manageable due to Delphi's prominence in the Six. Whatever hollow prophecies Ambrose spun for his supporters kept them content to wait peacefully. Alaric couldn't seek to punish or even disrespect Ambrose Delphi without risking civil war.

"We'd of course swiftly act to keep peace in Your Majesty's kingdom, but the ugliness of it." Hugo shuddered.

As the largest neighboring estates, the king would send Lennox and Bruis forces first against any Delphi unrest.

"The Graces abandoned House Delphi, and yet..." Alaric shook his head with a hollow chuckle.

"We'll find out what it is," Bruis vowed.

"Good." Not praise but an order. "As threats are levied against Proventium, I rely on the Six to be useful. The Six need to be guardians of Proventium, if not...adjustments will need to be made."

It was Bruis's response that kept him unchallenged in seniority. "Our fields are producing enough that our people are feeling no ill effects from the increased western exports."

The estates in the east were only able to provide so much aid to those whose crops suffered from proximity to the Wasting.

"Good"—King Alaric nodded—"divert any shipments intended for Merrifield land. Evenly distribute it between the Irons and Ravens instead."

"The Merrifields seem to be the most affected by the unrest." Uncle's statement was a question.

"Yes," the king confirmed. The quirk of his brow dared further argument. "Vaux's men will determine if the rebellion in Pine Grove was internal or if Tyth traitors gained a foothold on Merrifield land." Gaudy gold rings flashed under the light with the steady drum of his fingers.

"And if my men do find evidence of this?" Lord Vaux's poise was that of a perfect soldier.

"Wipe them out and leave the Merrifields with nothing. I'll gift the ruins to another house." His shrug was undermined by a restlessness that brought him to his feet, pacing the length of the study. "The Merrifields either do not take me seriously or are dangerously incompetent. Either reason makes them unfit to serve in my court."

"Incompetence is synonymous with Merrifield." Leith smiled at the king. Cocky and proud, it was a smile that had led to many boyhood brawls between us. Before I found amusement in his boasts, I had been eager to knock the arrogance out of him.

"The on-ground assessment has found no Tyth. As of yet," Uncle reported.

"And they won't," Leith agreed. "Finch Fjord said that Igor Merrifield is blaming the closure of Madam Midnight's for the unrest."

"The Merrifields lost their land because the whores moved out?" The king barked a laugh.

"The Madam emptied out her brothel in Pine Grove and took them to Kingslanding where more people can afford to pay for a fuck. Pine Grove revolted and the Merrifields were too occupied with their cocks in hand to do anything." Leith shrugged casually, but he glowed with pride under Alaric's attention.

House Merrifield, comprised of nature and water wielders, had taken up as much land as feasible with crops, but their magic was not able to sustain a continual harvest. Sugar and grain from the east kept them fed, but the Wasting and its strain were increasing.

Alaric's chuckle rolled through the room like a thunderstorm. "That's more pathetic than the fucking traitors moving in. The Merrifields should have put them all down. If they had any sense, they would have." He shook his head, smirk fixed in place. "If your men meet any resistance," he told Vaux, "I would never wish to overstep in telling you how to command your men. But..." Alaric trailed off meaningfully.

"They understand the need to establish a precedent." Vaux's nod was solemn.

"Good. Now, Mesgara." Alaric braced his hands on the back of his empty chair. "Bruis, what are you hearing from your contacts in Elvor?"

"They are committed to the alliance. They wish to end Mesgara's piracy by whatever means necessary. Their navy commandeered another Elvorian ship docked in Leopard's Bay. My nephew assured me that the ambassador's lack of retinue was not a sign of disrespect, rather a gesture of friendship, a display of their trust."

"The alliance will go through. If I have to send Gaëlle earlier than planned to ensure the marriage, I will."

"Shall we send one of the Stel's spies to monitor the ambassador's journey back to Elvor?"

"Good."

"I will see it done," Bruis pledged. The Stel were a house dominated by strength and speed. As House Vaux rose in prominence, House Stel aligned itself closely with House Bruis, preferring their orders over those of a competitor.

"I also trust that your late wife's sister, no matter how winsome she may be, understands that what she hears in Proventium will not travel back with her to Elvor. If she wants to return home one day, that is. Forgive me, Malcolm, I know she is not truly under your house, but we cannot have the knowledge of House Bruis disseminated through Elvor. The Rudyards have no claim on her anymore, so it must fall to you. Call me paranoid, or overly cautious, I know, but I must say it."

"Of course," Bruis dismissed the king's concern and threat with ease. "Clodia thinks of little but which gentleman's bed she'd like to visit next."

"Ah, the Wasting is far less pressing than which man will be so lucky."

Bruis and Uncle Hugo joined in the king's amusement, while Leith grimaced.

"The Rudyard's only contribution to Proventium is the beauty of their women," Uncle snickered.

My jaw clenched as Alaric and Uncle laughed. "I can think of a few houses resting on handsomeness," I said. My voice held a trace of warning. I coveted the dark hair and blue eyes of Rudyard beauty every day. Every man in the room knew Lavinia was the Rudyard legacy, like her mother.

"The Wards perhaps?" Alaric threw the name out with the glee of a mischievous child. House Ward had long been under weather wielders. No Harald woman was allowed to marry a Ward lest their strength come to rival the Royal House.

House Ward had also become one of House Vaux's closest allies under Julius.

The little Vaux whimpered, slinking further in his chair. I had no doubt, he'd crawl under the table if he could.

Unlike his brother, Lord Vaux didn't cower. "Lynx as well are lately resting on charm."

The disrespect to the queen's house should have been a challenge, but Vaux was not the type to be so bold. He'd only comment if he knew the king would accept it.

Fascination emerged on Alaric's face. He huffed and tilted his head, looking at Vaux like a favored pet had learned a new trick. "You may be correct."

"Speaking of the Lynx, Your Majesty," Uncle's voice was apologetic. "Is there action we could have done to aid Spruce Lynx? His manor that was seized...was that a rebellion issue as well?"

The king slowly pulled out his seat, dropping smoothly back in his chair. His silence loudly proclaimed that it was not a rebellion issue. Spruce was Queen Bryony's eldest brother.

"And Queen Bryony?" my uncle asked in the silence.

"The Lynx, I fear, have forgotten that they were risen at my hand. A reminder will help them."

I met Leith's eye. The king's temper at the mention of his wife was igniting quicker with each day.

"The Lynx are like ants," he continued, "a few crushed underfoot is unnoticeable."

The ants notice.

Leith obeyed his father's silent order with a sigh, asking, "Queen Bryony is not to join us at court this season?"

"This season?" Alaric raised his brows. "No, she will not be joining court again.

CHAPTER 8
LAVINIA

Blood shouldn't show overmuch. A lighter color would be more apt for the season, but then the dress may not recover. This dress, a deep navy with braids of silver silk accentuating my waist and chest, would survive the games today. Sleeves in fashion hit the knuckles of the hand in a sweep of fabric, but mine just kissed the top of my hand to maintain practicality for the day's event.

Wispy clouds streaked through the blue sky like ribbons. A perfect day for the start of the king's Solstice festivities.

"Good morning!" The door opened to bright poppy, Ruby's gown and lips as cheery as her greeting. Her hair was piled at the crown of her head, a few short corkscrew curls bouncing by her high cheekbones.

"You're in good spirits this morning. Excited for the games?"

"As long as Leith doesn't hurt his pretty face." She flashed a wicked grin.

"There." Thomasina, my ladies' maid since I was nine, smiled. She had braided my hair down my back before spiraling the braid into a low bun at the nape of my neck. She left a few tendrils out to frame my face. The hairstyle emphasized the subtle arch of my dark brows and the round set of my eyes.

"Thank you, Thomasina."

With one final pat on my arm, she left with gowns and undergarments to be laundered. Once the door closed, Ruby came to stand behind my chair. The vanity was situated with a view out of the large window that dominated the far side of the room. Outside the window, we could see the bright crimson awnings erected over the spectator stands for the day. The shock of red appeared brighter against the soft pink peonies lining the garden entrance to the right.

I had a vase of those peonies on the chest of drawers that sat next to the large four-poster bed. My room within the Bruis suite was small: dark furniture with sky blue and white fabric. Tidy and organized, here, I saved the clutter only for the bursting wardrobe on the wall opposite the window. Despite being my room for every court stay, this bedroom, lacking the familiar clutter of home, was akin to an inn. There were no trailing philodendrons over the wardrobe, no overflowing bookshelf organized by color, no stains of spilled paint on the stone floor. What Thomasina viewed as "mess", I labeled "comforts." Everything of value to me remained ensconced in the spacious sanctuary of my bedroom in Bruis Manor.

"You really do look lovely."

"As do you," I told her.

Ruby was petite with soft curves and warm skin. Her features were all notes of a beautiful song. They fit together perfectly, no feature too brash or sharp.

I was long slender lines, taller than was in style at court, with the ivory skin, blue eyes, and black hair of Rudyard beauty. All pretty on their own, but striking, almost harsh, in composition. A pleasant song played with a clumsy hand.

"I do hope Leith chose someone who won't cause a fuss when they lose." We both knew he'd never choose someone he was in danger of losing to. "Who do you think will get the most bloodied up today?"

I hummed in thought. "There is a Glenn boy who is arrogant as can be. I imagine he'll pick the wrong opponent." I mentally went through my last few patients, but there was nothing dire. "As long as it isn't Leith or Oran, I can't say that I truly care."

"Even Rhode?" Understanding and hesitancy softened her voice.

"Rhode is my friend. I thought, several years ago, I thought he and I were more, but…" The shame of it still bubbled in my gut at having to speak of it. I trusted Ruby. It was my pride that prevented me from telling her more. I had spoken the story only once to Opal before locking the humiliation away.

"Leith didn't tell me details. Only that Rhode abused your trust."

I nodded woodenly.

"Well, I never liked him anyway," she declared. "All that matters is your reputation is safe with me. No one will hear a word of it." At my nod, she gave a flippant toss of her head and smiled. "So really, no harm has been done!"

At Ruby's words, my mind went back. My eyes had long avoided the western corner of the gardens, but now I let them drift to where it all fell apart.

Pressed against the hedges, my mind was pleasantly blank. Here, safely trapped within the maze hedges of the garden, I thought of nothing but the press of Rhode's body against mine.

Mouth soft, his teeth scraped gently against my lower lip before his tongue gave a soothing lick. His hands were firm; one fisted in the back of my hair, the other gripped the thigh I had over his hip. As I drew back for breath, the hand on my thigh flexed harder, his lips making their descent down my neck.

"Graces, Lav," he mumbled as his lips reached the bodice of my gown. The hand in my hair left to dip a teasing finger along the bust of my gown. "Wanting you this much will drive me to madness. Will it ever stop?"

A breathless giggle left me as I stroked one hand from his neck down his chest. "I hope not."

The grin he gave me, straight, white teeth and black, endless eyes, made butterflies erupt in my stomach. It was when I was the sole focus of his attention, his desire, that I thought we could be happy together. That this was more than just attraction and infatuation. If I let myself loosen my grip on girlhood notions of love, maybe I could fall for Rhode.

He pressed his lips back to mine, more urgently this time. I hooked the leg slung over his hip tighter, bringing him closer. Untucking his shirt, I ran my nails over the smooth skin of his hip. Groaning, he pressed against me harder. The sound of my matching moan had drowned out their approach until it was too late.

I stumbled as Rhode was ripped away from me. My horrified gaze met a matching pair for a breath before Leith turned his ire to Rhode's prone form at his feet.

"We were looking for you," Oran rasped. I had thought this couldn't get worse, but I was wrong. The desire to squeeze my eyes shut faltered, conceding hopelessly to the insistent pull of grass-green. "I saw you head toward the gardens. I was worried." He spoke stiffly, a ragged quality to his usual deep timber. His body was just as tense as his voice. The tick in his jaw screamed at me to run. His hands

were encased in flames that he didn't seem to notice. It wasn't until they entered his line of vision when he reached for me that they disappeared. Placing a hand on my elbow, he drew me to the path opening, away from where Leith backed Rhode against the hedges.

"You son of a bitch." Leith's voice held a venom I had never heard before.

Rising, Rhode held his hands up placatingly. "Bruis, listen before you act rashly."

"Have you proposed marriage to her? Is that it? Because I assure you that is the only thing that will stay my hand."

"Yes," I started to say, only to be interrupted.

"You know my father," Rhode croaked. "He would never allow me to marry a healer, no matter how much I want to."

Breath left me with the same impact of Leith's fist against Rhode's face.

He had promised me. It wasn't a formal proposal. We weren't betrothed yet, but he had promised me. Confidently assured with a wink and the twining of his fingers with mine as we walked through the dark palace gardens. Whispered against the shell of my ear and sealed with a kiss to my neck among the quiet shelves of the palace library. Mumbled against my lips and assured with each stroke cocooned in the soft sheets of his bed.

"You'll love Thallium Manor. It backs up to the mountains. The best sunsets you'll ever see."

"I would be perfectly happy with daughters. I only care that our children get your eyes. We'll have two daughters, one named for each of our mothers. And they'll be as beautiful as you."

"I didn't know I could be this happy. The way you make me feel, Lav... Graces, I've never felt anything like it."

"My father won't be happy, but he will understand. I'm not his to control."

"I'm your best patient. You're stuck with me forever. I ache for you. I need you on hand to heal me at all times."

"Lady Lavinia Thallium, I love the sound of that."

I was such a fool. So desperate to fill the gaping loneliness in me, I had deserted my judgment. Years of longing, longing for someone to love me back, had left me imprudent. I had wanted to prove that my family's concerns for my prospects were unfounded. That I wasn't a liability because of my powers. That I could still be desired and cherished. And instead, all I had done was prove them right.

Rhode had proved them right.

I never should have given myself to Rhode without a formal betrothal. His father, I should have known. The only way he'd ever consent was if I were pregnant. Rhode had taken precautions to ensure I wouldn't be. An ugly, loathsome part of me whispered a wish that I was, so Rhode would be forced to keep his promises.

Of course, he had done this. I had let myself believe I was special. That he meant the precious words he gifted me. Idiot, a pathetic idiot. Now, I wondered how many others had heard the same promises in the comfort of Rhode's bed.

I gulped hiccupping breaths as I numbly watched Leith throw another punch. Tears silently tracked down my cheeks. I was too exhausted to fight their steady descent.

Spitting blood, Rhode's head snapped toward Leith, winding up for another hit. Leith's cocked arm froze in the air. Rhode held Leith's fist by his silver signet ring.

"Enough, Bruis. I let you get those because I deserved it."

Oran silently threw his dagger to the ground, his belt then followed. The only metal on him. A dagger of fire appeared poised at Rhode's throat.

"No," I gasped.

"What's going on? Lady Lavinia?"

A whimper seized my chest.

The blue flames of the dagger jumped less than an inch from Rhode's throat, illuminating the scene in the dark garden.

Lady Bryony. Her soft grey eyes filled with understanding.

Understanding that could bury me.

She was to be wed to the king next month, making her the most desired woman in the Lynx house. Court would listen to any gossip she brought forward. Anything to bring them closer to King Alaric, to their soon-to-be queen.

"Come," she beckoned.

My feet carried me to her without conscious thought. Even as I reached Bryony, my head remained turned over my shoulder to stare at Rhode and Oran.

Looping her arm through mine, she instructed Leith. "I'm retiring for the evening. Lady Lavinia looks tired as well. I'll escort her while you three rejoin the ball. I suggest you clean yourselves up and behave like gentlemen. Lest any of what transpired here follow you back."

Oran ignored her, throwing a flaming punch to Rhode's jaw.

"They are going to kill him," I breathed.

"No, they will not." She shook her head. Her hair, the color of spring wheat, swayed at her shoulders with the motion. She raised her voice to command over her shoulder, "If they care for your reputation, they will not." Already, she had the demeanor of a queen.

Leaving the three men behind, my frantic breathing became the only sound in the garden. No other witnesses—that was good, I thought distantly.

"Bryony," I started as we approached the final hedges of the garden. I kept my

eyes on the pale stone of the palace. The lights through the windows and the growing murmur of the crowd told me the revelry had not paused.

"Lavinia." She smiled at me with a gentle, almost maternal kindness, the sort I had been in search of my whole life. "More ladies have been in a similar position than they would have you believe. There is nothing for anyone to gossip about. We left the ball together and decided to catch up over a turn around the garden before retiring for the evening. Is that not right?"

I smiled back at her, shaky, fragile, and grateful.

"Yes, Collette?" Bryony promoted her maid, who trailed two steps behind us.

"Yes, my lady," she answered dutifully. "It was much too warm inside, so you and Lady Lavinia stepped out for some air."

"There are many tales that are to stay between ladies, between friends." Bryony squeezed my hand. "There are many a well-bred lady who marry and their husbands, they never find out these tales." She dropped her voice low. "A small cut to the bottom of your foot, just to get a drop or two of blood on the sheets. A good start to any marriage. Do you understand what I am telling you?"

I nodded. There wouldn't be a man who would have me knowing about Rhode. If I were to marry, everything depended on this secret.

The following morning, I had healed the burnt skin of Rhode's jaw. I didn't speak to him again for eight months.

"Well," I murmured, turning back to Ruby with a forced smile. "It's of no matter now." I stood and fluffed my skirts. "Shall we?"

CHAPTER 9
LAVINIA

Felix's speed and Brutus's strength made a compelling performance. In the second row we were close enough to be brushed by the dirt that whirled behind Felix. In front of me, Padgett was relaxed, his bald head growing pink under the midday sun. So far, there had been no serious injuries, only a cut or two healed under his watch.

Oran and Leith separated Ruby and me, so they could whisper between each other—identifying strengths and weaknesses of the competitors.

I looked across the stands to watch Julius drop a hand to Caius's shoulder. Speaking low in his ear, his other hand gestured toward the fighters.

Brutus caught Felix by the back of his tunic, throwing him across the ring. Felix righted himself as he flew almost the entire length of the 100-yard arena. Landing on his feet, he was back on Brutus in a breath. From behind, Felix pressed the flat of his sword against Brutus's side. His cousin didn't notice or simply ignored that Felix had won. Felix barely dodged the elbow Brutus threw at the side of his head. The speed of his duck left him vulnerable for just a moment. Long enough for Brutus to kick, sending Felix across the arena and into the boards at the far end of the ring.

The crowd erupted, some in outrage, others in celebration, as Felix lay with a hand clutching his ribs. King Alaric's voice boomed before I could step over the barrier and into the arena.

"What a show from House Vaux!"

Julius stood in the stands to give a deferential bow of his head. The expression on his face lacked any satisfaction. His pale eyes narrowed at the men in the ring.

"While that was a masterful performance from Brutus Vaux, our winner is Felix Vaux Appian!"

Brutus swept low for the king before leaving the ring without a glance at his cousin lying in the dirt.

At Padgett's nod, I rushed into the ring to kneel next to Felix.

"Fucking bastard broke my ribs," Felix wheezed.

"Yes." I grimaced. "We'll need to get your shirt off."

He choked on a groan without making any move to lift his arms.

"We'll have to cut it then." I kept a small dagger on a silver belt at my waist, gifted by Oran on my fourteenth birthday. The handle was decorated with small sapphires, to mimic stars in the night sky, that sparkled with the motion.

"Shouldn't have worn a shirt. Gives easy leverage to your opponent." Padgett, unconcerned with Felix's pain, finally joined us.

Felix gritted his teeth. "Old bastard."

Hand hovering over his side, I followed the silver threads in my mind to the injury. Internal bleeding was easy enough. The threads traced the blood to knit around the wound before my power wove around his ribs, straining to position them. Skin and blood were simple. I could heal them with a single pulse. Bones and cartilage were more challenging. My hand shook as I gave one more tug on the power crackling in my palms.

Felix's groan of pain stopped me from trying again.

"I don't think it's properly in place." I could almost see a ripple under his pale, reddened skin, showing the imperfection still in his ribs.

Padgett closed his eyes as he laid a weathered hand on Felix's side. At his sharp inhale, I watched the flesh contract. "There."

Felix threw a hand over his face to conceal his grimace.

"You're not going to coax it. You're going to force it. There is no finesse with bones. There is only broken and healed."

I nodded. "Yes, sir."

"You did well. Get some water before the next injury comes up."

His praise was sparse and hard-earned. This time, my nod was accompanied by a smile.

Padgett banded his arm around Felix's waist, guiding him to the Vaux rows in the stands. I felt the king's attention on me as I walked back to my seat. The flattering yet terrifying weight of it, almost made me stumble.

"Tunic off," Oran ordered Leith. "You saw what just happened."

"Yes, papa," Leith snarked as he obeyed.

"Be careful, sweetheart!" From the row behind us, Aunt Clodia wielded an ornate fan so large it threatened to scrape Father's chin with each flutter. Father ignored it all, her fan, her words, and Leith.

"On to our next match," King Alaric announced. "From House Lynx, we have Birch, and representing House Bruis, their heir Leith!"

The men who wished to compete picked their opponent before the day. A fight could only happen if both agreed. Some, like Felix and Brutus, preferred to keep their match an in-house competition. They trained together, eager to flaunt their dual strength in the ring. Others used their match to settle old scores against rivals.

And then there were those like Leith. He didn't want a challenge. He wanted an exhibition.

I noted the way Birch, a cousin through his father to Queen Bryony, avoided looking toward the royal box in the center of the stands even as he bowed.

Birch and Leith, resembling cousins themselves, circled each other. Leith's golden hair was a complement to Birch's strawberry blond, but where Leith's skin shone smooth and pale under the summer sun, the rays left Birch ruddy and freckled.

In all matches, Leith liked his opponent to make the first move.

"Scared Lynx?"

"Can't say I am, Bruis."

"You're shaking like a leaf. Trembling. Your parents should have named you dandelion."

Birch backed up a pace as roots shot up from the ground. Leith jumped to avoid the one threatening to tangle around his ankles. Glee lit up his face as ice shot to encase the roots. With a flick of his wrist, they shattered, coating the ground in ice chips.

Birch responded with a massive root erupting directly under Leith's feet. Falling back with a laugh, Leith praised, "Yes!"

Aunt Clodia screamed as if she were the one struck, but the rest of the spectators were familiar with Leith's displays. Cuffs of ice encircled

Birch's wrists and ankles. He stumbled but didn't fall, calling on more roots to break through the shackles. The two continued their dance in the ring, ice and roots clashing and shattering only to spring anew. All cheers from the raucous crowd were ignored by the men in the ring until Oran's shout of "end it."

Leith sent a smirk over his shoulder toward where we sat. Ice began crawling up Birch. Right hand extended, Leith encased Birch in a block of ice from the neck down. His left hand flicked, doing the same to the massive roots attempting to swarm him. One by one, they froze.

"Well?"

"Free my hand and I'll yield." Birch was a good sport even as his lips tinged blue with the cold.

"Is that a sufficient yield, Your Majesty?" Leith projected his voice up to the king.

"Leith Bruis is our winner!"

When Leith bowed, the ice on Birch disappeared. Birch braced his hands on his hips, taking a shaky breath. The roots slowly sank back into the ground, protesting their defeat.

"I dare say that was the most entertaining match we've had so far!"

The crowd's cheer rose to match the king's sentiment. I clapped along with Oran while Ruby shrieked in high-pitched glee. In the row behind us, Father stood to sedately clap for Leith.

Swaggering to his seat, the sheen of sweat on Leith's brow was the only physical mark of his match.

"Well done, my boy." Father's voice was gruff, but he did reach out to grasp Leith's shoulder, a moment I knew meant more to Leith than any celebratory crowd.

Showcasing the range of his skills as well as his stamina, pleased Father more than a swift victory. There were men with powerful magic that could not be sustained for more than a few minutes at a time. Leith's strength and endurance were a boast and a warning to other houses.

"Thank you for not making work for me," I told my brother.

Leith's grin grew. Kissing Ruby's hand, he then immediately turned to Oran. "Well?"

"It was good. You could have been faster when he whipped the vine with thorns at you. It shouldn't have come that close."

"Where is the fun in that? The people want a show." Leith leaned back to lounge like a spoiled champion.

Oran didn't smile back. "A show of strength, not comedy. You may as well have been playing with your food."

"I'll be timing your match then."

"Please do." With that, Oran stood and smoothly stripped his black tunic. In just a pair of black trousers bunched into worn boots, he walked to the ring.

I fought to tear my eyes away from the tan expanse of his back. The blush staining my cheeks and my wide eyes were too obvious, and yet I couldn't look away. Oran's broad shoulders blocked my view of the arena. Breadth and brawn, there was nothing subtle or lithe about his strength. He cracked his knuckles as he walked to the center of the ring, drawing my attention from his shoulders to the flex of his biceps. His arms were heavy and thick with corded muscle. His waist was a narrow taper made to look slimmer by the staggering width of his chest and shoulders. From the center of the arena, he turned back to us with a small smirk on his lips. I hardly noticed it. I got to see his face every day. The v of his abdominal muscles and the line of dark hair that descended into the waist of his trousers was a much more pressing view.

"It's time for our next match: The House Lennox heir versus the House Thallium heir! Oran Lennox and Rhode Thallium!"

My blood ran cold at the words. *He wouldn't.*

Rhode entered the ring displaying long, smooth lines of pale skin. His physique was vanity-based, lean muscle chiseled for looks, not strength. When I had first become close with Rhode, his torso had been littered with webs of silver scars. I remembered the awed look on his face after my magic had banished the physical reminder of Cadmium's discipline. Now, his skin no longer undermined the bravado he used as a shield. With his arms spread wide, Rhode turned a slow circle, inciting a roar from the audience.

Oran was a statue across from him. The only movement was the flicker of his flames, hands igniting on and off as Rhode incited the crowd into a frenzy.

It was rare for two heirs to spar. The spectacle risked unwanted scrutiny on the weakness of the loser. The rashness was so unlike Oran, I could scarcely believe it.

"Did you know?"

"Of course, I knew." Leith shrugged carelessly.

"Is he out to really hurt Rhode?" Ruby's brows pinched together.

Peering over Leith, she met my gaze. Worry pouted her lips. "People will talk."

"No," he scoffed. "Just some fun. Getting roughed up is not likely to kill Thallium. Though I'd have no objections if it did."

"Well, Lavinia won't let either of them die."

I had seen firsthand how strong Oran was. Growing up together, I had watched his power evolve from a spark to an inferno. Rhode, surely, knew what Oran was capable of.

But I didn't think anyone knew how strong Rhode was.

Like his father, the magnitude of Rhode's power was kept within the gilded walls of Thallium Manor. Any perceived weakness had been systematically targeted and beaten out of him. I doubted even Cadmium had yet to see Rhode's full capabilities.

The bell signaling the start of the match echoed in my already ringing ears.

"No sword. How disappointing." The smirk on Rhode's face instantly revealed his fear. I knew Rhode. The smirk was not his usual. Rather, it was the smirk he'd give after a confrontation with his father. The smirk he gave me when I went to mend his burnt face two years ago. One that was employed as a mask.

Oran's response was to send a ball of fire to Rhode's face.

Barely dodging in time, Rhode took another step back. He cracked his neck to the side before sending the dagger at his belt through the air. Without even having to flick his wrist, the dagger shot toward Oran.

I sucked in a breath, only to freeze in awe.

Oran's lips twitched, as close to a smile as he'd allow in front of court. He caught the dagger by the hilt, the point only an inch from piercing the tanned skin of his chest. He flicked the dagger in the air. Somersaulting above him, it ignited in flames. The fire-encased dagger fell to the ground between them. When he extinguished the flames, all that was left was a perfectly intact hilt. The dagger had been melted down to a pool of smoldering iron.

"Shit," Leith exhaled next to me.

Oran, too, had been holding back.

Rhode floundered, attention darting between his father and his opponent. Fighting to regain his composure, the line of his throat bobbed with a swallow.

He focused on the melted iron, trying to bend it back into a weapon. The iron writhed under his gaze but was quickly engulfed in flame once more.

Rhode panted a frustrated exhale. Thrusting his hand to the left, I knew what he was calling on. At his command, swords, javelins, arrows, and daggers rose in the weapons rack at the side of the arena. His hand shook as the effort beaded sweat on his forehead. Blue veins pulsed under the pale skin of his arm as he sent them hurtling toward Oran, one after the other.

A wall, as tall and wide as Oran, set ablaze in front of him. One hand extended, he braced against the impact of weapons hitting the shimmering wall of fire. Like the dagger, they too melted upon impact, the entire weapons rack left to pool on the arena floor.

The barrier fell away as a broadsword crafted in fire, resembling the one he usually wore at his waist, appeared in Oran's hand. He walked slowly to Rhode while the blue and orange flames crackled, stopping the sword an inch from Rhode's neck.

"Yield." His command was almost too low to hear.

"I yield," Rhode gritted the words between clenched teeth. He turned away from Oran's lowering arm, dutifully heading to his father. Displeasure flared Lord Thallium's nostrils.

I tried to silence my gasping breathing in the awed and unsettled hush of the crowd.

King Alaric recovered with a clap. "Our winner is the impressive Oran Lennox!"

At the king's enthusiasm, we stood with the rest of the crowd. Leith hollered and jumped, his fist pumping into the air. I felt a breathless laugh burst out of me. The fear fled my body, leaving me light-headed with relief.

Oran didn't smile at the praise. The sword of flames disappeared from his hand. He bent at the waist in deference to King Alaric, then walked from the ring.

The smile on my face dimmed as I looked to the royal box. Oran had just offered himself up to be used. When Proventium needed a fire wielder, Oran could be deployed the way legions of Vaux men patrolled the border with Tythmore.

Lord Lennox celebrated the feat like it were his own, standing and waving to the crowd.

Oran shrugged his black tunic over his sweat-covered torso. The material stuck to his skin from the sweat and heat that still radiated off him.

"That's how it's done!" Leith grabbed him by the shoulders and shook.

Oran gave a single nod. "Yes, it is."

"You say, 'You were right, Oran. That's far better than I did,'" I joked.

"What? He's going to cremate me if I don't?" Leith was still cackling as the two sat.

Oran's arm brushed mine, the usual heat between us amplified by exertion, searing through the fabric of my sleeves. Chest rising and falling rapidly, the adrenaline from the match was almost as intoxicating as the sight of him.

He was unharmed. He was here. It wasn't until he returned to me that I noticed how much easier it was to breathe when sharing his air.

"I cannot believe you did that." Any anger I felt with him for not telling me beforehand melted in relief.

"Vin," he started.

I dismissed him with a shake of my head. I didn't want to argue. "Well done." I smiled.

His eyes flicked down to the heaving of my chest for just a moment before his eyes met mine. "Thank you." The grin on his face emerged in its truest form—sparkling green eyes and cavernous dimples. "I wanted to impress you. Ending it in blood wouldn't charm you."

I giggled. "Impress me? I dare you say you succeeded in impressing everyone. Though I specifically do appreciate your restraint." I leaned closer to him.

"Happy to oblige." His voice dropped low. It was that sultry tone that tricked me every time into thinking that our flirtation could be more. That his interest could be genuine. "Admittedly, the restraint was as much for you as it was for me. A dagger through my throat is preferable to seeing your hands on him."

I bit my lip to stop a wistful smile from overtaking my face. Oran drew me in without trying. I had gravitated toward him since I could remember. It was an effort to remind myself that, for him, they were just empty words. Banter for amusement, not flirtation for attraction or love. No, I knew it was not that for Oran. Despite that knowledge, my stubborn heart refused to be swayed from him.

I mapped the pattern of veins running from his hands and up his arms. My heart discarded sensibility, traitorously remembering what it felt like to have those hands holding my hips.

It had happened six months after Rhode. At the time, I had thought it would change everything. That one kiss. A kiss I had dreamed about before it ever happened, and dreamed about even more after it had.

A kiss I now knew would never happen again.

I leaned against the bookshelf, soaking up Oran's attention like the final rays of summer sun. He watched me intently as I told him about the latest book I read.

"They have a passionate affair, and then he is deployed to battle. She spends six months believing her lover is dead. He returns just as she is about to marry someone else! It's quite a scandalous novel. Lots of passion, scenes of..." I trailed off in embarrassment. I had thought the story would make me seem mature, seductive. Now, I just felt foolish. "Well, you know."

His gaze heated, burning with sparks I struggled to name. He had recently been letting shadow grow to scruff instead of shaving every morning. The effect made him look older, more unattainable.

I began to babble out of nervousness. "And I know you know that I—" I shouldn't remind him about Rhode. "Well, we don't have to talk about that. It is just fun. Fun to read about passion. Love." The final word was a whisper.

His face pinched in pain. Staring at me with devastation etched into his features, he made no move to speak.

My embarrassment evaporated in concern. "Oran?" I placed my hand over his heart. "Are you alright?"

He looked down at my hand on his chest, and something seemed to snap. Suddenly, his hands gripped my face and pulled my mouth to his with a hunger that echoed my own. The hunger that had screamed at me since I was thirteen, and finally put a name to the reason I had never been able to look away from him. His lips were warm as they caressed mine, tongue tracing my lower lip. I opened to him, desperate for more. His hands left my face to clutch my hips. My own hands refused to release their grip on his neck. He kissed with the same confidence and skill with which he did everything. This was not a slow, hesitant first kiss. This was a kiss of lovers reunited. This was madness—the heat of him, the nip of his teeth on my lip, the slide of his tongue, the firm press of his body against mine. This was more than I ever thought possible. This wasn't just pleasure, it was all-consuming. I drew my head back to gasp a greedy breath. The loss of his lips on mine was soothed by the sucking kiss he pressed under my ear. The rasp of his stubble on the sensitive skin caused his name to leave me in a shaky moan.

Oran jumped back as if startled. As if my voice was the reminder of whose body he was touching. He ran the back of his palm over his mouth before straightening. "Forgive me, Lavinia."

We never spoke of it again, though the memory of it would haunt me as long as I lived. The stinging reminder that the infatuation I felt for Rhode was empty in comparison to what it could be with Oran. The painful proof that Oran was a man of passion, but not for me.

I snapped my face forward, even as the weight of his attention pressed against my profile. The memory was one I typically only indulged in when I was feeling particularly despondent.

The moment I had thought he had changed his mind.

I had tried on my sixteenth birthday to tell Oran how I felt.

It was no one's fault that neither of our minds had changed.

"Vin," Oran whispered. His voice was low, a secret just for us hidden under the roar of the crowd.

I turned to meet his gaze. *No,* I wouldn't fall for empty hope. My smile was pained. Quickly, I looked back to the match in the ring with unseeing eyes.

My foolish dreams were not his fault. He had rejected me as gently as possible. I would never forget the agony on his face. I think he would love me if he could, if only to avoid hurting me. Despite his rejection, I still couldn't think of Oran's flirtation as cruel. The burn of his rejection didn't change that away from the warmth of him, the cold was unbearable.

CHAPTER 10
LAVINIA

Laughter bloomed in the gardens as groups of the dispersing crowd made their way to the palace. Others clustered together, recapping the event. The activities of the court season were designed to prevent boredom among the nobles but fostered gossip and competition that lasted far longer than amusement.

The attention on Oran lacked subtlety, apprehension as loud as the surrounding chatter. He stood next to me, my hand hooked through his elbow, untroubled by their stares.

While Oran and Leith were still fresh after their displays of power, I felt like a cloth worn through from too much use. Repairing Arle Alexandrite's shattered collarbone had been particularly arduous, while reattaching Forest Haase's incisor had been surprisingly exacting.

I fought to catch Ruby or Leith's attention while he dramatically recounted his strategy to a group of her Southton cousins. Instead, I had the misfortune of meeting Heron Fjord's eye.

"Really?" I wanted a warm bath and a large cup of tea. I did not want to look at a bruise on Heron Fjord's leg.

"Do you want an actual injury?" Oran stood a step behind me. His bedside manner left much to be desired. Brows furrowed and arms crossed, Oran was intimidating enough without the day's performance.

Heron took a nervous step back. "But it hurts. You don't think it's going to get worse? You're here, it'll be quick."

A headache tapped at my temples. If I had the energy for Fjord's bruise, I'd instead use it on myself.

"Well, I guess I can try to," I began to agree.

Oran interrupted, "Fuck off, Fjord."

"Yes, sir," he sputtered. Scurrying away, Heron was unhindered by injury.

"Come on," Oran squeezed the back of my neck.

"Lennox! And the lovely Lady Lavinia!"

At the boom of the king's voice, his hand dropped. The crowds around us parted like a retreating tide to make room for King Alaric. Many, however, did not go far.

"Your Majesty."

I forced my features into geniality and dropped into a curtsy. Today was a glaring reminder of the violence that the king enjoyed. A violence I would never revel in despite my familiarity with it.

King Alaric was fitted in Harald crimson, though the velvet of his doublet put the banners surrounding us to shame. Gold stitching created a lattice pattern on the velvet. Intricate and expensive, he wore it like a plain tunic.

"Lady Lavinia, I must say I'm impressed. You displayed a level of extraordinary skill. Padgett is lucky to still have a job."

"Oh," I demurred, "you're too kind."

"I never give empty flattery, lady. Any compliments I bestow are fully deserved."

I ducked my head, a true smile overtaking my face. Years of feeling inferior had left me helplessly weak in the face of flattery. Compliments, from the king no less, had my chest swelling with pride.

My magic was useful. It may not be worthy of importance, but it was good and helpful. It wasn't something to hide away, a blight on the Bruis name forced into shameful seclusion.

"Thank you, Your Majesty. That means a great deal to me."

Oran stiffened next to me, the movement drawing King Alaric's attention. "Quite a show today! Melting iron." He blew out a breath. "Dare I say, I'm grateful you're following in your uncle's example and not your father's."

I fought to keep my face neutral. Worse than the king viewing Oran as a soldier to do his bidding would be the king viewing Oran as a threat to neutralize. Fear was a fine line; one Oran walked confidently, despite the storm that threatened to sway his balance.

"Thank you. I hope I made my uncle proud today." Oran's stance remained formal, his chin proud, and stare unwavering.

King Alaric clapped a rough hand on his shoulder. "I'm sure that you did."

The response was the perfect reminder of Oran's loyalties. Hugo had raised him to be a Lennox.

The king looked back at me. "House Bruis must be exceedingly proud of your showing today as well."

"Oh." I tilted my head the way Clodia so often did—better to keep his attention on me than on Oran. I searched for the words, unable to tell him that my healing was never something Father would view with pride.

"With your brother's betrothal, they must now be searching for a match for you?"

"Yes." I nodded. "They hope for a betrothal this season." I wrung my hands together, a habit I blamed Caius for. Noticing dried blood on the side of my hand, I rubbed my thumb over the rust stain.

Navy eyes tracked the movement. Reaching into the pocket of his trousers, he withdrew a handkerchief. I watched my hand as if it belonged to someone else pluck it from his grasp. A gold 'H' was stitched into fabric finer than that of my gown. Fabric now marred with a darkened streak. Was it rude to return a bloody handkerchief? The audacity of keeping anything at all from the king felt far ruder.

"Keep it, please." He raised his eyebrows as if pleading.

"Thank you, Your Majesty," I breathed. The sting on my teeth digging into my lower lip did nothing to distract from the nervousness I felt under the magnitude of his attention.

Flirting with the king felt like a dance I'd never learned.

With Rhode, the attention had been fun. I let myself be swept away by his words and affection, desperate for distraction. He was easy to flirt with because he himself did it so unapologetically. He could lead anyone in a seamless dance, never a missed step. Few men in court were as bold of a flirt as Rhode.

And no man in court made me as comfortable as Oran. While it was easy to get lost in the banter and flirtation, I knew tragically well that Oran was not serious. Oran's flirtation was bred from years of closeness. The familiarity made the steps as natural as breathing, even when each dance made my heart race.

No longer was I a carefree girl dancing for the enjoyment of it, uncaring about who my partner for the dance was. With the expectation of a marriage this season, I could hear the rhythm of the music but feared stepping on my partner's toes. But maybe throwing myself into the dance with the king of all men was the reminder I needed. The deadlines and consequences that threatened to paralyze me had no place in the choreography.

Under the king's appraisal, a thrill ran up my spine. If I could keep up with King Alaric, I could find the steps with any pick of suitors.

"Please, I've asked you before. Call me Alaric."

Oran stumbled back a step at Alaric's words as if struck. Pinned under a stormy blue gaze, I couldn't turn to question him.

"Only if you'll call me Lavinia." My tone held more confidence than I felt.

"Lavinia," he tested my name, drawing out the middle syllable. "Whoever Malcolm finds to be your husband will be the envy of court."

At his words, my soft smile froze. He was known to enjoy beautiful women. It couldn't be more than that. Mistresses weren't ladies of the Six. The king's mistresses were happy to be married off to a desperate courtier, content to live in opulence until they were cast off into a life of ridicule and scorn. By mere chance of being born a Bruis, I would never be lowered so. My last name provided protections that women like Temperance Sanctas were not so fortunate to have.

"Indeed," Oran's agreement came out in a growl. The tick in his jaw drew my attention. "We should all retire back to our rooms." Even in the face of the king, Oran did not ask, he informed.

Unperturbed, Alaric pressed a lingering kiss to the back of my hand. "I hope to see you tomorrow, Lavinia."

CHAPTER 11
ORAN

Call me Alaric.

The words mocked me in every moment of silence. The mindless crush of court had been whispering about the king's fixation on Lavinia. The speculation made me want to burn the palace to the ground. Maybe if the air were filled with ash, I would be able to breathe again.

Dimmer and brighter, I flickered the light from the vaulted chandelier to distract myself. With the light pouring in from the floor-to-ceiling windows on the far wall of the Chamber of Lords, no one noticed my manipulation of the flames. The wall behind me, in contrast, was painted to depict the storm that allowed King Vidar to triumph over Tythmore.

I didn't know King Vidar's storms, but I knew King Alaric's. My mother's fire had been helpless against the downpour that flooded our land. Harald storms were immortalized in my nightmares; the view of rising flood waters and blinding lightning from the roof of our cottage seared behind my eyelids.

My mother's hands shook, slipping from the deluge of rain. She didn't stop until I felt the rope connecting our waists, secure uncomfortably tight around me. "There. This way, no matter what happens, we'll stay together." Her voice was gentle, but I could hear the fear. It hadn't left her voice since she told me we'd have to go to the roof.

Call me Alaric, as if he were a smitten boy instead of a married man. I blinked out the flames in the chandelier entirely before sending roaring flames jumping toward the ceiling.

Call me Alaric was more pathetic than his bald threat. The caution in his estimation had been gratifying. The example of my father had loomed over me since I turned thirteen. It was his example that left me in the position of having to stand in silence at *call me Alaric.*

The traitor's son.

I couldn't let that harm Lavinia. I wouldn't.

The day of her sixteenth birthday, it had taken all my strength to deny her. She had looked up at me through thick, sooty lashes, those haunting eyes piercing my chest more efficiently than any blade. *I'll be introduced to court to find a husband, but I always thought, maybe…when I thought of marriage, I always thought of you.* It had to have been the fleeting notion of childhood. Her feelings just the shallow fancy of youth, brought on by proximity and friendship, nothing more. She was so brave, so good, and she deserved so much better. That bravery of hers, I had to meet with a gentle denial. *That will change once you go to court. You'll have your pick of suitors. Men who will make fine husbands. Who will make you happy.* I could make her happy as her husband, but the question was: For how long? How long until my stain spread to mar her, too?

I had crafted defenses and barriers against the draw of Lavinia. Each brick a reminder that she deserved more than a traitor. I had held out until seeing her with Rhode had ravaged my fortress like a hurricane. It was the endless expanse of creamy skin that made me do it. Seeing her long, smooth leg wrapped around him had driven me to insanity. I had been fighting my attraction to Lavinia since the spring she turned fourteen. When she had thrown her head back with a laugh and I found myself wanting to trace the line of her throat with my tongue. I was a seasoned soldier in the fight, and yet the sight of her in another man's arms completely undid years of barricades. Still, I held out, fighting with bloody knuckles for six months. But it was futile. It was always futile. My defense against Lavinia had been demolished the moment I saw her hands run down his chest. I was weakened by her already, always had been, but I'd not acted. Couldn't act. I'd fought every instinct to take her in my arms and never let go. Fought it so that I could protect her—until that one moment.

That moment of weakness was steeped in guilt. She had still been pining after Rhode. I had taken advantage of a woman who saw me as a friend, a protector. Graces fucking forbid a brother.

I hadn't touched anyone since. The women who had once been a pleasurable distraction were no longer enticing enough to shake the sound of Lavinia's soft moan. I couldn't touch another woman when I knew what the soft curve of her hips felt like under my palms. When I knew the taste of her lips.

My brain wouldn't let me have her, but my body would not let me have anyone else. My body had at least tried. My heart hadn't looked away from her since the spring of her fourteenth birthday.

And now I had to endure *call me Alaric*.

Rage burned hotter under my skin as I looked at the throne. The lords of the Six sat closest to the throne centered on the dais at the back wall. Three lords on each side of the stairs leading to the throne, each with their heir stood behind them. The large center of the room was left open, allowing room for debate and speeches. The rest of the nobles sat in three stacked rows along either side of the chamber walls.

Leith stood to my right, closest to the throne. Beamus Delphi stood to my left. At forty, he was the oldest heir of the group, but Ambrose showed no signs of relinquishing his seat. He retained his position through the execution of his niece and nephew. I imagined Ambrose Delphi would outlive everyone in this room.

After their overthrow as regent, the Delphi had never been challenged for their seat in the Six. They spoke on behalf of the Graces. A load of shit, but convincing enough to stay the hand of other houses. The Sands had talked of a challenge when Uncle was a boy. Ambrose had warned them their triumph would be short-lived, the Sand heir was to be born with little power. The Sand had balked at the threat but made no formal challenge. As foretold, Mace Sand had been born with the weather magic of a common peasant.

Ambrose's words hung over any house that thought to challenge them—unseat House Delphi from the Six and risk the wrath of the Graces.

Across from us were Thallium, Vaux, and Lynx. Usually, Alder Lynx was across from Malcolm Bruis, but today that seat was occupied by Cadmium Thallium. The Lynx lord relegated to the end, his face was set in a blank mask, but his hands were clenched in fists resting on his thighs. His son, Oak, kept his gaze on the floor. The Lynx heir had always been reserved, but typically was found looking around the chambers with a placid expression.

"Mesgara commandeered another trade ship." Uncle Hugo didn't look up from the report in his hand. Mesgara to the south had a royal navy that might as well be pirates: brutal, efficient, and lawless. To trade with Haloran in the north, they needed to pass the Strait of Tythmore or face the rough, unpredictable seas off Tythmore's western shores. Mesgara preferred to avoid the Proventium-imposed tariff on the Strait. Water wielders were efficient, but nature didn't tolerate being surpassed completely. When nature showcased the true magnitude of her power, Mesgara's fleet resorted to bloodshed to pass the Strait. They would bow to nature but never to Proventium.

Bruis shook his head. "There aren't enough men to patrol both borders and guard all the ships."

"Fucking water wielders," Leith grumbled.

Leith, like many others, believed that Mesgara's prolific water wielders were all bastards of the Crown. Far less shocking rumors passed between our kingdoms. Hearing stories of kings and princes doing as they pleased without a thought for what they left in their wake was akin to being told the sun will rise tomorrow in the east.

The doors opened for King Alaric, bringing all the lords to their feet. With the blight of the Wasting on his reign, he entered the Chamber of Lords as one would march into battle. Here, his usual humor was replaced with rugged determination.

"Sit, sit," he ordered with a wave of his hand.

Leith raised a brow in question. I answered with a shake of my head. The rumors had been swirling for weeks.

"A traitor faction attempted to land on our northwestern shore yesterday." Alaric remained standing before his throne. "Like the traitors before them, they were executed onsite. Proventium is a kingdom blessed by the Graces. Our enemies may try to harm us, but they will not succeed."

The lords began stamping their feet in agreement.

"Proventium is strong and will remain so. Two more legions of men have been sent to the border to deter any more unrest. I plan to visit in the coming weeks to assess the situation for myself. These uprisings cannot and will not go unpunished. That I assure you."

I gritted my teeth. All of Tythmore was punished daily, rebels and innocents alike were starved and desperate. Further force from the king did nothing but increase the very desperation that drove their attacks.

"An additional tax shall be levied on Tythmore, and will remain until every last traitor has been eradicated." Alaric gestured to the open circle in the center of the floor. "I open the floor to you."

"Your Majesty." Victor Iron walked to the center of the room and gave a low bow. "With the most humble respect, a tax is not enough. Those of us who live near the border know that the situation in Tythmore is worsening alongside the Wasting. Withstanding them both is proving a drain on our resources."

"The Wasting will be dealt with," Alaric dismissed.

When? The word seemed to buzz through the air like a harried hive. One lord to the next looked at each other.

"It would help to have more concrete reassurances to give our people back home. Concern is increasing. Will this harvest be our last before our land too is overtaken in the Wasting? Will trade goods arrive this autumn without interception by the traitors? Even in Iron lands, out of sight of the Wasting, our magic is being affected. Powers are weakened, leaving us and others living closest to the Wasting vulnerable to the traitors. Our families, our tenants, need more than the promises that have been offered."

He looked to Onyx Raven for support. The Ravens and Merrifields had land that bordered the Wasting directly. My mother had expressed the same concern. Living on the edge of Raven land, her magic drained with alarming speed.

Raven stood with a groan. "The effects of the Wasting are increasing. We assisted in quelling unrest in Merrifield lands, and it was a greater challenge than expected." His smile was as brittle as his thin shoulders.

"Yes," Evgeny Merrifield wheezed. His nods were frantic as he sought to meet Raven's eye. "That was our struggle. Our magic was draining rapidly, that's why—"

Raven interrupted him with a derisive snort. "My sons were still able to accomplish the task."

"Forgive me, but it sounds as if you are questioning your king?" Alaric had an unchallenged mastery of posing lethal questions in a temperate tone. "Surely, you do not question that your king holds the best interest of Proventium. Of my people."

Julius Vaux rose silently like a panther unfurling from his perch. "House Vaux has sent more men to the borders to lend their protection against the traitors. Where Lord Merrifield may struggle, we will not." Vaux was not one for public chest-beating. "I speak for all of the Six when I express the utmost confidence in the strength of our forces against the traitors."

Cautious support began as a murmur in the chambers. The king and Proventium relied on the individual armies of the governing lords. Spirit wielders of all levels knew Vaux offered good pay and training, giving him the largest army in the kingdom.

The look of satisfaction that crossed Alaric's face melted as Cadmium Thallium spoke.

He remained seated even as his voice sliced through the chambers. "In the matter of Tythmore and Proventium, Proventium is stronger. We will not fall to the traitors. It is for all of us to vanquish the traitor threat lest they sway more rebels with false promises. The Wasting," he reprimanded, "is a challenge for the Crown. If the Delphi prophecy is to be believed." He amended with a serene smile that did little to mask the venom poisoning his words.

Lord Delphi's umber skin was creased with deep-set wrinkles that carved further into his features with the squint of his protruding eyes. His sparse grey hair flapped helplessly as he tilted his head to look at Thallium. Beamus Delphi straightened in his posture. Amber eyes wide with feigned innocence, he raised his chin without any of the amused satisfaction of his father.

Leith's confusion mirrored my own. I scanned the crowd, noting who seemed surprised and who did not. The lords of the Six gave no reaction to Thallium's words. Beamus and Oak's countenances were heavy with understanding. Other lords looked between each other in shock. Burgundy whispered to Telis, who shook his head. Quinn and Glenn murmured together, heads bent low but eyes focused on the dais.

If Vaux was a panther, Alaric was a bull. He charged down the stairs. Iron fled to his seat, but the taunting red cloth of the Wasting had been waved.

Clouds darkened the sky, removing any trace of sunlight from the room. The windows rattled with rolling thunder.

"The Wasting will be taken care of. It started as the Graces' punishment for Tythmore. We are being tested by it as well because the Graces know that we are strong enough to overcome it. The challenge is designed to make us better. Cowardice and treachery have found home in Proventium, but it, too, will be dealt with swiftly."

Thallium corrected, "Since your reign began, we've not been free of insurgence in the west."

"Treachery is bred among the weak." Bruis made a show of adjusting his cuffs as he stood. He was undeterred by the king's wrath as he walked to the circle. "Bred among the weak, they target the strong. They know they cannot succeed us in power, in wealth, in strategy. They are reduced to subterfuge, to targeting our women and children. Fear is a weakness found in our enemy, not in us."

He knew nothing of the people across the border. The people who subjected themselves to abuse and disrespect in Proventium so that their families in Tythmore had enough to eat, the people who drowned under Harald storms.

Bruis turned to survey the lower lords, his words a chastisement of their concern. "The Wasting spreads in Tythmore because of that weakness, that cowardice. Doubt and fear will not stop the Wasting, it will only welcome the strain further into our borders. The prophecy foretelling the end of the Wasting will come to pass through strength and courage. The Crown will soon have all it needs to end the blight on our land and people." Bruis kept his steps measured, turning his back to the room. "If you have nothing to offer but self-involved fear, you may be better suited to life across the border."

The words were a long-ignored knife being twisted. I was familiar with breathing through the pain and ignoring the reason for the agony, but my lungs stuttered nonetheless.

Bruis left the other lords no choice but to make a raucous show of support. Support him or admit you're as cowardly as the Tyth rebels. The word had been spat in my presence my whole life. The insult of it dulled over the years, while the ache of the Tyth's suffering increased. I stared out the window as they clapped, ignoring the scalding heat of my uncle's hand digging into my knee. The clouds had gone, leaving sun bright enough to sting my eyes. I welcomed the burn. It was as familiar to me as breathing.

As the cheering died down, focus shot to the back of the chamber. The lords closest to the door fully turned to listen to the commotion outside the chamber.

"I will see him!"

I choked back a sigh. That voice, shrill and trembling. I couldn't bear to watch Bryony sign her own execution order. The hush that fell over the room amplified her echoing steps across the marble floor. I only opened my eyes when the click of her steps stopped.

Head held high in a gown of Harald red, Bryony Lynx stood in the center of the room. She fared better in the Lynx pastel court was accustomed to seeing her in. Crescents of deep purple marred her undereyes, making her grey eyes stormier. Oak and Alder kept their faces angled away. The Lynx were the largest house; they multiplied like weeds, more children, more cousins. As their numbers increased, it seemed their loyalty did not have the volume to extend to all.

"I don't believe I summoned you to court, madam." Rage simmered under Alaric words.

"I wished to see my husband. My letters have not received a response. I grew worried. I'm so relieved to see you well." Her tone was measured but contained the perfect amount of concern. Not so saturated as to be mocking or dramatic, the picture of a dutiful wife.

Bryony did not become queen by chance or luck. It was not a match of love but of calculation.

He wanted a beautiful woman with the promised innocence of youth. She had played her role perfectly. Bryony had smiled and demurred. She swore vows of sons and eternal love. She was devoted but not desperate, sensual but not suggestive, innocent but not frigid.

And unsurprisingly it had worked.

What was surprising was that it would end so soon.

King Alaric and the power he held were addictive like the sweetest wine. One never knew when they drank themselves to death until it was too late.

A boom of thunder crashed through the room, hard enough to rattle my teeth together. Alaric's power was heavy in the air like a damp, suffocating fog.

"I will visit you in your rooms when I am ready to see you," he dismissed.

"I will see you soon." Bryony's smile was brittle but she clung to the poise of a queen as she exited.

Once the doors closed behind her with the heavy snick of a coffin closing, the king spoke again. "I had hoped to postpone this out of lingering affection for the woman I thought that I had married, but with each day, more evidence comes to light that that woman does not exist. There is mounting evidence that the woman who was supposed to be your queen is working against Proventium."

Thunder rumbled like the low growls of a caged animal as he proclaimed his charges.

CHAPTER 12
LAVINIA

"Opal wrote." Ruby peeked at me through long lashes.

We had left the palace for the dressmakers in Tordenhold, the city situated at the foot of the sweeping palace grounds. Light from the window and ample candles lining the room reflected off the three floor-length mirrors, granting a glimmering sheen to the fabric of Ruby's wedding gown. The ivory against her rich tawny skin was worthy of a painting.

"She won't be able to come for the wedding if it is held at the palace. She'll be too far along in her pregnancy to risk the journey. So, if I want to see her, we'll have to have the wedding at either of our estates. Which isn't nearly as coveted. The king offered us a wedding here. He doesn't offer that lightly, and now we'll have to pass it up all because of Opal."

Despite the distance imposed after Opal's elopement, I knew Ruby loved her cousin too much to exclude her from such an important day, even if that meant passing up the prestige of a palace wedding. "I'm sorry, Ruby. I know how much it meant to you."

She met my eyes in the floor-length mirror. "It's fine. The new venue will be worth it. I just never get to see her. Even when we are back home and she is close... I can't go too often. It's poor form to associate."

Though Hugo would never have allowed Opal to marry Dean, court saw only the façade of a happy, blessed union.

"Leith, he said, Opal made her choice." I knew how much the words cost her. Ruby was never happy to speak against Leith.

"I don't think that's fair. That her choice for Dean meant choosing to be away from us. I don't think that at all."

"I don't begrudge her happiness, but sometimes… It is hard for me to not be angry with her." Ruby confessed the words in a whisper almost too low for me to hear. "Such a foolish choice, she knew what would happen." Her voice wobbled before she banished the emotion with a shake of her head. She fussed with the neckline of her gown while she composed herself. "She is so stubborn."

"Nothing will take away from your day, honey," Sapphire chided lightly. "Worry makes your face puffy." Eyes red-rimmed, she'd wept rather hysterically upon seeing Ruby in the gown. Sapphire had never shown any unhappiness at not having a son, looking at Ruby as if she could have never wanted more.

"Her happy life may look different than yours or mine," I said, "and that's okay."

The truth was that I envied Opal. She trusted herself implicitly, never wavering once a choice was made. When she eloped with Dean, I had felt immeasurable pride and envy. I longed for her courage. I wasn't brave enough to make such a leap. To risk the comforts that I had always known by disobeying my family.

Amethyst would love her daughter no matter her choices. I didn't have such security.

"Exactly," Clodia agreed. She was relaxed in the chair next to me. "Happiness is different for everyone. Who hasn't thought happiness was having a big stonemason in their bed?"

"Clodia," Sapphire's admonishment was diminished by the laughter shaking her voice.

"I suppose he is handsome enough." Ruby weighed her head side-to-side. "Aunt Am warned Uncle Hugo: Whatever she is forbidden from doing will be the first thing she does."

Headstrong to a fault, Opal had declared she'd marry Dean and eloped not three days later. Her blunt edges and cynicism were softened by love. The two had carved pieces of the other to take for themselves, sharing the good and bad in equal measure.

"Graces help them if the baby is a daughter. I expect it will be just like her, not a thought for what anyone else thinks." Ruby huffed a laugh, but I could still detect the stain of resentment in her tone. Be it gowns or relations, Ruby allowed for nothing unflattering to mar her image.

"Amethyst will have to leave shortly after your wedding for the birth, will she not?" I asked. Amethyst obeyed Hugo dutifully, but her devotion to her daughter was unrivaled.

"I expect she'll go after the baby is born," Sapphire said. "It won't look good to rush out of court on a moment's notice."

"Odds are he'll have her with another babe before the solstice." Clodia's brows were raised with glee.

"Oh, Clodia, I hope not."

"Young love, lust. Care for a bet?"

"I know better than to bet against you." Sapphire adjusted her skirts to hide her smirk.

"Girls." Clodia pointed a finger between us. "You'll see that I'm right."

"Sounds miserable." Ruby shuddered.

"Surely they would..." I glanced at Sapphire. I wasn't sure if she knew just how much Clodia had taught us about marital relations. "Take measures to prevent that."

"You'd think, but men can go a bit mad. There are men who love the sight of a pregnant woman. Etienne Westerly"—she rolled her eyes at the name—"for one. I always took a man saying he'd put a babe in me as a threat, but some women find it appealing in the heat of the moment. Poor fools."

Sapphire quirked a brow but said nothing.

"Is he the one with the pot belly?" Ruby asked. Her earlier discontent was eclipsed by familiar girlhood mischief.

"The one with three nipples?" I giggled.

"Girls!" Sapphire's sigh fought back a snicker. "This really is too much." She looked behind us at the empty shop, ensuring no one was there to eavesdrop.

"No," Clodia corrected. "The one with the lazy eye. Dreadfully unsettling for a man to have one eye on my face and the other down my bodice."

Ruby and I began cackling like little girls. My stomach hurt from the laughter and the constriction of my corset, but we couldn't stop. Sapphire pressed a handkerchief to her mouth to mask her smile.

"A lazy eye," Ruby shrieked.

"I think three nipples is the least offensive option." I barked a final laugh. "Were they all the same size?"

"Size, yes. Color, no." Clodia smirked.

"Girls, please. Edna, I apologize for the improper conversation. I hope you'll forgive us for such an indecent display." Sapphire's eyes narrowed at Clodia even as her lips rolled to contain her amusement.

My aunt shrugged, unbothered and unashamed. "Maybe pearls on the neckline?"

The seamstress, Edna, smiled, sorting through the drawers at her desk until she found an ornate silver box to present a blueberry-sized pearl.

Ruby's reply was interrupted by a boom of thunder sharp enough to rattle the mirrors. Pearls flew through the air at Edna's jump of surprise. Landing with soft plinks, they rolled across the floor and scattered through the room. I pressed a hand to my heaving chest, tensed for the next blast as I walked to the window.

Heavy, imposing clouds dominated what was once clear blue. The weather on the coast was often unpredictable, but this was different.

This was Harald power.

Clodia joined me at the window. The people once milling down the grey cobblestone walkways now rushed to take cover. While the street emptied, a singular carriage continued onward.

Red banners proudly adorned the doors and the horses' saddles. As the carriage passed in front of the shop, a thin hand moved the curtain to reveal the brush of wheat blonde hair against a pale cheek. Grey eyes scanned the street before the crimson curtain concealed her once more.

"Queen Bryony," I gasped. Looking to Ruby, I knew I wouldn't find the same care for Bryony as the one currently constricting my chest, but still, I searched for it.

"She's been invited back? Well, she'll be the subject of conversation for the rest of the season."

Clodia wrapped an arm around my shoulders. "Come away from the window, Lavinia." Her grave voice would have sounded like an impostor if not for the familiar, slow cadence of her words.

"Maybe she is finally with child," Ruby mumbled in a huff.

"Girls!" Sapphire nervously rubbed the diamond pendant of her necklace between her fingers.

"We will not speak of seeing her." Clodia ushered me to my seat.
"Surely, it is good that she is back."

My aunt's features were not crafted for solemnity. The frown made her mouth too large on her slender face. "She was not invited. Ambassador Vante was told in no uncertain terms that Proventium would soon have a new queen."

"No." The word exploded out of my chest.

"Vante is many things, over-eager, lewd, dim-witted, but a liar he is not. If he told me, he heard it from King Alaric himself."

"Enough," Sapphire begged. "Positive or negative, there is nothing to be said about Queen Bryony that will benefit us." She clapped her hands together with a forced frivolity. "Now, pearls? Edna, do we have any that aren't too gaudy? We don't wish to seem showy on the day."

Ruby shook her head at me in the mirror before matching her mother's cheer. "Lovely!"

Clodia pet a hand down my arm. Voice low in my ear, she cautioned, "The stench of scorned women spreads. The men can talk about Bryony all they want, but we must refrain. Anything said about her with reflect back on us."

I swallowed a reply, coarse sand scraping my throat.

To arrive unannounced and uninvited would be unthinkable. *She should run back to Borras Palace.* My gaze drifted back to the windows. *If Clodia is right, then it is too late for Bryony to run anywhere.*

CHAPTER 13
ORAN

The Lennox and Bruis chambers in the palace were next to each other. Convenient and unbearable all at once. As we walked to Lord Bruis's study, laughter could be heard through Lavinia's door. I gritted my teeth at the sound. Ruby or Thomasina didn't know how lucky they were. If the sound could be bottled and sold, the greed to hoard every last one would drive me to madness. When it came to her smiles and laughter, I was a miser counting each gold coin.

Lord Bruis's study was situated between the sitting room and his bedroom. His mahogany desk was positioned under a small stained-glass window—a knight kneeled in supplication before a dark-haired maiden. A hearth was at the back, while the rest of the walls were bookshelves, filled with volumes and tomes read and annotated in Bruis's careful hand.

The armchairs and rugs were awash in the Bruis colors: sparkling blues and pale greys. Lavinia's eyes and gowns.

My uncle, a booted foot resting on one knee, occupied the chair closest to the hearth on the left.

"Boys," Bruis greeted from the chair next to him. He called us boys to remind Leith of his place. The effect made Leith more intent on pleasing his father.

My uncle hadn't called me 'boy' since I was fifteen. Since the first time I fought back when he grabbed me by the scruff of my neck.

"Sit." Uncle Hugo gestured to the pair of armchairs in front of him.

Leith dutifully sat across from his father. I remained standing behind my intended chair.

"Queen Bryony has been moved to Mammatus Tower to await her trial for high treason," Bruis said this the way one would say the weather. "She will remain there for the duration of the trial, and then she will be executed."

Will be, not may be. I knew when the king made his claims that guilt would be the only conclusion. A trial was a farce that he had to follow. An animal feigning civility.

Not a full day after he proclaimed his suspicions, she was imprisoned.

"She has been formally charged with conspiracy to worsen the Wasting and infidelity with Sterling Mason." Bruis threw the decree papers detailing the charge on the low table in front of him.

"And did she?"

"Grow up, boy," Bruis ordered. Leith reared back with the blow. No real evidence of treason, then.

"And Mason?" I asked. He had come to apprentice in the palace blacksmith when he was a teen. He sent wages back to his mother in Tythmore. He was well-liked and crafted fine weapons. And he was a Tyth.

"He has admitted to the affair. In exchange for his confession, he will have a quick death."

After already undergoing torture by one of the king's men. Bron Harald specialized in precise, close-range lightning. A few minutes in a room with him and Mason would have admitted anything.

"The Wasting is worsening, that is a fact," Uncle said. "King Alaric has no heir, that is also a fact." He scratched his jowl in thought.

If court was an anthill under the king's boot, the Wasting was the boot looming over all of Proventium. No matter how we scattered, we found ourselves shrouded again under the threatening shadow.

Once, the Wasting would release its grip the moment one stepped onto fertile land. Now, crossing the Wasting could leave one powerless for hours. It had been allowed to grow into Tythmore for over two decades. The king had seen starving Tythmore as a benefit.

Fewer crops left them a weaker people. He'd have happily let it consume all of Tythmore, until it began moving east. As it encroached further into Proventium, the king was becoming increasingly desperate.

Bruis used his thumb to spin the wedding band he still wore. The polished silver shone under the dim light of the fire. "The Delphi seer during King Alaric's marriage to Queen Margaux foretold an end to the Wasting." Bruis began to recite:

Without the first son, the Wasting will further decay. At the whims of the Graces, prosperity and healing lay. The rot will spread until the chosen son prepares to reign. A cure to be passed in power from the mother's vein.

At the word 'healing', an involuntary spark came to my fingers. I smothered it back with a clench of my jaw.

"We've known he needs a son. So," Leith looked between his father and my uncle.

Bruis shook his head. "Bryony was meant to bring life back to the Wasting and deliver an heir. Barren in every sense of the word." He leaned forward. Elbows resting on his knees, he clasped his hands in front of him. "The king will move quickly. As soon as the execution is complete, he intends to wed again."

"Yesterday evening," Uncle's words were for Leith and me, but he kept his gaze on Bruis. "The king made a point to ask if there had ever been a Bruis queen on the throne."

"He's thinking of our house?" Leith's optimism made me clench my fists.

"No," I growled.

"We've discussed it," Bruis said with an incline of his head toward my uncle, "and Lavinia could very well secure the crown."

"Lavinia?" Leith sputtered.

As if we were brought here to discuss some distant cousin. I shook my head. I had no time for exasperation with Leith when the biggest threat to Lavinia was sitting in front of him. Disgust, horror, fury, the words were inadequate to describe the tumult ripping through me.

"No," I repeated.

"It's an opening that every house is going to be trying to fill." Uncle ignored Leith in favor of staring at me. The fact that he thought I could be convinced proved how little he knew me.

"Of course," Leith dismissed, "but Lavinia? Yes, she may be

pretty enough to catch his eye."

"That is not a difficult task for any lady when it wanders so."

Pretty enough, I wanted to scoff.

"She doesn't have a modicum of the power the past queens have held. Not just the most recent queens, but in all of Proventium history. Could you imagine? The heir to Proventium, a healer? We might as well relinquish Tythmore now. Or invite Mesgara into our borders."

"Leith," Lord Bruis cautioned.

"King Bergen has four water wielding sons. You think they will not see the weakness in a healer prince and invade?" Leith stood and began to pace. "What are the rough waters of the Southern Sea to four water wielding princes?" His voice continued to rise. "They'd be at our border tomorrow if they knew. Lavinia will never be seen as suitable."

"The prophecy does not say of what power the son will be, just that there will be one," Bruis dismissed.

"Any number of women can bear a son. Lavinia should not be in discussion." Arguing with them may be futile, but begging was suicide.

"Think about it, boy." Bruis stood, prompting Leith to follow. "He did not marry Bryony for the Lynx connection. He married her for her affinity with plants, to aid the Wasting. The prophecy calls for healing. Lavinia would give him that power, give him a son."

"You don't know that," Leith corrected in a huff.

"Your mother had a first-born son, did she not?" Uncle's voice was glib. "Lavinia bears a son, and the Graces handle the rest."

"You would be the brother of the queen." Bruis gripped his shoulders.

Leith grew contemplative, nodding slowly. "Of course, that'd be...but you don't know that the king will want her. The Rudyards, the Vaux, all have healers at court."

"We cannot ensure Lavinia will be chosen, but..." Uncle smirked. "Certainly, we can do our part to suggest it. From the way he has been looking at her, I think that we are already hurtling toward our goal."

The way Uncle and Bruis had watched her with the king at the Elvor banquet had made my hackles rise. I had thought they were merely eager for the interest Lavinia would capture from those witnessing her under the luster of Alaric's attention. Had I known the truth of what they were plotting, the horror would have made me tear his hand from her wrist.

"Lavinia is exactly the bride he is seeking," Bruis agreed, "despite her magic being less than ideal for other houses."

"And you think she could do it?" My head snapped to Leith. He was actually considering dangling her in front of Alaric. "Cure the Wasting?"

"She has proven her magic works on trees."

I wanted to scorch the smile off my uncle's face. Lavinia had been so proud of herself. Glowing like a star as we admired her success with the elm… and they would use that as justification to send her to slaughter.

Leith nodded once. "It is worth trying. And if she doesn't hold his attention, we'll betroth her to someone else. Seeing any interest from King Alaric will increase her value in the eyes of others."

"That is the kind of thinking I like to see from you, my boy." Bruis's meaty paw clasped the side of Leith's face. The two smiled at each other as if they weren't speaking of selling off the best member of House Bruis.

"You've all lost your minds." My voice shook with disgust. "You'd have her killed. That's what this is. The man has no sons, but soon to be three dead wives. You'd offer her up to be the fourth."

"Oran," Uncle barked. He sat up straighter in his chair but made no move to stand.

My hands were no longer heating, now fully encased in flames.

"The king will never cure the Wasting." I stalked around the chair toward Bruis. "Even if his next wife gives him a son, there is no guarantee he will keep her around. Another wife, another scapegoat for his failing."

"You don't speak like that outside of this room." Uncle stood then. "Do you understand?"

The laughter that left me, brittle and nocuous, was unrecognizable. "You're all cowards. You think you'll hide behind Lavinia? That her fate won't affect you? Tell me, do you think Alder or Oak Lynx will be unaffected by Bryony's execution? Ambrose Delphi had to banish his brother after the shame of Sevasti's execution. If you can't think of your sister, think of yourself," I urged Leith.

"You know family shame," Bruis reminded me.

"I am thinking of my sister," Leith's exclamation stopped me from turning my rage on Bruis. "The king's attention will get her a crown or a betrothal. King Alaric's attention will help her standing with the other houses. It will help her. It will help all of us."

"Help her?" The words charred my throat.

"I know you're fond of her, Or, but she isn't a child anymore." Leith crossed his arms. "I don't think King Alaric's interest in her goes beyond a pretty face. We'll use that to our advantage."

Bruis adjusted the cuffs of his cloud grey jacket. "Lavinia has his attention, and she will keep it."

"At what cost?" I fought to extinguish the flames licking up my arms.

"Everything has a cost."

CHAPTER 14
LAVINIA

With the crack of wood against stone, Oran's figure filled the door frame. He closed the door with more care than he opened it. Golden rays of afternoon sun dripped over his tan skin like honey.

"Oran?"

He opened his mouth, but no reply came. His jaw clenched with a snap. He shook his head, at himself or me, I wasn't certain. Running a hand through his hair, he paced a small circle with a huff. Remus awoke from his nap to monitor but didn't leave the pillow he had commandeered for a throne.

I rose from the bed. "What is it?" The sight of him unsettled sent my stomach into knots.

"Vin," he croaked. Oran closed the distance between us in two long strides, hands coming to hold my face. I could feel the tension in his frame despite the steady warmth of his hands.

"What's wrong?"

"Bryony is in Mammatus Tower. She has been charged with treason and infidelity." He rushed the words out as if that could soften the blow.

Tears rose to my eyes.

Not Bryony. Kind, beautiful Bryony, damned by the Graces.

We hadn't been friends, barely acquaintances, but I knew her to be kind. Kind and certainly not a fool. Only a fool would betray the king. I couldn't bear to think she'd take such a risk. To risk her life for an affair? To harm Proventium?

Aunt Clodia had been right. Arriving uninvited was rash and reckless. Bryony held her chin high even as she taunted a lion. Would she make such a move, designed to draw attention, if she were guilty?

Charmed by smiles and humor, it was easy to forget the cruelty the king was capable of, but he was feared by many and for good reason. Even still, it was difficult for me to imagine him killing a woman whom he had loved for years simply because there was no heir.

Father had been certain of Sevasti's guilt. Her own house had been ousted from the Crown by House Harald. A truth wielder, her guiding hand informed the king's decisions, slowly pushing the kingdom to ruin.

Betrayal by two queens. That was what we were to believe. Or was he using Sevasti's betrayal as a way to rid himself of a wife who had displeased him? The power the king held allowed him to do that and more. He answered to no one but the Graces. If he were violent or cruel, only the Graces could stop him.

"Did she..."

Oran's hands reluctantly fell from my face. "Sterling Mason has admitted to the affair."

"Graces," the air was punched from my lungs. There would be no recovery from his confession. He had damned them both.

My mind warred between them, victim and villain, but I couldn't say for certain which role suited who. As king and queen, they were unknowable to the masses of court, more projection than person.

The same power that Alaric exerted was by proxy Bryony's as well. That power could have steeped into her, arrogance a brine stronger than the kindness I associated with her. That power could have made her believe that there were no consequences to her actions, to having what she wanted.

Oran's jaw clenched, but his hands were gentle as they came to my waist. "There's nothing to be done for her. We need to focus on you."

I gave a small shake of my head, dislodging a tear from my lashes. "What about me?" My prospects were not so dire that they ranked with treason.

"Your father wants you to keep Alaric's attention." He ground the words out through his teeth.

Father wouldn't, surely not. Royal mistresses were from noble houses that wanted to gain an advantage. Land, attention, power. Father and Leith already had enough.

"He thinks the king could marry you."

The hoarse laugh that scraped my throat died at the darkening of Oran's expression. "Oran, be serious."

The thought of fluttering my lashes at a man capable of sentencing Bryony to die made bile rise in my throat. How was I supposed to ignore her fate? How could I not feel fear in his presence?

I was familiar with the cruelty of man, his capability to inflict harm. Surrounded by the safety of Leith and Oran, there were times I could ignore it. But that didn't mean it didn't exist. The brutality of man would forcefully grab my attention—in healing Honor's black eye, Ebony's burnt wrist, Laurel's broken rib. In Bryony's imprisonment.

The king was far from the only man capable of cruelty. Nor was he the only man who took what he wanted, whether it was freely given or not.

Even if I could believe her guilt, she didn't deserve such a fate.

I shook my head. Agonizing over this would do nothing but make me sick. It was all ridiculous. King Alaric married women of power, power that he needed either for himself or his heir. I was not that. I would never be that. Torturing myself over an implausibility was pointless.

Leith was not alone in his view of my power. A healer heir would not hold the throne for long.

"And my brother?" Leith may have often tried to be a barrier between Father and me, but he had never been a barrister for my desires.

"Leith thinks if the king pays you favor, it will secure another advantageous match for you."

Oran's hand was a soothing weight in my hair as I thought. Despite my family, I was not going to marry within the Six. That had been made all too clear to me. Unless…

"Maybe, that is possible," I conceded. The part of me that still clung to the idea of marrying for love ached at the thought. The practical part of me, the part that had been forced to grow stronger over the years, was eager for any potential to prevent a miserable marriage. "I could, yes"—I nodded, my head feeling heavy—"use it to our advantage."

"Vin," he croaked. Pain spilled through his features like ink.

"I know they want me to marry this season, but I wanted to ignore it. Father said if I find someone, he'll respect it. If they think the king speaking to me will help..." I trailed off with a shake of my head. "I expect one or two more conversations, and then King Alaric will be on to the next. They'll be sorely disappointed."

Better they be disappointed in the results of my efforts than in my obstinance. When I rejected Lord Merrifield's proposal, I knew I would not be afforded such an opportunity again. I just needed to secure a proposal before Father did.

"You're going to do as they say? Let them dangle you in front of the king?" His breath was warm against my cheek. I could feel the flutter of his heaving chest against my own through the scant inches between us.

"The king is not interested in me, Oran," I dismissed with a wave of my hand. "Nor I in him." *Graces, poor Bryony. How could I look at him without seeing her?* "I'm not going to waste time protesting. I can speak to the king. Maybe it will help them find me a suitable match."

I hoped I was convincing Oran because I was failing to convince myself.

King Alaric's favor was like a diamond. All gravitated toward it in the hope of the sparkle reflecting onto them too. When he bestowed his favor, court followed suit. If the king didn't overtly fear the liability of a healer heir, others could be swayed as well.

"So eager to be sent for show."

The words held a bite that made me take a step back to dislodge his hold. Oran followed me with a sigh. The tips of his worn black boots touched the hem of my dove grey skirt.

"I'm not cattle," I snapped.

"Fuck," he breathed. "I'm sorry, Vin. I didn't mean it like that." The fingertips of one hand grazed my waist. "Alaric is dangerous. The Wasting could end, he could have a son, and he'd still find a way to get rid of an unwanted wife on the crime of his displeasure."

"I'm not going to be that wife. But I will be *someone's* wife." I retreated another step. His touch never helped me think. I turned my back on him as I admitted, "I'm already unwanted." My voice cracked on the word despite my efforts. "If I can help things along, I have to." I nodded before facing him again. "Do you want me to be a mistress, a spinster, what?"

"Of course not! I'm trying to protect you. I don't trust your father." His long arms pulled me to him this time. While one remained on my waist, the other became a distracting pressure buried in the hair at the nape of my neck.

Despite my frustration, my hands gripped his shirt, holding him close. "He has protected me, Oran." Defending my father to Oran, a man who has truly protected me, felt like a betrayal.

Oran's reply was interrupted by the rapping of knuckles on the door. Leith strolled in before Oran had a chance to remove his hands. "We were talking." He didn't look at Leith as he spoke.

Leith snorted and pushed Oran a further step back from me with a gentle hand on his shoulder. "Please." He grinned. "No one would think you'd compromise Lavinia. We're family."

"Right," Oran muttered. I couldn't look away from that familiar tick in his jaw.

"He's told you then?"

Clearing my throat, I pinned my brother with a stare. "Leith, you need to temper Father's expectation. The king marrying me is preposterous."

"I agree, but if people think, even for a week, that King Alaric wants you, a line will gather. We just need to move quickly, lest you get a reputation like the Sanctas sisters." Leith's face contorted in disgust at the thought. "You won't do anything to harm your reputation." He pointed a stern finger at me.

"Yes, Leith," I snapped, batting his hand away.

Despite the inherent danger Alaric's power posed, I was in no danger of losing my head or my heart in a game of flirtation.

CHAPTER 15
LAVINIA

My cheeks ached from holding a smile.

Clodia and I were situated to the side of the hall, but from the line of greeters, we were at the center of the room. Our hands were kissed, compliments made, and then the next arrived. The initial attention had been flattering. Immensely so. But now the charm of being in demand was wearing thin.

One rumor about King Alaric's interest had made me appealing, enviable.

Radiating pride, Clodia's smile hadn't dimmed once. She knew exactly how to end a conversation that overstayed its welcome. Ushering it out with a hand so gentle, the conversation believed it was the one who decided to leave.

"Lady Lavinia." My name was spoken as smooth as velvet.

"Rhodium." I was met with not just Rhode but his two sisters as well. The girls, as fair as their brother, stood a step behind him. "I don't believe we've been introduced."

My aunt excused herself with a squeeze of my arm and a wink. She thought Rhode would apologize and beg to marry me. I couldn't blame her for the foolishness because that is what any man would have done for her. Clodia had no affections that weren't immediately and enthusiastically returned.

Rhode didn't glance at Aunt Clodia's departing form or his sisters. His dark eyes, usually dancing in flirtation, loitered on me with a foreign scrutiny. "My sisters are in their first season. And enjoying it immensely." The girls both conjured a smile, one more convincing than the other.

The banquet was not a distraction from the news about Queen Bryony. The two days of stillness after the news had created restless speculation, a frenzy for more, more gossip, more information. The king had yet to make an appearance, but the crimson banners and roses decorating the room acted as a reminder. Each hushed rumor was accompanied by a look over one's shoulder.

"Golda, Argenta, this is my dear friend, Lady Lavinia Bruis."

I smiled warmly, hoping to thaw their frozen composure. I remembered how daunting a girl's first season was. The girls were here without their mother, just as I was. Though their mother, Vera Thallium, still lived, Rhode had once confided that her illness made him wonder if death would be kinder. Cadmium never sought out the royal healers to treat her. *I think he prefers her sick,* Rhode had confessed.

I felt an aching sadness creep in, but fought to keep my face welcoming.

I had been excited for my first season, nervousness eclipsed by the joy of finally being included. Father and Lord Lennox had started bringing Leith and Oran to court when they were fifteen and fourteen. Summer and winter, two months at a time spent for them to learn their new role. Being forsaken made me far lonelier than each time Father's eyes avoided where I stood. At least that was a conscious decision. When he left me at home for court, he may have not thought of me at all until confronted with my presence upon his return.

"It's lovely to meet you both."

The twins wore matching gowns of rose. Platinum curls tumbled down their shoulders and were pinned from their faces in gold and silver combs, respectively. The combs mirrored the embroidery decorating the lower portion of their skirts and the hems of their sleeves with twisting vines of ivy.

"Perhaps, if your father agrees, you could join Lady Ruby Lennox and me for tea soon?"

The girls brightened at that, exchanging a covetous look. The twins were distinguished by the sharper point of Golda's chin and the dark freckle that marked the bow of Argenta's lip.

"Yes," Golda said with a nod. "The days are so boring. Father keeps us—" She was cut off by Rhode.

"Enough, Goldie." His voice was gentle. "I'm sure Father will have no issue with you two becoming friends with Lavinia and Ruby."

Argenta arched a delicate brow. "Really?"

Golda gave a huff. "He has a problem with everything."

"Hush." He pinched the side of her arm. "I'll handle it. Now, I think you both should go find Lady Philomena. I need to have a word with Lavinia."

"You're allowed to speak to a lady alone?" Golda was affronted. "We can't speak to anyone without you, Father, or Lady Philomena, but you get to do whatever you want?"

"He never has any rules," Argenta sighed. "There's no point in arguing."

"Because he's a boy!"

Rhode gave them a pleading look. "I'll make it up to you later, whatever you want."

"Whatever we want." Golda's eyes narrowed.

"Yes," he hissed. "Now, I see Lady Philomena. Go." He jerked his head toward Lady Vaux.

The girls left whispering, no doubt plotting what they could get out of their brother.

"Well, well, well," he drawled. Without the need to behave for his sisters, he slunk a step closer to me. His scent of mint and amber washed over me, familiar but not intoxicating. Outfitted in a black doublet trimmed in maroon velvet, the pale line of his throat almost blended into the crisp white shirt underneath.

I crossed my arms over my stomach as a barrier. "Your father will certainly have a problem with your sisters making my acquaintance. You should not have promised them anything." I offered to be kind because I remembered being lost before Ruby came to court, but I didn't think Lord Thallium would allow any real friendship between the girls and me.

"Oh, he will. Didn't you hear?" Black eyes twinkled with mischief.

"Hear what?"

"Hear that Lady Lavinia Bruis is the most desired woman in

court." Flirtation intruded on his smile. "I've known that for years, but it seems the rest of them are just catching on. They must have been blind for it to take this long."

"Oh, stop. It was two conversations."

"The rumors are saying the king desires much more than just your conversation. I don't blame him." His eyes ran down my body in appreciation.

Nervousness and frustration were wasps in my stomach where there used to be butterflies of anticipation. "Not you too," I whined.

"Ah, so I'm correct in thinking the Bruis father and son are encouraging this?" His brows jumped high on his forehead. "The line of suitors tonight must have them thrilled."

"Rumors are just that. Rumors. Queen Bryony is charged, not convicted," I deflected.

"So, they have designs to make you queen?" He said the question like a winning answer.

"Rhode," I admonished in a whisper. "It doesn't matter what people speculate. It's baseless and pointless."

We were interrupted by a footman with a tray. Rhode took two glasses with a grin. "Thank you, Egan. How is Marlene?" Rhode noticed people in a way that went beyond politeness, a peaceful rebellion against a father who would have him be a lord isolated above everyone else. He sought connection in any form. While his more amorous connections caused trouble, it didn't detract from those he made with people much of court overlooked.

"She is doing well, sir. Thank you, sir. She's started walking."

"Ah," Rhode cheered. "That's much too fast! I could have sworn she just learned to crawl a week ago!"

I took the glass of wine from Rhode as he finished his conversation. I felt my annoyance at his questioning melt away. If there was anyone who could understand my father's plan, my fear, it was Rhode. I could trust him, at the very least, to listen.

When Egan left, he turned back to me.

"Do you believe it? What she's accused of?"

"I was there for the decree. It's done." His shrug was light, but his voice was heavy. "Mason has admitted to the affair, and I can name another half dozen men that have fucked her."

"You're lying," I stuttered.

"Sadly, I'm not," he sighed. "The hubris of it, to think you can manipulate the king. It's so very in line with the man that Alder is that it's difficult to be surprised. I'm sure that was what he told her. 'Marry the king and you can still do as you please.' Shocking behavior until you think of who is behind it. I'd stay away from Dracaena Lynx."

"Excuse me?" I hadn't spoken to Dracaena in days. He wasn't a serious prospect then and certainly not now. My father would not allow any close associations with the Lynx family in the aftermath of Bryony's charges.

"Trying to make me jealous? Draped all over him, giggling. I know he isn't funny. Honestly, gorgeous, if you wanted my attention, you only need turn those eyes my way."

"What about Dracaena," I pressed impatiently.

"You don't see him tonight, do you? He's been arrested too. An affair with her own cousin. When you think it couldn't get worse, it does. They were going to put an inbred bastard on the throne."

The news felt like being trampled by a carriage, knocking the breath from my lungs and collapsing my ribs. So salacious, it didn't matter that it was unbelievable; people would circulate the rumor as a form of entertainment. "You can't believe that."

Lines marred the sides of Rhode's mouth as he frowned, weary with regret. "I believe she's fucked a handful of fools behind the king's back, Mason most often, but no, I don't believe one of them is Dracaena. But what I think, what we think, doesn't matter."

"Why do you think she is guilty?"

"Of infidelity?" At my nod, he dropped his voice even lower, "I know she is. Ash wanted her to marry Alaric. She wanted to marry Mason. He's been in her bed as often as the king. I saw him that night." Understanding dawned on me. "You left with Bryony, and as I was leaving, I saw Mason sneaking off the grounds. They were up to the same thing we were that night. Though unlike us, gorgeous, they didn't stop."

Bryony had done the unthinkable. She had committed adultery against the king.

"Graces' ever-loving fuck," Leith spat as he approached. "How does Clodia think this looks?"

I jolted, too caught up in Rhode's words to notice his approach.

Rhode held his hands up with a laugh. "And with that, my lady, I'll take my leave." He turned away with a parting shot at my brother.

"Bruis, you couldn't have combed your hair this evening?"

"Thallium, fuck." Leith rolled his eyes but ran a smoothing hand over his honey locks before adjusting his navy cuffs.

"Leith, do you believe the charges against Bryony?"

His eyes jumped from Rhode's back to meet mine, no shock or regret swimming in their icy depths. "She was fucking a Tyth behind the king's back." I had long heard others spit the word like a curse, but never Leith. The hatred in the word felt wrong in his voice. "That's charge enough." He looked at me like an imbecile.

Maybe I was an imbecile for scavenging after hope that Bryony would be exonerated.

CHAPTER 16
ORAN

"This all?" Fintan didn't leaf through or weigh the stack. He held the twine-bound letters firmly in both hands.

"Yes."

I was anxious to return to the banquet. Not because of the potential for my absence to be noticed, but because the persistent itch under my skin, *Lavinia*, was now accompanied by worry.

The itch, to be in her presence and earn her smiles, was not new. Lavinia was always running through my veins. What was new was the fear now frantically sprinting alongside her. I had learned to carry the desperate ache to be with her rather than buckle under its weight, but I didn't know how to also contain the consuming demand to protect her.

It had never been about wanting, though want I did. Lavinia was a vital need. Her safety, her well-being, came before everything.

The onslaught would begin tonight, and I didn't trust Leith to keep her safe. He was my brother and always would be, but with each disagreement, each secret, I had come to accept that the implicit trust we used to share had been altered. Leith should have been my ally in protecting her, but as long as he remained a slave to his father's wishes, I couldn't rely on him.

I had once trusted him with my life.

123

But now my life was Lavinia.

Fintan nodded, unbothered by the stillness of the stable that furthered my agitation. "Sionan will leave within the hour."

"I trust he'll deliver them with care." I knew Fintan understood, as Sionan did. Nothing was without risk. Meeting with a Tyth, the letters, Sionan's journey, all of it came with risk. It put them in far more jeopardy than it did me.

"On his life," Fintan swore.

I left the stables with a final nod, marching across the grounds to the palace. My power was warm at my fingertips should I need to extinguish the lanterns lining the path, but anyone roaming the grounds during the banquet wouldn't speak of seeing me. They wouldn't implicate themselves in the misdeeds of the shadows.

Whispers consumed the hall when I arrived, each group speculating about Bryony's fate and, no doubt, Lavinia. Bruis and Hugo had the ear of all of court. Their design would have easily passed through the masses during the stillness that followed Bryony's charges.

Like a bloodhound, I scanned the hall until I found raven hair and moonstone eyes. Pushing past Leith, she glided toward her aunt. More than just my eyes trailed her wake.

I couldn't interject in her every conversation, despite the avarice that nagged at me to covet every word and smile for myself.

No one would believe that you'd compromise Lavinia.

The sight of Leith roused his earlier words from where I'd banished them. The thought of compromising her, of leaving our families no choice was tempting. I was selfish through and through, of course, it was tempting. But temptation was a chronic condition I had learned to live with.

It was the aching desire to be a man worthy of Lavinia that stopped me. She deserved far better. Every piece of me was stitched together in the thread of Lavinia. She was woven into my favorite memories; the few that didn't include her gained importance only in recounting them to her, in watching her eyes light up, in hearing her gasp or giggle. The best parts of myself, each and every one, were held together by her. Each stitch learned and practiced so that I could be a man worthy of her.

A man worthy of her would not trick her into marriage.

She deserved a choice. She deserved to be happy.

Traitor's son. I'd never escape it. A traitor's wife was not the life she deserved.

"Problem?" I asked.

He looked at me with annoyance I knew was exaggerated. "Where have you been?"

"Things going well with Lavinia?" I deflected.

"The sheep! There's been a damned receiving line all night. The flock has been thrilled to chase after one little rumor."

"Any prospects?" I kept my tone bored even as I analyzed the room for who could potentially seal my fate.

"Thallium has circled back." My teeth met with a snap. "Burgundy has sought her out three times to speak. The bastard looks like he might faint every time she smiles at him. The king has yet to arrive."

Only an amateur admirer of Lavinia would deem their eyes the same color. Leith's were an empty sky, a cold new moon, compared to the constellations of Lavinia blue. I avoided his gaze, focusing instead on the tension shooting up my jaw and the faint glimpse of a head of onyx silk among the crowd.

"What's that look?" he asked. At my silence, he grew agitated. "What? Speak your mind."

"That's what your father cares about. He doesn't want this to lead to another suitor for Lavinia. He wants it to lead to the crown."

My earlier anger boiled anew under my skin. When you're intimately familiar with rage from a young age, you learn to control it. I mastered my anger before it could master me. I didn't need rage acting as another leash around my neck, but this was threatening to drag me back to the boy I had once been. The boy who had wanted to burn the world for taking his family away. Anger had done me no favors then. I certainly wouldn't let it rule my hand now when Lavinia was at risk. I would not lose my family again.

Those icy eyes, still the eyes of the boy who had first become my brother, were stern. "Watch what you say and where," he cautioned.

"You just believe every hollow word he says?"

"Of course not!"

"He'd respect you more if you took a stand." My voice was low and even. I wasn't trying to provoke him, I wanted to get through to him. "I know you think blindly following his every order will please him, but he'll respect you if you have principles. Your sister needs

125

you on her side."

"Like you?" Disdain twisted his features.

"Yes, like me. I care for her more than I care about the king's favor. Can you say the same?"

"She's my sister!" Leith shoved my chest with a huff.

"So tell your father that he's lost his senses."

"All he's done is help the rumor spread. Who are you to challenge how we handle her? She is our responsibility, mine and Father's. We'll decide what to do."

"And does this rumor include repeating the prophecy?"

"We know the prophecy is Delphi shit they spun when they were bored. Why anyone would trust them after Sevasti was fucking half the kingdom is beyond me," he dismissed. Leith's anger was heavy smoke, suffocating but impossible to hold, no matter how he tried to grab it.

"Your father is trying to convince himself that it isn't Delphi shit." I crossed my arms. "And he'll be trying to convince Alaric of it, too."

"The word of a Delphi holds little weight these days." He shrugged. A grin emerged on his face. "Lighten up!" Nudging his elbow against my arm, his smile grew. "Instead of worrying about the king's bed, you should worry about your own."

"I do just fine. Thank you for your concern."

Leith didn't need to know the emptiness of my bed nor the reason behind it.

"Graces, who knew it would be that easy?" Leith huffed a laugh and peered behind me.

CHAPTER 17
LAVINIA

The king's attention, heavy and imposing, was a persistent distraction from a lovely conversation. I smiled at Arrow, overly aware of how I might look to King Alaric.

My father's designs on the king were foolish, so my designs had to be strategic.

Several generations ago, the Burgundy family had been a member of the Six before their water magic weakened enough to be usurped by the Vaux.

Arrow was handsome. Shoulder-length dark brown hair and stubble accented the chiseled line of his jaw. He was lanky, almost as if trapped in the gangly stature of youth. I had to crane my neck to meet his eyes, a brown as warm and soft as his hair. He was respected but didn't radiate the reek of desperation so many lords did; aspiration did not drape over his shoulders like an ill-fitting cloak. I worried about being lonely in the north at his estate, but there would be time to ruminate on that later. For now, my focus was on piquing his attention just enough. He needed to stay an option while I collected others.

Placing a hand on his forearm, I looked at him through my lashes. "My lord," I began.

He straightened not with intrigue but alarm. "Your Majesty,"

Arrow quickly bowed his head.

The confidence I had been faking was becoming dangerously real and potent. I hadn't been trying to spur King Alaric to interject, and yet it had been almost as easy as calling Remus to heel.

Spinning slowly, I painted on a countenance of pleasant surprise. "Your Majesty." I dropped into a curtsey alongside Clodia.

"Lady Lavinia, I thought we agreed you'd call me Alaric."

At the king's familiarity, Arrow retreated, and Clodia beamed.

"Forgive me." I paused with a flutter of my lashes. "Alaric."

A bright cerulean doublet and matching shirt accented with gold trim stretched across Alaric's large chest. The color made his eyes, a deep ocean blue, sparkle. His copper hair was short on the sides, the length at the top parted and styled to one side. His matching beard was perfectly groomed. He had forgone a crown, though he never needed one. His position was etched into every line of his frame.

"Apologies, Burgundy, but I must steal her away." He didn't sound sorry in the least.

"Of course, Your Majesty." Arrow bowed again.

"It was lovely speaking with you." My plan would fail if the king scared away all prospective suitors. I held Arrow's gaze until he gave me a tentative grin.

Father and Clodia trailed behind us for propriety as I left the grand hall on Alaric's arm. Not even the king could disregard convention so boldly as to leave alone with a woman who was not his family. They gave us ample space, hopefully, enough that my father couldn't hear us. If I made a mess of this and lost Alaric's supposed affection as quickly as it appeared, I didn't need an audience.

He led us to the portrait gallery. The vaulted ceiling was crafted of glass panes lined in gold, allowing the night sky to glitter down the long hall. I looked up and felt impossibly small under the stark expanse of the palace and the world beyond.

Aunt Clodia and Father paused and turned to the first portrait, one of the earliest Delphi kings. "My, the lighting in this portrait is marvelous," Clodia exaggerated.

Neither knew a thing about art.

Their feigned conversation meant Alaric and I continued further into privacy. Faces of past kings and queens of Proventium, serene in their judgment. Only Queen Margaux was allowed to remain hanging next to King Alaric. Her expression was peaceful, her delicate features complemented by the soft curve of her lips. Loose curls of cinnamon brown hair framed her jaw. I saw touches of Princess Gaëlle in the thin line of her nose, the straight set of her brows.

Next to her portrait, the king was captured in all his splendor. The only portrait to have a full smile, his proud grin showcased a row of straight white teeth. The artist in me marveled at the brushwork, the way the light played off his crown, reflecting shadows and the faint glow of the inlaid rubies on his white doublet. The painter was wonderfully talented, capturing the magnificence of Alaric without erasing any of the flaws that made him human: an eyebrow that was longer than the other, a small gap between his left incisor and front tooth, the mole that sat at the edge of his beard. Studying the portrait also allowed me to avoid looking at the man. The painting was far less intimidating.

It didn't require conversation.

It wasn't imprisoning an unfaithful wife.

Now, as alone as we could be, anxiety sprouted in my gut. I felt her presence so strongly that Bryony may as well be on the wall watching us.

She could be guilty, but that didn't make him innocent.

"Lavinia," he began. His voice was gentle, tentative like a low tide on the beach. "Thank you for allowing me to speak with you."

"Of course," I stuttered. "I mean, it's my honor."

"No," he corrected, "I don't want you to speak with me as your king. I want to be Alaric and Lavinia. Please"

"I, well, Your Majesty, Alaric." A light laugh escaped me. "That is to say…I'm quite nervous." I felt a blush rising in my cheeks. Clodia would be horrified by the admission. I glanced back at her, desperate to draw on her self-assurance.

"I understand how I must look to you." He dropped his head to meet my eyes. "With news of the former queen's arrest, I must seem a tyrant. A monster."

Shock stole my breath. I never thought he'd be the one to broach the subject. Kings did not apologize, and they did not explain.

"It was shocking. To hear." He seemed to slump further. "No one knows the truth of the marriage but the two of you." It was as much a concession to him as it was a reminder to myself.

"The truth is embarrassing. I thought being perceived a tyrant was better than a fool, but I find that I cannot bear for you to see me as

129

such."

"The two previous queens..." I trailed off.

The weariness that sank into his features hollowed his face, emphasizing his age. "Margaux and I were not a love match, but she grew to be my dearest friend. After her death, I felt unmoored. Sevasti... I loved Sevasti. I'm embarrassed by how quickly and how much. She took me by surprise. She was unapologetic and wild. I felt because she was so outspoken that she was inherently honest. A truth wielder who would always be frank with me." He smiled, sad and self-deprecating. "When I discovered that she had been lying..." He paused, unable to find the words. "The woman I married never existed. She had always planned to incite chaos. She had hoped that in this chaos of civil unrest and rebel attacks, that I'd be overthrown or killed, and House Delphi reinstated. She and her brother seemed to be the sole figures behind the plan, but it left me feeling very alone. I felt I couldn't trust anyone."

His honesty was hypnotic. A man above consequence and challenge, choosing to expose himself was aberrant. Alaric trusting me enough to be vulnerable had a new tenderness blooming behind my ribs.

"Bryony." He looked up to the skylight, searching the night sky for answers. "She took me for a fool. Her affection was addictive, given and rescinded at whim. There was a time when I would do anything for her smiles. Make any promises, give any gifts. She'd grow quiet, and I'd blame myself. I see now it was never love."

I knew from the stories that circulated court how fickle love was for some. Love that burned too fast and hot to sustain itself, and love that was a fragile ember extinguished in a moment. Looking at Alaric, it made sense that he would be built of bright, sparking passion rather than the steady, enduring burn of devotion.

The unrequited love that had plagued me since childhood was painful, but there was a comfort in its permanence. Loving Oran was something that was mine. The thought of being without it brought me far more pain than the lack of his affection. I'd claw at that love. I'd dig my nails in until they broke before I surrendered it.

"I gave all of myself, hoping to get part of her in return, but she always kept her heart from me. I know why now." His hoarse bark of laughter sounded like a shattering. The pattern on the marble flooring, grey cracking and crawling through the pale stone, resembled the agony on his face.

"There was no room for me in her heart with Mason there. They planned to run away together. To Tythmore. They hoped to use her power to stop the Wasting in Tythmore but send it further into Proventium."

"It was more than infidelity," I murmured.

"Yes. If she were just unfaithful... well, I don't know what I would do because it was always more than that. Her plans to harm Proventium were far greater than my pride. What little I have left. Had she rejected my courtship to marry Mason, I would have wished her well. Instead..." He shook his head with a sigh.

Love.

It was a blessing and a curse. Bryony's love for Mason and Mason's love for Tythmore made them desperate. Reckless. Dangerous.

To die for love. Even in the tragedy of how avoidable it all was, they'd be together in the end. A modicum of relief.

I understood the pressures of pleasing family. Of fitting the mold that court forced ladies into, unyielding and constricting. And yet, love would be the only thing that I could think worth defying my family for.

The silver shine of tears lining his navy eyes was what broke me. I had never seen a grown man cry. Father had snapped at ten-year-old Leith that he was too old for tears, and he never cried again. Oran had always been steady. In all our years together, I had no memories of him wavering. To see not just a man, but a king, brought to tears wrung my heart.

My hand didn't shake as I ran it down one velvet-covered bicep. Alaric's lips curved, gratitude emerging through the sheen of devastation. His large hand, smooth and warm, covered my own, holding it on his arm.

"I'm sorry," I said. "It is cruel what happened." I felt dizzy with the shifts that had happened. How had my heart broken for Bryony just this morning, and now Alaric had a share of my sympathy?

His hand squeezed mine. "I couldn't bear the thought of you thinking the worst of me. I needed you to know."

"Thank you for telling me. I hope you know how much I appreciate your trust."

"I find myself thoroughly enraptured with you."

I sharply inhaled, but a calm settled over me as understanding danced between shades of blue. The flutter in my stomach was no longer fear or anxiety. It felt dangerously like excitement. A feeling that summoned a small smile to my face. When it threatened to grow, I bit my lip to hold it at bay.

Success and pride were intoxicating in their novelty.

The sound of his breath was loud in the stillness of the gallery. As the kings and queens of Proventium looked on, Alaric bent his head and pressed a lingering kiss under my jaw. The intimacy of it made me freeze. Not my hand or my cheek, but the soft curve of my neck. The rough scratch of his beard on the sensitive skin shocked my excitement into a hasty retreat.

I needed to maintain the right amount of attention. The wrong amount, and I'd be another woman taking him for a fool.

"Forgive me, Lavinia." He peeked at me from under his brow like a giddy boy. "I speak too much in your presence. I feel very comfortable with you. I hope with time you can feel that as well."

CHAPTER 18
LAVINIA

I stared at the small scrape on my neck. A crimson tear on ivory silk left by the abrasion of the king's beard. Proof that yesterday was real. Alaric was enraptured. A giggle escaped me. Remus, lying in a beam of sunlight on the floor, perked up at the sound.

I had believed myself a difficult person to love. Chasing my father's affection and approval had left a wound that scarred. A jagged reminder to be biddable and likable. Father was sad enough when he looked at me without adding my own sadness, so I hid it under a thick plaster of pleasantry

When you're told constantly of your own ordinariness, you begin to think of it as something to overcome. Charming, happy, pretty, all practiced to distract from the disappointment of the averageness running through my veins. I had long hoped that being average perfectly would be enough. Surely, it was better to be average perfectly than to be extraordinary poorly.

Recently, the fear that even that was not enough, would never be enough, had made the sadness harder to pack away.

A smile, slow and soft, emerged like a winter dawn. I wouldn't heal the mark on my neck. I'd keep it as proof that I was more than the burden my family saw. If I could enrapture King Alaric, I could do it to another.

The thought invaded my mind before I could fight it back: *Oran*.

Alaric was charmed, but he didn't know the truth of me. He knew shine and trimmings. Oran knew the very heart of me, no blemish or flaw escaping his notice.

Maybe that was why.

Where I saw comfort and safety, Oran saw boring familiarity. My body and mind felt instant assurance around him. I knew I was safe no matter what, as long as he was near, and yet my heart still raced. Speeding to match his, my naive heart was desperate to be as close to his as possible; running my blood hotter in my veins and sending butterflies fluttering in my stomach. A balm and a torment all at once. But maybe for Oran, familiarity had bred a familial affection.

A sigh refusing to be trapped deflated my chest and the hope it harbored. It was never productive to agonize over Oran, especially this early in the day. I brought my hair forward, spilling inky strands down the sage green of my gown.

In the privacy of the Lennox drawing room, the twins were bold. Rhode had not exaggerated their loneliness. Giddy at the prospect of fresh conversation, our tea had been spent fielding their questions that ranged from obvious to audacious. Golda especially reminded me of Opal. If Ruby felt the same, it wasn't helping her patience.

"I think your husband is very handsome. Have you kissed?" Argenta's attention was riveted to Ruby.

"He's not her husband yet. He's not allowed, is he? Rhode says he's never kissed anyone, but I think he's a liar," Golda declared around of mouthful of pastry.

"That's not appropriate." That had been Ruby's mantra all afternoon. "A kiss on the cheek or the hand during courtship. A small peck on the lips after a betrothal. Nothing more until marriage."

Argenta nodded. Mystified by Ruby's wisdom, her dark eyes were cavernous in her slender face. Golda huffed, tongue teasing the edge of her front teeth in thought, before looking to her sister. A silent conversation passed between squinted eyes and pursed mauve lips.

"Lavinia," Argenta started with a coy smile. "Father says the king wants a new paramour. He then mentioned your name."

"Well"—Golda's brows raised—"That wasn't exactly what he said."

"What did he say?" I asked.

Argenta looked at her sister, pleading replaced her earlier glee.

Golda's head tilted. "He said, 'the king is looking for a new trollop to crown.'" The words were mumbled through the teeth biting her lower lip.

Ruby's cup clattered back into its saucer. The sharp noise and her accompanying gasp incited the girls.

"Goldie! I was being polite. Have you ever tried it? Obviously, Lady Lavinia doesn't want to know Father thinks she is a trollop. She isn't! She and Lady Ruby just said you don't kiss before marriage."

"You repeated it wrong, Gen! Wrong means it's a lie."

"Girls." My voice was thin. I clutched my teacup to stop my hand from rising to the mark on my neck. Graces, if any rumor of impropriety had already started, Father would have me married within the week.

"I'm so sorry. Please don't be mad." The darkness of Argenta's panicked gaze made her look even paler, the pretty flush wiped from her cheeks.

"It's fine. Honestly."

"It's not fine," Ruby shrieked.

At her tone, tears rose to line Argenta's eyes. Golda was solemn but steady as she watched me. "I'm sorry," they said in unison.

"I don't think that about you." Argenta shook her head frantically, dislodging a single tear.

"I don't either," Golda huffed. "Obviously."

"It's okay, truly," I told them, taking one of each of their hands in mine. "You don't ever need to apologize for what your father says or thinks." I waited for them to nod before I withdrew my hold.

I brightened my smile to fight off the worry rimming their eyes. "I didn't expect the rumors to travel quite so fast," I finished with a self-deprecating laugh.

"He's smitten." Ruby glowed with triumph. "Everyone says so."

"It's overwhelming," I admitted lowly. "Intimidating."

"Why?" She looked at me as if I had grown a second head. "There is no greater honor. For you, your family!"

Ruby would be better suited for the attention. She'd play the role perfectly. "I don't like being the subject of gossip."

"Anyone negative is jealous," she dismissed. "The attention of the king is what everyone covets, and you have it."

"For now," I conceded.

Her attention cut to Golda and Argenta before tilting her head closer to mine. "Don't speak as if you wish it to be fleeting. The position you're in is enviable. Papa and Uncle Hugo were raving about how well you've done. You should be proud. You just need to continue as you have and you'll keep his attention. I know you will."

"King Alaric is handsome, too," Argenta said.

"He is." I fought to lighten my voice. The twins saw finding a husband as a fun game: picking the most handsome man and getting married. I had thought that way once. They, at least, were aided by their magic, though I doubted their father would let them have much say in who they wed. "Is there anyone you ladies have your eye on?"

"I'm going to marry Caius Vaux," Golda crowed.

"Goldie," Argenta groaned.

"He's so handsome. Don't you think?"

"Caius is very handsome," I agreed. A look of amusement passed between Ruby and me. How many first-season girls made a similar declaration about a crush? I remembered Ruby declaring Cosmos Stel to be her future husband.

"Gen doesn't have an eye for anyone at court."

"Goldie," she begged through her teeth.

They shared another look of silent communication. Golda agreed to whatever Argenta was asking with a roll of her eyes. Looking back at me, Golda began, "Lavinia——" She was interrupted by the door opening.

"Ladies," Oran's greeting sounded more like an assessment.

"Oran," Ruby cheered. "Oh, Graces, is it so late that you're back already? Leith?"

"Leith should be heading back to his rooms."

Ruby flashed me a grin. "I told him I would see him once his meeting was done. I really must go find him. Mother! So lovely getting to know you girls." Neither she nor Sapphire looked at the twins as they cheerily brushed past Oran.

Unbothered, the girls' focus was fixated on Oran. "Hello," Argenta squeaked. A blush crept from her neck to her cheeks.

I couldn't contain my grin then. "Oran, these are Rhode's sisters. Ladies Argenta and Golda Thallium."

"Ladies." He nodded again.

The girls giggled to each other before gleeful eyes tracked over

Oran's large frame.

"We should be off." I strolled to where Oran remained by the door. "Seeing as our hostess had to leave. Ladies." I pressed at their stunned stares.

"I'll escort you to your room," Oran told me. He smoothed a hand down my hair to rest at my waist. I leaned back into the warmth of him.

"We'll accompany both of you to your room first." It was out of the way, but it would give me more time around Oran.

"How gallant of you, Lord Lennox." Argenta was far too enthusiastic to be coy.

"Lord Lennox is my uncle," he gruffly corrected.

"You can call him Oran," I told the girls.

"Oran!" Infused with glee, it seemed like their new favorite word.

My amusement-filled gaze found embarrassment and exasperation in Oran's as we led the girls to the Thallium chambers in the southern wing.

"Oran," Golda chirped, "are you smitten with Lady Lavinia like the king is?"

Argenta nodded. "Our brother, do you know our brother? Rhode, he said, it's tough to get Lady Lavinia away from you."

"Rhode said you don't like him," Golda added. "I don't like him either sometimes."

"You shouldn't say that about him."

Oran coughed and looked down at me again. "Lady Lavinia is my closest friend."

My heart thumped in my chest. I wanted more than to be just his closest friend, and yet, Oran acknowledging our connection sent a heat through me to rival the chill of longing. Though never enough, it was a closeness I cherished.

Nothing would be enough unless I was able to remain curled into the space between his neck and shoulder forever.

The girls continued to chatter until we reached the Thallium chambers. Argenta wrinkled her nose in annoyance at being returned to their rooms.

"We'll do this again soon," I promised.

The door opened to Rhode. "There you are," he scolded lightly. "You were supposed to return an hour ago." He was met with a mumbled apology from Argenta. "Gorgeous, what a surprise." He grinned.

"That's not appropriate," the twins mimicked Ruby's earlier chastisement.

"Please go inside," he begged.

"Thank you for such a delightful afternoon." I smiled widely at them, elbowing Oran when the girls remained fixed in place.

"Lovely to meet you both." His tone lacked any sincerity, but they beamed back and went inside in a flurry of farewells and giggles.

Crossing his arms over his chest, Rhode smirked. "Well, Lennox, does the king know that you're skulking about the hall with Lavinia?"

"We aren't skulking, Rhode. We were with your sisters."

"I'm just playing, Lav. You know the rumor mill," he lamented with faux concern. "Your father and his uncle have been feeding it."

"They have," Oran agreed. "So certainly, anything negative about Lavinia wouldn't come from them. I guess if I hear any rumors that I don't like, I'll be looking at you." With a step forward, Oran challenged, "But you wouldn't want to hurt Lavinia more than you already have. You know what happens when you do. It doesn't go well for you."

Rhode grinned at the threat. "Of course! We're all friends."

"Is there a point to this, Rhode?" I fought the urge to stamp my foot.

Hands raised in innocence, he shrugged. "Just want to make sure you know that people are talking. And everyone has taken notice. Everyone."

I knew they would. "Goodbye, Rhodium," I snipped. Turning away from Rhode, Oran placed his hand back on my waist as he followed.

"Be careful, Lav." Rhode's voice was thick with worry.

My hair swung as at looked back at him. Oran's hand clenched on my waist. Apprehension prevented me from interrogating Rhode's worry. "I will be," I breathed.

Oran's hand remained firm on my waist while we walked until I felt a heat rise, not painful but noticeable even through my gown and corset. He dropped his hand then and shook it at his side, sighing in annoyance. I knew he didn't like Rhode, but I didn't think the interaction was so frustrating as to ignite his magic. When the threat of flames was gone from his hand, it stroked down the ends of my hair. We walked slowly, which suited me just fine. Worry was inconsequential when I could instead savor being alone with Oran.

"It'll all be okay," I assured us both.

"Of course. I'd never let it be otherwise."

I was never scared of falling when Oran was near. He would catch me. He always had.

He had caught me before either of us realized that I had fallen so hopelessly in love.

"How was your day?" I asked as we entered our wing of the palace.

"Good."

"Good, how?"

"The financial planning went well." His face was pensive. Leith and Oran had been involved in the financial running of the villages that were tenants of Bruis and Lennox land for years. "A blessing that we are removed enough, and sustainable enough, that none under our care will go hungry. How was your day?"

"Oh, nothing exciting or important." I breathed a laugh. Tea and gossip felt incredibly silly in the face of Oran's responsibilities.

"I love hearing you speak. All your stories are important to me."

When I was a girl, Clodia had once let me eat as much honey cake as I wanted. I devoured slice after slice, licking my fingers to not waste a drop. Each bite made me want more until one bite became one too many. The sweetness I had savored suddenly became cloying. Vomiting honey cake for the rest of the night, I vowed never to touch it again. Excess and indulgence turned something I loved into a revulsion.

Despite this, I was still a glutton. An affliction Oran didn't suffer from. No amount of time with him felt like enough. I would take more and more, as much as I could. I'd crave Oran even if every second of his time belonged to me.

I worried that in my voraciousness for all of him, I'd become who he'd tire of.

I spent so long endeavoring to be worthy of love, to earn it. How could I know how to keep it? Oran loved me, not in the way I wanted, but I knew he cared for me. But the time would come when I would be the last slice of honey cake. I had to enjoy him while I could, because by the time he was tired of me, there'd be nothing I could do to stop it.

"Well, Golda and Argenta are quite lonely, so Ruby and I hosted them for tea. They're very sweet but very sheltered. Their mother is ill, so they are learning much of the rules and ways of court from Lady

Philomena, and I suppose, now, Ruby and me. The afternoon got away from us because they hardly pause to draw breath. Well, unless you're in the room and then they are stunned speechless," I teased.

"Oh, that was what it was?"

"As if that is new to you!" I smacked his arm with the back of my fingers. "Ladies fall all over themselves around you. They have for years." I leaned my back against the wall outside the entrance to the Bruis chambers.

"Is there a reason you're still standing then? Have I not charmed you, Vin?" He looked down at me, dimples punctuating the question. His long lashes cast shadows like imitations of the freckles sprinkled over his nose and cheekbones.

"Hopelessly!" I felt adoration saturate my voice, sweet and thick like fresh honey. "Tragically, I have had to pick myself up many times." I wrinkled my nose in jest to disguise the truth of my words.

"That's fortunate as I much prefer ladies who stand on their own two feet. Ladies with dark hair and blue eyes. Ladies who bite their lip when they think…Ladies who snore as if underwater." His grin grew crooked and self-satisfied.

"Oran," I gasped with a giggle. "Don't say that! Ladies do not snore. How dare you?"

"Well, I considered a joke about you falling to your knees for me, but that felt more salacious."

I drank in his face like a woman parched. "Think about that often, do you?"

Oran took a step closer to me. He rested a hand on the wall next to my head, caging me in. "A fantasy like that is capable of driving a man mad." I felt dizzy from his words, from the low hypnotic tone of his voice. Heat pooled in my belly as his voice dropped even further. "Thinking about it would bring me to my knees."

"Oran," I breathed. I grasped the loose fabric of his tunic at his waist and pulled him another step closer to me.

His free hand grasped my chin. The thumb that stroked down the center of my chin made my lips part eagerly. "Lavinia," he groaned. "You have to know that I—"

Whatever he was going to say was interrupted by Aunt Clodia opening the door. "Oh!"

Oran dropped his hands and took a step back. I was slower to react, my hand refusing to loosen its grip on his shirt.

Grinning with a secret, Clodia's eyes bounced between us. "I hate interrupting, so I'll just wait for you inside, darling. Take your time. Oran, it's lovely to see you! So handsome, dimples like your mother."

The door closed behind her with a heavy click in the now-silent hall. The sound of my breathing was frantic between us, trying to keep pace with the rush of blood pounding in my ears.

Jaw clenched, Oran's face was solemn. I was shaking my head before he could speak. "She won't say anything." I tried to assure him.

"I'm sorry, Vin. I lose my head around you."

"No, please." The plea caught in my throat. "What were you going to say?"

"It was selfish, what I was going to say."

"You're never selfish," I chastised. "But I am. And I very selfishly need to know what you were going to say."

I was selfish but also a coward. I had tried once. Handed my heart out to Oran, only to have him gently close my own fingers around it instead of taking what I offered for himself. I wasn't brave enough to try again.

He brushed my hair behind my ear, his thumb stroked my cheek once before he withdrew. "You have to know that I will do anything for you," he vowed. Oran's features were smooth granite that still failed to overlay the sadness in his eyes. "No matter what happens, I will always be by your side. For whatever you need."

In a storm of uncertainty, he would be there. I was grateful for that, even as I burned for more.

At my nod, he bent to press a lingering kiss to my forehead. I closed my eyes, breathing in the scent of whiskey vanilla. I would take any part of him I could have.

CHAPTER 19
ORAN

That mark on her neck. I'd not felt the burn of jealousy with such searing pain since seeing her and Rhode in the garden.

Jealousy was not the familiar heat of my flames. It was the burn of poison, scorching down my throat and corroding my lungs.

My mother. That was what stopped me. Clodia delighted in Lavinia's happiness. Her seeing us felt of no consequence until she mentioned my mother.

My mother, who was a shell of a woman after the death of her traitor husband.

I couldn't do that to Lavinia.

The fantasy I called upon when I couldn't sleep, Lavinia safe and happy as Lady Lennox, was becoming harder to summon. That fantasy required me to turn my back on my father's people, on the Tyth suffering under the Wasting and the cruelty of Proventium. I had never been able to abandon them fully, and the pull of the cause was becoming a riptide. Lavinia was better protected on shore, oblivious to current that gripped me. Even if they took me away from her.

Away from my only happiness.

"Ruby was looking for you." I hadn't been able to bring myself to return to the Lennox rooms, preferring to languish in the hallway.

Leith ambled toward me with a stormy expression. "Was she?" he asked, but then shook his head to dismiss the question. "That fucking Quinn. He is cheating at cards, but I haven't figured out how."

"Which one?"

"Benedict," he spat like a curse.

"You think he's smart enough to cheat?" None of the Quinns were burdened with intellect.

"No! But he is. Somehow, he is."

"Sounds like Quinn is smart enough. It's the rest of you that aren't."

His eyes lit with idea. "Come on! I'll play and you tell me how the fuck he is doing this."

I'd latch on to any distraction. In Tordenhold, I would be removed from the temptation of knocking on Vin's door. Leith mumbled to himself as we wound through the cavernous palace. The silence allowed me to count each step away from Lavinia.

"I wasn't planning on losing any more today, so watch him like a hawk. He's doing something." Leith quickened his pace as we approached the main entrance of the palace. "After being so financially responsible today, I deserve it."

I snorted a laugh. "Only had to talk you into the more reserved budget five times."

A breeze of cool evening air ruffled my hair. The line of readied carriages indicated how many men of court had made a similar escape from the palace. The thought of the potential crowds at the gaming hall had me weary already. Empty carriages wouldn't be making their way to Tordenhold for pick-up for at least another two hours.

"Last year, it had to be more than seven." Leith hopped into a carriage with a grin.

"Graces, help all of Bruis land when you take over."

"That's what I'll have you for. You'll keep us on the right track."

"Unless you lose it all tonight." I leaned against the door as the carriage jostled over the stone road out of the palace grounds.

Temptation didn't subside, but the physical distance was a much-needed barrier between Lavinia and the words that were clamoring to escape my lungs.

"Benedict fucking Quinn! That's another thing. The buy-in came from where? He's the fourth son. Big brother giving him an allowance? Beckett is a cheap fuck. I refuse to believe that he handed

Benedict enough of an allowance. The cheat. I'm telling you, I had him in the second round." At my silence, his voice rose. "I did!"

I forced myself to relax into the drone of his rant and the rocking of the carriage as we moved to the dirt road through Tordenhold. Though built in the same grey stone, the buildings, stained with the smoke and grime of the city, lacked the shine of the palace. Tordenhold was shuttered until we entered the entertainment district. Men laughed and stumbled down the street illuminated by the lanterns, glowing in the windows and outside the doors, that beckoned to gamblers, drinkers, and those looking for an evening companion.

It took me a moment to notice when Leith's voice trailed off.

"Are you alright, Or?"

"Just thinking."

"I hate when you do that. Never good for your health," he joked. "If you ever want to talk, I can listen for once," he offered with a kindness that had become chipped away by his father's unflinching demands.

I felt a pang of regret at seeing the earnestness of the boy who had first befriended me. "Thanks, Le."

There were three things I couldn't talk to Leith about: Lavinia, Tythmore, and my fear of the two becoming intertwined.

Pushing open the door to the Drunken Hare, we left the filth of Tordenhold's back streets for the loud, smoky excess of the gaming hall. The men of court dominated the tables in the back while the men of Tordenhold occupied those in front. Leith pushed through the raucous crowd without a glance to lead us to a table of familiar, loathsome faces. Seeing Burgundy did nothing to quell the temptation that still roiled inside me. Leith grabbed two chairs from the neighboring table. The protests from its occupants quickly quieted under his glare.

Vigo Iron groaned, "I'm dead. I'm going to have to flee the kingdom."

Benedict laughed. "It's not my fault you don't know when to quit."

"That's my entire allowance for the summer." Vigo buried his head in his hands.

"Going to have to beg Papa for more, are you, Iron?" Arrow Burgundy's taunt was light, but his eyes were curious.

"Fuck." Vigo's voice trembled, teetering on the edge of tears. At seventeen, Vigo was an acne-spotted boy playing at a man.

"Come on, Iron," Leith laughed. "I'll give you three silver to win it back from the bastard."

"Hey," Benedict protested. Squat, round features and a croaking voice, Ruby had once compared him to a bullfrog.

"Can I have the three silver and just keep it?" As the youngest Iron brother, Vigo had been sheltered. Now he was set to learn the games of men the hard way.

"No," Leith spat. "You're going to let a Quinn, a Quinn of all people, do this to you?"

"Piss off, Bruis. I won, get over it." Benedict struggled to hold Leith's eye.

"Iron, I'm not just going to give you the coin for nothing." Leith shook the boy's shoulder with a rough playfulness. "Come on!"

"Why? Your father has coin, I know he does. The king, he'll probably start giving you more just to be able to speak with your sister. You don't need the money, I do."

Leith removed his hand from Vigo to throw both his hands up in exasperation. He looked around the table for commiseration.

"I need to go home." Vigo pouted. "I'm fucked."

"Pull yourself together," Benedict scoffed.

"You don't understand. Vance is going to kill me."

"Stop crying." Bear Glenn pointed a stern finger at Vigo. "If I wanted to be around tears, I'd spend the night with my wife."

"So, the Irons are in need of coin?" Burgundy braced his elbow on the table. "Interesting. Do the Thalliums not help? No loyalty to Lady Thallium's family?"

"Your father and brother can't be mad at you when it's their fault." Reed Growley attempted to comfort Vigo with a pat on the arm. The pitch of his voice matched his name and thin face.

"It's not their fault." His chin wobbled as he defended them. "The Wasting has fucked us. The town, they were…we had to do something. The Haase are charging too much for grain, but we had no choice. The Placino aren't any better. Two gold for a single bushel of wheat!"

Even as neighbors threatened to starve, there were men content to feast on greed.

"Fuck. They are going to kill me. Why did I do this?" He pulled at his dark hair in frustration. "Oh." His hands went to his ear, removing the small gold hoop. "What if I give you this," his voice cracked, "and you give me some coin back?" The trembling hand extended was smooth with no veins or calluses.

"Toughen up, Iron." Leith's head dropped back on his neck with a groan.

Benedict's head shook in dismissal before lowering to count his coins. A smirk was poorly concealed by the limp hair falling over his brow.

It wasn't tears that made a coward, it was inaction.

"Give him his coin back." At my words, Benedict's gaze snapped to me. I remained reclined next to Leith. "Give the Iron boy his coin back." If the likes of Benedict Quinn thought they only had to fear me in the sparring ring, they were mistaken.

"What? No. He lost, I won." Benedict averted his gaze as he protested.

"Fine, then bet everything, what you won and what you came with, and let's play again. But I get to shuffle."

"He volunteered to shuffle the deck every game," Leith breathed.

The table erupted in accusations. A chair fell to the ground with a crash as Crow Fjord grabbed Benedict by the shirt.

"Fucking cheat!" Bear Glenn spat as he stood behind Fjord.

I remained seated as the chaos descended. Benedict's stumbling pleas and excuses went unheard.

"Never trust a Quinn. I fucking knew it!" Leith began re-collecting the coin he'd lost with a laugh.

"Take your coin back," I instructed Vigo. Gaping in shock, his hands were frozen fists on the table. I repeated the words, finally spurring him into action.

"Lennox," he started, voice wobbling more than a newborn colt's legs.

"Go." I tilted my chin toward the door.

The disgust I felt for Benedict Quinn was only overshadowed by the disgust I felt with myself. Vigo Iron was another victim of the Wasting. One who was still in the fight, though not a soldier I saw fit to win or even survive. The Irons faced the effects of the Wasting every day while I played at the edges. I swallowed the bile that rose in my throat as I watched the others berate Quinn. Offering charity was a paltry sacrifice.

It wasn't enough. None of what I had been doing was enough.

CHAPTER 20
LAVINIA

One hour, if it went poorly. One hour and a half, if it went well. That was the rule Aunt Clodia proclaimed for an initial meeting.

"Painting! How marvelous. I admire it greatly, though it is a skill I very much lack."

"Well," I replied, "no one can be perfect."

"It's especially impressive considering that a woman as beautiful as you is far more suited to inspiring art than creating it."

Arrow Burgundy was pleasant. Hopelessly so. He possessed a disarming level of averageness. He was fine-looking without drawing excessive notice. He matched in conversation without saying any opinion too strongly. Even his laugh, a low chuckle, was agreeable, never erring toward boisterous or amusing. As such, the tea, accompanied by his mother and my aunt, passed without any thought for more or less time.

An hour or an hour and a half was… fine. Pleasant.

The words were right, but I felt no thrill at the rapport. I had always thought attraction to be glaringly loud, unignorable, but with Arrow, it was quiet. Not silent, but I had to strain my ear to notice it.

"Our land has beautiful views of the mountains. I'm sure an artist could get great inspiration there."

"Oh, yes," I encouraged. "You're neighbors with the Thalliums."

"Yes, I forgot that you were... friends with Rhodium."

My smile was etched in granite. Whether Arrow was searching for information or implying he already knew, I refused to acknowledge it.

"I may be biased, but I do think the views from Burgundy Manor are better. Though the estate lacks the opulence of Thallium Manor." He quirked a brow in a show of self-deprecation. "Their mines are impossible to compete with, so we settle for being best positioned to watch the sun drop behind the mountains each evening."

At Clodia's count, an hour and a half exactly, we rose. I curtsied to his mother before allowing Burgundy to press a kiss to my hand.

The moment we exited the Burgundy suite, Clodia sighed. "That woman." She clicked her tongue in distaste, the rhythm matching the clack of our shoes against the stone floor. "She was rude. I feel like we must know each other, and I've just forgotten."

"She was cold," I granted. Lady Burgundy had scrutinized me from head to toe upon arrival and then spent an hour and a half avoiding looking in my direction again. "But I don't think that she necessarily means to be rude."

"Lark Burgundy. Cow," she mumbled. "Well, what did you think?"

"Very nice, don't you agree?" I found myself searching for some encouragement from Clodia. Burgundy was my best prospect. I needed Clodia to see potential. Hopefully potential that I was blind to under the fog of *pleasant.*

"And tall! I don't think your father could have any objections." She clutched my hand in hers, still decorated with the substantial diamonds from her first and second husbands.

"But we aren't there yet."

Clodia tilted her head back and forth as if weighing options. "It's not difficult to speed these things along. An outing with another gentleman, one Burgundy doesn't like, preferably, and we'll have a betrothal before your father can blink."

My feet stumbled, but I was unable to look away from the conniving quirk of Clodia's brow.

"Men like competition."

"Right." I knew what I was aiming for. I couldn't let the reality of a loveless marriage deter me from choosing for myself.

"But they won't enter a competition they feel set to lose. They need to feel as if they have a chance of winning."

The tense set of my mouth failed to contain a groan. The game had far too many rules. I understood why women consigned themselves to whichever husband was selected for them.

"I think he's attracted to me, so we've got half of it, I suppose."

"Certainly! But we must be careful. It's about being beautiful and unsuspecting. Beautiful and proud means vanity. We need to be very careful about that," she cautioned. "They love to call us vain. A beautiful woman must be vain! They put the impetuous on us when really, men think about our looks more than we ever could. Beautiful women are coveted and lusted after, with or without the woman trying to be desired. That's the weakness of men. Never forget that weak men are dangerous men. If they see something beautiful that they cannot keep, they'd rather crush it in their hands than let another possess it."

Clodia's gaze held the same stern trepidation as in the dressmakers. "I understand." I was learning that while Clodia was bold, she wasn't reckless. If Clodia, confident and experienced, was cautious about the whims of men, I needed to be wary.

"Lady Rosemary," Clodia greeted as we passed her and her maid.

"Ladies." Rosemary's brown eyes were always narrowed in suspicion.

"Oh, give my best to your mother." Clodia turned to me, "Mink, Lady Sand is a fantastic card player. When I would visit with my second husband, we'd always play. Lady Piper Fjord was a card shark!"

I grinned while Rosemary simply blinked.

"Lark Fjord," Clodia exclaimed. She dismissed Rosemary with a saccharine smirk. "Excuse us." Ushering me along, Clodia continued. "Before Burgundy, she was being courted by Hymn Growley." She hummed in thought. "His courtship didn't seem very earnest with his head up my skirt."

I barked a laugh loud enough for Rosemary to hear down the hall. "No!"

"Honestly, holding a grudge after all these years is an insult to her husband."

I was still fighting back giggles as we entered the Bruis suite.

"Hello?" I called. Clodia floated to her room with a parting smile, as Remus, dragging a boot in his mouth, emerged to greet me.

I wiggled the toe until he released it, damp with slobber and dented by his teeth. At least it wasn't mine. After throwing the boot in the direction of Leith's door, I picked Remus up in my arms, earning a scratchy lick to my chin.

"Lavinia." Father's voice dripped with impatience.

Entering the study, Father, Leith, Oran, and Lord Lennox surrounded the hearth.

"Put that mutt down," Father ordered.

Stealing his future hunting dog for my lapdog was just one of my many transgressions. The moment I released Remus, he lumbered over to butt his head against Oran's shin.

"Burgundy, was it?" Bronze scrutiny fell on me, squinted in calculation.

"Yes. It was nice. All went very well." I didn't know what Father wanted to hear.

Oran met my gaze for a breath before looking back down at the book in his lap, running one hand over Remus's ear.

"Nice." Leith chuckled. "What all men hope to hear. I'll let him know your review."

I rolled my eyes at his input.

"Be careful with Burgundy. Last night, he proved he's a dreadful gambler. You'll have to keep the purse strings tight." Leith threw the papers from his lap onto the low table between the chairs.

"I'm not talking to you," I snapped.

"Lavinia," Father cautioned. His navy doublet was perfectly pressed, unharmed by the rigid posture that kept him separated from the seat cushions.

I straightened my back, feeling each feature of my face drop into a mask of obedience.

"Nothing wrong with nice," Lord Lennox kindly told me.

Father twisted his wedding band around his finger. "That means all went well? Everyone behaved appropriately?"

"Yes." I certainly wouldn't mention Clodia's issues with Lady Burgundy.

"Plans for another outing?" Oran focused on the flames dancing dangerously high in the fireplace.

"Not yet. But he was very eager for things to continue." I exaggerated in hopes of getting him to look at me, but I received not even a nod.

"Well," Father said, "he and his father are shrewd. The

151

Burgundies are in no place to take risks. They need all the support they can get against the Thalliums."

"I'm sorry?" With the Thallium's wealth, I couldn't conceive of why they'd bother the Burgundies.

"I mentioned your outing to the king. He was eager to see you himself."

"Oh? Lovely."

They won't enter a competition they feel set to lose. If Father were setting up a competition, the king as a contender would disrupt my plans. He was just supposed to spark interest among the other lords, not challenge their suits with his own.

"And you will act appropriately enthusiastic when he does seek you out."

"Not too enthusiastic," Leith snorted. "She's not Temperance Sanctas."

"Boy," Father snapped.

Lord Lennox straightened his pine green doublet as he stood. "The invitations that we've received since the banquet prove just how well Lavinia has done. I have no doubts that she'll continue to impress."

"I don't like taking risks either, Lavinia." Father rose from the chair with intimidating grace. I held my breath, but not even a glance touched me as he prowled past. "Do not make me regret trusting you to conduct yourself well."

I shrank back. Today had gone well, and yet I was being chastised for a possibility. He paused with his back to me, waiting for an answer I didn't have.

"I won't."

He nodded with the finality of a death before exiting the study.

Lord Lennox, in his hollow nicety, gave me a wink. "We look forward to it."

Leith scrambled after them like Remus would, but not before pinching my cheek. I swatted at him, but his parting grin made me feel lighter despite my frustration.

Oran was slower to follow. I finally felt the caress of his gaze against me, but stubbornly, I waited to raise my eyes until he spoke.

"Don't let him make you feel bad."

"But he's so good at it," I weakly joked.

"He's bitter at having to rely on you. That's his weakness."

"Nobody relies on me." I admitted the words to the line of his throat and collarbone bared by his black tunic.

"I do." He swayed toward me. "You're the only person who doesn't test my nerves." A dimple kissed his cheek for a moment only.

"High praise." I felt the tension lift from my shoulders.

"And your father is relying on you to ensure that the Thalliums don't push us from the king's right hand. We can't compete with their wealth or Vaux's men, so your father and my uncle need to be likable. They have knowledge Alaric wants, but he's testing the extent of their usefulness. Everyone keeps the Delphi happy." He shrugged. "The Lynx are out, but the Thalliums have gold to throw at Proventium's problems. If our houses don't succeed in giving Alaric what he wants, he'll move them aside for Thallium to try. That's why they need your help. Don't ever let them make you feel lesser."

Green eyes pinned me in place until I nodded. The ghost of his hand brushed the length of my hair. "I'll leave you to it." Oran handed me his book before he left.

I watched his exit with an ache in my chest. An hour and a half with Arrow Burgundy banished with a single dimpled grin. I looked down at the book in my hands, The Theory of Magical Farming. I'd picked it up months ago from Lennox library, only for Amethyst to scold me. Unladylike and unnecessary, she'd deemed it. But Oran had left it for me to keep.

It was gestures like this where the affection I felt for him threatened to consume me. It was an excess, a love that spilled over only to refill to the brim with one look.

To avoid languishing in the wanting that stood to destroy me, I perused Father's study. I'd never been left here alone. I cataloged the books on the shelf, titles embossed in gold and silver. The stack of leather-bound notebooks on his desk felt intrusive to open, but the papers Leith had left strewn on the low table… if I righted them into a neat stack and skimmed a few words, there was no harm in that.

What I had expected to find, I couldn't truly say. But it certainly was not this.

My hands crumpled the edges of the paper as I read. Counts of crops, profit for the last five years for Lennox and Bruis land, maintenance costs for the mill, fields that needed to increase production, imports promised to the Ravens, Merrifields, Irons, and

Wards.

My father's annotations littered the margins of each page, but one note froze my inhale. *Delphi* was scrawled in the margins next to information on one of the northern fields. Written and then underlined in Father's careful hand: *must monitor.* I knew the Delphi proximity to our land had long worried Father and Lord Lennox. If the Delphi wanted more land, if the Graces told them they needed more, our estate would be looked at first.

My eyes drifted lower to words even more troubling.

Sustainable for two years.

The words were circled several times like a horn blaring. I knew that as the Wasting rotted the west, more was demanded of the estates in the east and north. I'd never realized just how much was required of us or how desperate other estates had become.

Father was smart. He could design new increases, he just needed time. Time, he wouldn't get if King Alaric found us failing.

He didn't have to sincerely court me for affection to color his view of House Bruis. If Father and Leith needed me, then I would help.

CHAPTER 21
LAVINIA

"You best go. Off to the king, I hear. My niece is heartbroken." Lady Pilar straightened from her recline. I thought she would have lovely eyes, rich chocolate brown framed by thick lashes, if only she'd stop glaring at me. "Are you with child then? Is that why he is so eager to kill the queen?"

The reason Lady Pilar had requested my assistance this morning became clear. I'd found no ailment but hadn't wished to waste time arguing when I was expected in the gardens to watch the archery. Now, I understood her summons was to chastise me on Temperance's behalf.

"Excuse me?" Shock came first, anger dutifully racing after it.

"Don't play dumb, girl."

"Dumb is the last thing I am. I was being polite, though you clearly have no interest in it." It was rare for me to stand up to my father, but the games women played were familiar. Clodia played them better than anyone. I preferred to avoid them, however there were times, like now, when it was impossible. In my mind, I saw the smirk Clodia wielded like a dagger, invisible to men but capable of cutting other women with precision. I brought that same smirk to my own face. It felt odd but empowering, like when I was a little girl parading around the lawn in my aunt's fine jewelry.

Pilar pursed her lips but continued as if I hadn't spoken. "My poor niece. She's absolutely devastated."

"She has time for devastation?" I threw the question over my shoulder as I walked to where Thomasina waited at the door, her silent ire trained on Lady Pilar.

"King Alaric took up much of her time."

"Time she can now fill with her husband and child."

"You insolent girl! You think what?" She heaved herself up to stand on unsteady feet, cane wobbling under her weight. "You think that you are above us?"

No. But I was above her brother. Happy to have his fortunes preserved on the backs of his daughters.

Alaric's shifting affections were not an emotional blow to the Sanctas family, but a financial and social one.

The luck of birth saved me from being in such a position. My father was a proud man. He'd find debt almost as abhorrent as compromising my reputation.

"Oh, but you're not," she hissed, sending drops of spittle into the air. "All women sell themselves. It's the price that varies. My brother's wife never had the stomach for it. The girls would have no hope of a husband better than a pauper if it were left up to her. You don't have that problem, I'd venture. Not with that aunt of yours coaching you. Coached her sister, too. That's how your mother rose from a no-name Rudyard cousin to Lady Bruis."

Outrage and malice didn't scream, instead, they schemed. I remembered Leith's disgust with the sisters. The smirk on my face grew. "The king granted you your late husband's estate, didn't he?" I turned to watch the words hit their mark. "Took it from your husband's brother, if I'm not mistaken. Temperance hasn't done enough? Maybe you should have aimed higher yourself instead of expecting your nieces to do it for you." I shrugged in a show of being exactly the insolent girl she accused me of. "Goodbye, my lady. I can't keep them waiting any longer. King Alaric will be sick with worry looking for me."

"Lav," Leith cheered as I approached the entrance of the sporting gardens. When I reached him, he bent low to whisper in my ear. "What the fuck. I ran out of charming stories ten minutes ago."

"I got caught up," I tried to dismiss.

"He won't start without you. Everyone is just standing around. I said I would go find you, but I've been pacing out here with my dick in my hand."

"First, you're disgusting. Second, calm down. Lady Pilar needed healing."

"Who gives a fuck about her? You're not the Sanctas's servant."

"Leith. It's done. Thank you, Thomasina." I squeezed her hand in mine. Maintaining the distance between our stations had been a condition of her employment set by Father, but when married, I was determined to take her with me and do away with the imposed propriety to forge a true companionship. I watched her leave with a knot of dread in my stomach. I knew the part I had to play, I just hoped that I would do well without rehearsal. "Shall we?"

The overly saccharine smile that scrunched my face was one my brother hated. Eyes narrowing in return, he glared at me until we entered the view of the others.

King Alaric stood with Lord Beamus, who looked distinctly uncomfortable. Beamus's umber skin was coated in a light sheen of sweat. He wore his sable hair tied back at the nape of his neck. The style emphasized the harsh cut of his cheekbones.

"I'm so sorry for my lack of punctuality."

As we still walked the remaining few steps to the king, he extended his hand to me. The press of his lips to the back of my hand quieted the garden like a shot.

"Lavinia," he crooned. "Now the event can begin." He smoothly threaded my arm through his own, bringing me fully to his side.

"You're too kind to have waited for me. I'm sorry to have stalled the festivities."

"Nonsense." He grinned wider. "I'm just happy you're here."

Beamus cleared his throat. His amber eyes turned down at the end, making him look slightly sad even with the close-lipped smile on his face. "Lady Lavinia, pleasure."

"Lord Beamus," I greeted. "Are you much of an archer?"

"I try to be. We Delphi, well, it's a useful skill."

The Delphi needed skills like archery since their magic would do little in combat. Thankfully, Father was meeting with Lord Vaux and Lord Thallium. I could hear his chastisement as if he were next to me.

"Try to be doesn't sound very confident, Beamus, but I know you." Leith wagged a playful finger. "Downplaying to try and catch us off guard." He chuckled.

I breathed a sigh of relief as Alaric and Beamus joined in.

"Lead us off, Beamus." Alaric clapped a hand on his shoulder.

As he stepped to line up his first shot, I took in the rest of the event. Tables with white cloths covered in tea and cakes made my mouth water. The group in attendance was intimate, only a few Lennox, Delphi, Stel, and Telis members joined Leith, Aunt Clodia, and I. Ruby sat with her father, mother, aunt, and Clodia at the table nearest the shooting range. Hercule warily eyed Clodia as she gesticulated through a story sloshing the floral teacup in her hand.

At the neighboring table, Oran lounged with his long legs outstretched. Disinterest emanated from his crossed arms and furrowed brows, but he occasionally nodded along with what Lady Lyra Telis was saying. A curtain of scarlet hair brushed his shoulder as an ivory hand touched his bicep.

Hugo would never let him marry a Telis.

The thought scorched through my mind before I could stop it. Lyra didn't deserve my contempt, but the sight of them together sent an all too familiar wash of envy over me, as green as Oran's eyes. It deepened to the deep pine green of the Lennox crest when he turned to look at Lyra, asking a question that made her lean further into him.

Cast under the glow of summer, he was a devastating sight without adding the torment of jealousy. The summer sun shone on Oran with extra favor, painting shimmering streaks of bronze in his hair and warming his tan skin. My favorite, though, was the extra freckles she dotted on his nose. It was unfair, really, how someone so handsome was capable of becoming even more so. The temptation of Oran was enough without the sun's taunting hand. But of course, even the sun would be smitten with Oran.

It was petty, but I arched into Alaric's side and widened my smile. The king's attention was far more important than the simpering of Lyra Telis.

"I hear you're one of the best marksmen in the kingdom," I said.

He beamed. "I endeavor to live up to your expectations. In all things."

"I don't see how you, of all men, could not."

Alaric's grin softened as his eyes trailed down me. Once they made their circuit back up to meet mine, he tossed a command over my shoulder. "Leith, why don't you go and sit with your lovely betrothed?"

After one round of shooting, Alaric took my hand in his. "Have you seen the temple on the eastern grounds?"

"Only from afar."

"Come." He pulled me closer to him.

I paused, seeking Aunt Clodia. I couldn't be seen leaving alone with a suitor, let alone the king.

"I forget myself, Lavinia. I always do around you." He smiled apologetically. With the snap of his fingers, two maids left their positions at the edge of the shooting range. The conversation of feigned disinterest around us increased. "I hate to bother your aunt with such a walk. Especially in this afternoon heat." He began leading me away as he spoke. "I wouldn't want to drag your brother away from his betrothed either."

The maids trailed ten feet behind us. I looked at Alaric through my lashes. "Very thoughtful. They do act as if they won't have the rest of their lives to spend together."

"Love will do that. Infatuation is addictive."

I knew the insatiability of love well.

"I never come this way." I attempted to steer us toward a safer topic.

Alaric filled the walk with jovial stories of exploring the palace as a boy, of the designs his father added to the palace, and his mother's love of the gardens. Each giggle pried a finger off anxiety's grip.

The Temple of the Graces gleamed like a diamond among the rolling grass. The light danced off the pristine white stone columns that comprised the circular temple. Nestled near the cliffs, the sound of the ocean was a soothing rumble as we approached.

Standing on the entrance steps, I craned my neck up. The temple was a private place of worship for the Haralds and those they invited. Each column curved into an arch to form the paneling of a roof. In the center, they held aloft a gold star that seemed to kiss the sky, reaching to take its place alongside the blazing sun. The blue sky peeking between the white arches made a hypnotic pattern.

"It's beautiful." The stillness of the temple was broken only by the soft chirp of two mourning doves sitting atop one of the columns.

"You fit right in." His voice was smooth, suede caressing my neck.

I peeked over my shoulder at him. "As do you."

Alaric had his hands clasped behind his back, maintaining a space between us. I could lean into the game when I wasn't nervous and fixated on what might come along with it.

Navy eyes sparkled, trailing down me before rising to the sky. "My mother would bring me here once a week as a boy. To express our gratitude for the blessings given to us by the Graces. They chose the Haralds to rule Proventium because we understood our duty to the kingdom, its people, and the Graces. The Delphi saw the will of the Graces, but it was my family that would fulfill that will. I'm ashamed to say the habit of visiting fell away after she died. Maybe if I had continued, things would not be the way they are."

"It's never too late. You can still be the man she raised, the man who comes every week, who is grateful for his blessings."

"Recently, I haven't felt blessed," he confessed in a whisper. "Looking at you now, that feels the peak of insanity, but… I've been isolated with this problem that I cannot solve on my own. The burden is mine, but being able to share it with someone, someone who will listen and understand, well, that is a gift from the Graces. Another gift, I should say."

Mesmerized, I stared into his eyes. "I understand. It can feel silly or impossible even to feel lonely when surrounded by so many people, but I understand how lonely it is to feel like no one *sees* you."

"Yes," he breathed.

I looked down, tracking shiny black boots inch closer to me. A breeze and my skirts would stroke his legs.

"I struggle," he said, "with opening up to people. When I have in the past, I've put my trust in the wrong person. I thought I'd never open myself up again… and then a dark-haired maiden smiled at me."

The smile that overtook my face was not the practiced smile of a court temptress. It engulfed my face with unrestrained joy before I could mold it into something prettier, more fitting. Alaric raised a hand to his chest and sighed as if overcome by the sight.

"You're a dream," he told me. "What are your dreams, Lavinia?

I'd give you anything I have."

I saw a slender opening. One I must attempt to clumsily squeeze through. "Dreams," I exhaled a laugh. "Growing up on Bruis Estate was a dream. I'm envious that Leith and Ruby get to stay there forever. There is no more beautiful place to live. But I know my brother and Ruby will do a beautiful job preserving the childhood home I love so dearly."

"Your father has created a fine heir for Bruis lands." Relief flushed through me. "And a fine lady to be mistress of another estate. I'm only sorry that Bruis lands can't all be yours."

"As long as they are in the care of my brother and Ruby, I'll be grateful."

He nodded once, decisively, before his gaze turned pensive. "And a new dream? A dream for your future?

To help my family stay in the king's favor. That was a good dream. A helpful dream. A worthy goal. Not the childish fancy of my other dreams.

I had the wish to be a painter once, but that was frivolous. Being helpful was more important. I couldn't expect to find love and happiness if my secondary dream were so shallow. The depth of love I dreamed of, an abyss and excess of *more*, was selfish as it was. Perfection was impossible, but I struggled to shake the notion that love could only be attainable through its pursuit. Ironically, the greed for love was my inadequacy that was most challenging to contend with.

I'd come close to acceptance of a lesser love in the past, but I knew even if I did renounce my dream of true love, the appetite for it would never leave. A life of bread knowing others feasted—a lesser love could sustain me, I could even learn to cherish it, but it'd never dull the gnawing want.

"A new dream? I suppose I always dreamed of…"

I couldn't tell him what I truly dreamed. I'd have to blur the subject, casting it in a haze instead of allowing myself to paint the picture of the life I'd always envisioned. A life that included the man I've etched from years of memories. The man I loved so much it colored everything around me, even as the hunger for his affection was sometimes so acute it blackened the edges of my vision.

"A family of my own."

People to love me.

"You'll have it," he said the words as if making a decision. "You'll be beautiful at it. A family is the most precious thing the Graces can give."

"Yes."

"My daughter," he smiled, "she adored you. Couldn't stop talking about how lovely you were to her."

"Oh, she's a very sweet girl."

"Before Gaëlle, I didn't know such a love existed. With each pregnancy, Margaux and I would come here and make an offering. Her excitement never dimmed. I felt it harder to let go of the losses. My own weakness, I fear. When Gaëlle was born, healthy, screaming." His laugh reminded me of the wind echoing through the glens. "I was overwhelmed by how much I loved her. But it made the losses harder. Loving Gaëlle made me aware of how we'd feel if another baby came."

"I'm sorry." I placed a hand on his arm.

"If the Graces wanted to punish me, I'd rather they do it to me. Not to the innocent."

"Do you think it's the Graces punishing you?" My voice was tentative as I asked.

The Wasting, the lack of an heir, to whisper about them as designs by the Graces against the Haralds would be treason.

"Testing me, perhaps. At least in my last two, there was nothing, no ruined hopes." He looked down at me, determination triumphing over sadness. "I love my daughter. But I need a son. All this, everything my family has built, will fall apart. Proventium will be thrown into a civil war to decide a new king. People will lose their lives, and it will be my fault."

"It's not too late. Your next marriage, the Graces could bless with multiple sons." That's what this was all about. He wanted a wife to give him a son.

"I don't know if the Graces will be so kind to me. But I couldn't imagine the Graces not being kind to a woman like you."

My exhale wavered to match the trembling in my hands. He'd never been so forward about his intentions. I couldn't imagine how I looked to him, gawking in shock. My breath stuttered again in my chest as he took a step forward. Those meaty hands, no longer safely clasped behind his back, now grabbed my waist. As he lowered his head to meet mine, I felt like a voyeur. I watched Alaric take my lips with his, but I didn't feel heat pooling in my stomach. Didn't feel the warm caresses of his tongue against my lower lip. Didn't feel the scratch of his beard against my cheeks. My movements met his from instinct, from memory.

The rhythm of the kiss was soft and exploratory, but nerves, not desire, were the frenzy in my gut. I was being kissed by the king.

Did he think this would go further?

Before my thoughts could spiral, I pulled back and gasped a breath. My eyes opened to meet Alaric's, shining with joy.

"Forgive me, I couldn't help myself." His hands freed my waist to grab one hand in his. He pressed a firm kiss to my palm.

My relief resembled a grin. "Forgiven."

As we exited the temple, the two maids rejoined us from where they had been standing, backs to the temple.

I focused on counting my breaths. He was desperate for an heir. Alaric was likely searching for that in many women, not just me. He wasn't serious about me. He couldn't be. Once he did find the woman he was looking for, I just had to hope that lingering fondness for me would protect House Bruis.

My heart lurched at the sight of a figure ambling toward us. *Too far away to have seen anything,* I assured myself.

Ambrose Delphi. His weight leaned heavily onto an obsidian cane, favoring his right ankle as he walked toward us. Even limping, Delphi carried himself with confidence.

"Delphi." Alaric's greeting was not outwardly hostile nor welcoming.

"Your Majesty and Lady Lavinia. Charmed."

"My lord." I curtsied. "Are you on your way to the temple?"

"Yes, I convene with the Graces often. They were insistent in my dreams last night that I visit this afternoon." What he lacked in chin, he made up for in eyes: protruding, round eyes of bright amber.

Eyes that paralyzed me under their knowledge.

I knew there were followers of the Delphi family who believed they truly spoke with the Graces, but I had never heard a Delphi claim so outright.

"Lady Lavinia and I were just speaking with the Graces ourselves." Alaric's smile was thin. "We'll leave you to it."

Delphi tilted his head in farewell, but stumbled as he stepped past us. His cane wobbled under the weight of righting himself.

He waved away my concern. "I have a pain in my ankle, comes with age. I hate to bother Padgett with the aches of an old man."

"I'd be happy to see if I can help." I knelt, my skirts a blooming puddle of periwinkle around me.

"Padgett's job is to see anyone who comes to him." Alaric spoke the words in correction to Delphi and me.

"It's no trouble," I insisted.

Ambrose extended his ankle to me. Silver uncoiled behind my eyes to wrap his ankle in a soothing thread. I could dull the ache, but my magic would only be a temporary solution.

"Better?" I asked. Alaric's hand on my elbow tugged me to my feet the moment I started to rise. "The effects should last for a few days. When they start back up, I'll be happy to heal it again."

"I know." Ambrose smiled at me, not with gratitude but as if sharing in some secret. One only he and the Graces knew. "We'll have more to discuss soon."

CHAPTER 22
ORAN

Lyra Telis was a proficient gossip. Her sister, Artemis, was a truth wielder, eager to pass her knowledge to her sister. I had avoided Artemis in the two seasons she'd been at court to mitigate risk and avoid the boredom of her conversation. Lyra, I had sought out once. Once, and now, at any function, I could count on her eyes hunting for mine. Silence died a violent death in her presence. I needed do no more than raise an eyebrow or hum to propel her on.

Leaving the archery with Lyra on my arm would stir talk, which suited my purposes just fine. As did any distraction to quiet the snarling beast that lived behind my ribs. A beast that was gnashing its teeth to follow Lavinia.

"Artemis hasn't been asked to go see the queen, but she did speak with Mason and... well, it's been a long-standing affair between them." So that part was true then. I suspected as much, even if I had hoped Mason was smarter than that. "They brought him out of the tower rather than bring her in. It was a whole spectacle, but apparently, getting into the tower is a production and a half. Gaudy eyesore in the river. But"—she waved the complaint away—"overly careful if you ask me, can't have the full scandal of it all falling into the wrong hands."

"They don't consider Artemis the wrong hands?"

She doubled over with a giggle, clutching my arm tighter. "Artemis? A traitor?" She flickered her hair as her laughter faded—red, obnoxiously bright.

I noticed a strand clinging to my sleeve. I had tried to subvert my preference for black hair and blue eyes, but each diversion only further solidified my tastes. Grimacing, I plucked the stray hair off me.

"The traitors who should be worried are anyone who has been friends with Mason. Artemis said they were discussing a raid on the blacksmiths. Bron wasn't lying when he said Mason wasn't her only lover. Scandalous, I know! Was she having an assignation with all the blacksmiths?"

"Oh?" I prompted.

Her eyes, a dull watery blue, were wide. Not even the thrill of gossip was enough to brighten their lackluster shallows. "Shocking, but I wouldn't rule it out. Even if they weren't involved with Bryony, Bron said that surely Mason was working with them in more ways than one. The Tyth," she clarified. "A never-ending scandal."

Poe and Arren. Those were the Tyth who also worked in the blacksmith on the grounds. Men who didn't deserve torture or death for their association with Mason. Certainly not for association with Bryony. Poe couldn't speak in the presence of a woman, let alone bed a married one. Arren had a pregnant wife who may as well be the only woman in the kingdom.

"Honestly, it's shocking that they allow so many Tyth to work together."

Graces help us all if Lyra's notion became an actual decree.

I steered us in the direction of the Telis rooms while Lyra prattled on about the upcoming masquerade ball. Without a queen to oversee planning, Ladies Telis and Vaux had stepped in. "Mother told King Alaric that he couldn't arrive any earlier without causing a stir or any later without seeming uninterested. Can you believe it? Dictating the arrival of the king? That's Mama for you."

Graces, it was too easy to keep her talking. Lyra was in the middle of yet another story when we reached the door to the Telis suite.

"Lady Lyra," I interrupted, "it's always a pleasure."

Her maid silently shuffled past us and inside. I wondered if the woman spoke at all or if a condition of her employ was being Lyra's mute audience.

"All my family is still at the archery?" She shifted closer, chocking me with the scent of jasmine.

I preferred rose. Rose and moonstone eyes framed with sooty lashes.

"I really must be off." I kissed her hand in apology. Lyra Telis was a beauty. But there was only one beauty that I yearned for. A beauty that was in the gardens on the arm of the fucking king.

By the time I reached the royal blacksmith situated on the southern grounds, I was actively fighting the flames that tickled my palms. A fire on the grounds would bring an end to the archery, an end to the smiles Lavinia was awarding him.

"Lord Oran, sir," Arren greeted. He wiped his hands on a rag, leaning a hip against his work table to face me. Arren was as tall and thin as a stalk of wheat. His brown hair had started to grey at the temples. The deep grooves in his forehead gave the impression that he was in the middle of solving a puzzle.

I scanned the workshop. "Arren. Are you alone today?"

"Yusuf is off making a delivery to the Sands."

"Good. I want you"—I extracted a pouch from my pocket—"and Poe to make me a new sword." I tossed him the pouch, coins rattling. "This should more than cover the expenses. I'd also like to commission you both as the Lennox house personal smiths. There'll be further payment, of course."

"Sir?" Arren's eyes narrowed. He made no move to lower the pouch from where he caught it against his chest.

While I knew about Poe and Arren, all they knew of me was that I was a Tyth. *Everyone* knew the Lennox heir was a reformed Tyth. They didn't know that since I was fifteen, I endeavored to learn about every Tyth that worked on the palace grounds.

We look out for each other. It was a lesson from my parents that survived the flood that destroyed our lives. The Tyth didn't know which village would be targeted as a rebellion den, didn't know which shops and fields would be burnt as punishment. *We look out for each other.*

"Best you mention this to no one but Poe and your wife. You'll leave today to Merce village and see the tailor. You'll let him know that Oran Lennox has hired you both, and he'll see you settled."

"Sir?" Blinking rapidly, the lines on his forehead deepened. "We have a good life here. My wife won't be uprooted even for coin." He extended his hand with the coins toward me.

"Will she be uprooted so that she doesn't become a widow before your babe is born?"

At my words, his extended arm dropped to his side with a clank.

"In the eyes of the crown, it doesn't end with Mason Sterling." I watched his throat bob with a gulp. "Fintan can assuage any doubts you have. Today," I ordered.

CHAPTER 23
LAVINIA

White roses, pink peonies, and purple hydrangeas transformed the table in our sitting room into a florist's shop. As wide as the table and several feet high, I'd never seen such an arrangement outside the royal ballroom. The smell was intoxicating, the colors entrancing. Remus stood on his little legs to inspect them. The sound of his inquisitive sniffing was in harmony with the rapid fluttering of my heart.

The note that had accompanied them was no effusive love note, signed simply *Alaric x.*

Father had read the note this morning, satisfaction relaxing some of the perpetual tension in his frame. "Two meetings in three days," he rasped. Father had long held a remarkable talent for making statements sound like interrogatives, facts like faults, and compliments like deficiencies.

Twice in three days. How many more until Alaric grew bored? Until he realized that a healer was no prospect for a queen?

Father would know if Alaric had been seen with other ladies. The query perched on my tongue, but I knew better than allow it out. Instead, I foolishly waited for him to look at me with pride or praise. It was only Clodia beckoning me to get ready that pulled me away. Empty-handed as always, I left Father with my note as proof of my success. However unacknowledged and fleeting that success would be.

Leith and Ruby, as well as Thomasina and Ruby's maid, Simonette, had been drafted as our chaperones. Lilac seemed a fitting choice for my dress, an attempt to banish the heavy hang of clouds that smothered the sky above the grounds like stubborn smoke.

"You don't own anything lower cut?"

"Aunt Clodia!"

"Gifting a floral arrangement like that, a man wants something nice to look at in return." She gave a tug to the neckline of my dress, revealing another inch of cleavage accented by a delicate trim of lavender lace. Cleavage that was far more than I usually possessed, thanks to the Halorian undergarments Clodia gifted me. The corset was scandalously low, the intricate boning of it pushing every advantage while restricting each breath. She claimed to wear them exclusively. How? I'd yell the question if only my lungs could allow for more than a feathery simper. "There. You do look beautiful, darling girl. You too, Ruby."

"I hope it doesn't properly rain. My hair will become a wreck. The parasol I have doesn't go with this dress. I should bring it in case, shouldn't I? I can't have frizzy hair in the presence of the king." Ruby stared in the hand mirror with distress. "Leith! Hurry up," she called. "Do you have a parasol that matches our outfits?" Her dress was a deep, cool red. The grey gloves she wore chosen to match the pale slate of Leith's attire.

"You aren't embarrassed that your hair takes longer than ours?" I couldn't resist teasing. I snapped my fingers to bring Remus away from the flowers that were in danger of being eaten.

"Remember when you cut your own hair and looked like a boy for a year?" he retorted.

"Shut up," I huffed.

"You were a dashing boy," Clodia told me. "A very pretty boy."

"I trust you on what makes a pretty boy," I told her solemnly. I couldn't look at Leith as my lips twitched with amusement.

"Pretty boys, stable boys," Leith listed under his breath.

Clodia's brief romance with one of the stable boys on our estate, years later, remained an endless source of amusement.

"Stop," I mouthed. Laughter made the constricting corset suffocating.

His hand was too slow to cover the snorting laugh that escaped him.

Ruby looked between us with confusion. "I think those boots were the right choice."

Leith smothered his amusement and turned to her. "You're always right, sweetheart. You look gorgeous." Glancing back at me, he said, "you could cover up."

"Don't be prudish," Clodia clucked. She handed me gloves made of the same lavender lace that trimmed my bodice and sleeves.

"I've never been accused of that in my life."

Leith's exploits didn't rival Clodia's, but if rumors were true, they were not prudish either.

"How tense you are says otherwise." She propped one hand on her hip. "Sex would help you loosen up. You'll understand soon." Clodia patted a hand on his arm, ignoring his exaggerated shiver and hack of disgust. "Oh"—she turned to me—"I have the perfect earrings." In a slink of emerald silk, she departed.

"So here is where everyone is." Oran's worn boots were nearly silent on the stone floor. His hands were in the pockets of his dark brown trousers. Wearing a shirt of Lennox green, his eyes were impossibly bright. "And looking..." He trailed off, looking away from me to glance toward Leith.

Leith spared his best friend only a nod in greeting before taking Ruby's hands and bending his head to trade whispers.

Oran focused back on me, coming so close that I had to tilt my head back to meet his eyes.

"Looking like what?" I was not above begging for his attention.

Wanting was an immortal creature that was never quiet and rarely proud.

"A dream."

The compliment stirred a memory of another conversation—a masterpiece showing the faults of its imitations—the thought fled as quickly as it intruded. Under Oran's attention, it was nearly impossible to focus on anything else.

"Oh?" I bite my lip. "Do I feature in your dreams often?"

"Not every night, so not as often as I'd like."

The smolder in his gaze made my stomach clench. "So only when you're lucky?" My admiration trailed over his face before descending to the tan skin of collarbone revealed by the opening of his tunic.

"If only I were more lucky and less lonely." The start of his crooked grin teased at one side of his mouth. The same spark was in his eyes as when he had pressed me against the hall. When I had thought he'd kiss me again.

"Lonely?" I fluttered my lashes at him with a smile.

"Unbearably so."

The rumble of his voice was my favorite sound, one I'd brand on me if I could. In another world, there would be no king calling. I'd stay here with Oran, watching the dent of dimples rather than the tick of his jaw. "You'll be devastated to hear I can't help with that for very long. We are to leave soon."

"My bed is cold if you're looking for other ways to help me."

"I find that hard to believe." My voice sounded brittle even to my own ears. His bed no doubt had a line of warmers, eager for their turn.

"Come and see for yourself."

My breath hitched. Hollow flirtation, I reminded myself. "You can't just warm the bed yourself?"

"Alone? No fun in that." His resonant voice was like a tender hand stroking down my spine. I fisted my hands in the fabric of my skirt before they could betray me with the stupidity of doing something like dragging his face down to meet mine. "Though I do try."

"To the thought of me?" I purred. Desire was remarkable at banishing jealousy. The image of Oran alone in bed was too enticing to waste a moment on the thought of the girls who knew the image intimately.

He leaned closer, voice dropping lower as if following the heat pooling between my thighs. "So many thoughts of you, it's almost impossible to pick."

"Here!" Clodia's voice shocked me a step back.

She gave Oran a feline smile before moving between us. The diamond earrings she dropped into my hand were ostentatious. I'd have a headache from the weight of them pulling my ears before the afternoon was through. "It's important to remind the king that you're no village girl. You're a Bruis."

"Alaric again?" Oran asked, something shuttered in his eyes, as Clodia moved on to fuss over Leith's attire. He brushed my hair behind my shoulders with the back of one hand. The other took an earring from my palm. The rough brush of his fingers against my jaw and ears as he gently fastened each earring sent the tickle of goosebumps up the back of my neck.

"Yes," I confirmed.

His hands left their task with a final caress of his thumb along the line of my jaw. His stare darkened as his touch left me.

"It's temporary," I reminded. "A few more outings and he'll be looking to the next."

My confidence in the fickle nature of the king did little to brighten the cloud over Oran's expression. "I can only hope he is so blind," he murmured.

I looked out the carriage window at the dreary sky as we descended the winding path to the beaches below the cliffs. The gulls grew louder with each rock and sway of the descending carriage. The waves battering the rocky shore were a soothing sound compared to their piercing calls.

You'll start to bore him soon. The nagging in my head had a measured rasp. Father could be unhappy all he liked when it ended, but he wouldn't be surprised by my failure, my inadequacy.

Desired, sought-after, coveted, I should try and enjoy the attention while it lasted. I hoped I could one day fondly call upon the image of me on the arm of the king. A memento I could hang on the wall of the shadowy corner reserved for the Bruis healer daughter.

I painted a precise curve to my lips, soft and suggestive, decorating the canvas in my mind: a confident woman in a low-cut gown and a charmed suitor. I'd have the sun shining on them instead of being shrouded in gloom. I'd have her eyes smiling to match her lips, but her expression would have none of the eager, earnestness of her caller. I tossed my hair, the beautiful girl in the painting would certainly toss her hair, before opening the door.

Waiting to hold the carriage door, Alaric was worthy of a portrait. The cerulean shirt that revealed a tuft of dark auburn chest hair, utterly too fine for the stormy day, was perfectly suited for the canvas I'd sketch.

The warmth of his hands made the final nerves disappear. My smile didn't waver as my feet touched the ground. The copper of his hair began shining to match his smile. We were standing in a perfect sunbeam. My practiced expression transformed into real delight, a giggle escaping me.

Alaric had parted the storm around us.

Here, in the warm daylight, my painting came together. The sketch was brought to life by getting to know a man who should be unknowable. Each brushstroke comprised of a laugh. Each detail arose from a story. Each color mixed charm and wit for brightness and vulnerability for contrast.

CHAPTER 24
ORAN

A pale hand, glowing in the darkness of the corridor, grabbed my arm. If someone was waiting for me, tracking my movements, then I had made a grave error. This late at night, the cavernous halls of the palace were always empty of the milling groups and harried servants. I allowed myself to be pulled a single step before flipping our positions and pressing a forearm against their neck. The bright flames, a party trick, were meant to threaten, not burn, but when I saw Thallium's startled face, I considered allowing the heat to consume my arm as it longed to.

"Feeling suicidal, Thallium?" If Rhode was the one monitoring me, I'd have no hesitation in ending him.

"Let up, Lennox." He struggled but made no progress. "I didn't realize you were so jumpy. Guilty conscience? What are you doing out so late?"

I released him with another shove. "Who would be the better question."

He straightened his doublet with a huff. Thallium appraised me before his expression grew mischievous. "Not in the bed you really desired to be in, though, is it? Not unless you're feeling suicidal, too?"

"What are you driveling on about?" I failed at restraining the rage

175

in my voice, which only served to increase his amusement. How long Thallium had known about my feelings for Lavinia, I wasn't sure. But there was no mistaking the knowledge roosted in his smirk.

Clapping me on the shoulder as if we were friends, he snorted a laugh. "Right. Come on, Lennox."

"I don't take orders from you."

"Are you going to be as difficult as Bruis?" Hands on his hips, he groaned. "He's throwing enough of a tantrum without waiting further. So, please, come with me. Just a conversation. Please."

"Leith is waiting to speak with you?" Leith would only go with the enticement of a bribe.

"With *us*. Look," he lowered his voice. "I'm not doing this out here because I value my neck. So, please."

"Not good enough," I dismissed. The gossip Leith traded in was of no interest to me, especially when it came from Thallium.

As I turned to leave, he raised his voice just a fraction. "It's about Lavinia."

The flash of panic at her name made a burst of magic throw the dim torches along the wall up to the ceiling. Thallium startled but remained where he stood. I was devolving into an adolescent again. When it came to Vin, maybe I never stopped being one. I clawed back my magic, letting it swirl in my gut alongside the dread that I hadn't been able to banish since *call me Alaric*.

"Is that a threat, Thallium?" I extinguished the torches in the hall.

"No! The opposite. I want Lavinia safe, too. You're not the only one who cares about her." The darkness of the corridor couldn't conceal his sincerity.

Allowing the torches to relight, I followed Thallium through the hall. He continued past his chambers, leading us further into the southern end of the palace. The yellow banner on the door depicted two soldiers, their swords forming a V in the center of the Vaux crest. Marigold yellow, Lavinia had called it, like the flowers she once braided into my horse's mane.

Leith lounged on the divan in the sitting room, surrounded by an excess of gold pillows. "Took you long enough. The little Vaux isn't much entertainment."

The kid wrung his hands by the window. He met my eyes and wiped them on his trousers, a look of determination arrived and retreated in a blink of crumpled brows.

Mahogany wood and gold upholstery absorbed the faint glow from the fireplace and candles, but even in the muted light, I could make out the fine craftsmanship of the furniture, the rich tapestries covering the walls, and the flower arrangements throughout the room. Lady Vaux had good taste let to run rampant by her son. A son who was paid very well indeed for his soldiers.

"Cai isn't a jester for your entertainment, Bruis." Thallium kept his tone measured. He threw a pointed look to the open armchair next to him, which ushered the little Vaux over.

"You begged me to come here," Leith drawled. He, like me, wore a simple tunic and trousers, contrasting Vaux and Thallium's formal doublets. "Said it was so important, secret information about my sister. Begged, and then left me for a fucking hour to go find Oran. He's not her brother as well, in case you fucking forgot." He threw the words at Thallium with an ill-disguised glee in the malice of it. "Where were you?" Leith turned his focus to me.

I ignored his question. While I made to join him on the divan, a movement in the back of the sitting room caught my eye. There, leaning against the door to the inner rooms, was Julius Vaux. Blanketed in shadow, he looked over his shoulder for a moment before returning to his observation.

His glance drew Cadmium Thallium, with the silence of a wraith, from the inner chamber to his side. Sitting on the divan, Leith and I would not just have to pass the little Vaux and Thallium to leave, but also the doorway where the lords waited.

"Let's get to the point of this," I demanded.

Annoyance had been replaced by apprehension. I wouldn't give Lord Thallium the satisfaction of labeling it fear, even just to myself. Lord Vaux and Lord Thallium weren't here for idle gossip.

Cadmium had no need of more gold. Favors and fear were his desired currency. A bargain with him was one of brutality. If Cadmium was deigning to speak with us, he wanted something. Something I worried would destroy us.

Leith winked at me. "Ah, you can tell me all about her later."

"Speak," I barked. My eyes didn't leave Cadmium Thallium and Julius Vaux.

Thallium, *Rhode*, I forced myself to acknowledge his name, avoided looking to where his father stood. Clearing his throat, he seemed to regain some of his grating confidence. "By now, it seems

177

you've been very successful in using Lavinia to catch the king's eye." Rhode looked not to me but to Leith. "This week's romantic beach stroll is all anyone will talk about."

Infatuated, that was the word on every courtier's lips. King Alaric was infatuated with Lady Lavinia Bruis. *Fucking imbeciles.*

Leith's response was a smug grin. He and Bruis were getting exactly what they wanted.

"The question is: do you really think you'll achieve your goal? What happens to Lavinia after you needle a marriage out of him?"

"Don't say her name." Leith pointed a stern finger in correction. "My sister is not your concern. Whom she marries is not your concern. You made sure of that. Unless you actually have information to offer, then we're done." He shrugged but made no move to stand.

Despite his sincerity, Rhode even thinking of Lavinia made long-simmering hatred boil anew under my skin.

"Alaric's wives last less and less time. That should concern you, if you're offering up your sister to be next." Elbows perched on his knees, Rhode laced his fingers together as he stared at Leith.

Agreeing with Rhode over Leith was a sign of how terrible things had become.

"Now, who said that? Rumors are a nasty thing, but such is life at court." His grin grew. Leith was a scholar of assholery who had ascended to a level not even Rhodium Thallium could match. He thought he was just toying with Rhode. He didn't see the lords in the shadows. Or understand the truth of Rhode's concerns. "Is this all we are here to discuss? You trying to get information with none of your own? My sister is not betrothed to anyone. No offers have been made. When, not if, when one is made, I'll not be consulting you. Or the little Vaux."

The little Vaux missed the accompanying glare of contempt, too focused on the twisting of his fingers in his lap.

"Leith Bruis and Oran Lennox." Cadmium's words slithered from the shadows before he followed to stand next to his son's chair.

The little Vaux straightened instantly at his brother's approach. Though the hand Julius placed on top of the seat behind the little Vaux's neck was gentle, it provided him little comfort.

Cadmium's head tilted back and forth in a serpentine assessment. Crafty was the word my uncle had labeled him. A compliment and a concern.

Leith's jaw dropped before the arrogant heir was replaced by the one his father had molded: obedient, respectful, and composed. "My lords." He cleared his throat. Humiliation and defiance battled on his face.

"Rhodium, you've wasted enough time."

"Yes, Father." Rhode remained focused on Leith and me. A mouse offering up its brethren in hopes of avoiding the viper's strike.

"It's late. My patience has long since left me," I interrupted. I refused to surrender to the apprehension chilling my spine, whispering advice to run. Cowardice was an illness I was determined to sweat out. This would be good exertion. "My lords, what is it you wish to speak to us about?"

A puff of air that was supposed to be amusement left Julius. "Don't flatter yourselves. Hugo and Malcolm wouldn't speak to us when we tried to raise the subject. My brother said Lavinia trusts you both. He also said that Lord Bruis doesn't know everything his daughter gets up to." Knowing lent a shine to his pale eyes.

"Son of a bitch." The implication sent Leith out of his chair. "I'm going to fucking kill you."

"Sit down, Leith Bruis." Cadmium's strike was swift. The metal fastenings of Leith's boots and belt halted his steps. "I do not give my time to lordlings often."

Rhode remained seated, hands gripping the arms of his chair. "He's not going to tell anyone."

Leith's anger was all-consuming. "Fucking bastard! I told you what would happen if you said anything."

A shock of ice to his face jolted Thallium from his seat, only for his father to throw him back by his belt.

"Enough," Cadmium hissed. I watched in fascination as the gold and silver rings on his hands began slithering over his fingers and palms.

"Everyone, calm down," Julius ordered. He was as composed as I'd always seen him, but I noted the way he considered Cadmium's hands.

The little Vaux, still seated, collapsed in on himself at the command.

The tension slumped out of Leith as Cadmium released him. His rings remained agitated, gold and silver thrashing along his knuckles, even as he nodded to Julius.

"Rhode here seems to think you are a part of your father's plan to," Vaux paused, searching for the right word, "entice Alaric to marry Lavinia, but I think you're smarter than that. Surely you understand the danger that puts her in."

Appealing to Leith's ego was wise. He failed to hide his satisfaction at the compliment, preening under Julius's praise. "My father, well, he has his ideas for her. I have my own. I think Lavinia is on her way to being the most sought-after lady in court. Then she can have her pick of the appropriate options."

"And will it be you who determines who is an appropriate match? Does she listen to you? Caius seems to think Lavinia trusts Lennox's judgment over yours."

The little Vaux sank lower into his seat, shoulders by his ears, to hide in the cushions.

"Cause Oran is soft on her." Leith threw a hand in my direction. "She only listens to him over me if it gives in to what she wants. She is my responsibility. I know what's best for her even if it's difficult for her to accept," he finished with a huff. "No offense," he belatedly offered me the condolence.

Vaux was leading the discussion, but I knew better than to believe he was in charge. Cadmium didn't align with any lord he couldn't steer. Julius had been the new lord who survived a challenge, the boy with no one he could trust, when Cadmium offered his alliance.

I addressed my question to Lord Thallium. "Lavinia and Alaric concern you, why?" Just saying their names together like a couple threatened to choke me. "It's not out of the kindness of your heart so get to the fucking point. You want what?"

"Oran Lennox." Cadmium shook his head. "You're smarter than that. Smarter than your uncle, I always thought."

"You want to spurn the king?" I searched his expression for any clue. "You want House Bruis to spurn the king and lose their standing?"

A choking gasp left Leith. Of course, he never considered all the ways his father's plan could turn against House Bruis.

The twist of Cadmium's mouth lacked any smugness. Despite the tension in the room, his face was placid. He ignored Vaux's stare; the dark abyss of his gaze trained on me.

"We don't want the king to get what he wants." Julius's arms crossed over his chest. "As it appears he wants Lavinia, we'd like her to marry someone else." Julius raised a hand to gesture to Rhode. "Our kind volunteer will be approaching her this week."

Numbness slowly wrapped her icy fingers around my heart. I fought to recover, to hide the devastation on my face. My muscles wouldn't obey.

"We tell you this because we'd like you both to support the match. To help convince her, if need be."

"Flattering," Rhode griped. "Convinced, Graces, don't stroke my ego further."

"Why," I rasped. "Why are you doing this?" I demanded from Vaux.

I couldn't keep looking at Thallium. If I saw any fucking satisfaction on his face, at winning, at getting what he wanted, my Lavinia, I'd kill him before I could stop myself.

Would Lavinia forgive me if I did? She might not. The jolt of pain the thought sent through me was enough to be in control of my body again. Earning her hatred would be worse than watching her marry another. The grind of my molars was the only distraction preventing my body from incinerating the room. "Alaric's attention is fickle. He'll move on before marriage crosses his mind." I repeated that hollow, hopeful assurance daily.

"The prophecy," Cadmium mused. "Lavinia is not an obvious connection, but a clear one. Once suggested. Did you think Malcolm Bruis's aim had any subtlety?"

"What the fuck?" Leith blinked rapidly, trying to connect the prophecy to Vaux and Thallium.

"You don't want the prophecy to be fulfilled." My voice was stronger as the pieces came together. Lavinia was a pawn to thwart the king.

Cadmium's head tilted again, calculating where to strike. "It's not in our best interest for Lavinia Bruis to cure the Wasting."

Leith's laugh was acidic. "Lord Thallium and Lord Vaux don't want the Wasting cured? What? So far away in the north, you don't care? You think it won't affect you?"

"No." I shook my head. "Thallium doesn't want *King Alaric* to cure the Wasting."

Lord Thallium's answer was a narrow and cold grin. "I knew Oran Lennox was smart. The question now is... is he useful?"

181

A Union in Thunder

I refused to shrink back. I turned my head to Vaux. "And you?"

Julius was calm as he looked at me, but his hands flexed on top of Caius's armchair. "My brother would be sent to propose had Cadmium not agreed to let his son do so." The little Vaux sank further into his chair.

"Young love reunited," the words twisted and writhed out of Cadmium's mouth. "Finally, we've found an area where Rhodium may excel."

"To think," I said, "I've spent my life with the stain on a traitor when it's Vaux and Thallium who would see the kingdom fall." They shied from the label I knew intimately.

"The Harald king, not Proventium." Julius's correction was an admission.

"No," Leith stuttered. His head shook with a desperation that made the small motion look like a convulsion. "Fuck," he breathed. "You." He looked away from Lord Vaux and pointed to Lord Thallium. "You, you want to be king, is that it? Overthrow the Harald for the Thallium rule?"

"Alaric Harald is unfit. He's let our kingdom descend into turmoil in pursuit of money he doesn't have."

Money the Thallium mines had.

"The tariffs on Tythmore Strait don't cover the losses from Mesgara. Nor do they cover the soldiers he's deploying to Tythmore. What worthy king is defeated by land and pirates?"

"It is my soldiers bearing the cost of his failure," Julius seethed. "For centuries, House Vaux has welcomed any Spirit wielders a place among us. The villages on our land are filled with hardworking men, good men. Alaric, like his father, thinks nothing of risking their lives for his cause. My responsibility is to the men who depend on me, to their families. Not to the Harald king."

The Vaux soldiers were impressive, especially against the rebels with little to no magic, but that did not make them invincible. If Alaric saw the Lynx as ants to crush, then the legions of Vaux soldiers would be rats to drown.

I studied Lord Thallium. Any opening, any weakness, was masked under a layer of cold silver. "And Tythmore?"

Was this it? Was the price for Tythmore giving up Lavinia forever? Surrendering my home in exchange for my country.

"Oran Cahill," he mused.

The name I held for five years. Oran Cahill was a boy I didn't remember, and a man I wouldn't recognize. "That's not my name." I felt the candles in front of me hissing at me to react, to burn, to fight.

He acknowledged me with another tilt of his head. "Starving masses are troublesome. Once Lavinia Bruis cures the Wasting, they'll be eternally grateful. A lower tax and food on their table, there won't be an uprising left."

"Nothing to fight over." Rhode grinned. "The Tyth will be so grateful that a little tax will feel like nothing." He shrugged as if the conflict that'd lasted our entire lives were already solved.

"You actually believe the shit Ambrose Delphi is selling?" Leith asked, his fight reemerging after the drain of shock.

"It's not shit," Julius corrected. "The sight of the Delphi has never been wrong. A healer queen will bring the end of the Wasting. Who would it be if not Lavinia?"

"Maybe the Wasting isn't meant to end in our lifetime," Leith countered.

"Maybe"—Julius shrugged—"but Alaric is desperate. He sees Lavinia as the answer. And we don't want him to have her."

"No," the word came out of Leith like the crack of a whip. "Unless you have something to offer me, the answer is no." He stood and adjusted the cuffs of his shirt. Chin raised, he stared at Thallium and Vaux with defiance. Bruis pride was dangerous.

"Something to offer you?" Vaux's voice dropped, the threat in his voice wrapped around each word. "You forget that you aren't Lord Bruis, yet."

"Well, isn't Papa proud," Rhode breathed.

"You can't say the same," Leith quipped. "That's why you brought us here. Because you think your son will fail." He pointed his finger in accusation at Cadmium. "I fucking can't wait for it either." He looked down at me. "I think we're done here."

Leaving this room wouldn't stop their plan.

"Talk of her choosing from eligible suitors was a lie then?" Julius was in front of Leith in an instant. The speed of the motion pushed a breeze through Leith's hair. Only two inches shorter than Julius, Leith crowded the final step between them with a snarl. "Your father will put the chance for the king's favor above his daughter? You're a fool, boy."

I saw the impact of the word on Leith. He took a step back at the contempt in the word. 'Boy', Bruis's favorite reminder of his son's shortcomings.

Recovering his pride, Leith looked Julius up and down. "Would be a shame for your plans to leave this room. You've given me such leverage. You're the fool," he finished with a grin.

"Leith," I cautioned.

"I *know* you won't say anything," Julius dismissed.

"For now. Because your plan will come to nothing."

"She could die." The little Vaux's voice trembled. The little Vaux cared more for Lavinia than the others. He understood the price of this was greater than the Wasting, than the king. Vin was the true price. "You'll risk her life for pride, for…for." He stopped with a shake of his head. The kid looked on the verge of tears, which only made me angrier with myself.

He couldn't fight for Lavinia, but I would. She'd had enough forced upon her.

Lavinia's life had been defined and dictated from the day she was born. Choices weren't denied if she were never given one. Bruis let her think he agreed with her decision to deny Merrifield, but I knew Merrifield was too lowly for Bruis to ever consider. He'd deemed Merrifield unsuitable long before Lavinia's rejection.

She deserved a real choice. I couldn't offer myself as I longed to, but I could give her this. This chance to choose something for herself.

"Leith." I stood and forced him to face me. The words felt like knives in my throat. "Let Lavinia choose. She deserves to choose for herself." Even if it killed me.

CHAPTER 25
LAVINIA

"Oh, no!" I drew the words out in mock dismay. "Not another knight!"

"No one likes an ungracious victor."

"It's hard to be gracious when the competition is so paltry."

"Well, look at that," Caius pointed at the window next to us. Turning my head, I felt the soft rush of air as he moved his knight into a better position on the board in a split second.

I flipped back to face him. "Cai, you do this every time!" We were cocooned in an alcove among the expansive library of the palace, accompanied only by the scent of old pages and leather. On our third game of chess this morning, my aunt had yet to check in since we arrived. Clodia had promised with a wink to be reading in the next alcove over.

A rare, unrestrained smile brightened Caius's face. "Can you let me win one time?" His brows raised in pleading. "For what little pride I have left?" His voice bounced off the floor-to-ceiling shelves.

"You're the least proud person I know," I snorted.

"Papa was a good teacher, but after…" He trailed off before banishing the grief away with a rough shake of his head. "Mama was the only one who had time to play, and she's dreadful."

"Your brother?" I asked softly.

"Childish amusements," he grumbled, "don't interest Julius."

The sympathy on my face made Caius turn the conversation back to me. "And your brother? Is it Leith who taught you?"

"At first. Once I started beating him, Oran then took over. I only win against him on occasion. I suspect when he lets me." I wrinkled my nose. The last time we'd played, he made a foolish move that was without a doubt designed to concede the match.

Hands twisting in the open space between his knees, Cai opened and closed his mouth in aborted conversation. At my raised brows, he sighed. "About Oran…"

"What?" My voice was too harsh for Caius, but the dread that flashed in my stomach got ahead of my tongue. "Sorry," I amended.

"See, well, the thing is, Lav, is that we spoke with him and your brother. Me and Rhode."

"Rhode spoke with my brother?" The fine hairs on the back of my neck rose, chilled despite the kiss of sun through the small window to my right.

"Yesterday. Julius thought, he was there, too, he thought Rhode needed to be there, that Oran and Leith would listen to him. Lord Thallium, well, he, he didn't help things. I don't think, that is, well." Caius did this when he was upset. His discomfort made him stutter around the crux of the issue. "They weren't in favor of the idea, but Oran, he said, he told them you should get to decide."

"Decide what, Cai? What are you talking about?" I fought for control over my volume even as building panic urged me to scream. Lord Thallium? Nothing good could come from him interacting with Leith or Oran.

"I'm sorry, I shouldn't have said anything. You, well, you will, but you should hear it from Rhode." Pleading eyes held mine. "I shouldn't have said anything, but I know… I know you, that you," he sighed. "Oran, well, he didn't volunteer." Caius looked so sad as he stumbled through the words, face wrinkled in a pity I didn't understand.

"You're not making sense. Volunteer for what?"

"No, I'm sorry. I shouldn't have said anything. Well, other than what he asked me to. Rhode, he, Rhode asked me to tell you. 'Remember how good we were at sneaking around.'" Furrowed brows raised with insinuation.

An insinuation that was as clear as it was insulting.

"Rhode is not getting a moment of my time unless you explain."
"I can't. Please just, tonight."

I kept my steps quick but light as I wove through the hall. At this time of night, I had never before run into anyone, but I wouldn't risk making noise that could draw someone from their rooms. The insult of Rhode's request quieted my worry about *Rhode and Oran*, but didn't silence it. I wanted answers, needed answers. If Cai couldn't explain, I had no choice but to make a trek I hadn't made in two years.

As a shadow grew on the corridor, I threw myself around the corner. Pressed against the hall, the stone wall dug into my back, scratching through the thin fabric of my robe. A mass of black shadow came to form an outline of broad shoulders and a strong jawline. The hammering of my heart was loud enough to match the swift, confident steps of the man. A warm fragrance tickled my nose before I trapped the breath in my lungs. I counted to thirty in my head, letting the shadowy figure of the man become distorted and then finally disappear.

The palace librarian, Percy, had rooms off the corridor to the library, but Rhode had discovered that Percy had been sleeping in the dessert chef's room. He left each evening an hour after sunset to Asa's bed and wouldn't return until sunrise the next morning.

I paused outside the door. The flash of jealousy that struck me was surprising in its intensity. I never asked if I were the first woman he had brought here. If he found this room because he was so desperate to be with me and only me. I never asked because I preferred not to know.

I didn't miss Rhode often. But I longed for the comfort that came from feeling so important to him. To someone.

The door opened as silently as it always had. Barely more than a closet, a desk, bed, and armoire dominated the room, leaving only a narrow path for Rhode to pace. Here, he took up so much space that there was no air left in the stuffy chambers. The charm of Rhode Thallium could run the expanse of an open field and still need more space.

"Lav." Relief relaxed the line of his mouth.

Against my will, I felt some of the fight drain out of me. This scene was so familiar. Littered sketches in my mind featured this room, this man. "Rhode," I sighed. "What is this? What's going on?"

He touched the end of my braided hair that hung over one shoulder. "Well, gorgeous." The rumble of his voice cracked through another defense. Here in the dark, his voice was deeper, huskier, matching the expanse of his eyes. "Graces, I have missed you."

"Rhode," I cautioned. Retreating a step allowed a gulping breath unscented by mint and amber. "If you think we're doing this again, you're a fool, or you think I'm one. We're friends. Nothing more."

Rhode growled playfully. "I'd never think you're stupid. I'm doing this poorly. You've got me out of sorts. I'd never complain about a woman's lack of clothing, especially you, gorgeous, but it's distracting."

I glanced down. My robe had opened, revealing the nearly transparent fabric of my nightgown. The lines of my figure were outlined under the silver sheen of moonlight. I closed my robe tightly and, for good measure, crossed my arms over my chest. "I know you've never complained about undressed women. That's just one of the many reasons that I don't trust you." Old anger, buried under friendship, leaked into my voice.

"Fuck." A white hand ran through equally pale hair. "I'm alone with you for the first time in years, and I've lost my ability to speak. Please, gorgeous. You know if I could have, two years ago, if I could have narrowed my world to just you, I would have."

He could have, and he didn't. "Why am I here? You asked Caius to get me here. Why?"

"The circumstances. That was the issue two years ago. Not the friendship, not the love." His dark eyes were wide. "Certainly not the sex." Pleading was replaced with a familiar smirk.

My face heated in a hidden blush. "Rhode."

"What if circumstances have changed?"

Had the rumors spun so out of my control that people thought I was in the king's bed? "I'm not a mistress," I growled, "so you can choke on your circumstances."

"Shit, I keep messing this up. The circumstance I'm talking about is marriage."

I froze. That word was one I never expected to hear fall from his lips. Not again.

He cornered me against the door with a smile. "What if we could have that life? The one we dreamed about. You and me, a few blue-eyed daughters running around Thallium manor."

The picture was not as hypnotic as it was two years ago, and yet I was tempted to reach out. If I touched it, would it be as beautiful as it looked from afar?

His lips took mine the way he had almost taken my heart two years ago—slowly, with confidence overlaying tenderness. I fell into the kiss like an old habit, losing myself in the familiarity of it, the rhythm and slide of his tongue against mine. His fingers teased at my hips before running up to my breasts. My robe was so thin I may as well have been naked. The scratch of my fingernails along his scalp made him groan as I knew it would. We were both slow to draw back. His hands leisurely descended to my waist. He seemed to understand that I wouldn't go further. Couldn't.

"I really have missed you." The words were spoken against my lips like a final kiss. "We can do it. We can get married."

I squeezed my eyes shut lest I plunge into those familiar depths. "Rhode."

"We can. I'm telling you. You can be Lady Thallium tomorrow."

The promise had been fool's gold two years ago. I feared I was no better at telling real from false. The shine was so enticing. "Your father..." I trailed off. Studying him, I saw only a hint of the boy who had eagerly made me countless promises.

"He's given his blessing." When Rhode lied, one hand scratched at his neck. Now, his hands remained steady on my waist.

"Really?" I felt a rush of hope blooming in me. Did the king's attention make me worthy of a Thallium? I had planned for Alaric to secure attention for me, but never that of Lord Thallium.

"He has. I'm not worried about the king either. His displeasure is to be expected, but we can handle it. Father knows what he is doing."

My smile quivered, a newly bloomed daisy in a winter breeze. "And what is he doing? He had refused to risk a healer heir for his son, but now..."

"He sees King Alaric." He waved one hand dismissively. "Everyone has. And if the king doesn't fear a healer son, then..." He shrugged with forced levity. "Come now. You can't honestly say your search has turned up a husband you'd prefer over me."

"He doesn't fear a healer son for you?"

"Nor does he fear the king's displeasure. Lav, I promise. This time we truly can."

No, Cadmium Thallium didn't fear, but he did covet the fear of others.

"He doesn't fear King Alaric's displeasure," I repeated slowly, struggling to form a picture around the words Rhode avoided.

Respect, power, standing all were difficult if you made an enemy of the king.

"As my father loves to remind me, there is little to fear when Thallium mines are the richest in the kingdom. Lennox may wish to stay close to the king, but we have no concerns about that. If we have to leave, we leave. Father will handle Alaric's tantrum, and we can enjoy Thallium Manor to ourselves. Think of it, gorgeous, just you and me for days, weeks. We can make up for the two years apart."

"Ah," I sighed. "Your father told you to marry me. That's why you're here." Foolishness clogged my throat.

He had started to pull me back.

I had thought it was genuine.

There had been whispers of Thallium's aspirations. Father had dismissed them as rumors. But this was it. House Thallium was to be an adolescent boy taking a new toy from a playmate. Cadmium wanted to test the extent of his influence. If the king would ignore being bested or slighted.

I was to be used as a test.

And Rhode, as always, would do as his father instructed.

"You can see it as told me, or let me." His eyes still gleamed with hope. Embarrassingly, I knew why. Rhode believed I would fling myself into his affection as I had two years ago. A desperate girl willing to equate affection with devotion.

No. I was not so starved as to be grateful for discarded affection.

He stumbled back a step at my shove. Pacing in the minuscule space in front of the door did little to lessen the agitation itching under my skin. Tears stung my eyes from frustration and… disappointment.

I could see how easy it would have been. Not a bond forged anew, but a broken habit reforming, strengthening into a vice. Sentiment and friendship would offer marriage as an escape from failure's dogged pursuit.

"Rhode, if you wanted to marry me, you would have." He shook his head, but I continued. "Your father has no other heir. His pride would never let him name a husband of one of your sisters."

Running into his arms would be running away. It wouldn't be love.

"I want to marry you," he insisted.

Oran said you should get to decide.

My choices were rarely considered. Having one now felt overwhelming but empowering. I knew what the easy option would be, and yet, I didn't want easy.

"But not enough." I shook my head. Fondness was not love.

The decision settled in me, certain and firm. I wouldn't spend my life begging for the scraps Rhode's father would allow him to throw me. I had charmed Alaric, and I would find another when he soon grew bored.

There were no guarantees that I would find happiness in my next suitor. But I wanted to try.

I wanted a husband who would damn the world to have me.

CHAPTER 26
ORAN

Leith's magic encased me like the final frost of winter, vengeful and frigid. The smothered flames inside me broke through the hold with no effort.

With red cheeks and sweat on his forehead, he cheered. "Good!"

We'd both needed this. Leith had taken convincing to accept giving Lavinia a choice. He'd pouted and raged about his father needing to know everything concerning her prospects.

"She's too good for Thallium, and she knows that now."

Whether my words would hold true or not, they were enough. Leith became eager for the prospect of Rhode's rejection. My disposition was not so easily buoyed. If she picked Rhode, would she be safe from the prophecy's demands? If she rejected Rhode, was her fate as Alaric's wife sealed? I'd suffer any torment, even her marriage to another, as long as she remained safe.

I couldn't dwell on the little Vaux's concern without bile rising in my throat. *Fuck*, maybe it would be better if she said yes to Rhode.

I wasn't one for wishing or praying. I knew what I could have and what I couldn't. What I could make happen and what I couldn't risk.

I wouldn't risk tarnishing Lavinia with the Cahill dishonor.

The further Tythmore pulled me in, the more danger I posed to Lavinia. But damn if I wasn't pleading with the Graces for Alaric,

192

fickle and foolish, to forget her. I prayed to the Graces who had long since abandoned me. I had nothing to bargain with, so I simply begged.

It's temporary. Her shrug had been medicine for a fever. I would keep repeating her words until I saw them become true.

I released the magic I had wrapped around Leith to cover my sword in flames. Matching me step for step and strike for strike, we clashed in ice and fire, filling the air with pops of boiling water and angry steam. I let my mind go blank, focusing on nothing but each movement until the burn of my muscles and my magic was all I could feel. The heat was comforting.

"He's burning up. Are you sure he isn't sick?"

"Look at him, darling. He's fine! Just my son." My mother's voice rang with pride.

"Oh? Are you your mama's boy or are you going to be your papa's boy?" My father's callused fingers ran over me, tickling my stomach the way his stubble tickled my cheek with a kiss.

It was one of the only memories I had of my father. Of my family being happy. They were like insistent flies recently, coming back not long after I'd swatted them away.

Leith spun and ducked, sending an icy kick to my chest. I staggered back and sent a wall of flame between us. I saw it grow, allowing the flames to reach above our heads.

"Now that's what I like to see!"

Leith's ice met my fire, the walls pushing at each other as we circled the arena. His grin was unmistakable through the clashing gaps in the wall. My magic hummed under my skin, thrilled at the challenge, at the sport. The trial of using my magic was holding it back, keeping it tame when it longed to blaze through the continent.

I'd always seen fire. It lived in me, ruthless, merciless, charging and retreating at my command. Unleashing it has always been easy. Calling it to heel took practice. As a child, I had no choice but to learn how to become a general the flames would respect. Exert control or be burnt alive.

"Scared?" He goaded. Steam rose to join the clouds above the arena as I pushed the wall, hotter, taller.

Some things had not changed since we were boys. I continued to circle the arena, planning my next move. I pulled my flames back slightly, letting Leith's ice gain a few feet. His cheer was cut short as I erected a second wall of fire at his back.

"Fuck!" He stumbled as he turned, his ice falling with him.

I dropped my flames. The laughter that came from the sight of him, wide-eyed in the dirt, was a relief. Happiness had become elusive, only attainable when I was fixed under moonstone attention.

The watching nobles cheered. Leith stood to give an exaggerated bow. He was still chuckling as he clapped me on the shoulder.

"Fuck." He twisted to look up, squinting into the sun. "Do you think we missed lunch?"

"I'd say so." I had little appetite these days. I should get used to the relentless ache. Rhode or Alaric—degrees of agony were difficult to measure.

"I'm supposed to look at...flowers?" His brow wrinkled. "Or menus? Something."

"A doting groom, you are."

"It's been easiest to just let Ruby do as she wishes. I nod and she smiles. We're both happy." His face softened, not with love, I knew it wasn't love yet, but with growing infatuation.

"She's not going to be happy with you now."

Leith grabbed his shirt from where it lay on the first row of spectator seats. "You lost horribly, and I injured you." He grinned. "That's why I'm late. Had to see your wounds tended to."

"Ruby isn't so stupid in love as to believe that."

"If she's unhappy, I know several ways to earn back her favor." He winked owlish and clumsy in his haste.

I prowled to the sporting garden, looking for any distraction from the restlessness clawing under my skin. Stillness gave the beast an opportunity to escape.

It'd been three days. Thallium hadn't come to boast yet, so they either hadn't spoken yet or she was taking time to assess his proposal. If she did reject him, maybe another would be bold enough to propose under the king's attention. Burgundy, she seemed to favor. A marriage to him, and I'd hardly ever see her. The restlessness bared its teeth, howling for release.

That would be far worse.

I could endure seeing her on the arm of another as long as I still got to see her.

Arrow Burgundy laughed with perfect timing as I approached the archery field. Bows in hand, Burgundy and Crow Fjord watched Bear

Glenn take a sloppy shot. Glenn groaned and returned to Fjord's side. Fjord and Burgundy had their backs to me, but Glenn's ugly profile was on display. His smile had far too many teeth.

"I hope you're better than Glenn or you'll have no chance of surviving Bruis." Fjord's cackle was as soft as an avalanche.

"Isn't that why you fuck a healer? To survive a disapproving family?" Glenn shrugged, too focused on his friends to notice me.

"My father understands the appeal," Burgundy's voice was light. "She's lovely, but now, she's a death sentence." He stepped forward and lined up his shot with an amateur stance. "If King Alaric is truly going to pursue her, I'll not risk my neck." He released the arrow, catching the left side of the target.

"He pants after her like a dog ready to hump her leg." Glenn cackled, grating and boisterous. "I don't blame him. Any bastard would happily take her to bed."

"Beautiful is not worth dying for." Burgundy turned, toeing at the dirt with a smirk. His voice held the same callousness with which he questioned Vigo Iron at the gaming hall.

No, Lavinia being isolated with a spineless coward for a husband would be worse than enduring Thallium for the rest of my life.

He joined Glenn as Fjord approached for his shot.

"Her pussy might be worth dying for." Glenn elbowed Burgundy.

I absorbed the blow of their words as embers turned to an inferno. It was years of control that kept my magic from incinerating the garden.

Fjord turned, his bow hanging at his side. "You'd not die," he squawked. "A healer would ruin the kingdom."

"He can't risk it, but you could, Burgundy!" Glenn clapped him on the shoulder. "I guess if healing is to be accepted as a dowry at least you'd get a good fuck every night."

"Better than you've got!"

Burgundy shrugged. "I can get that without risking my children being stuck healing skinned knees."

I'd fight to give Vin a choice, but that choice would not be Arrow Burgundy. Fucking bastard.

The ball of fire I sent to the back of his shirt danced despite the anger that wanted to consume. He spun, falling to the gravel below.

"Lennox!" Fjord's voice cracked like an adolescent.

There would be greater satisfaction in using my bare hands.

"Stand up."

Kneeling, Burgundy rose slowly, like he didn't know whether to play dead or flee. "We meant—" He cleared his throat. "We meant no disrespect."

Glenn took off in a run. His stout frame stumbled in his haste. Fjord was faster in his terror, overtaking Glenn without another glance at Burgundy. A cowardly flock behaving exactly as expected.

I took a step closer. "You will never speak of or to Lavinia again." The crack of my fist against his jaw didn't slake the beast's thirst. The second punch was harder. The third I let be aflame. I extinguished the flame for the fourth. The crunch of teeth and cartilage more gratifying than the all-too-familiar burn.

My left hand released its grip on his shirt, sending Burgundy tumbling to the ground with a groan. I hoped the water he brought to his hand, cradling his jaw to soothe the burn, drowned him.

"Every day when you wake up the same pathetic coward that you are now, you will remember that you're still breathing because I allowed it. You won't get that healed, since healing is so beneath House Burgundy," I spat. "Your season at court is done. If I see you again, you won't have a home to go back to."

CHAPTER 27
LAVINIA

For tonight, Alaric x

A mask and dress of matching silver had already been delivered. Now, a marquis-cut diamond necklace, the center stone almost the length of my smallest finger.

Extravagance and grand gestures didn't change the impermanence of Alaric's attention. Even with the necklace in my hands, I wouldn't mistake his affections for holding the diamond's durability when I knew them to have a flower's fragility.

Spending the evening on Alaric's arm while wearing such a piece was sure to incite more rumors. I placed the necklace back in the box with a shaking hand. No man would approach me tonight, but I hoped to leave an impression. When the king's attention moved on, I needed more than just Rhode to view me as a desired prospect.

Looking at the necklace, I allowed myself a moment to enjoy the beauty of it. Just as I was determined to enjoy tonight. Both would be another mark of my success.

See Father, don't you see?

The masquerade transformed the already magnificent ballroom into overwhelming opulence. My senses scrambled to find a focus. The flowers woven into the window frames and arches, dripping down like a lady's earrings over the large stained-glass windows. The tables laden with rich roasted meats and decadently sweet desserts. The fizzing bubbles of sparkling wine. The flicker of chandeliers casting shadows on the masked masses. All magnificent, but I found myself hypnotized by the dancing crowd. Colorful skirts fluttered with the steps, like delicate butterfly wings readying for flight.

"Tell me honestly, Lady Clodia. How does a Proventium ball compare to Elvor?"

The silk of her turquoise dress swished as she adjusted her stance. "It's been some time since I've been to a masquerade. It's marvelous," she purred. Her mask of navy lifted at the upper corners, mirroring the set of her eyes.

"Has it helped to charm you back to our kingdom permanently?" Alaric tilted his head down to grin at Clodia. His mask matched his crown, gleaming gold accented in rubies.

The masquerade allusion of anonymity succeeded for few, and certainly not kings who accompanied their mask with a crown.

"Permanently?" One black brow arched over her mask.

"Lavinia has told me how happy she is to have you close. Whatever I must to sway you from the arms of Elvor and back to Proventium, I shall." He looked down at me with affection. "Anything to keep a smile on Lavinia's face." The hand on my waist stroked up my ribs, before finding its place again.

Laughter and conversation rose above the quintet of musicians playing a jaunty melody on the stage at the far wall. The energy of the crowd was joyous, but still, I felt the weight of inquisitive eyes. I felt naked already without the crowd's scrutiny.

My silver gown bared my shoulders, a style that was considered bold for unwed ladies. The sleeves started in line with the top of the low-cut bodice before flowing down in a sweep of fabric that kissed my knuckles. The skirt resembled smooth, poured metal. For the bodice, that shiny silk draped and swept lowly on my chest, accenting my figure with a romantic softness that belied the harsh, structured boning of the corset. My hair was a waterfall of night down my back, exposing the pale skin of my decolletage and shoulders. Father and Clodia preferred my hair tucked behind my ears, left to fall behind me. I couldn't hide behind the strands as I tended to. As I wished to now.

On display like a statue or blank canvas. I longed to move us from the center of the room, a corner, or even under a table would be more comfortable. The exhilaration of attention lasted only a moment before exhaustion set in. Alaric's endurance for attention was a product of ignorance. He knew no other way of being.

I looked up at him through my lashes. "You'd rob my cousin of the comfort of his mother living near to give me my aunt?"

"Of course." He winked. I did not doubt that Alaric would give me anything because he believed he possessed everything anyone could ever want.

"Your Majesty, such charm." Clodia assessed him with satisfaction. "I adore being with my niece, but I trust that she'll be in good hands during my visits back to Elvor." Pursing her lips and raising her brows, she might as well have been shrieking in glee. My smile grew in response.

If Father couldn't be proud, I'd savor Clodia's approval.

"Tell me about Lavinia's cousin. A vital member of the Elvor court, if I'm not mistaken?" He drummed a finger against his chin in thought.

I caught a commotion out of the corner of my eye. An empty goblet hung from Oran's fingertips while wine dripped down Ruby's bodice and Sapphire's skirt like blood. Oran placed the goblet down before his hands lifted, one placating, the other waving Leith over. He spoke low in my brother's ear. Ruby looked on the verge of tears, frantically scanning for witnesses to her embarrassment.

As Leith took Ruby and her mother on his arm, I forced myself to focus back on Alaric and Clodia. I had let the harmony of his deep burr and her melodic chimes fade into the orchestra's tune.

"I can't imagine why he wouldn't beg me to come back." Clodia giggled.

"See—" Alaric gestured a hand accented in a large ruby signet toward her. "Elvor can't compare. Name your price, lady, and you shall have it. Lavinia's happiness is invaluable."

"Excuse me." Father approached. His expression, tempered by a plain grey mask, held a far more subdued satisfaction than Clodia's.

I schooled my features into serene composure. If I were smiling too widely or flirting too blatantly, Father would find that in poor taste. "Father."

"Malcolm, is that really the best mask you were able to acquire?"

Clodia clicked her tongue in reprimand. "Not flattering."

Father ignored her. "Your Majesty. A magnificent evening."

"Bruis," Alaric cheered. His hand left my waist to clasp my father's hand in greeting. "It's been my favorite evening in as long as I can remember."

Father's dark eyes tracked the movement of Alaric's hand coming down to squeeze my own. His brows relaxed as Alaric's grip retreated. "Yes." His smile was thin. "I apologize, but Clodia, I was asked to escort you to assist Ruby. Something about her gown."

"Oh." Clodia's eyes widened in surprise.

"In selecting a replacement," I said. A flush came to my cheeks as I realized I shouldn't know about the accident. "I caught a glimpse of wine on her skirts," I excused. "She must need your eye to ensure her new gown complements her mask."

"I'll return with Ruby looking gorgeous in no time. Your Majesty, a pleasure."

Father sighed as Clodia took his offered arm. He bestowed me a small nod before escorting her out, leaving me unchaperoned with Alaric in a ballroom surrounded by all of court. Speculation had already been traveling between ears with alarming speed. This was setting fresh horses on a carriage.

"Lady Ruby's accident is my good fortune, it seems."

I smiled and took a step back as if I merely wanted to face him rather than stand at his side. Really, I needed the distance to prevent him from touching me further in front of such an audience. "She had been so excited about her gown. I feel horrible for her."

Alaric nodded before his eyes tracked over my shoulder. I turned to see the approach of Thallium and Vaux. Rhode and Caius trailed them. I took a further step back to accommodate the addition. More distance between me and Alaric.

"Your Majesty." Lord Thallium nodded. His narrowed gaze passed over me with dismissal before focusing back on Alaric.

"Thallium and Vaux." Neither his voice nor smile held any enthusiasm. In a deliberate showing of his favor, he moved to stand next to me.

"Lady Lavinia." I couldn't remember the last time Rhode had called me 'lady' without grinning at the absurdity of the formality or smirking in flirtation.

I nodded, too scared to address him. If I misstep into too familiar territory, it would spell disaster for us both. "Enjoying the evening?" I addressed my question to Caius.

Shining grey eyes met mine for only a moment before dropping to the ground. "Yes. Yes, that is, it is a wonderful evening."

"Matching masks," I observed with quiet mischief.

He looked up to grin at Rhode. "Well, it, it was his idea of course." The masks were a deep red, so dark they were almost black. A sharp diversion from the pristine white mask of Lord Thallium and the bright azure mask of Lord Vaux.

"I like them." I smothered a giggle.

"They're fine enough." The Rhode I knew emerged despite his efforts. "I always preferred silver." His eyes trailed over me. The lascivious grin was typical of Rhode, but in present company lacked self-preservation.

Alaric stiffened next to me. I was saved from desperately floundering for conversation by Lord Thallium.

"Lady Lavinia Bruis," he spoke to me for the first time in all my time at court. I could see the resemblance to Rhode in his coloring and the sharpness of his jaw, but Thallium's features lacked the delicate symmetry of his son. Rhode's almond-shaped eyes, full lips, and chiseled cheekbones were so pretty they were wasted on a man. Cadmium was handsome in the way of a serpent or python. His looks an unforgiving warning. "My daughters were grateful for the welcome you and Lady Ruby Lennox showed them."

"It was my pleasure, my lord. They are lovely girls." I rushed the words out with an eager smile.

Lord Vaux placed a hand on Caius's tense shoulder. "They are. We cannot wait to welcome Golda into our family."

My mouth gaped. Julius was older than Leith, and Golda was only sixteen. It was common for girls to come to court at that age but not to wed.

"What news is this, Vaux?" Alaric demanded. His navy gaze held a silent storm. Dark waves rolled, only belying a hint of the tumult churning under the sea depths.

"I'll be submitting a wedding date request to you tomorrow," Thallium said. "Golda Thallium is betrothed to Caius Vaux." It wasn't pride that brightened his dark eyes, but something like a challenge—one that prickled at the nape of my neck.

Caius had said nothing. At least he was closer to Golda's age, and

Caius, I knew, would be a kind husband to her. I schooled my features. "Congratulations!"

"What happy and surprising news." Alaric studied Thallium and Vaux like the predator it was all too easy to forget he was. "Forgive me if I am confused, but before I approve wedding dates, I approve betrothals where it concerns house heirs. Is Caius no longer your heir? Did you sire a bastard somewhere to replace your brother?" He made a show of looking around the ballroom. "No," he tutted. "I don't think that would...fit your tastes."

Chosen with precision, Alaric's words hit the soft underbelly of his prey. Julius's throat bobbed with a swallow.

Thallium shrugged. His mask of pleasantry remained firmly plastered to the lower half of his face. "The news can't be too surprising. House Thallium and Vaux have a longstanding friendship, one we are overjoyed to solidify in marriage."

Alaric cocked his head. "How do you think it looks were I to make exceptions for certain houses? Where is the equity in that?" He gave Lord Thallium no chance to respond before turning to my friend. "Caius, does a good king give preferential treatment to certain lords? No, I think a good king holds his houses to the same standards."

Caius's pleading gaze met mine before snapping to the king's boots.

Alaric would not stand for being made a fool, yet Thallium seemed determined to provoke him.

"Approving a wedding date," Alaric mused. "Doing that for someone who has put me in this position... If I approve it despite your lack of protocol, I'm an unjust king. I reject it, and I am disloyal to two houses that have been valuable, trusted advisors. Do you think it was fair to create such a quandary?"

"I'm sure it was done with no malice," I placated. If Thallium and Vaux, the engineers of this betrothal, wouldn't stand up for Caius, I would. To draw Alaric's attention, I ran a hand down his forearm. "I'm sure the proper approvals just escaped them due to their excitement. Love is said to scramble the mind after all." Relief washed over me as Alaric smiled back.

"I guess I can be understanding of that," Alaric murmured.

"Maybe a winter wedding?" I raised my brows in command at Caius until he nodded. "My soon-to-be sister would so hate to have her upcoming nuptials overshadowed."

"Yes, a winter date is one I will approve."

"Thank you, Your Majesty." Rhode nodded. "Caius and my sister are delighted with the match."

"Thank Lady Lavinia," he commanded.

My expression faltered as heat licked up my spine like a lover's teasing caress. I glanced over my shoulder to find Oran's green eyes tracking leisurely down my frame, a mischievous tilt to that familiar crooked grin. Dressed in all black, his wide shoulders stretched the fabric across his chest. One chestnut wave fell over his forehead. As his tongue peeked out to wet his lips, I was overcome with the urge, the need, to rip the black mask from his face to see if it was lust swimming in his eyes. Lust, like I felt scalding through my blood, growing with each step he took toward us. Focused on the heat of his approach, I could barely feel the brush of Alaric's arm against mine.

"Traitor!" My stomach dropped. Alaric cheered the word as if in jest.

"Your Majesty." Oran tilted his head down slightly. "Vin," he greeted me next.

Alaric leaned closer to me at the nickname. "Oran," I began.

The king interrupted, the hand gripping my waist was a firm shackle. Looking at Cadmium and Julius, he said, "You know the story of our favorite traitor here, don't you?"

Thallium appraised Alaric before nodding. "I think everyone has at one point. Oran Cahill."

If the name drew shock or pain, Oran gave no indication.

"I think he's done well." Alaric looked back at Oran. "All things considered. Don't you?"

Oran's attention fell on Rhode and Caius instead of Alaric. "I endeavor to uphold the values of my people. As we all should."

"If only your mother shared the sentiment." Julius's words made me gasp in indignation.

Oran's eyes darkened swiftly while his answering smirk emerged slowly. "But then you wouldn't have the pleasure of my company. Without my friendship, what would you do?"

"Be better friends with Bruis, I imagine." There was a warning in Rhode's tone that I couldn't understand.

"That'd be a sight to see." Oran then looked down at me. "May I steal you for a moment?"

"Yes," I agreed before realizing I should look to the king. "If you'll excuse us just one moment."

"Not for too long." Alaric pressed a kiss to my hand. Displeasure like thunder shrouded his brows.

I gave him a final flirtatious smile as the tension left my body. I had once dreaded Rhode and Oran being near each other. Now my concern was for Oran when near Alaric.

Oran wrapped his arm around my waist, leading us to the exit of the ballroom.

"Should you do that?" I asked. I didn't risk checking if the king was watching our departure.

His lips silently quirked. His strong arm, banded around me, gave my feet no choice but to keep up with his pace. He used his free hand to remove his mask, providing me an unimpeded view of his profile. My eyes lingered on the small bump in his nose from a break before my magic had developed. I had never offered to fix the small white scar on the bridge of his nose because I was inexplicably fond of it.

"Where are we going?" The words had barely left me before an explosion knocked me to my knees.

CHAPTER 28
ORAN

They were fucking early.

I covered Lavinia's fallen frame with my own. Plastering my chest to her back, I bracketed my arms on either side of her head as shards of glass rained through the room.

It had been going to plan. A spill of wine on Ruby and Aunt Sapph to ruin their gowns. A plucked pin from Aunt Am's hair to undo its careful construction. My uncles and Lavinia's brother, father, and aunt all sent to escort and assist. All safely removed.

It had been going so well.

I hadn't let myself be distracted despite the way Lavinia's gown molded to the curve of her waist and hips, cascading down her body like molten silver. I hadn't let myself waste time with the jealousy that ripped through me each time Alaric's hands strayed to her waist and his eyes to the soft swell of creamy skin above her bodice.

I had kept to the plan and those fucking bastards didn't.

I felt each of her trembling breaths as if they were my own. I needed to get her out of this room. I looked behind me to see if we could run.

The second chandelier in the center of the room dropped with a crash, raining more glass and metal on the crowd. A clap of thunder, so loud I felt the tremor of it in my knees, replied.

Alaric was at a disadvantage. This wasn't an open battlefield that he could flood. Alaric's power was too great to be contained to a room, unless he wanted his storms to collapse the walls of his own palace.

Several men converged near the windows, being drawn to the image of a group of fire wielders. The dozen men were cast by a single illusion wielder, Landon. An approaching Sand dropped with the impact of an arrow. The archer, Nash, had hidden himself in the gardens this afternoon. The shattered glass announced his positioning. Two Alexandrite jumped through the broken window in pursuit. I hoped the darkness of the gardens was enough protection.

I gripped Lavinia's waist, bringing her with me as I stood. I kept my chest to her back, ushering her away from the mayhem behind us. Her breathing was too fast, the strained flutter of her ribs and spine pattered against my chest. "It's okay, love. It's okay."

I couldn't make out the words Lavinia was gasping over the screaming crowd and clashing metal. Others had begun to run for the exit. If I could get her out the doors, she would be safe.

I checked over my shoulder again. Lord Iron sent a broken piece of chandelier through one of the rebel's shoulder. A ball of fire from Slate Raven blazed through the illusion of rebels to scorch the wood paneling around the window. He threw his flames indiscriminately. I couldn't tell if, in his panic, he had seen through the projection. If his rapid blasts were meant to hit the illusion wielder, he was looking in the wrong place. Ember Placino held a flaming dagger in hand but retreated as the image of rebels approached. He ducked, narrowly avoiding a fake flame. As always, Ember had been drinking heavily. Disoriented, his head swayed on his neck as he crouched on the floor.

I scanned for the crimson of the king as another clap of thunder shook the palace. Ieuan stood on the dais in the back of the room, his water matching the efforts of an approaching Fjord, waves arching and clashing.

We were almost through the door when Lavinia dug her feet in. "No! We need to help them."

She gave a kick as I lifted her feet off the ground. She could be mad at me all she liked. Tomorrow she could be mad. Tomorrow meant she'd live through today.

"There's nothing you can do right now. You can help when it's over."

"Oran," she protested, thrashing in my arms. "Put me down. We need to help."

"No." I lifted her higher in my arms. "I need you safe."

"Oran," her voice shook. I could picture the tears of frustration and fear pooling in her eyes.

Finally, out of the ballroom, I loosened my grip enough to let her feet touch the ground, but not so much that she could run back in.

She ripped her mask off, discarding it with a ragged exhale. "What's happening? Is it…" Her body heaved, turning in my arms to press her face into my neck.

"Tythmore," I confirmed. I cradled the back of her head, grounding myself with the familiarity of the silken strands against my palm.

She pushed back with a sniffle, but stayed close enough that her forehead brushed my chin. "You need to help them."

"Go up to your room and I will."

"No, I need to be here for when it's over." She pulled back further to meet my eyes. The franticness that had seemed to ebb in my arms returned with a fervor. "Go. Go, and I promise to stay here."

I move my hand to the side of her neck, brushing a thumb against the drum of her pulse. I left the constellations of her eyes to look at the fleeing figures in the hallway. A few were running toward the ballroom instead of away.

"No," I breathed as Leith sprinted toward us.

"Go," Lavinia urged. "I'll stand right here. Please!"

"Rebels," I called to Leith.

"Fuck," he growled. He spared Vin one glance before throwing himself through the doors.

That was why I wanted him gone. Leith was foolhardy in his talent. It would pain me to see him fight the rebels, but I wouldn't live with my brother being injured in the fray. He had more magic than most of the rebels, but where they planned, Leith acted, impulsive and reckless.

Lavinia stared after him with wet eyes. Her gulping breaths were the only sound I could hear.

"Look at me. Love, look at me." I stroked the hair away from her face, drawing her gaze back to me. "It's okay. It'll be okay."

"You have to help them," she croaked. "I'll stay here, I promise."

"Vin," I begged, "you stay where you are, or I let everyone in there burn." I waited for her wide-eyed nod before returning to the chaos.

I wanted to look for Leith, to protect him, but he more than anyone knew what my magic was capable of. I couldn't risk him asking questions. Catching a glimpse of him running left toward the windows, I went right.

Two women, Southton cousins, had fallen. I pulled them to their feet, pushing them in the direction of the exit before I focused on the scene in the ballroom. A wall of fire blazed out of me toward the exit to bracket a safe path as more ran past.

I hadn't cared about the casualties before. Now, I felt a knife twist in my chest with each person that fled. This was war, I tried to remind myself.

Proventium, the Wasting, didn't care about the innocents. But I did. *Fuck.*

Ieuan was gone from the dais.

The two Thalliums were standing in my view, holding six rebels in place by the buckles on their boots. Each could impale the rebels where they stood, but the Thalliums merely restrained. The rebels sent useless spears of ice and roots toward the Thalliums that Lord Vaux easily deflected with quick slashes of his blade.

Cadmium and Julius did want Alaric to fail.

"Go," Julius shouted over his shoulder as his short sword cut through another root.

Mystified, the little Vaux took in the destruction around him.

"Go!"

The boy obeyed the second command. Stumbling backward a few steps, he then disappeared with speed that blew a gust of wind through the room.

The illusion of the fire wielders had advanced to the center of the room. Leith's spears of ice sliced through the image, but didn't disrupt the illusion. The projection of the dozen fire wielders pushed toward Leith, a few Ravens, Growley, and Quinn. Not many were trained in combat with illusion wielders. Landon was powerful enough to affect the entire room. Leith, Lord Growley, and Beckett Quinn sent a barge of ice, so much that I felt the chill from where I stood, through the unaffected figures. I erected a real wall of flame in front of the illusion to further the distraction.

I played with the wall, elevating and dropping it until an ice wielding rebel joined the illusion. Dropping the wall, I ran further into the fray to search for Ieuan's familiar freckled face. He was smart. I wanted to believe he had jumped from the dais. The alternative that he had been knocked down—I couldn't think it.

My steps faltered when a blast in the back of the room sent the illusion crumbling. The group of fire wielders disappeared into nothing. I met Leith's wild gaze and watched understanding dawn. He hadn't realized they were fake.

Landon. His illusion failing meant he was either dead or injured.

The thunder that boomed now felt like a conclusion. Tythmore was never going to have enough men. Even with the advantage of surprise, it wasn't enough. My chest heaved with a contained scream as I finally spotted Ieuan prone on the floor. Electrocuted in the water he wielded. My hands burned as I frantically looked around to see how many others had died.

"Oran!" Aunt Am ran toward me. Uncle Hugo chased at her heels. His hand floundered, desperately trying to grab her arm, but she was faster.

"It's okay." My voice was hoarse.

Aunt Am crashed into my chest with a sob. I allowed myself a breath to collapse my head on her shoulder. The only apology I could give her, though she deserved more.

Uncle Hugo's eyes swept over me as he reached us. He rested a hand on his wife's back, the other became a gentle weight on my shoulder. "The traitors?" His gaze was wary. He knew better than to accuse me in front of Aunt Am.

Aunt Am who loved me.

Who was never scared of me.

Who I was betraying.

"Dead or captured, it seems," I mumbled to hide the tremor in my voice. Scanning the room, for once, I was hoping not to find a head of onyx hair. I didn't want Lavinia anywhere near the carnage. As I swept the room, Alaric found me. I schooled my features to match the anger etched into his face.

"When I heard the thunder, I was so worried. I ran down and then"—she looked to Hugo with accusation in her eyes—"I couldn't get in."

"I'm glad you were safe," I told her.

She collapsed back against my chest. "Lavinia is safe," she murmured. "I saw her in the hall with the Vaux boy."

Aunt Am knew more than I could bear to acknowledge. What she didn't know, I knew, would break her heart.

She had defended me for so long, and that love would be for

nothing.

For a traitor.

Hugo wouldn't hold it against her. He'd pity her soft heart, fooled by the traitor in their home. He wouldn't blame her for any of it. He'd rightfully blame me.

"Lennox." Alaric had sent Bron. "We have need of Oran."

CHAPTER 29
LAVINIA

Blood dripped down my fingertips to the marble floor.

"It's okay."

Padgett focused on healing the damage to Adder Glenn's glass-littered chest. Saving his wife from a crashing chandelier, spears of glass punctured his lungs and tore through his body.

His wife, Flora, knelt on the other side of his chest. Shaking with tears, she sobbed into the hand that she clutched in both of hers. She made no assurances or pleas, only heaved with agony.

"It's okay." My voice was as shaky as my hands. The chandelier had severed through his thigh. I had stopped the bleeding, but was struggling to hold it back to seal his skin. Like pushing a wine cork into a geyser, the damage fought against me. Exhaustion pulled at my magic. The silver threads in my mind were becoming harder to hold onto, bowstrings taut and ready to fly out of my hands at the smallest release. I blinked rapidly against the salty sting of sweat dripping in my eyes.

I tried to block out the sound of Flora's tears. I wouldn't be annoyed by the volume of her grief, no matter how distracting it was, but I needed no reminder of what happens when healers fail. My hands trembled on his leg as I gave a final push. The skin, a raw, angry pink, closed at the center of his thigh, just above where his knee had once been. Like the rough edges of a cliff, jagged skin was both a success and a failure. It was ugly, but it was healed. Panting, I allowed myself one heartbeat to close my eyes, then I looked up at Padgett.

He never spoke while he worked, his unseeing eyes directed at the closed skin of Adder's chest. I held my breath as I waited for his confirmation.

He'll live, he'll be fine, he'll live, he'll be fine.

Finally, Padgett blinked with a weary but relieved nod. "He'll be fine."

Flora collapsed onto her husband's shoulder with a whimper.

Padgett, still steady despite the work, left his position by Adder's chest to come beside me. "It's not pretty, but he won't complain."

I squeezed my eyes shut in sorrow. Too panicked, I hadn't even tried to salvage the leg.

"You did well," Padgett assured me. He helped me rise, my knees aching from the stone floor, and chucked me under the chin with the knuckles of his pointer finger. "Reattaching a limb would require multiple healers, more than we have. He'll be grateful for his life."

"Even when he has to hop?" I tried to infuse some levity in my words, but they came out despondent. Blinking away the threatening dizziness of exhaustion, I scanned the ballroom in a daze.

Padgett had sent his wife, Mariana, to the far side of the ballroom. A line of men with minor injuries, burns, and cuts stood waiting for her mending. One Telis, Eliana, no more than eighteen years old, assisted her.

Nero and Alba Rudyard knelt over Porter Ward, working on the shattered bones of his leg. Destroyed from ankle to hip, their healing would need to be precise to mend his leg enough for him to walk again. Porter was conscious, his head of ruddy brown hair pillowed on his brother, Poet's lap. His eldest brother, Scholar, stood vigil.

Their mother, Lady Karissa Ward, stormed toward her brother.

"Tell me!" she shrieked. Lord Judge Ward wrapped a restraining band around her waist.

Beamus Delphi shook his head. Water dripped from the end of his loose ponytail and his doublet to the floor. His solemn expression held none of his sister's anger.

"I hate you!" Her scream was ragged.

I moved to help Porter when a cry rang from the opposite side of the ballroom.

Zeno Vaux had been stabbed in the fight. Padgett had instructed a Lynx on how to wrap his thigh. Not critical, he could wait. That's what we had thought.

"He's not breathing!"

Padgett's stride got him there first. He placed his hands on either side of Zeno's head. Blood seeped out between the fingers of Padgett's left hand. I stumbled forward, the hem of my skirt sweeping against his foot, before another shout rang out.

"Get me a fucking healer!"

Padgett was the best there was. He would help him. Zeno was a cousin of Caius's father. Padgett could do more than I could for him. I held on to that belief as I left them behind.

Herleif Harald, a cousin who made up the king's inner circle of strategists, seized my arm as soon as I was within reach. "This way," he barked.

I dug my feet in when I realized where he was leading me. "I'm not leaving, people need help."

"The person that I need you to help is out here," he gritted through his teeth. "Fucking Bron."

"Bron is injured?" The king's mountain of a cousin seemed above something as human as injury.

"No."

Outside in the hall, the agony of the ballroom seemed to flood out to echo off the stones. Most of the women and many of the men had fled. Only the injured and those who volunteered to help remained inside. Another Lynx brushed past us carrying the herbs I had requested. Sleeping Ferns. They just needed to be crushed and steeped in hot water. I wanted to call out to him, but the words died in my throat when I spotted the figure slumped against the hall.

Bron stood over him, suffocating the boy's prone form under his shadow. That's what he was, a boy. He couldn't be older than sixteen. Head tilted back on his neck, blood matted in his hair while fresh crimson dribbled down his chin and bubbled between his lips.

"Turn his head," I shrieked. "He's choking!"

Bron made no move to help the boy.

The cold stone sent a shock through my knees. With one hand, I propped up his back, the other turned his head to the side. I didn't ask what happened. They wouldn't tell me, and I didn't have time.

The boy didn't have time.

Pain erupted behind my eyes, silver threads unfurling into his chest. Pushing my drained magic to give more, gasping breaths were all I could manage. Broken ribs, a collapsed lung, and internal bleeding. My magic wrapped around the damage, refusing to surrender until all was healed, even as it fueled the agony pulsing at my temples.

The unconscious boy slipped back, torso collapsing onto the floor. I bowed my head, focusing on the steadiness of his breath and heartbeat. My hands and arms fell limp at my side, but the tremors continued through the muscles.

"He wasn't fucking talking."

"Dead men don't talk either," Herleif snapped. "And this fucking kid is not the one who can answer how they got Mesgarian blades."

"Fucking Tyth scum."

"He'll die like a traitor. Death like this would be too good for him."

The boy had survived the fight only to almost lose his life to Bron's beating. Dread was strong enough to overcome the haze of pain.

I'd healed a boy so he could be interrogated. Tortured.

I watched Bron heave the boy like a sack of wheat over his shoulder with tears stinging in my eyes.

Each step back in the hall reverberated pain up my spine. The blurriness distorting the edge of my vision was fading, but the ache in my head was not.

The boy.

The thought ripped through me, a worse pain than the one that settled in my muscles.

He'd helped execute the attack. But he was just a boy.

I met Padgett's eyes as he stood talking to a woman, her back to me. A marigold gown, another Vaux. At the small shake of his head, I understood his regret. Zeno Vaux hadn't been saved.

I made it back to my bed just before sunrise. Leaving my silver dress, now streaked with shades of crimson, ruby, and rust, in a pile on the floor, I plunged into a cold bath. As each drop of sweat and blood washed away, terror and guilt burrowed further under my skin.

Wrapping my arms around my knees, I cried for them all. Those I treated and those I didn't. Those we saved and those we didn't. For Clarence, for Adder, for Aster, for Ronan, for Zeno. And for the boy.

The boy whose suffering wasn't over like the others.

Suffering that was beginning anew.

Suffering that I had prolonged.

CHAPTER 30
ORAN

Under the bright sunlight that flooded through the three glass walls of the Bruis Atrium, Lavinia's inky strands reflected an almost blue gleam. Dissatisfaction creased the skin between her brows. As talented as she was at painting, she was even more adept at finding non-existent flaws in her work. I moved closer to get a better view, only to find myself. At my inhale, Lavinia turned. Her cheeks deepened with an enticing blush.

My face wasn't visible, but I recognized the color and curl of my hair. Facing the rose sunset, the Oran of Lavinia's eye leaned back on his palms in the tall grass, Remus bounding toward him. The brushwork made my hand twitch to reach out as if I could feel the downy softness of his fur. Two horses were small in the distance, grazing in the autumn evening. I recognized the scene from a few weeks ago. My eyes eagerly searched for Lavinia, but I knew they wouldn't find her replicated. She never painted herself.

"I think the grass needs work."

"No." I shook my head. The grass was the exact color of the autumn fields, bleached by the dry season and the cold nights. Looking at the grass, I could feel the breeze sweeping across the painting and the rough texture against my bare feet. "You're very talented."

"Thank you." Vin looked away from me with her full lower lip trapped between her teeth. "You're a nice subject to work with." An indent appeared between her brows. "I'm sorry I didn't tell you before I started."

215

"Don't be. It's a nice surprise." My bicep brushed her shoulder as I joined her. I couldn't stop the proud grin that came to my face.

Vin smiled then, eyes sparkling with uncharted constellations. "Leith will certainly protest another painting of you in the house." She giggled.

I only knew of one other. A painting depicting Leith and I laughing in the horse stables was hanging in one of the guest suites in Bruis Manor. "I'll hang it in my house then. He's just jealous."

"Don't tell me, Oran Lennox is secretly vain?" she teased. At my bark of laughter, she continued. "I'll allow it only because you are a good subject." I preened under her attention. "Well, not so good as Remus. You're handsome, but Remus, he's stunning!"

"I'm in competition with Remus?"

"All men are." She shrugged prettily.

I huffed an exaggerated sigh. "I guess I have no choice but to challenge him to a duel."

"No! I couldn't bear to lose either of you." She turned fully toward me. Eyes, larger in her face with a show of pleading, glittered with amusement.

"So, you do have enough room in your heart for us both?"

She pursed her lips in thought. "I suppose. Though you'll, of course, be in second place."

"If he were a lesser man, I wouldn't accept it. But against Remus, I can concede."

"Accepting defeat like a gentleman? I may swoon!" She tossed her head dramatically.

"Well, Vin. I'm flattered, but you're in stiff competition with Tivali."

"The barn cat? You have horrible taste! Not to besmirch her, but do we even know if all her kittens have the same father?"

"Played for a fool again," I lamented.

"Love makes fools of us all."

I felt myself lean further into her, hypnotized by the flutter of her dark lashes. "It really does." The husk of my voice made her eyes flicker closed for a breath before they opened to search mine.

In another life, I would have been able to kiss her. There would have been nothing to stop me from taking her into my arms and keeping her there. In another life, I could have given her everything. But in this life, all I could do was press a kiss to her forehead.

My stare finally rose from the damp stone floor. Daydreaming of Lavinia felt wrong. I detested bringing her into this room, even if it were only in memory. But I needed to escape this room. She was my favorite escape, even when I did not deserve it.

The Tyth's raspy panting was an intermission from his desperate screams. Camden, they said his name was. I didn't recognize him, but I knew Fintan would.

I hadn't asked many questions. I had answered their questions and provided intel, but asked few questions of my own. I didn't want to know too much.

The plan, as Fintan told me, was to cause havoc and stoke dissent. Force people to see that the unrest had not been smothered. Prove they could infiltrate the palace, and cast doubt on how King Alaric handled his affairs.

So close to the king, of course, they had to try.

And of course, they failed.

Two dozen men were never going to be enough. Most of those men hadn't lived to see the torture Camden was enduring.

Landon and Ieuan.

Landon had been a projector like my father. Seeing his magic had been a strange ache when I had no memory of my father's magic.

He'd play like you two were explorers. Transform the house into a ship in the middle of the ocean, my mother had told me once, reverence and grief saturating her voice.

The pain of experiencing Landon's magic paled in comparison to the agony of my inaction. I provided the knowledge they needed to get into the palace, the times of the guard change, but once they were in, any support would have secured my place alongside them at the gallows.

But maybe that was better than living as a coward. A failure.

I'd gotten Lavinia out. That relief was powerful enough to push back the self-hatred that threatened to choke me.

My mother had informed me of my father's responsibility to his people and absolved me of it in the same breath. But even as a teenager, I felt the weight of it lowering onto my shoulders. As a member of court, I was able to pass along key information to the rebels. I had lied to myself for years that that was enough. That if I jeopardized my position, they would lose all knowledge of court and the king.

With Camden's screams ringing in my ear, I had to face my failings.

The time for loitering at the edges of the rebellion was done. Or every further drop of rebel blood would be on my hands.

I had remained silent while Bron worked. His lightning paled in comparison to the magnitude of Alaric's, but they used its weakness to their advantage. Crackling across his knuckles with each hit, it inflicted intense pain without killing. Bron didn't care whether it was a lie or the truth; he knew what Alaric wanted to hear, and it was his job to extract it.

Another strike scorched through Camden. His eyes screwed shut in pain as a hoarse scream tore out of his throat. Shaking hands clawed at the arms of the chair, rattling the chains on his wrist.

"Still don't want to talk?" Sweat dripped from Bron's temple down a reddened cheek.

Camden had done well. Bron thought him the leader of the surviving rebels. By his bravery, I ventured he was correct. A weaker man would have told Bron whatever he wanted to hear hours ago.

"Fuck you," Camden spat. He wouldn't remain conscious for much longer.

Bron knelt in front of the chair. Grabbing Camden by the shirt, he gave a single shake. "You're all going to be hanged as traitors anyway. You don't want to tell us how many you're working with? How you got into the palace? No?" Bron looked over his shoulder at me.

His sadistic grin reignited my hatred. I let it burn inside me.

"Oran can do a lot with fire. We've got days. You talk, we'll leave you alone until the hanging." He raised his brows as if bargaining. "You don't talk...I keep you begging for death for days, weeks." Bron's grin widened, displaying jagged yellowing teeth while he lazily shrugged. "Maybe we'll bring the pretty healer down here to keep putting you back together so our fun doesn't have to end."

Camden looked past Bron's shoulder with recognition. Had Fintan passed along my name, or had the rebels figured out who was prominent enough in court to have the information they wanted? Holding my stare, he silently entreated me for mercy.

As Bron backed away, I lowered my chin a fraction of an inch. An agreement. Gratitude flashed in his eyes for a moment only before all light left them. Though death in the tower was not dignified, this was the kindest I could offer. His body dissolved into ash, swirling from the chair and into the air. Hopefully through the grate above us and into the river. That would be a far better resting place than having his head spiked on the border of the Wasting.

Bron jolted forward before retreating in shock. "What the fuck did you just do?"

Burnt to ash from the inside so quickly that Camden wouldn't have felt anything. I hoped. I clawed back the fire that screamed at me to finish the job, begging to go after Bron. "Shit." My voice was gravelly with disuse. "Sometimes my powers get away from me." Bron shrank back from the emptiness in my eyes.

The tunnel groaned with the rushing river surrounding us. Bron kept me in front of him. Good. Scared men kept quiet. If he challenged my killing of Camden, I'd not be so generous in granting his own death. Threatening to bring Lavinia into that miserable room had sealed his fate. Only the timing was undecided.

I walked swiftly through the dark tunnel, eager to leave the memory of Camden's screams behind. I did the right thing, but the necessity of it scaled my spine with jagged claws. With each breath, they dug in deeper with renewed strength.

They all deserved better.

I needed to do better.

The damp stone strained my lungs until finally, I spotted the taunting pockets of light from the exit grate shrouded at the end of the tunnel. I climbed the ladder rungs, calling out to the Lynx we'd left waiting above ground. "Ficus!"

Light blinded me as thick, gnarled branches, armed with thorns and brambles, receded under Ficus's guidance. I batted away the bony hand he extended to me after peeling up the grate.

"All well?" His eyes, the pale brown of dry soil, bounced between mine and Bron's emerging figure.

"The rebels didn't talk," I told him.

Ficus's attention went over my shoulder. Back to the tower.

Mammatus Tower sat in the center of the raging Sacris River. Prisoners were brought in by boat to the single dock entrance. Only a select few knew about the existence of the tunnel that ran from the grassy knoll on the shore under the river and into the base of the tower. Even fewer knew how to access it.

Ficus Lynx. Forced to guard the knowledge of the tunnel. Knowledge that could help his doomed cousin.

"No," Bron mumbled. "Nothing to be done.

CHAPTER 31
LAVINIA

I did not want to be here.

Despite the newly scrubbed floors, my nose still stung with the tang of blood and the burn of smoke. Not even the breeze through the shattered windows was enough to banish the stench of death.

I swayed where I stood. Father's sudden grip on my arm was destabilizing rather than steadying. Why had he agreed for me to be here? Why had King Alaric asked?

Thank the Graces, you're unharmed.

He'd breathed the words between us, hands bruising on my hips. His concern yesterday afternoon was a fleeting moment of humanity before Alaric the man was replaced with King Alaric the general.

Standing in the back of the decimated ballroom, five steps behind him, I was a silent observer. The reception was not focused on his words of condolence, though there were plenty. The priority was for the people of Proventium to see the strength of the king.

A leader worth following. A leader ready to defeat our enemies.

Even on the brink of war, with Tythmore and Mesgara, I struggled to see any enemies. Instead of the faceless villain, *the savage Tyth*, I saw a thin face with freckles scattered across the bridge of an upturned nose.

I saw the boy.

A boy doesn't go into the battles of men unless certain he has nothing to lose. I was unable to stop wondering just how many other children were that desperate.

In mourning black, Alaric looked pale, shadows like pressed thumbprints under his eyes, but he did not waver. His sympathy was accompanied by a resolute promise: Tythmore would be punished.

The lords and heirs of the Six stood behind him, completing the show of strength. I was the only piece that didn't fit. The ghastly girl in black. Leith and Father, tall and dignified, bracketed me. To Father's left were the Lennox, Thallium, and Lynx. To Leith's right were the Delphi and Vaux.

The final family to approach, Lord Ward and Scholar marched forward. Lady Ward held Porter's arm, his steps slow.

"Sister," Beamus acknowledged Karissa.

Her lips pursed in a denied reply.

Poet, the only brother to have received their father's coloring, buttery blonde hair and cornflower blue eyes, was last. His focus pinned over the king's left shoulder.

"I expect Tythmore to be flooding as we speak." Judge Ward made no move to bow to Alaric.

"The storm I sent last night was just a warning of what is to come."

"If Your Majesty requires assistance, our house would be happy to help." Scholar's strong features were made even harsher by the shaved sides of his head. In the center, his dark hair was wild and unkempt, falling on his forehead and covering the nape of his neck.

King Alaric rolled his shoulders back. "I'll be leaving shortly to get closer to the border." Whatever was in Alaric's face made Scholar step to the side, putting himself in front of his brothers. "Maybe young Porter would like to join me? Since you are so eager to offer the assistance of House Ward. Oh…my apologies."

Porter had inherited his mother's sight instead of his father's weather.

"All is forgiven." Poet's grin was overly-wide in compensation.

Vaux took a step forward, disrupting the line behind the king. "Your Majesty, I must recommend we leave with all haste should we wish to make it to our stopping point before nightfall." Lord Vaux and his best soldiers would be joining King Alaric and his guard on their journey.

The loud worry that had marred Poet's features was replaced with quiet appreciation. He reached forward to usher his mother and younger brother away.

Alaric turned his back on the Wards in dismissal. Judge's nostrils flared before he turned Scholar by the shoulder to follow.

Rhode ducked his head as Thallium stepped forward. "More than enough time has been given to court. The people understand how preoccupied a king is, especially as we now face war on two fronts."

Father approached to meet Thallium. Leith jolted to follow. "The Stel spies are en route to Mesgara now. We need confirmation that they are willingly and knowingly arming the Tyth before we hasten to war."

I looked at a brush of heat down my sleeve. Oran bridged the gap left by Father with a touch that was as searing as it was gentle. Under the cuff of my sleeve, his thumb stroked the bone of my wrist. My lungs released a long-held breath, meeting the rolling green fields of *home*.

"And you think that the Tyth just purchased Mesgarian blades? Which shop in Tythmore is this?"

"You sound like a warmonger," Lord Lennox tutted.

Oran's hand left me with a final sweep of his thumb. At my nod, *understanding, gratitude*, he stepped forward to support his uncle's challenge.

"We know war will fill the coffers of the Thallium mines and smiths, but the people deserve proof before"—Lennox stressed with a glare—"we take any action."

"Enough!" King Alaric's reprimand cracked through the room.

As the men awaited his instruction like a pack of hounds, I squeezed behind Leith's shoulder.

I did not want to be here.

"Forgive me, Your Majesty." Thallium's hiss of the title was almost mocking.

Quickening my step, I chanced a glance over my shoulder. Only green eyes tracked my exit.

"Wait," I called.

A wide smile was on Poet's face before he turned. "Lady Lavinia." Poet was handsome without being intimidating, clefted chin and square jaw dwarfed by too-large ears. The feature was as disarming as it was endearing.

223

The heel of my boots clicked loudly on the stone floor. I was moving far too quickly to be dignified, but I couldn't care. I refused to look to where the boy had been slumped in the hall and risk collapsing in front of the Wards.

"I'd like to take a look at your brother's leg, if I may?"

"Lord Vaux said you were far too kind for King Alaric." Poet Ward was audacious, especially for a second son. "And too pretty, if I may be so bold." His grin widened, showing off a small gap in the center of his lower teeth.

"Thank you," Lady Ward breathed. Tears welled in her eyes, which only strayed from her son for a moment.

Pain strained the line of Porter's brow. His dark hair, which fell neatly to his shoulders, was marked with sweat at the temples.

"That might be easiest," I gestured toward the bench on the other side of the hall. *Not on the ground, not slumped against the wall. No.*

"Come on." Scholar and Poet took Porter's weight between them, depositing him gently on the bench.

"I'm sorry that I wasn't able to help you earlier." Only a full day had passed since the attack, and yet I felt like I had failed Porter.

"No apology needed, Lavinia. The Rudyards did their best." His face scrunched as if bracing for further pain.

"Your cousins." Scholar's eyes swept between my dark hair and pale eyes, an acknowledgment and accusation.

"On my mother's side," I confirmed. Resting my hand gently on the side of Porter's thigh, I noticed the small line of stitching by the knee of his trousers. A rip carefully mended in thread that was just a touch too dark to match the navy fabric.

Nero and Alba had done well. The shattered bones were strong. What they missed, either in haste or exhaustion, was a fracture at the top of his hip, erupting like the impact of throwing a rock on a frozen lake. With an inhale, I flooded my magic into the fracture. The frayed silver threads behind my eyes snapped back as the bone smoothed.

"Fuck." The word fell from Porter's lips as an exhale of relief.

"Porter!" Lady Ward chastised in a whisper even as she smiled.

Rising to my feet, Porter followed, free of his earlier stilted slowness.

"Thank you." Porter pressed a kiss to the back of my hand with an exaggerated and gleeful smack.

"It's fixed." The weight of Scholar's scrutiny had an urgency I couldn't understand.

"Can you do anything about his face?" Poet's laugh was bright as a spring morning.

"My pleasure. If you all are well"—I looked over each of them—"I need to be getting back."

"Lady Lavinia," Lady Ward faltered, amber eyes narrowed in concern. She seemed to measure the words that waited on her tongue as she tentatively approached me. "My father starts each morning by seeing how the day will end. I hope you'll be careful." She turned back to her sons without another word.

A warning or advice, but certainly not a prophecy. I was too lowly for the Graces to concern themselves with.

Shouting stopped me outside the ballroom.

"My father began the campaign, and I finished it! That will be my legacy. Not the Wasting. I'll not be the Harald King who relinquished the throne."

A warning.

A king was dangerous. A king at war was lethal. I didn't need to be a Delphi to know that.

CHAPTER 32
LAVINIA

Bryony Lynx was executed on a cloudy day. The pending storm seemed to mock her further—her husband as inescapable as her fate.

I didn't know if the hang of clouds was the king's doing, but the executioner's blade above her was. He'd returned yesterday from his campaign near the border after three days of storms. Unlike the impersonal warfare of his storms that slaughtered the people of Tythmore, this was intimate. People would look into his wife's eyes as the blade dropped. A crowd would hear the choking gasps of the surviving rebels as they were hanged for the attack.

Sitting in front of my window, I kept my eyes fixed on the clouds.

Adultery and treason. Bryony had not seemed capable of either and yet... It was a lesson I would keep learning: in court, none were completely themselves.

Guilt and shame churned in my stomach. Bryony had given me a kindness when she had no reason to. She saw a scared girl and decided to help. This was how I repaid her?

Flirting with her husband.

Accepting her crimes.

Hiding instead of facing her cruel fate.

Each sin stacked upon each other, worse than the last. My lungs labored under their crushing indictment.

I barely remembered Queen Sevasti's execution. Abandoned by House Delphi, her guilt felt irrefutable. Father had sent me home from the season early, so it wasn't until Father and Leith returned days later that I realized it was done.

I had never spoken to her. Any concern or regret for her death had been abstract, a swirl of colors rather than a clear image.

Unlike this.

The portrait of kindness, wheat blonde hair, and soft grey eyes, as she took my arm.

A picture that would haunt me.

The gloom obscured the sun's descent from morning to afternoon. I was frozen, even while the day moved too fast. As if at any moment, like Bryony, my time, too, would run out. She shared with me the secrets of women. To protect me from the cruelty of man. And yet she had been unable to protect herself.

This was another lesson she was giving me.

A final lesson.

I could not marry the king.

I wanted to blame my father. This was his design. He encouraged this.

But it was my fault.

My need to please, to be pleasant and accommodating. My foolish ego, flattered by the attention of the most powerful man in the kingdom.

There was still time, I reminded myself. The king would grow bored, and then I would be free. Free to move swiftly to secure a match.

His affections were inherently ephemeral. They were a torrent of passion and promise. A hurricane sweeping one under a shower of gifts and compliments. But in the eye of the storm, I could see those waters were empty of devotion.

CHAPTER 33
ORAN

"Tell my husband, I forgive him."

Bryony didn't tremble or cry before the crowd gathered in front of the palace. The poise of a queen, even when being led to her death. I forced myself to watch as the blade dropped. Bryony was not cowardly, so I would give that same respect.

Bruis's lip trembled as he looked at Bryony. Good. I hoped he was plagued by the vision I was: Lavinia in a plain gown with her hair bundled under a dark cap, facing death at the king's hand.

Bryony's execution would haunt my nightmares, Lavinia in her place.

I had always thought Malcolm Bruis was motivated by protecting his children, that he knew no way to do so other than force them into the mold of what succeeds in the Harald court. But looking at him now, I wondered if I was wrong. Was the fear in his eyes for himself or Lavinia?

The coward.

Rage surged in me. I was no better. I had let my uncle make me into a coward. My fear of what would happen to my mother, to Lavinia, had paralyzed me. Just as I loathed them for using Lavinia as a pawn, I had become one as well.

My fear that I couldn't protect her from being a traitor's wife in the

Harald court had caused all this. I should have married her. I should have told her how I feel.

The nine surviving rebels to be executed alongside Bryony had struggled and wept, raged and begged. I forced myself to watch them too.

Traitor.

It'd been spat, whispered, and roared at me my whole life. I'd hidden from the word. Denied and ignored the call for years. But now, to leave my mother and my people to face their fate alone was not something I could tolerate.

I would no longer be a traitor to myself, to my people.

Once she was safe, I would burn it all to ash. I may have failed many of my countrymen, but I would not fail Lavinia.

No matter the blood in my veins, the responsibility I bore, the house I belonged to, Lavinia was the true call I must heed.

The crowd, once roaring for blood, was quieting at an alarming rate.

Rats scurrying away from refuse at a flash of light.

I shouldered through without a word. Uncle hurried to keep pace as I entered the arched path that led from the front of the palace into the inner courtyard. I allowed him to pull me against one of the courtyard's stone arches, taking my destination, the stairs leading to the east wing of the palace, from my view. I allowed him because I needed to play the obedient heir, especially in the wake of the attack.

"Whatever foolish notions you have in your head end now."

As a boy, Hugo had accepted me because he had to, but there was a brief time when he had found me an adequate son. It wasn't until I was twelve, understanding the picturesque life I lived at Lennox Manor was built on the wreckage of the life I should have had, that the title of Lennox heir began to chafe. My uncle knew the true nature of my discontent before I had the understanding or tools to hide it. Our relationship shifted then. Along with his frustration came a renewed fear. His threats soon followed.

I regarded him with surly boredom. I already knew everything he would say. "I have to get back to speak with Lavinia."

"Lavinia," he hissed. Uncle looked around the courtyard to for prying ears. "Opal's son could have power." This did take me by surprise. "If you upset the king, I'll send you back to Tythmore and take Opal's boy for my heir. Better one of Dean's weak, water wielding spawn over a traitor. Silent," he scoffed, "like you're sad. The only reason you're not a fucking traitor is because I made it so. I'll not have you ruining my efforts, making me look like I sympathize with the fucking Tyth. Do you understand? You and your mother are safe from the Wasting. From the stain of treachery. Do you want that to be you up there?"

Safety? He thought safety, safety that was fading with each moment, was what would sway me.

"Lavinia won't be safe either if you fall off the line I've set for you."

"I don't think you'll be safe either." Fury deepened my voice. "You and Bruis are the ones claiming she's the king's salvation." Looking down on him, I enjoyed the flash of apprehension in his eyes. "If she fails, you'll look like you were sabotaging our kingdom."

"Vin?"

Curled by the windowsill, she looked young and scared. "It's done then." Tears saturated her voice and the smooth skin of her cheeks. I felt each one like the slice of a razor.

I knew her. I knew she was desperate for a way out. But I also knew Lavinia couldn't see that Bruis would always be unworthy of her.

"There was a boy. A blonde boy. Was he…" Her breath hitched, hiding from the word. Executed. Killed.

I recalled the boy's face, wet, hiccupping sobs escaping uncontrollably. They never should have included him. Fintan and the others were as responsible for his death as the king. A child who should have been safe at home, not fighting like a man. Proventium saw soldiers as expendable, Tythmore was supposed to be better.

"Yes," I told her simply.

She buried her head in her hands. I moved without hesitation, drawing her into me. As her frame shook and tears soaked the collar of my shirt, I tightened my arms.

"Don't be sad," I begged when her trembling slowed. I'd get on my knees, crawl through glass, fight the ocean's current, anything to stop her sadness.

She drew back to meet my eyes. "Tell me something happy." A tear fell while another clung to her lash like morning dew.

I was at a loss. My happiness was her. It always had been.

Carding my fingers through her hair, I vowed, "We'll always have each other." That was as happy a thought as I could muster.

"Always."

CHAPTER 34
LAVINIA

My movements were stilted, my facial expression strained, my voice shaky. I was aware of how horribly I was concealing my emotions. However, it only seemed to spur the king's efforts. He was animated and grinning, filling the silence with stories and compliments.

We hadn't talked about it. The Execution. But it was all-consuming. Every time I closed my eyes, I saw Bryony as she had been—confident, smiling, beautiful.

The boy scared and bleeding on the floor.

This part of the library was for royals only, an outing designed to impress and distract. Clodia and Thomasina feigned occupation with one of the shelves closest to the doors while King Alaric and I proceeded further into the room. Shelves bloomed up toward the vaulted ceiling like plants toward the light. Only here, the shelves weren't just filled with books. Some had tomes, some glass vials, some scrolls, and others held pieces of art or weaponry encased in glass.

"Spectacular, isn't it? I'm embarrassed to admit, I've not done as much reading as one likely should."

"What is it all?" I studied the ceiling, painted with the delicate oranges and pinks of a sunset dotted with cream clouds, to avoid looking at him.

He encroached so that I could feel the heat of his body against my back, the tickle of his breath on my neck. "The royal wing has writings and artifacts going back as far as the very first king of Proventium. Journals, accounts, treaties, and prophecies." He paused after the last word, an emphasis that made my breath pause.

"Oh," I prompted. I moved further down the shelf, wiping my clammy hands on the skirt of my dress.

"Yes, not a generation has passed without a powerful seer being bestowed on House Delphi." He matched me step for step. "Each prophecy as it pertains to the royal house or a member of the Six is recorded and stored here."

A light touch on my waist guided me to turn toward the shelf of glass vials behind us. Inside each was a small scroll of parchment.

I squinted to make out the small plaques decorating the shelves and dividing the prophecies. I searched for 'Bruis', finding it in the corner, only a dozen vials behind the name. Only less was 'Vaux', two lone vials behind the plaque.

'Harald' prophecies consumed the entirety of the upper shelves. Crowded together, the vials' glass curves pressed against each other, hip to hip. If one fell, it would take down every Harald prophecy on the shelf.

King Alaric's suffocating proximity abated for only a moment before he returned with a wheeled ladder. The wooden steps groaned under his climb. He plucked a single glass vial from its spot directly under the Harald plaque. Extended between his thumb and forefinger with an eager smile, he offered it to me like a diamond.

"This one"—his brows raised—"is a very important prophecy. One I have been waiting years for. One that I feel, I hope, is in my reach."

The glass was cool in my hand. My fingers felt clumsy as I pulled the small cork out of the top. At the tipping of the bottle, the scrolled parchment slid onto my palm. I secured the vial between my arm and ribs before unfurling the paper.

Without the first son, the Wasting will further decay. At the whims of the Graces, prosperity and healing lay. The rot will spread until the chosen son prepares to reign. A cure to be passed in power from the mother's vein.

The words were a positive fate, and yet I felt the impact of them like an attack. Healing. My mind stuttered on the word. The glass slipped from against me, shattering on the floor at my feet. A shriek that sounded like it couldn't possibly belong to me bounced off the shelves. I jumped, but my fingers refused to uncurl, denting the paper in my hands.

I'd rip the paper to shreds if I thought that would fix this.

Smile, don't look so alarmed. I met his eyes once I managed to curve my lips. "I apologize. Just shock, I suppose." Shock sounded terrible. "Surprise," I corrected with a wince. My smile felt like a cornered animal baring its teeth.

King Alaric stepped forward, the broken glass crunching under his feet. Manageable pieces became minuscule shards that would embed themselves under the skin, invisible and impossible to extract.

Uncurling one of my hands, he held it in his own. "Lavinia." My name was invoked like a prayer. "You're everything I have been searching for. I'm certain of it. I'm so very ashamed of my past choices. Each was such a folly that I can hardly stand to look at you. But I pray that you can forgive me for not knowing better. Knowing that if I just waited, I would find you and everything would make sense." His smile was a plea, not a command. A smile that I once would have found captivating. "I spent so long searching, now that I've found you, I can scarcely believe that I ever thought I found my salvation before you."

"When—" My voice cracked on the word. "When was this foretold?"

If my question were a disconcerting response to his declaration, he didn't show it. "Right before Gaëlle's first birthday. I interpreted it how I wished to at the time, a confirmation that Margaux would have a son. After her passing, I began taking it more seriously. My search..." He sighed, "I was too headstrong to understand how explicitly the seer was trying to guide me. Guide me to you. Proventium needs this prophecy. You will think me selfish to say this, but I need you more. The prophecy is merely"—navy eyes searched my face for the words—"an additional blessing. A fortuitous sign of what we will accomplish together for Proventium. Without the prophecy, or even if it were to be in spite of it, you have ensnared me." He crowded another step, trapping me in place, entreating me to believe him. "I know that you are the woman for me. I feel it in the depths of my soul. I love you, Lavinia."

Graces, what have I done?

"Forgive me." He took my face in his hands. "I pictured this to be done with more romance in my head, but my senses got away from me." He flashed a self-deprecating smile. "I just needed you to be assured of my intentions. The formality, I promise you, I will endeavor to make it worthy of you."

Keep smiling, I repeated in my head again.

I had put a noose around my own neck. Slower, more agonizing than the swift death found at the end of the executioner's blade.

CHAPTER 35
LAVINIA

Anxiety, fear, helplessness, and rage flooded over me. Like spilled paint, the colors bleed together until they become one ugly, dark, indelible mess. My frantic, gulping breaths did nothing to ameliorate the stain.

"Lavinia!" Father barked.

I hadn't heard anyone come in. I took note of how I stood, my hunched posture over the back of the couch, fingers clenched like claws in the rich fabric—the intense, suffocating pressure on my stomach and lungs.

"Apologies." Creaked through my unmoving lips.

"What's wrong?"

Leith was here too?

"There was…the king showed me a prophecy."

Blue and brown met in faces separated by twenty-five years. I watched in horror as Father's face transformed into a small grin. He was never one to smile, wide and uninhibited. His lips stayed closed, satisfaction rather than joy.

"You know what I'm talking about?

"Lav," Leith sighed. His gaze darted between Father and me like an animal deciding between fighting or fleeing.

"Of course." Annoyance replaced Father's minuscule pride. "I would never have thought you'd capture the king's attention without the prophecy. Healing," he mused. "The king mentioned it in the spring. The possibility was slight but worth exploring. I didn't have much hope until he raised the issue with me again after the Elvor banquet."

I had thought this was something I had brought on myself, but no, Father and the king had been planning this.

I wasn't to be a wife. I was to be a tool. Provide the son and cure the Wasting, or be removed to make room for another to try.

"You knew?" My words were heavy with betrayal.

Marriage was supposed to mean freedom. It was supposed to allow me the space to regenerate the limbs Father had pruned with the shears of his disapproval. Marriage to the king, to the prophecy, would trim branches until there was nothing left of me.

His lips flattened into a familiar stern line. "You're finally doing well, Lavinia. Do not test my patience with the petulance you had as a girl. You didn't want Merrifield," he reminded. "And how fortunate. Merrifield wouldn't have made you a queen."

"I did you a favor," I croaked. "This was supposed to be temporary." Backing away from the couch, I began to pace.

"A favor?" His scoff cracked through the room like a whip.

Leith's silence was louder.

"You didn't tell me that all we were exporting west was not sustainable. You didn't tell me that the Delphi are antagonizing our border. You didn't—" My words died in a choking gasp as Father advanced a step.

"If I didn't tell you, how did you know?" The words were the clipped sentencing of a judge. No matter the answer, the punishment would be the same.

The portrait of a good daughter was hard to summon, but I tried. Hands laced in front of me, chin high, eyes lowered. "I found papers in your study."

"And you think we needed your help?" He spoke the words with an exaggerated, patronizing patience.

Leith drifted to the side of the couch that divided Father and I. Whose side he fell on, I knew already.

"You did," escaped my clenched teeth. "I did this to help because I thought it would be temporary."

"You did it for us? Now you care about how you affect the standing of our house?" His brows raised as his voice dropped. "No, Lavinia. You did it for yourself. You didn't want to trust my judgment in your future husband. It's my fault, really"—he placed his hands in the pockets of his trousers—"that you've been such a spoiled girl. But for once, it'll be a benefit to House Bruis."

For once, *I* was a benefit to House Bruis.

The chill of his words imbued the room. Father never released magic on accident or emotion. This was purposeful, a reminder of what he had that I lacked. The prickle of bumps rising on my skin was nothing compared to the sting of tears in my eyes.

"I'm glad to be of use." The latch on the ache behind my ribs shattered.

"And you will continue to be of use."

Father's order was clear. I would not jeopardize his plans, the king's plans.

My plans were the foolish scribbles of a little girl. I was the only one who had ever been dumb enough to think them, scrawled in paint with my fingers, capable of rivaling the calculated and meticulously recorded plans of men.

I couldn't bear to force my face into the smile I had long practiced in his presence. I managed only a nod.

Father hesitated before walking around the couch to meet me. "I am proud of you. You did what I hoped you would." He touched his knuckles to my chin in a loveless caress. A caress that comprised the entirety of paternal affection I was bestowed throughout my childhood.

Those words. I had been striving to earn them my whole life. Scratching and clawing to dig them out. I thought if I could only earn them, everything would fall into place—this gaping wound inside me would close without a scar.

I didn't even raise my hands to catch the words. They fell limp at my feet while fresh blood bubbled.

Whatever further explanation he was giving was drowned out by the increasingly shrill ringing in my ears. *Oh, please let me have hit my head. Let this be a hallucination.*

The door shut with a thud heavy enough to stop the ringing. The fog around me cleared, burnt away by the orange glow of rage. Grabbing a book off the table next to me, I threw it at Leith's head.

He ducked with a yelp. "Lav." His voice was stern, but his eyes were nervous. "Listen, Lav, we didn't tell you about the prophecy because, honestly, I didn't believe it."

"Didn't believe it?" I sent a pillow at him next.

"No," he huffed, "the Delphi prophecies are shit. I thought it would be a week or two of interest before he was on to the next."

His shrug made me even angrier. That I was so unworthy, so unremarkable, that I was not enough for lasting interest. "Oh, you did?" I spat.

He approached me like a spooked horse, hands raised and voice low. "Lav, I didn't think it'd go this far. I didn't, but isn't this a good thing? He'll offer for you, and then you'll be queen." His eyes lit with the possibilities. "You'll be free to do whatever the fuck you want."

"As long as I have a son and cure the Wasting." I counted on my fingers. "How am I supposed to do anything about the Wasting? 'Chosen son,'" I seethed, "When I fail, everyone will blame me, and then what?" I couldn't bear to say it, but Bryony's fate pressed against my neck.

"Why do you have to go to the worst possible outcome?" He threw his hands up. "Anyone else would be fucking thrilled. You're going to be queen. Don't you see how this will change things for us?"

"And what if I don't want to be queen?"

He rolled his eyes. "You were happy to hang all over him, and what? Now that we are about the be elevated to the highest level in court, you want to change your mind? Queen," he repeated. "I don't think you're understanding what this will do for us. House Bruis has never dreamed of rising so high."

"I don't care about that!"

"Yeah, I fucking know. You never have. You spread your legs for Thallium because you don't give a fuck about our reputation."

I lashed out like a drowning cat. The side of my fist clipped his shoulder. My foot connected with his shin. My nails raked at his neck. Grabbing me by the tops of my arms, Leith shook once before forcing my eyes to meet his.

"I'm sorry," he ground out. Leith was the one prone to outbursts and tantrums. He was shocked to be on the receiving end of one. "I didn't mean it. You know I didn't." Even his apology made me struggle anew in his grasp. "You're looking at this like it's bad when it could be great. You'll be queen, but you won't be alone. Fuck the Wasting! We'll figure it out together."

Exhaustion overwhelmed the fight in me. "For how long? If we fail, how long do I have until I lose my head too?"

The Lynx disavowal of Bryony kept their lives, but they were specters in court. Would Leith abandon me, too? Or would I one day be responsible for my brother's place on the execution block?

His breath was shaky as he shook his head. "No, no. Lav, you'll be fine. We don't know that your powers won't help the Wasting."

We didn't know that they would either.

"You didn't think to warn me?" Tears broke free of the levee of my lower lash line, flooding my cheeks.

Agony and anger were sisters, similar but distinct. Agony was far more familiar with living within the walls of my heart. She ushered anger out with a firm hand before making herself at home in my chest.

His brows creased, but he made no move to comfort me. "It's done, Lav. You won't change his mind."

CHAPTER 36
LAVINIA

"Did you know?"

Oran had followed me this morning without question, first to the stables and then to the cliffs.

"Yes." His voice was thick with guilt. I knew Leith had spoken to him last night and informed him of the precipice I balanced on. "I assumed Leith had told you. I shouldn't have trusted that he would. I should have ensured you knew myself. I'm sorry."

The words offered some comfort. At least he hadn't knowingly concealed it.

The sight of Oran made a new ache bloom behind my ribs. The breeze ruffled one chestnut wave over his strong brow and sad eyes. I was desolate, and yet an insistent part of me yearned to make him smile. Maybe the sight of his crooked grin and dimples would make me feel better. Would help dull the throbbing in my chest.

I dismounted Camelia to stave off the fresh tears I felt tapping behind my eyes. Overlooking the cliffs, I kept my gaze on the horizon to avoid looking at the beach below the drop. The beach where I had thought King Alaric was charming. The beach where I had flirted because I could, because I thought it was fun. The beach where I'd felt confident, desired, hopeful.

Stupid girl.

I'd lived a privileged life, but that never stopped me wanting, dreaming.

A bright library to read in. A field to teach my children riding. A dining room that could fit everyone I loved around one table. A husband to hold me in his arms through the night.

What I wanted was always simple, even if acquiring it was not so.

Marrying a king would stomp that sweet, simple life under its heel. My children, to be molded into rulers, would not be mine to raise. My husband, wedded to the kingdom, would not be mine either.

The life I wanted, the husband I wanted, would be lost to me forever.

Despite my efforts to make this fantasy husband some handsome, faceless, nameless man, it was Oran. That had never wavered even in the wake of his gentle rejection. It was his laugh, his green eyes, his crooked grin.

I collapsed in the grass, legs folded under me. Oran lowered himself slowly, knee brushing mine as we looked over the Southern Sea.

"I wanted to marry for love," I confessed. Oran likely already knew, but I hoped saying it aloud would help release the desire into the breeze, carrying it far away from my stubborn heart.

I had to let go of that elusive, impossible wish.

"Being in love is not as wonderful as it may seem." His words were stilted and forced, matching the strained line of his jaw.

Oran had many paramours over the years. Ladies gone as quickly as they came.

Apart from Lady Cressida Burgundy.

Cressida, with hair like spun gold, had held Oran's attention, and apparently his heart, for a whole season. He never spoke of what transpired between them, but by the next season, the eldest Burgundy niece was married to Beckett Quinn.

Through the lump in my throat, I agreed. "In my experience, love is quite painful. But even still, I think I would feel rather lonely without it." I clenched my hands in the grass to stop from rubbing at the pain in my chest.

"Lavinia…"

"Did you love Cressida very much?" I was a masochist when it came to Oran. This agony, the agony of wanting, was an old friend, unlike the new agony of helplessness. The one I had met in the royal library, and now refused to leave my side.

"No." Bewilderment unclenched his jaw. "That courting was at the bidding of my uncles."

"Oh." My mind jumped between the other ladies I had seen him with. Not knowing the object of my envy only made the feeling grow stronger.

"And you? Rhode?" The usual acid with which he spoke the name was diluted with pain. He cleared his throat. "I know he made you many promises."

I winced. Had I made a grave mistake in rejecting him?

"I was never in love with Rhode. I liked, like, him very much. He's handsome and charming." I couldn't look at Oran as I spoke. "It was nice feeling desired. But I know the feeling of being in love, and that was not it. I thought maybe with time I could have fallen in love with him." I looked down at my lap. "He was not in love with me either, obviously."

"Any man who had a moment of your affection and didn't fall madly in love is a blind fool," Oran growled.

I studied him. If I were in love with a fool, then what did that make me?

"Vin, who was it if not Rhode? Who were you in love with?" The question was hoarse and raw.

"Am," I corrected softly, "in love with. A blind fool, according to you." I exhaled a laugh that I hoped did not sound as hollow as it felt. "There is nothing to be done. I hope with time, the feeling will fade. I can't know as I haven't been in love any other time to compare. But I imagine it will eventually dull," I lied.

"Then I pity him even more."

"I'm scared," I admitted, not to Oran but to the vast expanse of sky and sea. "But...Leith is right." I looked back at Oran. "It's too late."

"Vin." He shook his head, fist clenched on his knee.

"Even if I were to beg Rhode to have me, or Arrow, or—" I stopped before I could say his own name. "The king told me how Sevasti and Bryony made him a fool. Any husband I could find would be at risk of retaliation. I'd be putting them in danger when it's my fault. I did this to myself. I'm so stupid. I thought it was just a game." Pleading crept into my voice, begging for understanding.

"You deserve a man who'd go to war for you. Who'd proudly lose his head for a day in your company. That is what you are worthy of, Vin. So much more than Alaric or Rhode or Arrow."

I squeezed my eyes shut, but that failed to stop the escaping tears. If only it could be Oran.

No, I would never risk his life for my selfishness. For my stupidity.

"Tell me something happy."

"Every time I smell roses, I think of you." The right side of his lips lifted, but the sadness in his eyes did not. "I think of when I found you crawling into the rose bush at the side of the manor to get that baby bird. It was fine once you put it back in the nest, but you were covered in scratches from the thorns. You let me hold your hand while you healed all your cuts. You've always smelled like roses. It's my favorite because it makes me think of you."

I buried my head against his shoulder. His arm wrapped around my waist, holding me against his side. How ever he loved me, be it a raindrop compared to the ocean that ran through me, I would hold on to it. In a loveless marriage, at least I would have this.

CHAPTER 37
LAVINIA

"I believe Lord Delphi has need of a healer."

Thomasina remained by the door, hands clasped behind her back. I knew the effort it took her to watch me instead of dropping her eyes to the ground.

Ambrose Delphi was unsurprised, and worse, impatient.

"Lady Lavinia, finally."

I had thought the Bruis chambers large, but the Delphi suite was expansive. The sitting room alone was twice the size. Fabric of Delphi purple, deep and rich, draped over every seat and framed the windows. The largest window in the center was stained glass depicting two men.

The golden laurel crown of the Graces sat atop the standing man's fair head, bowed slightly to the man kneeling at his feet. Adorned in a crown of thistle, black robes pooled around Death, the fallen brother of the Graces. Despite his supplication, Death's lips curved in a smile, eagerly accepting his banishment from the Graces for the domain of death. When Death pulled at a soul, the Graces had to release their hold.

Limping to the settee, Delphi called for his son.

Beamus emerged from a door down the long hall branching off the center of the room. "Lady Lavinia." His smile was apologetic. "Lovely to see you."

Lord Delphi waved a hand toward the plush bench seat across from him. "I know why you're here, of course. My cousin was Queen Sevasti's father. He'd demanded to know what we'd seen. But fates come when they need to, when they choose to. By the time her fate was delivered to me, she was already wed."

Beamus lowered himself gently next to his father. The molten amber of his eyes entreated me to understand, to forgive. "Bad things happen when people fight their fate. They bring more strife, more death, and the fate still comes to be. It always will."

"My cousin's daughter and son were killed, as was their fate. My cousin's fate was to be one of the only members of court to know," Delphi stressed the word, "of his children's innocence."

Like Sevasti, her father was a truth wielder. The Graces seemed as cruel as their fallen brother, Death—dooming a man to know the truth but rendering him helpless against the lies that took his children's lives.

"And my fate?" I perched on the edge of the seat. One knuckle cracked with how tightly I laced my fingers together. "You foretold an end to the Wasting, but that has nothing to do with me. Does it?"

"That prophecy was my mother." Beamus rubbed his forehead with a thin hand. "She never enjoyed court. She was a peasant, did you know?" His face brightened. "My grandfather had the most delightful trick. Each evening, he could see the price the fishmonger would charge the next day. My mother, well, her sight is a great deal more powerful."

"I heard tell of a girl on my lands who could see"—Delphi's grin blanketed his face in wrinkles so deep that I could no longer see the amber of his eyes—"everything. I purchased her within the week. She was waiting for me, bags packed, and had already informed her father of the price I'd offer." Father and son shared an affectionate and amused look.

"Despite her talent, she has journeyed to court only three or four times. And always because of something she has seen. She told Alaric the prophecy herself, right here in this room." Beamus's awe of his mother's talent saturated his voice. "King Alaric, he's never content with prophecies. He wants more details than can be offered."

"Seers are able to see the destination," Ambrose grumbled, "not the path one takes on the journey."

"The Wasting will end," Beamus nodded.

"The reference to healing is nothing to do with me." My voice shook, but I refused to scream as I longed to.

"Prophecies are never to indicate a singular path. If they removed all choice, people would expect a prophecy for every decision."

"But they cannot be ignored." Ambrose's words struck me with enough force to shrink back in my seat. "There is a reason, Lady Lavinia, that House Delphi was the stewards of this kingdom for so long." Ambrose's fingers, gnarled with age, tapped a rhythm on his knee. "There is a sickness that corrodes the mind of man." Even unsmiling, wrinkles sliced his cheeks like scars. "A man who is sick with an unending greed for more will ignore the good in front of him for the fruitless pursuit of better until there is nothing of worth left. That was a prophecy I didn't tell King Alaric." The title was spoken like a curse.

"Please," I entreated. "There are so many of them. Not all of them can be true. Not all fates can co-exist. Fates can change."

"Is that what you think?" Ambrose used his cane to lean forward in his seat.

Beamus squeezed his eyes shut, hiding a pity that chafed, as he corrected. "Seers don't choose what they will see, the Graces do. To fight a prophecy is to fight the Graces themselves. Fates do not change."

"Once they are spoken, they are given a life that cannot be killed. Prophecies come to fruition oftentimes in the most surprising of ways." Ambrose's stark white brow quirked.

"The Harald prophecy will have to come to fruition through someone else." Defiance didn't feel as uncomfortable as I feared. I raised my chin higher. "Tell me a new one. Give me one of my own."

"It doesn't work that way, Lady Lavinia." Beamus shook his head.

"And if I see you on the correct path?" Ambrose challenged.

"Then I won't argue."

"Father," Beamus sighed.

"This cannot be my fate." The Delphi saw what the Graces gave to them. They weren't meant to abide by favors or requests. Yet, I would demand and beg. "Please tell the king that the prophecy has nothing to do with me. This path is not mine."

Amber eyes began to glow gold. Lord Delphi's head tilted as he saw through me. I counted thirty heartbeats before gold faded back to amber.

"You're on the right path for your fate."

"No," I whispered. This couldn't be inescapable.

"Yes," he corrected, "there is nothing to stop the path you are on." Satisfaction curled his lips. Delphi didn't care what my fate meant for me. He cared that the Delphi were correct.

The suspicion that had been a whispered nagging began shouting. "My father has been concerned about the Delphi pushing into our land."

"Malcolm is a cautious man." Ambrose nodded.

"Were you?" My voice was harsh. "Or did you just need him to think you were?"

"There are many parts to a prophecy," he demurred. The smile that remained on his face was the confirmation I needed.

"And your part was making my father feel like his standing with the king was in jeopardy."

"I said fate cannot be stopped or delayed; I didn't say it could not be aided along. We are the stewards of the Graces, of Fate, for a reason."

Another chess player for whom I was a pawn.

"Steward of the Graces," I spat. "I wonder how they feel about you playing at being a Grace yourself." The anger I felt wavered as the aching knowledge of my entrapment closed around my throat.

His smile grew. "The Graces picked well with you."

"The path is right." Beamus tried to comfort me. "Your fate is your own. Don't think of King Alaric's fate or Lord Bruis's. It is your fate."

My fate. My path. A path I had taken, assuming there would be a divergence. A path I had foolishly taken, unaware of the gates locking, barring my way back.

CHAPTER 38
LAVINIA

Any shade of red now made me feel sick. They all amounted to Harald crimson in my mind. At least I didn't have to look at the wine to drink it. I was going to look horrible in red.

Ruby tried to move my glass away from me, but the servants were all too happy to bring me more. *A future queen can have all the wine she'd like.* The thought was biting in my head. Anger was good. The urge to scream felt a lighter burden to carry than the constant desire to weep. I'd become intimate friends with anger to keep agony away.

"I don't know," Ruby murmured to Leith. "Maybe we should all retire for the night."

"Father said it's good for people to see her." I didn't feel the grip on my arm when he leaned behind Ruby to chastise me. "Stop embarrassing yourself."

I sat straighter and tried to focus on the stage. "I'm fine." The assurance would have had more impact had it not been so mumbled. The heaviness of wine that sank into my limbs was better than the chill that refused to release me.

The room and my emotions were cloaked in a pleasant haze. The song sounded the same as earlier in the night. Had the song ever changed, or was the evening a performance of one long song? The music was concluding, and everyone was clapping. Surely, I'd remember clapping. People were leaving around me when two maids approached. The rumble of Leith's voice was so familiar that I forgot to listen to the words that began confidently before trailing off. My mind and muscles were sluggish. I was following them out of the hall before the words caught up with me.

"Excuse me, my lady. You're needed."

I swung my head, looking for Ruby and Leith. I met Ruby's troubled gaze for only a moment. She glanced up at my brother, but he wouldn't look at me as he tugged her along.

Oh, Graces, if someone needed healing, I was ruined. I felt around in my mind but found not a single thread of silver.

"I'm sorry." Shaking my head brought spots to my vision. "I don't think I can help."

The maids didn't respond or slow as they led me through the castle. The perpetual noise of court dimmed with each turn. Everything looked the same in this Graces forsaken castle.

The sight of Bron cleared away some of the fog in my mind. Shocking up my spine, fear held a startling clarity. The maids were gone. I couldn't hear that croaking voice over the dull roar of understanding. I should have heard it earlier.

Like approaching a waterfall, I hadn't recognized the faint rumble. Now that it was in view, the sound was deafening.

They brought me here to be alone with the king. He can't do this to a Bruis. My father would never agree to this. I would never agree to this.

The king's grin was greedy with glee. He was kissing me before I could move. At the slam of the door, panic overwhelmed my senses. My heart raced like a rabbit fleeing a circling hawk.

"Your Majesty, no, I—" The hold he had on my waist was firmer than the grip of intoxication. "No, we can't. A child," I scrambled for an excuse he would hear, "we can't conceive a child until after we wed. The Graces, they don't…" The shaking of my head made the edges of my vision darken. The room moved around me, a boat rocking in rough waters.

He shushed me with a calm control. "Everything is alright. You don't need to worry." The hand he stroked over the side of my head was too heavy, too cold.

His pupils were the black expanse of a storm settling over shadowy waters. I thought I had resigned myself to my fate, but now, thrashing against the current, I realized how wrong I was.

"We can't risk a child." My voice was a grating demand, so different from the acquiescent girl he'd met.

"If we have to marry in haste, all the better. I'll have you, Lavinia." He still smiled, but the tempest in his eyes darkened.

He wanted me. And he would have me. Whether it was now or in a few months, Ambrose's words repeated in my head. *No, there is nothing to stop the path you are on.* The pounding in my head made me squeeze my eyes closed. I felt like a child—if only what I couldn't see didn't exist.

What was the point of fighting? Angering him would do me no favors.

This was my fate.

On his decision, this was my fate.

He wouldn't be dissuaded. He would marry me. Whether he treated me with affection or retribution depended on me. A lesson I'd been learning all my life: be biddable, be appeasing, be loveable. The admonishment of childhood, I knew, would be far kinder than what the king could inflict on me.

The fight left me with a sigh. Abandoned me. Fingertips grazed its fleeing form but found no hold.

The grip on his hand on my waist tightened before spinning me. The sound of my laces being untied cracked through the room like lightning, deafening and devastating.

Bryony's advice. I had never thought to need it pertaining to the king. I was supposed to employ it with a nice, handsome husband. Or maybe I wouldn't have needed it, so caught up in newlywed bliss that such things wouldn't matter.

I hadn't even remembered the advice until I was back in my room, led through the empty halls of the palace in the dead of night by a nameless guard. I couldn't bear to look at my naked body, scrubbing myself in a tub of scalding water in the dark. Lighting a candle would bring to focus what had happened. What I had allowed. What I had done. I'd find no comfort in the familiar warmth of a flame.

With each scrub, I kept my eye on the shadow of the door. The locked door didn't feel like enough.

Should I have screamed? Scratched and kicked? No, it would have made things worse. He had not been rough in the act, the way he could

251

have in anger. I had only been with Rhode before, an insistent reminder of how wrong this was. Being with Rhode, I felt powerful, desirable, and adored. Being with the king, I felt like a trophy to be polished and encased in glass.

I had been outside my pliant body, waiting for it to be over. If he felt my sadness, he made no indication. After, lying next to me, he had grinned. The scratch of his beard against my shoulder, the silk sheets under us, that was when I returned to myself.

Was I ruined? Did it matter?

Stupid girl.

CHAPTER 39
ORAN

"Your plan was ill-conceived, underdeveloped, and too small."

I couldn't bring myself to care if anyone saw me with Fintan. Usually, I was cautious about anyone seeing me with a Tyth, but caution died with the declaration of the king's intent.

He wasn't responsible for the rebel deaths, and yet each time I thought of Fintan, I thought of Camden begging for death. The rage, as much for myself as it was for Fintan, pulsed outwards and inwards. With each beat, it threatened to consume me.

Voice solemn, he told me, "We couldn't get a nature wielder from Tythmore in time." His brows pinched low, deepening the carved line between them.

"I'm not talking about the rescue." That never happened despite the details I provided on how to get into Mammatus Tower. "I'm talking about the entire attack. All of it was too small. Tythmore won't accomplish anything until we think bigger."

"We don't have the resources to go bigger."

"Not yet, but we will. We aren't the only people Alaric has made enemies of. It's time for us to stop thinking of this as Tythmore against Proventium. We won't win. But Tythmore versus the Harald?"

"You think we'd have allies in Proventium?"

"I know we do."

The relief I expected to accompany taking up my father's position didn't come, instead, eclipsed by responsibility.

This was just a piece of what I needed to do. The largest piece had yet to come. Until then, each step, each breath would remind me of my failure.

Until I had Lavinia away from Alaric, nothing mattered.

"Oran Lennox, I always wondered if your uncle knew what he was doing with you." Lord Thallium spun a silver coin between his fingers before it melted to form a ring on his pointer finger.

The problem with the plan would always be the possibility of betrayal. How much Thallium and Vaux wanted power, and how appealing we looked as allies.

Vaux nodded but kept his gaze on the toes of his boots. "It's a good plan."

"Your men at the border, where do their loyalties lie?"

For years, the Vaux had the largest army. Where other noble houses were comprised of the fighting men on their lands, Vaux drew strength and speed from across Proventium. There were tales of mothers moving to Vaux lands upon their son developing magic.

"They are loyal to me. Not the Harald. My father offered low-level wielders protection. Fair wages and work. He showed our people that they are not workhorses to be whipped and ridden into the ground. Still, he tolerated more than I am willing to accept."

"Good." I nodded. "While Alaric thinks that the border is being secured by your men, the rebels will have time to organize their forces."

"And the prophecy?" Vaux looked up then, head cocked to the side.

"The prophecy is Delphi shit."

The Graces could find someone else to burden with the Wasting. Damn them all. I'd fight the Graces myself if I had to.

"Funny, Cai said the same thing." Thallium, Rhode, piped up from where he huddled against the wall behind his father.

"Lavinia will not be involved much longer." Rhode didn't sink into the wall at my glare. With his father between us, he merely smirked.

"I see," Vaux mused. I wonder what he knew from the little Vaux and what he'd guessed on his own.

"I do not," Cadmium hissed. He rose from the armchair to advance on me. "Our plan to deal with Lavinia Bruis was interrupted. Was that the word the boys used?" he asked Vaux before looking over his shoulder to his son. "Failed would be my descriptor."

Rhode straightened his posture but dropped his chin to avoid Cadmium's contempt.

"Lavinia Bruis is not your concern. I will handle it." If Thallium thought I'd cower like his son, he was mistaken.

"How?"

"It's not up for discussion." I recognized the glint in his dark eyes. It was the same one my uncle got when one of his threats landed. "I make a good ally," I continued, "but I promise you, I make an even better enemy."

A man like Cadmium wouldn't respond to diplomacy. A bully only respected his own reflection.

"If I have to incinerate this entire kingdom to stop her name from even leaving your lips, I will."

"I don't know if the traitor is in a position to be making threats. The masquerade attack, just knowing about it would get you hanged. Planning it?" Thallium quirked a dark blonde brow.

"All I know about the attack was that you and your son were purposefully absent from the fight. Hoping the rebels would kill him, no doubt." If they turned on me, I would not go quietly. "I'd lose my head with a smile on my face knowing you and your son are on the executioner's block with me."

Cadmium's answering grin was slow and serpentine. "Allies."

"I don't know, Father," Rhode drawled. "Is jealousy really a motivation you trust? He doesn't care about the Harald outside of his pick of wife. He's been dying to get under Lavinia's skirts. Even before I got under there."

I only took one step toward Rhode before Cadmium interceded.

Prowling toward the real prey, he ordered, "Watch your tongue." The rings on each finger of Cadmium's clenched hands, gold on his right and silver on his left, raised into spikes.

Rhode flinched at the warning before quickly masking it with a shrug. "Am I wrong? I never thought I'd see the day when Oran Lennox defies his family."

"I think you've forgotten who my father was."

"And your brother," he goaded. "Leith?"

"Leith isn't involved in this." I wouldn't let it show how the blow landed, even as I searched for an exit wound.

"Of course," Vaux agreed. "Leave the Bruis out of this. All of them," he told Rhode. "And Caius. I will decide my brother's level of involvement in this. Not you."

"'Yes, sir,'" Cadmium prompted Rhode, leaving fang marks on each word.

"Yes, sir," he dutifully repeated.

Vaux ignored him. "You want to protect Lady Lavinia. I understand. You need something from House Vaux, you come to me."

Vaux's need to shelter his brother from harm was one I was achingly familiar with. "Agreed."

Rhode followed me when I left the Thallium chambers. "The king will move fast," he drawled. "What's your plan for Lav? If he goes through with the wedding, it'll prove a challenge to stop all of the rebels from convicting her of his crimes."

I was unsurprised to find genuine concern etched in his face. "I'll protect Lavinia." Rhode was another moth desperate to stay near the light.

"That's all I get? Lennox, come now." He increased his pace to stay alongside me. "You can trust me. After all, we have so much in common. Our politics, our taste in women." His worry verged on desperation, lending a manic edge to his usual smirk.

"Lavinia will be safe." Lavinia would be the first to hear my plan. I wouldn't betray her by speaking as if the decision has been made for her. If she didn't agree, I'd change my course. Any course that would ensure I stayed near her was the one I would take.

"Cai will be worried about her."

"Then he can speak to his brother."

"Don't tell me you're scared of him, too." Rhode was better at masking his disdain for his father than his loathing of Lord Vaux.

"Fuck off, Thallium," I sighed.

Rhode had the narrow view of a child. Thallium hit his son for sport. Vaux hit his brother so he would stand a chance when someone else did.

Turning a corner, Bruis and King Alaric walked side by side.

"Oran," Bruis greeted. He observed me like a wild dog he had caged and chained. He had never believed me to be fully leashed by my uncle. "With Rhodium. What a surprise."

"Lord Bruis, Your Majesty." Thallium bowed. "I'll leave you to it." He turned around the same way we had come.

Idiot.

I bowed my head before meeting Bruis's gaze.

"You and Thallium have overcome your boyhood rivalry? My daughter will be pleased there are no injuries to attend to."

"We have a few things in common."

"I hope this doesn't mean we won't get to see any further sparring displays. Selfish, I know, but it was the best show we've had in quite some time." Alaric laughed as if we were friends sharing a joke.

"I wouldn't worry about that."

"You should be off." Bruis raised his brows.

We were leaving for the wedding, another piece of Bruis's plans falling into place.

"Ah, we were just talking about the nuptials," Alaric said. "I hope you've expressed my regrets to your cousin for having to miss it."

I nodded. "Of course. Excuse me, I need to go check with Lavinia on when she will be ready to leave."

"Lavinia," Alaric drew her name out. Despite the need to avoid undue attention, I reveled in the unease creeping into his posture. "You'll be seeing Lady Bruis home?"

"Yes, her brother and aunt have already left. You won't be joining us until tomorrow, my lord?" I couldn't remember the last time I formally addressed Bruis. The sarcastic bite of the title threatened to coax a grin to my face.

Bruis cleared his throat. "Oran is the only family left to accompany her and her maid."

"She'll be waiting for me." I gave a final nod to them both.

This was the first step. Once we were away from the palace, the rest would come.

The contentment I expected from having Lavinia to myself for the ride back to Bruis Manor was extinguished like the missing constellations in her eyes. Gaze fixed out the window, one hand stroked unconsciously over Remus's back. He was pressed tightly against her stomach, providing comfort he knew she needed. The few conversations I tried to start were met with the same detachment. I allowed her this silence, even as it stoked desperation in my chest.

My hands, aching to smooth away the pinch between her brows, were clenched on my lap, flames flickering against my will. It was only when I watched her shiver despite the summer heat that my resolve crumbled.

"Vin." My voice was soft, and yet even a whisper felt disruptive. "Come here. Let me…" I trailed off as I fumbled for the cloak folded in the small trunk at my feet.

At the touch of my hand on her wrist, her shoulders rose with coiled tension before dropping in an exhale.

"This side first," I mumbled. I knelt in the well of the carriage, sliding the cloak over her right shoulder and then her left. My fingers felt clumsy with haste as I adjusted the cloak around her, encasing her and Remus in dark green velvet.

A flicker of starlight came back into her gaze as she slowly blinked. "Thank you," she murmured. Lavinia's attention was gone from the window, instead staring down at the cloak for the rest of the journey.

CHAPTER 40
LAVINIA

When I was a girl, I was enthralled by Clodia's stories of my mother. I'd watch enraptured, unsure whether to focus on the gesticulation of her hands or the expression on her face. I'd recall her stories often, like re-reading a book whose pages were weathered from love.

Clodia's account of my parents' wedding was my favorite chapter. My mother had laughed with unrestrained joy as the skies opened up right when my father pressed their hands together in the blood tie. Forgetting the cut on his palm, my father had left a streak of rust on the hip of her white gown as they embraced under the downpour.

Leith and Ruby's wedding day was fit for the same chronicle. Cast in a celestial golden glow, they vowed to honor each other until the end of their days.

Ruby's parents shone with a pride that put my father's quiet satisfaction to shame.

I kept my arm laced through Opal's. If my grip on her slipped, so would my smile. Envy bubbled in my stomach, thick and ugly, which only made me angrier with myself. It was my fault that I wouldn't have a wedding day like this.

I wouldn't let my faults spoil Ruby and Leith's day.

I would not let my anger and envy further turn me into someone I loathed.

I would ignore the pain in my chest and the churning in my gut.

I would be happy while I could find reasons to be so.

"Oh," Opal breathed as we made our way from the temple to Bruis Manor for the festivities. "It's the most disturbing feeling." Nose scrunched in disgust, she placed my hand on her belly to feel the baby's kick.

This, these moments, I would not allow to be taken from me.

Dean's hand rubbed the top of her stomach. "Please don't refer to our daughter as disturbing."

"I'm referring to our son as disturbing." Opal's cheeks had rounded along with her stomach, making her usual smirk softer.

"Do you really think it's another boy?" I asked.

"She just likes to be contrary," Dean hummed. Barely taller than me, the side of Opal's curly head kissed Dean's cheek when she leaned into his broad chest.

"Why, I've never heard such lies in my life! Vile blasphemy from my own husband!"

The hall of Bruis Manor had been transformed under Ruby and Sapphire's instruction. Chains of white roses line the ceiling like stars. The scent hung heavy in the room, florals masking the scent of the banquet along the back wall. Pale Bruis blue cloth covered the long tables arranged in the hall to leave the left side of the room free for dancing.

Opal sank into the chair Dean offered with a heavy sigh. "Ruby just couldn't wait another month. She had to drag me here when I'm the size of a cow."

Opal had the same tawny skin as Ruby, but her curls were darker, only a shade lighter than mine. Her face lacked the angles of Ruby's arched brows and high cheekbones, but next to each other, the resemblance was clear in the set of their brown eyes and the pout of their lips. Though where Ruby's rested curved in a demure smile, Opal's were often contorted in a mischievous smirk.

"At least at my own wedding, I was still small with child." She snickered, unashamed if anyone heard.

Ruby was almost too beautiful to look at. When I would fantasize about weddings as a little girl, my imagination lacked the picture of what a bride should be—corkscrew curls framing pomegranate-flushed cheeks, white gown glowing against skin bathed gold by the afternoon sun.

I fell into her embrace before being pulled into my brother's arms. He lifted my feet and swung us side to side. The motion, the way he'd hugged me since I could remember, made me dig my nails in tighter to the fabric at his shoulders.

After Leith put me down, a caress that was as familiar as it was thrilling ran down my hair. Oran's hand came to rest on my back.

"Dean, Opal." Leith nodded.

"I've missed you so much!" Ruby pressed a kiss to Opal's cheek. Leaning against Leith, she looked at him with an order carved into her expression.

"It's great to see you both." Despite Leith's forced cheer in the words, we all knew he didn't mean them. He'd never liked Opal and thought even less of her after her elopement. "Thank you for coming. Any advice, Dean?" Leith snaked an arm around Ruby. "The most experienced husband of our—" He paused, reading the word in the expectant set of Ruby's brow. "Friends."

"I think luck is the only thing a man can hope for to survive the Southton-Lennox ladies." He winked at Opal.

"Mrs. Branch and Lady Bruis now." Opal flicked her hair. "The Branch name will go on without you, so I'd watch what I say if I were you."

He picked up her hand and pressed a tender kiss to her palm.

Oran's hand slid from my back to my waist. I smiled brighter than the tempest roiling in me.

"I'm so excited for our new baby," Ruby squealed.

"This boy has overstayed his welcome." Opal's words were gruff, but her hands were affectionate as she traced secret patterns on her stomach.

"Oh," Ruby breathed. She straightened with a fresh sense of pride. "The king is here."

My muscles locked. A rabbit unaware of a circling hawk had nothing to fear, but I was already paralyzed in the grip of its talons.

Oran's hand, comforting in the burn of his presence, tightened on my waist to ground me.

While Ruby was surprised, Leith was not. The knowledge landed like a punch. He raised a hand in greeting. The show intentionally casual.

The gold and crimson of King Alaric's doublet seemed aggressive against the soft blues and whites of the wedding decor. His shiny black boots lacked any marks, the leather stiff and new. The large gold buckle on them rattled with each step.

"Lavinia," Opal whispered. She reached up to thread her fingers through mine. A kindness I repaid by squeezing with all my strength.

It had been a lie so enticing that I had tricked myself into believing it. Now I was the stupid girl who had told herself a fairytale would always be just that—a story.

"Your Majesty," Ruby gushed. "We are so honored." Her dazed, rapid blinks did nothing to disguise the elation in her eyes.

Leith bowed. "Thank you for coming."

"I would never miss a chance to celebrate the Bruis family." He smiled at the couple before he turned to me. I felt the weight of his stare fall to Oran's hand anchored on my waist before trailing up to my face.

"Lavinia," he breathed my name, pulling me out of Oran's arms into his. I held Opal's hand until I couldn't any longer. The scrape of his beard against my cheek sent a fresh wave of nausea through my stomach.

The scratch of his beard on my shoulder and silk sheets on my back.

"Your Majesty, what a pleasant surprise."

"I missed you. Two days felt too long."

As he led me away from my friends to dance, my hand trembled in his. A life led by him, doing and saying as dictated by the king, would be agonizing.

Joining the spinning couples on the dance floor, I nodded and grinned when the pauses in his rumbling seemed to call for it. We twirled closer to the windows that flooded the hall with light and allowed for a view of the knolls behind the manor. I squinted as if I could see over the hills to where I knew a single cherry tree stood.

Planted by Bryony.

Her visit had been brief, an inaugural tour of Proventium. A mature fruit tree was gifted to each village she visited. Wherever she went, abundance followed. Fruit trees were scattered like evidence through the kingdom, her magic living on in each harvest.

When the song reached its conclusion, my head was still turned toward the windows. I checked the smile on my face before looking up at the king. Under the clapping, the whispers had an edge of anxiety. The guests invited from the village maintained a wide berth. The crowd was right to be wary of his presence, but I couldn't let that show.

It's an act, I reminded myself. One I now knew too well. I looked up at him through my lashes, the flirtation in my face chiseling away at the tension in his brow.

"Come," I urged him. "I think you'll love the pistachio cake. It's even better than the one at the palace."

"High praise indeed."

"Promise not to tell, Miss Forth?"

"Your secret is safe with me." He winked.

I steered the king's attention away from the curled lip of Mr. Huffman and the scowl of Mrs. Bain.

Caius had told me tales of demands for an end to the Wasting delivered in bloodshed and destruction. The nearer one got to the Wasting, the less respect they held for the king. If even on our lands, sheltered from the draining starvation in the west, King Alaric was scrutinized, then the instability was greater than I had known.

"Such a lovely home and village. I'm disappointed in myself that I haven't visited before." King Alaric placidly surveyed the banquet, balancing his cake on one hand while my fork clattered against the edge of my clutched plate.

Father and Leith left the full burden of entertaining the king with me. At least here, surrounded by the celebrating crowd, I was sheltered from his full focus.

"Very different from Tordenhold." Our small village must seem inconsequential compared to the city that was home to thousands.

"Far more charming than Tordenhold," he told me kindly.

The flattery fell flat, but I beamed anyway.

Finally, Father approached. I had yet to decide how to tell him about the Delphi without revealing the reason for my conversation with them. Despite my disappointment in him, he still deserved the assurance that our lands were in no danger. A cruel part of me, growing in size and fervor, insisted I gloat that Ambrose Delphi had played Father for a fool.

"Malcolm! What a day! If I may be so bold, House Bruis should be very proud."

Father bowed his head at the praise. "Thank you. Is your room to your liking?"

The largest room, of course, had been given to the king. Father planning and concealing his arrival was salt in an already stinging wound.

"It's perfect." King Alaric grinned. "I only regret that we'll have to leave tomorrow afternoon. I'm sorry to drag you away from your celebrations, Malcolm. And even sadder to drag myself away." He chuckled.

"So soon?" I kept the hope from my voice even as it brightened my gaze.

"Yes," he grimaced. "The duties of Proventium never rest for long, and certainly not during such times." His concern about the looming war was gone in a breeze. His expression grew playful. "I can spare you a day or two to celebrate with your brother, but no longer."

The walls of the hall seemed to shrink, crowding against me.

I was saved from responding by a commotion near the banquet tables. The scrutiny jumped off the king and landed onto Opal, doubled over in her seat.

I pushed through the crowd, uncaring if Father and the king followed me.

"It's okay, Lav." She smiled through the pain. The bones and veins in her hand seemed to pulse as she squeezed Dean's arm. "The boy has horrid timing."

"Can't imagine why he'd be so eager to meet you." I brushed my hand over her contracted stomach.

Leith, Ruby, Oran, Hugo, and Amethyst closed in around us. Amethyst's concern was only tempered by Hugo's restraining grip.

Ruby's smile was brittle. The moment was a cloud hanging over her day, obscuring the sun meant to shine only on her.

"Jericho, we'll need a carriage readied immediately to take Mr. and Mrs. Branch home," Leith ordered. Grinning at the crowd, he raised his voice. "Nothing to worry about. What's a wedding day without a little drama?"

Oran's hands steadied me as I stood. Dean lifted Opal from her seat in a cacophony of groans and huffs.

"I hate this already. I'm not doing this again," she growled to her husband.

Amethyst shrugged off Hugo's hand to kiss Opal's cheek. The touch she ran down Opal's arm, more to soothe herself than her daughter. "We'll come visit tomorrow. We can't wait to meet the new baby. It's all going to be fine, honey."

"More to celebrate!" Hugo boasted while surveying the crowd before pressing a swift peck to the top of Opal's head.

I pulled Leith and then Ruby into my arms. "I'm sorry. I'm so happy for you."

"Go," Ruby whispered. "But don't let the king leave. His leaving early would be…"

"Don't worry." I shook my head. I wasn't surprised that the king's presence and what it meant were most important to Ruby, but the acknowledgment of it had something dangerously close to resentment itching under my skin.

My progress after Dean and Opal was halted by Father's glare.

"I have to go assist the birth," I spoke the words to the silver buckle on his boots.

"Labor takes hours, no need to go now."

I bristled at the callousness. "No, I do need to go now." I raised my glare to meet his for only a moment.

As I wilted, I felt Oran's presence press against my back. "Go change," Oran told me. "We'll follow after them once you're ready."

I looked to the king standing at Father's side. I'd employ what I had practiced to my advantage. Stepping forward, I clasped his forearm. "I'm so terribly sorry to leave during your visit. You understand, don't you?"

Another man who knew intimately the perils of childbirth. Unlike Father, flattery could garner his agreement. "Of course. Selfishly, I am sorry to see you go. Maybe it will progress quickly, and I'll be able to see you before I leave tomorrow." His brows raised.

"Yes."

He kissed my cheek, uncaring about my Father's presence. "Until then." Pulling away, he looked behind me to Oran. "Take good care of her."

Oran's expression was smooth and unyielding. He held the king's eye for a breath but made no response. Looking at me, a softness entered his gaze. I took his extended hand as greedily as I always had.

CHAPTER 41
LAVINIA

Even with my added weight, Declyn did not slow until we reached the small cottage nestled at the edge of the village.

I heard Opal through the open door of the bedroom the moment we stepped into the house. They'd been home just long enough for her to strip to her shift and get into bed. Sweat already beading at her brow, one hand rested softly on Dale's back, while the other clawed at Dean's hand. "Thank the Graces!"

Dale's lower lip wobbled. He was a mirror image of Opal, dotted with his father's freckles.

"Hi, sweetie," I cooed at Dale. "Your Uncle Oran is here. He told me that his horse really wants to meet you."

"No," he chirped. Of his limited vocabulary, 'no' was his favorite word.

Leith had screamed and begged to stay with Mother when she went into labor. The maids had dragged him away, threads from her chemise clutched in his fingers. They hadn't made him go farther than the closed door that did nothing to block the sound of Father's scream when she took her final breath.

"Declyn will be so sad. He was so excited to meet you."

"No!" He shook his head, but his stubbornness was no match for Opal.

She clicked her tongue. "That's no way to greet your Uncle Oran. You go until Aunt Lavinia comes and gets you. No, no, off you go. Take Papa with you."

Dean pressed a lingering kiss to her forehead as she fought through another wave of pain pinching her features. The hand he placed on my shoulder as he passed trembled.

The village midwife, Lucy, arrived shortly after they left. I kept a cool towel pressed to Opal's forehead while Lucy dictated her breathing. Lucy had no magic, but her years of experience were of far more value. She'd attended dozens of births, while this would only be my third.

Dale had been the second, Winter Alexandrite the first, an alarmingly small, blue baby born at court when I was seventeen. Lady Autumn had expected the baby to arrive in the spring, but had gone into labor one short week into the winter season at court. Padgett had attended all of Queen Margaux's pregnancies and births. He'd delivered a stillborn daughter and a son who only lived for a day. He had told Autumn not to worry, but I would remember the dread in his eyes for as long as I lived. Death marking a newborn was the greatest cruelty the Graces could allow.

Winter had not cried on her entry into the world. Padgett's hand spanned the entirety of her chest, forcing her lungs to breathe. Padgett, Mariana, and I had taken turns sustaining Winter until the fourth day, when I felt a push against the silver threads wrapped around her lungs. Winter began breathing on her own, but Autumn's terror remained for weeks.

I reminded myself of each story Autumn had told me of the child Winter had grown into. A playful, sensitive little girl.

Opal and her child would be fine.

I stroked a hand over the downy head of Pearl Branch as she rubbed her face against her mother's shoulder.

"She's perfect." Ruby, Sapphire, and Amethyst had repeated the same sentiment during their afternoon visit. They could say little else. Lord Lennox had dragged them away once Opal's eyes started to droop with exhaustion.

Opal smiled, sleepy and soft. "She is." She met my eyes. "Thank you."

"Of course." I shook my head. "Always."

"I would have been scared if you weren't here."

Pearl screamed into the world just before dawn emerged over the horizon. While Lucy tended to Pearl, I had whispered congratulations to Opal, stroking her hair to distract her from the threads of magic that stopped the blood pooling onto the sheets.

"You're not going to cry, are you?" I asked to lighten the grave crumple of her mouth.

She snorted and hacked. "Disgusting! I'd never."

I breathed a giggle, before studying her face. "Are you in any pain?"

"Just sore. But it's good. She's here." A sigh of relief floated out of her, dissipating through the quiet room.

Night had fallen outside the window. Pearl had been alive for over half of a day. I'd spend the night watching her breathe. Once she made it a full day, then I'd believe it was real. That she was here and healthy.

"Dale was so gentle with her."

"Just wait until he realizes that she is here to stay. Jealous little terror." Her eyes gleamed with affection, but her smile was fleeting. It set like the evening sun, shadowing her face in concern. "What are you going to do, Lav?"

"What do you mean?" Playing dumb with Opal never worked, but I hoped she was too exhausted to press.

"Lavinia." Her reprimand was piercing.

"It's done, Opal." I forced my voice to be light, my shrug casual, my face serene.

"No, it's not. If I thought you really loved him or even just fancied him, I wouldn't say anything. You know that, don't you? If I thought you were happy, I would support it, no matter how moronic."

I refused to meet her eyes. The solace I wanted to find in baby Pearl was a hollow consolation that opened into a new, gaping desperation. I longed for a life like Opal's.

The envy in me was a boiling pot. I held the lid firmly lest I scald others.

"I think…it's up to each of us to make ourselves as happy as we can within our circumstances."

"Bullshit," she spat. "We can hide you, say you were kidnapped by bandits and killed. Something!"

"Opal," I sighed. Temptation was a familiar plague that needed no further strength for its torment. "It'll all be fine. Really, I don't want

268

you to worry about me."

"No." She shook her head. Running a soothing hand down Pearl's back, she continued. "You don't want to burden anyone with your problems, but it's not a burden. That's what friendship is. You're always there for me, but you won't let people be there for you. Not truly." Her lower lip trembled. "I want to support you."

"You do," I insisted. To confess my stupidity would do nothing to ameliorate my fate.

"You don't have to be perfect for people to love you."

Her words were a mirror held in front of me. I would close my eyes rather than confront my reflection. "Will you visit me?"

Resignation passed over her face before settling into a forced levity. "Of course, nothing could stop me. As your guest, my return to court will be quite a triumph. Ugh, Papa will be insufferable. Is it too late to pretend you don't know the Lennox family?"

CHAPTER 42
ORAN

Seeing Lavinia hold Pearl Branch sent a wave of longing through me that nearly took me to my knees. I stroked the side of my pointer finger against Pearl's chubby cheek, earning me an owlish blink from her and a soft beam from Lavinia. My other hand clenched at my side against the urge to take this image of Lavinia, me, and a baby and make it our own.

"Don't hoard all the baby time," Ruby begged. "You've had two days with her," she told Lavinia, "and you'll have her for the rest of your life." She pointed at Opal.

Opal's laugh was more of a sigh than her usual cackle. "I see how it is. You only like me for my babies now." She turned her focus back to the meal tray on her lap.

"I'll go wake up Dale if I can't hold Pearl. First, you disrupt my wedding, and now you deny me my baby? Don't be so cruel to me, Opal."

"You're cruel to me! Lav, hand her over." Opal rolled her eyes with a contentment that only came around the family she and Dean created.

Lavinia swayed a step without Pearl to anchor her. I hooked my arm around her waist, bringing her weight into me.

Leith observed from against the wall, but had yet to touch either Pearl or Dale.

"Vin." I kept my voice low. "Come." She hesitated, worrying her lower lip between her teeth. "Opal and Pearl are both fine. You did a good job."

We left Leith and Ruby to their visit. Lifting Lavinia onto Declyn, I pulled myself behind her as quickly as possible. Her slim neck swayed under the weight of the past two days.

"Was all well at home?" she asked as Declyn walked us through the village.

"All was well," I confirmed. "Your father entertained the king sufficiently. Though Alaric dragged his feet leaving. Hoping to see you."

The sight of Alaric stalling outside yesterday would have been pitiful if it weren't so enraging. Bruis and Uncle Hugo returned to the palace with him. The rest of us would join them in another two days. It could be two years and still feel too soon.

I wished I had a clearer view of Vin's face, but caught a flash of white teeth in the plush of her lower lip, before her mouth curved, sardonic rather than playful. "Can you blame him?"

"Not at all, but you can. You haven't seemed happy around him."

She shrugged one shoulder. "A king's attention, there's much to be happy about. Ask Ruby, Father, Leith, they'll all tell you how well things are working out."

"But not you."

"Please," she dismissed.

"You can talk to me." I kept my voice gentle. "You said it yourself, it's a different life than you envisioned."

"I was just nervous." She shook her head. The movement brushed midnight silk against my throat. "I've realized now how exciting it all is. It's an honor."

"You don't want to marry him. You don't, Vin." My voice grew harsh with insistence.

"I'm sick of people telling me what I think. What I want. It's not enough to dictate what I know, no, now what I feel has to be dictated by others as well."

"That's not what this is," I insisted.

"You're doing it right now!"

"I know you, Vin. I'm not telling you what you want. I'm just acknowledging it."

She huffed and jerked forward in the saddle so that her back was

271

no longer pressed to my chest.

"You won't say what you want because you think you can't have it. You're used to hiding how you feel." My hands clenched the reins. I needed Lavinia to fight, not resign herself to what we both knew was a fate akin to that of a canary in a cage.

"I'm not hiding." Her shoulders drew in further at the denial.

"You don't want the king."

"At least *he* wants *me*!" The words left her in a shriek.

Shock, echoing through my chest, stole my breath. "That's what you think? That he is the only one who wants you?"

She laughed, hollow and callous. "Many men want me in their bed."

I ground my teeth to stop from screaming.

"But it's nice to be wanted for more. To be with a man who doesn't see my power as a liability. Not just a man, a king." Her voice wobbled on the final word, along with the mask she had in place to distance herself from the situation, from me.

"Vin," I sighed. "You don't have to lie to me. Please."

"You're one to talk!" Anger roared back in her voice. Good, if she had to fight with me to remember herself, so be it. "Shall we list all of the things you'd prefer to do over talking about how you feel?"

"Last I checked, my life wasn't dependent on an impossible task."

"Oh, so you don't think I can have a son? You don't think I can cure the Wasting?"

"I have to believe the Wasting can be cured," I corrected slowly, "but I don't think any one person will do it."

"You're not a Delphi. You don't know anything about it."

"Take it from a Tyth." My teeth gnashed through the word. "The Wasting is far worse than you know. Than most of Proventium know."

"I forgot that means you know everything." The acid in her voice was the same one corroding the stars in her eyes. "I'll remind you that we were attacked, people were killed, but I guess the Tythmore courier must have forgotten to deliver the announcement to you."

Lavinia's words sliced through me as sharply as the guilt I felt from her witnessing the devastation of the rebel attack. Telling Lavinia the full truth was the only remaining path. The others would be appalled that I thought it an option at all. Even my mother, petrified to overstep the careful boundaries of our relationship, would try and dissuade me.

Love made people stupid.

And it was incredibly stupid to tell anyone, especially the object of the king's affection, about the rebellion.

I had always lost my sense around Lavinia, but I couldn't believe this to be the wrong decision. I knew implicitly that I could trust her with everything.

The guilt I felt at dragging her into the danger of the rebellion ached. That guilt, however, was manageable compared to the fatal guilt of leaving her with Alaric. I'd bleed out from that long before I knew Lavinia's fate.

I was responsible for the constellations dimming in her eyes. This time, I would not fail to keep her safe. The certainty of it mixed with the fire in my blood.

"Vin." The fear in my voice made her spine go rigid. "Let's wait until we are in the stables. Then we can have it out."

"Fine," she huffed, "but I'm still mad at you."

Once Declyn was settled in the stable that sat in the rolling fields between Lennox and Bruis Manor, I took Lavinia's hand in mine, pulling her outside of the dust and dark wood and into the golden sunlight and emerald hills of our home.

Our home. For the little time we had left here.

Lavinia shook off my grasp to stomp through the grass.

"Vin, let's talk. Yell at me if you need."

She whipped around to face me, hair flying, eyes blazing. "I don't want to talk because nobody listens to me! I say I'm fine, and everyone tells me that I'm not. I'm sick of it."

"Fine, we won't talk about it." I crowded into her space, a part of me preening as she didn't back away.

"Really?" Her head tilted back, defiant as she held my gaze.

"Yes, we have something else to discuss anyway. Something I need to tell you."

Concern seeped into her features, softening her moonstone eyes and the stubborn set of her chin, though the pinch between her brows remained.

Here, we were as alone as we could be. I needed to make use of this time, but the words eluded me. An agile hare evading a hunting dog.

"My parents," I began.

"Is your mother okay? Is she safe?"

"Yes. Fuck," I breathed. "I don't know where to start."

"You can tell me anything." Lavinia, far too patient with my silence, ran a hand down my arm in encouragement.

"The Tyth infiltrated the palace because I told them how." The words fell out, artless and clumsy. I looked to the sky to save myself from seeing betrayal on Lavinia's face.

"Explain." Her demand was steady but held the gentleness that was innately, uniquely *Lavinia*.

"I helped them." My head dropped to focus on the ripple of Lavinia's hem in the breeze.

Years poured out of me like a burst dam. Every struggle and worry flooded out to muddy the waters of the only safe harbor I had ever known. Lavinia took it all in. Her eyes drifted from my face to a point over my shoulder, arms wrapped around her stomach in protection. I just prayed that my words wouldn't wash away the affection that usually swam in her gaze. Could it navigate such rough waters? If it didn't, would I survive its loss?

"They have no hope for things to get better under Proventium's rule. And I agree," I finally admitted. "My mother has always believed in what my father died for. She told me when I was a teenager how bad things were, and I ignored it for a time, but no longer."

"He wants to cure the Wasting," she mumbled. Not a dispute but a query.

"Not for Tythmore but for himself. He wants Proventium's farmlands restored, and Tythmore reduced to rubble. They are starved and helpless, exactly as he wants them. If he gets his way, Tythmore will be a quarry and a shipping passage."

She blinked rapidly in a daze. "He's said this?"

"Yes. All the lords know it to be true."

Breath stuttering, Lavinia raised a hand to rub over her heart. "You...I sent you into the attack. I made you go back to the ballroom."

"I told them I would aide in planning as long as I was able to get you out. We were supposed to be out of the ballroom before they attacked. You weren't meant to be in danger. I went back in to help more women flee, but I couldn't interfere otherwise."

"Why not? You could have killed the king or Lord Delphi, Lord Lynx. You probably could have incinerated the entire room." The way she studied me, like I was a stranger, threatened to gut me.

"Because then I would have lost you. I told the rebels that without my position, there would be no further information of use. That is true, but keeping my position also meant I could stay near you."

"Oran." Her face crumpled.

"I am a traitor to the Lennox name. To Proventium. I think I've known for years that eventually I'd be a traitor like my uncle always feared."

"Because Tythmore is...it is that bad what he's doing." Her eyes glittered as the light reflected off the tears lining her eyes.

"Yes."

She stumbled back a step before taking two hasty steps forward. "Thank you for telling me."

"Vin."

"I helped kill that boy." A tear fell then, agonizingly descending her pale cheek. "I revived him, and then he was tortured and killed. He could have died in the hallway. His suffering would have been done and instead—" She sucked in a ragged breath. "He must have been so scared."

"That's not your fault." My voice was harsh, anger not at her but at Bron, Alaric, and all the others.

"I was ignorant of a lot, but it's no excuse—"

"No," I interrupted. Lavinia had been sheltered away from the truth. She didn't bear the shame that the lords and heirs of Proventium did.

She looked to the sky, her eyes reading unwritten words among the clouds. When her gaze lowered, the resignation from the carriage ride mixed with a new determination. "If the prophecy is truly about me, if I can do it, I promise you I will cure it for everyone. I won't leave Tythmore to suffer."

"Vin, it's not for you to fix." I reached for her then, one hand on her jaw, the other on the base of her neck. "We don't know that anyone can end the Wasting."

"I spoke with Lord Delphi. He said I was on the right path. I, the Wasting, I have to try. I don't know that my power can do anything for it, but I have to try. He is marrying me for the prophecy. That is what is expected of me. I promise that if I can help, I'll help everyone."

"You don't have to marry him. Fuck him and fuck Delphi." The right path for her was with me. If the Graces were speaking to Delphi, they were wrong. I'd stop Delphi, the king, the Graces, all of them.

"Oran." She looked at me with pity that jolted fresh panic through my stomach. She was resigned to navigate life in shackles rather than fight until she broke them.

"Vin."

"I don't want to talk about this anymore." She shook her head against the grip of her hand on her jaw. "Thank you for telling me. I hope you know that I will never speak of this to anyone."

"Of course, I know that," I dismissed. I knew I needed to give her time. She had enough to process now, without the final piece, the largest piece, to contend with. "I trust you above all else."

Time. I couldn't give her much, but I could give her the night.

CHAPTER 43
LAVINIA

"I'm never getting married!" Opal declared. At seven, every opinion felt permanent.

"I am." I looked up from my letters to find her hacking in exaggerated disgust.

"To who?"

"Oran." The answer was so obvious, I didn't know why she needed it explained.

"Gross." She shuddered, dark curls messily bouncing around her shoulders.

"Don't be mean," I whined.

Our tutor, Miss Remi, softly laughed next to us in the library of Lennox house. "Girls, no one is getting married until they have proper penmanship."

"Then I don't need to do my letters." Opal's smile was gummy from the two teeth she'd knocked out falling in the river the week prior.

I loved dance and art lessons best. Penmanship may not be as enjoyable, but there was something satisfying in exacting each letter to perfectly match the letters of Miss Remi's hand. Having a matching letter, or even better, a matching word, was an accomplishment that left no room for argument. Unlike dancing and art, there was a right and a wrong. The swoops of my L's were too grand. They were loud, unlike the quiet elegance of Miss Remi's L. My first name needed a lot of work, but my family name, that I had mastered. Each letter was one I felt pleased with. If Father saw it, he may even be unable to discern my 'Bruis' from Miss Remi's 'Bruis'.

"Opal," she sighed. "You had a full hour of art this morning. We cannot have

time for lessons like art and dancing if you will not do all the lessons. Penmanship is vital for—"

Miss Remi's words stopped at the opening of the door. Father and Lord Lennox entered, trailed by Leith and Oran.

"Is everything going well?" Father asked the question to Miss Remi, but focused on me.

I straightened in my chair and smoothed a hand down my braid. "Come look at my letters!"

He peered over my shoulder. The only acknowledgment of their quality was a low hum in his throat.

"Opal, let me see." Lord Lennox rubbed a hand over her slumped shoulders as he looked. "You haven't made it very far. Let's see some more," he encouraged.

She twisted in her chair to look up at him. "Papa." Opal's face scrunched in thought. "Are you going to make me marry Leith?"

"No!" Leith shouted in horror from where he and Oran stood near the door.

"No, sweetheart." Lord Lennox indulged her with a patient grin. "Aren't you too young to be thinking about marriage?"

"Are you going to make Oran marry Lavinia? She'd say yes." Opal nodded. "But you can't make me marry Leith."

"I don't want to marry you," Leith snapped.

I kicked Opal's leg under the table, warm with embarrassment.

"No." Father's voice lacked the patient amusement of Lord Lennox.

I was familiar with the furrow of his brow. Disappointment. I'd tried to overcome the misstep with smiles and tales of our day, but nothing relaxed the tense line of his frame.

Later, as Father had led Leith and me home, he'd told us. Leith had huffed that he already knew, but I had not.

"Without Hugo's guidance, Oran would be just like his parents. A traitor to Proventium and a danger to us all. He can be your friend, but Proventium will always come first. Bruis are loyal servants of the kingdom."

I hadn't viewed him differently then, and I didn't view him differently now.

The confession fit perfectly with what I knew of Oran. Kind, honorable, brave, of course, he would not tolerate the weight of injustice on his conscience. Oran had also always possessed a ruthlessness about him. Maybe it should have scared me, but instead, I had always found safety in it.

The things I shied away from, Oran would face.

Sitting in the silence of my cluttered room, I stared out the round window across from my bed. If I squinted, I could make out the sandstone shape of Lennox Manor, no bigger than a fingernail in the distance.

Usually, I would fight thinking about Oran, but after his confession today, the effort would be futile. The bread I'd been able to stomach for dinner threatened to reappear as the magnitude of just how little I could control churned in my gut.

Oran wouldn't stay forever, he couldn't. He'd have to leave for Tythmore at some point. How long he would stay, I didn't know, but I would have to accept the possibility of forever. Better separated by kingdoms than by death. I wouldn't beg him to stay, to abandon his cause. I had been selfish enough.

Now I had to be better.

My fate in Cirrus Palace was set. The pain of separation, of loneliness, of worry, would be a poison. The clear direction in front of me was a distraction, not an antidote. But it would be enough.

I couldn't wallow in my malaise, not with the task that lay before me.

Maybe I should be angry about the attack. That he helped Zeno Vaux be killed. That he helped Adder Glenn lose his leg. My acceptance of this stung far more than the knowledge itself.

Oran's morality had always allowed him to justify wrongs for a greater end. But what was happening to Tythmore was for no greater end.

The suffering of Tythmore had been a fact my whole life. Ever present, it faded into the background. I didn't note the moldings on the wall of my bedroom because I saw them every day. Now the moldings on the wall had caught fire.

I couldn't look away.

I was kept ignorant, but I was the one who had been too self-involved to demand answers. Too focused on my own future.

I had denied the prophecy because it was not compatible with the life I dreamed. I wouldn't part with the love in my heart. This would simply be an act of that love. I'd spend every ounce of myself on curing the Wasting. To help Oran and his people.

To do something good, something useful.

Delphi's confirmation of my fate had felt like a tragedy, but now it sparked with something like purpose. My fate and Tythmore's were intertwined, lying at the mercy of the king and the Graces.

I had always done what was asked of me. This was one more expectation. I'd bend and break to make it so.

Resolve settled in me. I couldn't fight my fate, but I would fight the Wasting.

In the light of a new day, my resolve shook but did not falter. Sadness and fear held an endurance I was determined to outlast.

I watched the water bubbling and singing over the rocks. To accept my new life, gilded walls instead of open sky, I needed to first say farewell to the life I had known. Following the stream to the lake it fed had been a favorite childhood activity. When we were girls, Opal and I would lift our skirts and wade in. Ruby would dip a toe in at our insistence, before watching from the shore. Opal would be scolded once her mother spied her damp hem. Father never looked at me enough to notice.

"Can I help you?" I didn't turn around as I asked.

"We never finished our conversation, so I'm here for when you're ready to talk."

"What's there to talk about?" I knew I was being obstinate and yet couldn't help myself. My resolve felt fragile next to Oran's strength. He knew just where to strike to topple the defenses I had crafted the night prior.

"When you want to talk about what's happening to you, I'm here."

I turned to him then. The calm, even burr of his voice incited mine to a shrill demand. "What's happening to me? I'm making the best choice I can. I'm choosing to do the right thing."

"You're not." He shook his head, chestnut waves ruffled in the breeze.

"Yes, I am."

"Your father has denied you any choice. This courtship with Alaric has been their doing, not yours. You're not happy about it. I'd say you're furious about where it has led."

"What good does that do?" His hand gripped my upper arm as I made to brush past him. Firm but with his ever-present underlying gentleness. "You should be happy. You'll have an ally against the Wasting."

He ignored my words, insisting, "You don't tell your father and brother how you feel. You're scared to be angry with them because you don't want to ruin things. Admit it."

"Stop!" My determination was not fit to withstand his sympathy or his challenge.

"You can yell and scream at me. I'm not going anywhere, not even the Graces themselves could ever make me leave you."

"Stop it." My voice shook.

"I'm so tired of your fake smiles. Aren't you tired? You don't look like a maiden eager for her pending betrothal. Say it. Nothing you say could be worse than what I told you yesterday."

"Graces, Oran, what do you want me to say? That I'm terrified? That throwing myself into the ocean feels preferable? What does it matter? I cannot reject the king. There is no way out."

"This, your honesty, yes, that is what I want. I want to know everything about you. Of course, I want to know how you feel."

"But how I feel doesn't matter," I cried. I closed my eyes to protect my heart from the endless well of kindness in his gaze. "The only option left is to try. To endure the marriage and try and help the Wasting. I will marry him. And I will stop the Wasting."

"Fuck Delphi! He's a manipulative bastard who speaks more lies than fates," he seethed. Oran's chest rose and fell with a heavy pant before he softened. "How you feel matters to me more than anything. We'll figure a way out of this for you. I understand what it's like to not want to burden others with the truth. To worry about compromising or endangering people with the truth. Why do you think I never told you about Tythmore?"

I shook my head. "You don't understand how far it's gone. There is no going back now." My voice was hollow, matching the chasm that had opened in my chest. "It's my responsibility."

"What do you mean?" His voice was so earnest. Such honesty after the artifice of court made the longing in my heart scream louder.

Telling Oran would be the ultimate shame. He'd see just how stupid I was. The girl who thought she was in control, only to find out she was trapped.

Ruined.

It was humiliating, and yet this secret was suffocating. I couldn't look at him while I said it. While the most valued opinion of me was irrevocably changed. I kept my back to him, the words raced out of me, eager to escape. With the release of speaking it aloud, I felt like I could finally fill my lungs again.

"Vin," he breathed. "Vin." His voice was insistent. "It's not your fault. It's his. He should have respected you enough to never even ask that of you. He had you brought there when you'd been drinking?" His voice rose before forcing it back down. "This is what he wants. He wants you to think that you're trapped, but you're not."

"I am trapped." By my foolishness, by the king, by fate.

While my eyes were closed, he placed himself in front of me. The soft hand that ran down the length of my hair didn't track up to my neck as it usually did. This time, it paused and gave a gentle tug to the ends, forcing my eyes open. "You're better than him, than all of them. Don't accept anything that you don't want."

"I can't be so selfish as to condemn others with me. I can't." My happiness was inconsequential against the plague of the Wasting. I'd peacefully sentence myself if it meant I could help those suffering.

"Selfish." The word came, slow and thick like molasses. Oran shook his head. "I've tried very hard to not be selfish with you, Vin. But here I'm telling you to fight for what you want when I've...fuck. I've been a coward for years." I let myself sink into green eyes of welcoming spring grass. "You should be mad at me. I thought I knew better than you. That I was only hurting myself. Could you love someone selfish better than you could love a coward?"

"What?" The rushing of the stream was eclipsed by the roar of blood in my ears.

"I understand it's selfish of me to ask you to leave everything behind and run away with me."

"Oran, be serious." Hope was dangerous. It flared too brightly. The temptation of the flame vanquished the memory of past burns. "You have Tythmore to focus on. You said yourself you have to maintain your position for now."

"I am serious. I can help Tythmore from beyond the border now that there are others in place in court." He took another step toward me, the sun dwarfed behind his frame. "We could marry and run away together right now."

I'd not let him put an obligation to me over the obligation of his birth. "I know you like to fix things, but I don't want you to pity me, Oran. I can't stand for you to look at me like I'm so pathetic," I spat the word, "that you have to destroy your own life, your plans, to save me."

"It's not pity. Running away together would be as much for me as it is for you."

"What does that mean?" As rapid as a hummingbird's wings, my heart fluttered in my chest. I tracked the long line of his throat as he swallowed. He seemed more nervous now than he had during his confession yesterday.

"Before your first season. Do you remember what you said to me?"

I could never forget the way his rejection, however gentle, ripped through me.

"It would have been selfish, but I wanted to take you for myself even then. I didn't, because I knew I didn't deserve you. I said no, even though I wanted you more than anything I've ever wanted in my life. I lied to you then, but I swear I'll give you nothing but the truth now."

"Oran." My voice trembled.

"I thought there was no greater torture than seeing you and knowing I could not have you. Then it was the profound torture of seeing you with someone else...now I know the real torture is you being in a moment of pain, feeling even a hint of fear. I cannot bear it. I would suffer anything if it meant you were happy."

"I'm only truly happy when I'm with you," I confessed.

He closed the final step between us. "I've been drowning in you for years. I love you. I have loved you for so long, in truth, I don't know who I'd be without it. Lavinia, you are branded into me."

The words burrowed under my skin, settling the restless longing that had been there since I could remember. Now, it was replaced with the certainty of *Oran*. I leaned into the hands holding the back of my neck and my cheek. "I love you. It's always been you."

"I'm yours, Vin."

I stole the words from his lips. Oran, the heat of his body and the spark of the kiss, eclipsed everything around us. I pressed myself against the hard lines of his body, desperate with years of longing. A want that had grown and would never be satisfied. Wrapping my hair around his fist, he pulled my head back to scrape his teeth against the sensitive flesh of my neck.

This kiss was not like the rushed craze of before. We kissed like time had stopped, like nothing mattered but the slide of his lips against mine, the press of our hips, the taste of him. Addictive. Inevitable. This was jumping from a cliff and being caught in strong arms all at once.

I was not made to chase love. I had been doing it all my life, giving love and working tirelessly to earn it back. Seeking love was not what

I was meant to do. Not when it had been within me all along. In front of me, next to me, the great love I had always dreamed of was there. Even when I thought it was unrequited, it was there. Oran. It could never be anyone else. I didn't need to earn his love, just as he didn't need to earn mine. It was unwavering and unconditional. Its presence was so integral that I didn't notice the weight of it. It would only be noticeable if I lost it; the absence would pull at me like a phantom limb.

I wouldn't lose it. Nothing could pry me away from this now. Saying goodbye to the life I knew didn't scare me when I had the most important piece of that life standing with me.

Damn, the Graces. They were wrong. My fate was green-eyed, holding me as tightly as I was holding him. Even if we spent the rest of our days running from the king, from Graces, I knew that we wouldn't let go of each other.

Oran retreated with a wet pull to my lower lip and a groan but kept his hands firmly around my waist. "Wait," he panted. My favorite crooked smile teased at his lips, but this time I was able to take it for myself before pulling back to eagerly memorize the way his eyes deepened in a haze of pleasure.

"I want to do this right."

I scratched my nails down the back of his neck as I smiled.

"Fuck, how am I going to be able to think about anything but kissing you ever again?" He shook his head. His lips took mine in another kiss. Longing, lust, and love narrowed my world to the man in front of me.

Pulling back, he dropped to kneel in the grass. Refusing to separate, I hunched over him, my hands on either side of his neck.

"What are you doing?" My laugh was breathy. Everything felt so light, it was dizzying. I'd have to learn to breathe without the pressing weight of pining on my chest.

"Marry me. Lavinia Bruis, I didn't know love until you. You were fourteen, wearing a green dress, and the way you laughed sounded like forever. It took the heart out of my chest. You've had it ever since, and it'll always be yours. I want to be with you until the end of my days and beyond. Marry me."

"I love you," I breathed in answer. I fell into him, collapsing onto his bent knee and throwing myself into his chest. He caught me around the waist, as he always had. As he always would.

The elm tree, slowly healing, didn't stand proud and impressive above us as I had pictured as a girl dreaming of a wedding. But with the man I'd dreamed of marrying holding my hands in his, it did not matter. Nothing mattered except the love I greedily drank from his eyes. Being covetous for so long, I didn't know how long it would take to break the habit. But we had years to learn. To learn that love was not rapacious longing but an equal exchange. If I reached out, he would meet me.

The wind whispered its congratulations as the grass that witnessed our childhood now witnessed our vows.

Oran had interrupted his vows to whisper an apology for the pain of the blood tie, but I welcomed the cut across my palm. He had been in my blood for years. With that first smile, I had been lit aflame. Holding our palms together, I felt my blood run hotter. The steady flame glowed brighter, each ember entwining us further.

"By the Graces, I vow to love you under storm and sun, in hardship and joy. I vow to never be parted from you in this life or any that follows."

The vow danced in the air around us, twirling to join the Graces above us. We breathed each other in, disbelief transforming into joy. A joy so large I didn't know how I could contain it. As a grin consumed Oran's face, I knew I wouldn't have to hold it alone.

Our lips met with softness that was quickly overtaken by the need for more. Our intertwined hands dropped to grab and hold each other in any way we could, greedy and gluttonous and deserved. My lungs ached as I refused to part from him. A breath without him was a waste. Oran was gentle as we sank to the ground. Each movement erased all memories of the past. The rightness of *us* eclipsed any others.

I was made of moonlight, but Oran was the sun, blinding intensity and warmth. Every touch, every kiss before Oran had been a mere shadow: fleeting, insubstantial, and cold. This was all-consuming, the sun casting shadows and extinguishing them.

I lost myself in the pleasure of being as connected as two people could be. *Mine*, the truth of it sang in my chest and hummed through my veins. There, cushioned in the soft grass, blanketed by Oran's body and the endless summer sky, I felt the ecstasy of forever settle over me.

I would wear his love like a crown. An adornment to be proud of.

It'd fit far better than a real crown.

CHAPTER 44
ORAN

I ran my hand down Lavinia's back, marveling at the feel of her—silken black hair curtained over soft ivory skin.

She propped her chin on my chest. "Tell me something happy."

"We're married." Joy and disbelief saturated each word.

"We're married," she repeated.

I took her smiling lips with mine, rolling her back against the grass.

Fingers interlocked, we walked slowly back to Bruis Manor. The sun's low perch in the sky was a ticking clock.

"I'm not scared of leaving. Not when it's with you. As long as we are together, everything will be fine."

We'd leave in the early hours of tomorrow, racing against dawn to make it as far west as we could before we were found missing. From there, we'd ride north. The Cape of Thieves, the only pass between Tythmore and Proventium that didn't require crossing the Wasting, was a heavily guarded landing spot. Manned by Vaux soldiers. We'd land on the northern coast of Tythmore and from there ride south to the Cahill lands.

I stopped to look at her. Running my free hand down her mussed hair, I vowed, "I won't let anything happen to you." The plan was imperfect, but I would protect her. I'd die before I let anyone harm her, and then patiently wait for her in the afterlife.

"I trust you." The constellations in her eyes sparkled. "Do you trust me?"

"With my life." She had been my life for years.

"Then you have to trust me to at least try. I have to try and cure the Wasting. I know you think Delphi is a liar, but I need you to support me."

Delphi was careful with his words. He didn't bestow assurances or guarantees, only hints. Enough information to impress his power, but never any more. I should have known that once she was aware of the true magnitude of strife, she'd take the cause on herself.

"I don't believe in much, but I believe in you."

The hand not held in mine reached across to run up and down my forearm in a maddening caress. She beamed at me. The sight so beautiful it stole my breath. "I think I'll like Tythmore," she mused.

"I hope so." I cupped her cheek. "Once everything is done, we can come back here. I hope this could still be our home one day." This I didn't promise. I didn't know how Lennox Manor could ever be a home for us.

But I hoped.

Lavinia loved her home. We couldn't keep it, but I would fight to get it back. For her.

"Lavinia Lennox," she mused. Rising on her toes, she pressed a kiss to my mouth. A sweet, fleeting kiss that I was too greedy to allow. I took her lips with mine, teasing my tongue at the seam until she opened.

"What the fuck!"

I tore back from Lavinia. Leith's mouth was open in shock, staring at his sister as if he'd never seen her before.

"Leith," she croaked. Her wide eyes looked to me.

I gently guided her a step behind me. Leith would never hurt her on purpose, but his temper was a danger nonetheless.

His mouth closed with an audible snap. Rage barreled into his eyes as they met mine. "My fucking sister?"

"Calm down." I hoped my years of diffusing his anger would lend enough experience to do so again.

"I know you've been fucking your way through court but Lavinia?"

"That's not what this is, Leith."

He ignored me. "Fuck, Lavinia, have you learned nothing? I thought after Rhode you'd finally got it through your head to stop spreading your legs for a fucking compliment like a cheap whore!"

"Don't fucking call her that!" I exploded toward him, any thought of pacifying his anger gone.

He met my advance with his own. Chest to chest, I could see the vein throbbing at his temple. "Or what? You fucking bastard, I was your best friend! Do you know what will happen if anyone finds out that you took her for your whore?"

"Don't use that word. You will not disrespect my wife."

Leith stumbled a step back at the title. He blinked in a daze before shaking his head. "No. She's to marry the king."

"Not anymore."

"We just did it today," Lavinia whispered. "Leith, please listen. I never wanted to marry the king. You know this. It would have killed me."

"Married?" Leith's focus and ire remained on me.

I cataloged every tick I knew about him as a fighter, the shift of his stance, the clench of his fists. "Yes." Even with the battle before me, I couldn't help the pride in my voice.

He barked a humorless laugh. "It's not enough to fuck my sister, you have to fuck over all of us? Do you have any idea what you've done?" He gripped my shoulders, shaking and then shoving. The moment I righted my balance, he swung.

Leith's fist against my jaw ruptured with fresh and long-healed wounds. I met him strike for strike, refusing to stumble even as my head snapped to the side. With each hit of my own, I pushed into his space to move us further from Lavinia.

It was the magic-less brawling of childhood. The men we were replaced by the boys we'd been. The boys who used their fists to work through their differences. We'd scraped viciously until one day Leith had fallen to the ground, and I had extended a hand. Laughter had burst out of both of us, and a brotherhood replaced rivalry.

A friendship born through fighting.

Now come to die as it had begun.

"Stop," Lavinia begged.

Everything slowed as I watched Lavinia's hand grab at my arm. Leith's fist swung forward. Too close, it was too close to her. I found my magic then, buried under anger and fear. I retreated several steps, pulling Lavinia with me as a wall of flame pushed Leith back.

The reflection of the fire matched the rage burning in his eyes. Eyes so like Lavinia's, but where hers were rimmed in tears, his were edged in hatred. I let the flames fall with a sigh.

Leith stomped toward us, his movements heavier than before. "You'll get her killed. Don't you see that?" Leith punctuated his scream with a push to my shoulders. His breath was ragged as he croaked, "He will either kill her as a traitor or marry her as a widow."

"He won't find us beyond the Wasting."

"Oran," he breathed, "You idiot. Fuck." He clapped his hand over his mouth as he crumpled.

While Leith turned away from us, I looked at Lavinia. She clutched a hand over her stomach, swaying in physical pain. I took her hand in mine, thumb running a mindless pattern over hers to soothe and distract.

No matter what Leith said, I wouldn't part from Lavinia. She was my wife.

Leith turned back, the anger in his eyes dulled by tears. "I will not let you get yourself or my sister killed. She stands a chance of living as the king's wife. Being your wife is a death sentence. How do you think the king was waiting and ready for your father's attack? He has spies among them. Don't you get it? They'll sell you both to the king within a week."

No, my father hadn't been betrayed by his people. No, I couldn't accept that. "Once we are in Tythmore, we'll be safe. I'll keep her safe."

"Fuck you," he burst. "No, you think the fucking traitors will stop him? The Tyth can't fight because they are weak! If they could do more than throw a tantrum, they'd have done it already."

"Leith, you don't," Lavinia began.

"No, you don't understand anything"—He threw his hands up— "Graces ever loving fuck! You think happiness, fucking childhood dreams, does what? You think Father got where he is on happiness? Grandfather? Me? You think happiness keeps our lands, our money? Our heads?"

Lavinia shrank back under his renewed rage.

"Don't speak to her like that, Leith. I'm not going to tell you again."

"You're going to be the most powerful woman in the kingdom. You, a healer." Leith punched the fist of his right hand into his open palm. "You ungrateful fucking brat."

Flames licked up my wrists at his words, but I couldn't hurt Leith. Despite his cruelty, Lavinia loved him.

"Leith," she cried. "Stop acting like I'm doing this *to* you. Please, will you listen?" I followed next to her as she approached him.

"The Tyth can't protect you!" He was frantic in his fury.

I knew at that moment it didn't matter that he was once my brother. I could not trust him with the truth of our plan. He'd see the Vaux killed along with every last rebel.

"We have a plan. A plan that keeps Lavinia safe. Far safer than shackled to the king."

"Of course." He laughed again, humorless and biting. "Not shackled to a king but a traitor." That word from Leith's lips would have been a fatal blow if not for Lavinia at my side and the mark of our blood tie on my palm.

"How long have you been planning this?" The suspicion that I'd use Lavinia was more cutting than his anger. "Biting the hand that fed you," he seethed. "You think you've won? Or maybe this was the plan, to take my sister down with you."

I continued on as if he hadn't spoken. "The plan is far bigger than just me, but I'm not going to tell you anything about it. I don't trust you. I don't trust you to protect your sister." I laced my fingers through hers. "I don't trust you to do the right thing. I'm a traitor and you're a coward."

"You went behind my back, took my sister, and will see us all killed, yet you have the gall to be self-righteous with me." He shook his head in disgust. Lavinia's hand squeezed mine harder as those hate-filled eyes met hers. "We're all dead if you don't fall back in line."

"No," she mumbled. The tears that had been lying in wait began their tortuous descent.

"We're leaving," I said, "and you and your father, my uncle, you'll all say you don't know where we are."

"You think I won't tell them where to find you? If you won't protect her, I will. I will tell them you fucking stole her away. That you've manipulated a girl who's too stupid to know what's good for her. Traitor scum like your father. You won't make it far before he sends every Graces-damned guard after you. He'll level all of Tythmore under a storm like he did last time."

I choked back the fear of a little boy, crowded on the dining table in his mother's arms as flood waters rose around them.

Leith's nostrils flared as he stepped closer to me. "I'll see you hang."

"Leith," Lavinia shrieked in horror.

"I will," he promised before looking at Lavinia. "I will see you crowned even if it means he has to die."

Her hand left mine before she threw her weight at Leith's chest, making him stumble a single step back. "He's your best friend." She pushed him again. "He's my husband."

Leith's arms hung heavy at his side. "I thought he was, but he's not. It's him or all of us."

"No, no, please. Leith." Her breathing grew rapid, eyes darting between Leith and me.

His features smoothed into a stone mask, befitting Malcolm Bruis's heir. "No one has to know about the marriage. We don't say anything, it doesn't exist. Fuck what the Graces know."

A dead, frost-bitten olive branch thrown at my feet.

"You play the part expected of you, you don't cause any problems, and he keeps his head."

"You can't be serious." She took a shaky step forward, hands raising at her sides to grab him. As if touching him would bring back the brother she knew.

"If you'd rather he be executed..." He shrugged. Triumph flashed across his face.

Lavinia turned back to me. Her devastation pulled me under. I thought I was used to drowning, but the waters of her pain crushed my lungs anew.

"If you run, I will send him after you before you make it off our lands." His smirk dimmed. "Your choice," he told me, "but I can't guarantee he'll believe she's innocent. He may kill you both."

I didn't want to think Leith could be so callous with her life, but I had to believe his words. If I couldn't trust our history, I had to trust in his threats.

Leith saw the moment the weight of his threat made impact. A cruel grin twisted his features. "The Lennox heir and the soon-to-be queen."

CHAPTER 45
LAVINIA

Leith's grip was as cold as his eyes.

We were to go back to Bruis Manor, while Oran went to Lennox Manor. Separated for the night until we all journeyed back to the palace tomorrow. The threat to inform Father and Lord Lennox was a hand around my neck, the squeeze to remind, not choke. It was hardly a concern compared to the crushing asphyxiation of Leith's threat against Oran.

I would do whatever I must to protect Oran.

If I had to sever the part of myself that had always been his, to protect him, I'd bleed out remembering the joy of being in his arms.

But not yet. Not until there was no other choice.

I stumbled a step after Leith before ripping my arm away. Throwing myself into Oran's chest, I pressed my face into his neck.

"Give us a moment." Oran's voice left no room for argument. "Over there."

I heard Leith huff and mutter, the sound of his footsteps retreating a relief.

"What are we going to do?" I hated the whiny helplessness of my voice. I would draw on Oran's strength and gather my own. And I would fight. To save myself. Oran. Tythmore.

"Delay the wedding for as long as possible, whatever excuses you can come up with. I will find a way to get us across the border."

Ending the Wasting had been the extent of how I had thought to help Tythmore, but no longer. Their cause, Oran's cause, was now mine. The king, my family, I'd fight anyone separating us.

I wouldn't betray myself for House Bruis.

"You swear you won't leave me."

He pressed a firm kiss to the crown of my head. "Never. I will never leave. You're mine and I'm yours. This is temporary, but we are not."

I nodded against his chest, the thick cotton scratching my forehead. I needed him, but he needed me too. "I love you. I'll delay the wedding, I'll tell him I need to try and help the Wasting first, I'll tell him...I promise we'll find a way to fight this."

"Listen to me, love. We have to be strong and we have to be smart."

"Lavinia!" Leith's bark made my shoulder tense. I wanted to claw his face off.

"You can trust Caius," Oran whispered. "Caius and Rhode. I don't have time to explain now, but you can trust them."

"Now," Leith ordered.

"Tell me something happy," I begged. I would allow myself this one moment of weakness while I was in my sanctuary, the space between Oran's neck and shoulder, before I crafted and donned an armor that could withstand what would come.

"I love you," he spoke low in my ear. "I've always loved you and I always will. Even in death, I will love you. This will not stop us."

"I love you." A plea, a promise, a prayer.

CHAPTER 46
LAVINIA

I focused on my breathing, one of the few things I could control. Inhale, hold, exhale, hold. Thomasina and Clodia had pinched my cheeks half a dozen times, but the color wouldn't take. Ruby's cheek stain was far too bright on my pale skin. My jaw ached from the grinding of my teeth behind the smile frozen on my lips.

We'd been back at court for a week. A week of smiling through a pain that increased with each minute. I'd often comfort patients by telling them the pain would lessen. *Breathe deeply and the pain will begin to dull.* In extreme cases, numbness takes hold too quickly to feel anything at all. Shock is often more powerful than pain.

I was still waiting for that to happen.

Looking at fighting an enemy as large as Proventium was being unmoored in the ocean with no sign of land on the horizon. I didn't know where to look, where to go. A rushed plan was doomed to fail, so for now, I delayed. I watched. I plotted.

I avoided looking at my father and brother. My family now adversaries.

Never again would I doubt Leith's threats. The one secret we held between us, the marriage, was the only one I trusted him to keep. We both knew Father would blame Leith as much as he blamed me. This secret was the sole tie that remained between us.

One I'd sever as soon as I could.

I avoided looking at Oran. My favorite sight now unendurable. His sadness would take an axe to the carefully sculpted statue of a maiden that masked my anger and agony.

I spotted Caius in the crowd next to Lady Philomena, her purple gown was so dark, it resembled the black of mourning. His brother's hand rested on his shoulder. I caught a glimpse of Golda's white blonde hair, dwarfed by the surrounding masses. I looked to Lord Vaux to save me the sympathy in Caius's gray eyes. Lord Vaux tilted his chin, something terrifyingly close to knowing on his face.

I forced my attention away as King Alaric began to speak, focusing on my posture and my smile. King Alaric's arm wrapped around my shoulders like vines of ivy. I looked out numbly at the crowd in front of the dais. His voice filled the room, but I could hear nothing over their scrutiny.

Unworthy.

The word was clear in their stares.

They didn't know the truth of how much so.

I looked down at my gloved hand and saw red. A large ruby ring on display and a scarlet scab hidden under white silk gloves. I couldn't bring myself to heal it. Would it still be real without the mark? The evidence of the blood tie adorned the hand betrothed to another.

"Lavinia Bruis, your next queen of Proventium."

ACKNOWLEDGMENTS

Union was the most insistent story I ever dreamed up. Lavinia and Oran arrived in the summer of 2024, crystal clear and fully formed. The rest of the characters and plot came together over the remainder of the year. Creating this story made me fall in love with writing all over again. Before Union, I had taken a long break from writing, and it was only through this story that I realized how integral writing was to my life.

My love of writing would not have been born if not for the love of reading instilled in me early on. Thank you to my parents for your endless support. Especially my mom, who I roped in to acting as a beta reader, an editor, and a cheerleader. Thank you for believing in me and encouraging me to take the leap and publish this story.

Thank you to anyone who has picked this book up. I appreciate you being here more than I can say, and I hope you'll join me for the conclusion of Lavinia and Oran's story soon.

ABOUT THE AUTHOR

Hannah Eaton is an east-coaster living in Colorado with her Chihuahua-mix, Arlo. She has a degree in Classical Studies and Comparative Literature from the University of St Andrews, Scotland. When not writing, you can find her reading, hiking, or analyzing the Real Housewives.

www.ingramcontent.com/pod-product-compliance
Lightning Source LLC
Chambersburg PA
CBHW021409110726
47901CB00008B/2118